Risking It All

Also by Nina Darnton

The Perfect Mother
An African Affair

Risking It All

Nina Darnton

 St. Martin's Griffin ✿ New York

RISKING IT ALL. Copyright © 2017 by Nina Darnton. All rights reserved. Printed in the United States of America. For information, address St. Martin's Press, 175 Fifth Avenue, New York, N.Y. 10010.

www.stmartins.com

Designed by Anna Gorovoy

The Library of Congress Cataloging-in-Publication Data is available upon request.

ISBN 978-1-250-07525-3 (trade paperback)
ISBN 978-1-4668-8664-3 (ebook)

Our books may be purchased in bulk for promotional, educational, or business use. Please contact your local bookseller or the Macmillan Corporate and Premium Sales Department at 1-800-221-7945, extension 5442, or by email at MacmillanSpecialMarkets@macmillan.com.

First Edition: September 2017

10 9 8 7 6 5 4 3 2 1

For John
Again, Always, Forever

Acknowledgments

There are many people whose help I sought and received in writing this novel. I'd like to single them out to express my profound gratitude.

To Phyllis Grann, my dear friend, in-law and first editor on every book I've written, my eternal thanks for everything you've done to help me make the transition from reporter to novelist. I wouldn't have written this or any other novel without your help. To Jennifer Weis, my wonderful editor at St. Martin's, my gratitude for initial conversations that helped me shape the plot and later edits that deepened the characters and the story. To Sylvan Creekmore, her assistant, thank you for your help in shepherding the manuscript through all the stages of production. To Karen Richardson, thank you for your copy edits and for saving me from embarrassing mistakes.

To Kathy Robbins, my close friend and agent, thank you for everything from editorial comments to reassurance when necessary to finding just the right publisher for my work to patiently answering my many questions. To Kathy's husband, the excellent writer Richard Cohen, thank you for joining Kathy, Jennifer Weis, my husband, John, and me in perusing the endless lists of possible titles looking for the perfect one, even those suggestions I e-mailed to you all in the middle of the night. To the staff at The Robbins Office, thank you for all your help.

To my daughter Liza Darnton, an excellent professional editor in her own right, thank you for your love and support, your sensitive, insightful comments on the text in many stages of its development, and for not charging me for your work. To my son, Dr. James Darnton, and his wife, Dr. Blythe Darnton, thank you for your encouragement and support and for your invaluable help in guiding me through the medical scenes, instructing me about hospital procedure and illnesses. To my daughter Kyra Darnton and her husband, David Grann, thank you for encouraging me, rejoicing in any success I have had and sharing your lives, children and careers with me. To my five amazing grandchildren, Zachary, Ella, Asher, Adara and Lucy, thank you for bringing so much love and light into my life. I am so proud of all of you.

That leaves the best for last. Thank you to my husband of fifty years, John Darnton, whose help, support, advice, editorial suggestions, wisdom, humor and love I simply don't think I could live without.

1

Marcia was sopping wet when she entered the lobby of her building on West End Avenue. She kicked off her soaked shoes in the doorway. They were probably ruined, she thought, but she was too excited to care. She went straight to her bedroom, dripping little rain puddles onto the Oriental rug in the entry hallway, changed out of her clothes and pulled on a pair of sweatpants and a T-shirt. Catching a glimpse of herself in the bedroom mirror, she noticed her wet hair plastered around her face and towel-dried it with one hand while opening her briefcase. She ignored the manuscript she had brought home to edit and extracted three pamphlets she'd picked up in her doctor's office that afternoon. Clutching them in her hand, she curled up on her bed to read them again.

Surrogacy. Her last chance, her last hope. She had tried everything else. Surely this would work. But she knew getting Jeff to accept it would be an uphill fight. At least it wasn't adoption; she knew he would never give in on that. But he'd also been resistant to every form of conception other than as a by-product of their love-making. She would have preferred it to have happened naturally too, but it hadn't. They had tried to conceive a baby for three years with nothing to show for it but a less spontaneous and thus less exciting sex life. She had taken her temperature every day for months to determine when she was ovulating. She'd rush home when she was and miss dinner dates or parties required for her work. Making love became so separated from seduction it began to seem like a job. They'd been to doctors and they'd had every test anyone could think of and nothing explained why she couldn't conceive. Yes, they'd told her, he had a slightly low sperm count, but others with the condition still had children. Whether that was the problem or it was something else entirely, she remained barren and it had become the heartbreak of her life.

Convincing Jeff to try any medical intervention hadn't been easy. After the first two years of disappointments he was ready to give up. That had been a year ago but she remembered every detail of their conversation as if it were yesterday. She had just emerged from the bathroom, fighting tears.

"I got my period," she'd said disconsolately.

She'd climbed into bed, pulled up the blanket and turned away from him, staring silently into space.

"Don't react like this, Marcia. It's only one time."

"One more time after two years of only one more time. I feel so sad and so stressed I don't know what to do."

"Maybe it's the stress that's stopping it from happening," he said.

"I don't know, that sounds vaguely like it's my fault somehow."

"No, I'm not saying that. We're both tense."

"Look, if being tense prevented conception, rape victims would never get pregnant."

He paused for what seemed like a long time before venturing his next suggestion. "Listen, honey, please, turn around. I want to say something."

She sighed and turned to face him.

"Maybe we just can't do this," he said gently.

She didn't look at him. Her thoughts were far away. "Maybe not like this," she said quietly. "But there are other ways."

He looked perplexed.

"We could try IUI," she said.

"What's that?"

"It's intrauterine insemination."

He looked puzzled.

"You know," she added with a little smile, "the turkey baster method."

He withdrew his arm from her shoulder. "That's a turn-on," he said.

"It's not supposed to be a turn-on," she countered. "It's not about sex. It's about conception."

"I thought those two went together."

"Well, I guess this is for when they don't," she said softly, getting out of bed and leaving the room.

He'd gone along with it after that, but she knew he did so grudgingly. He hated the idea and he hated the process, and she knew, and appreciated, that he submitted only because he understood how important it was to her. But when that method also repeatedly failed, he was more than ready to give up. She'd begged him to talk to her doctor about another possibility and so, reluctantly, he went with her to discuss the next step with her gynecologist.

The doctor had suggested in-vitro fertilization: Marcia's egg would be harvested in a minor surgical procedure and then fertilized by Jeff's sperm outside her body. It would then be inserted into her uterus. The doctor explained that to increase the odds of success she would insert several fertilized eggs at the same time. The process, she said, would cost about $15,000.

They were shocked. Insurance wouldn't pay any of it and although they could afford it—Jeff had a good job in a law firm and Marcia was a senior editor at a publishing house—this was not a price they could shrug off. Besides, they realized that it might not take the first time around. Each cycle would multiply the cost by the same amount. How far were they ready to go?

"What if more than one egg takes?" Jeff had asked one night as they were lying in bed talking about it.

"That's very rare," Marcia answered.

"Not so rare. I can just imagine it. The Naiman Quintuplets," he said. He pretended to roll up his sleeves like a circus barker. "Come and see them. A modern miracle."

Marcia laughed. "Well, we'd be sure to get lots of presents. And five of each. Can't you just see them lined up in their cribs, all of them with your chin dimple?"

"It's not funny, Marcia. What if we did have twins? That's not rare at all in this procedure."

"We'd be done, then," she whispered. "There'd be a few tough years, but we wouldn't have to do this part ever again."

They had gone through with it. There had been no way to turn back—Marcia wanted a baby too much. She'd have tried anything, paid anything, borrowed if she had to. And Jeff had gotten into the spirit of it. It had become a challenge, a kind of high-stakes game and, as usual, he simply didn't want to lose. He seemed equally devastated when it didn't work, Marcia thought. But when she insisted they try it again, he balked. And when she'd convinced him, promising this would be the last time, and once again failed to conceive, he refused to try a third time. The subject had been dropped. They stopped taking her temperature and consciously trying to conceive. But Marcia never really let it go. She was painfully aware that her thirty-ninth birthday was approaching and that soon she might lose her chance completely. She'd taken her temperature without telling him and made sure they made love when she thought she was ovulating. Still, nothing had happened and she felt bereft every month when she got her period. Continually disappointed, her usual optimism failed her and she fell into a depression from which she couldn't seem to emerge.

Now hope slowly stirred again, like a cat stretching

after a long sleep. She felt a renewed sense of possibility and purpose, and resolved to research the subject thoroughly starting tomorrow. She knew Jeff would be against it—they had discussed surrogacy early on and both had rejected the idea—but that was before it was clear it was their only chance. She'd taken it up with her doctor today, and she believed that she had finally hit upon the right solution and that nothing now could stand in her way. Nothing, that is, except Jeff.

2

She spent the next two hours reading about surrogacy on the Internet, pulling up articles, criticisms, and testimonials from happy parents. She learned there were agencies that provided guidance through the process of surrogacy, companies with names like Conceptual Options and Growing Generations, and she made a note of their numbers, resolving to speak to their representatives. Maybe there is a book in it, she thought, featuring different couples talking about their experience. If not, there should be, she noted mechanically—she was an editor, after all.

She heard the door open and close—Jeff coming home. She decided not to discuss it with him right away. It would be prudent to wait until she had more hard facts with which to counter his arguments. But she was so excited that she was barely able to wait until they finished dinner. She fidgeted and fussed around the kitchen and when he started to tell her about a run-in he'd had with a colleague, he noticed she hardly heard a word he said. Seeing that something was preoccupying her, he asked what was going on. He didn't need to ask twice.

"Jeff, I saw Dr. Gordon today," she blurted, barely restraining her excitement.

Dr. Gordon was her gynecologist and Jeff stiffened. "Is everything okay?"

"Yes, everything's fine. It was just a checkup. But we discussed something I really want to talk to you about."

"Sure."

"She thinks maybe we should try surrogacy."

He let out an exasperated sigh. "Marcia, we already discussed surrogacy. That was one area I thought we agreed on. It's wrong. It's exploitive. It's rich people renting the wombs of poor people who do it only because they need the money."

"I've been reading up on it. Some women say they do it to help people who can't have children."

"I think that's bullshit."

She bristled. He was already turning this into an argument. "Why is the only scenario you can accept a selfish one? Believe it or not some people actually get pleasure from helping others."

"You used to say it was all about class," Jeff countered.

She nodded. "I did and I still see that," she said evenly, "but I have to admit I'm open to a different interpretation now. I mean, if there's psychological testing, if the birth mother really knows what she's getting into—

maybe it should only be allowed for women who already have children of their own, for example. And if the birth mother or family really need the added income, maybe it's a way of doing something good for both families."

He looked at her with feigned admiration. "It's amazing how you can adapt your principles to your needs," he said.

"No, I'm just able to let go of my prejudices when I have more information," she snapped.

He got up to get a beer. He hesitated at the refrigerator, clearly deciding whether to come back and resume the conversation, or settle down in the living room and look for a game on ESPN. She knew he didn't want to return, but he finally came back to the table and sat down heavily.

"It just feels wrong, Marcia. Unnatural. A woman isn't an incubator; she has feelings. You can't predict how she'll feel if she bonds with the child during her pregnancy and then has to give it away. What if she changes her mind? Remember that case you used to talk about? That woman who went through the whole surrogacy, signed a contract and everything, and then backed out when the baby was born? What was her name?"

"Mary Beth Whitehead. I followed that story compulsively." She frowned. "I was very much on her side at the time. But things have changed. When she did it, they used her egg. The baby really was her baby, biologically as well as emotionally. Whatever she thought before, whatever she signed up for, she was that baby's mother and it was heartbreaking to watch her pain."

"I know. And I don't think any woman can know how she'll feel about giving up her baby until she actually experiences childbirth," Jeff answered, grateful for even this slight concession. "That's not something you can just sign away without the option to change your mind. I mean, think about it. What if we did this and at the last minute, the mother changed her mind?"

"I don't know. But I'd like to find out how often something like that happens. One of the articles said that now it's not usually the surrogate's egg that's used. That's one of the good things that came out of the Whitehead case. If we did this, the baby would be genetically ours. We need to do more research. There are lots of families who have done it. I think the odds of success are knowable."

"I don't know. It just involves three people when it should involve two—like adoption, which I also never wanted."

"I've always known how you feel about adoption and that's why I never pushed it. But maybe we should revisit it. Would it really bother you so much to not have the baby come from us?"

"Come from us? You mean you think it comes from us when it's born to another mother? I'd call that the definition of not coming from us."

"Not really. But if you can't stand that idea, what is it actually about adoption that makes you so against it?"

"It's not about the genes. For me the worst part in adoption and in surrogacy too is the complications and intrusions it makes in your life. These days you don't just adopt a baby. You have to have a 'relationship' with the birth mother. Even if you don't, the child has a right to know who she is. Families become more complicated. I don't want any of that."

"Jeff, you're confusing things. If the surrogate gives birth to our baby there wouldn't be any reason to maintain a relationship with her after the pregnancy and delivery."

"Who knows? All I know is that our child should come from us in a normal way. I agreed to try to increase our chances and that didn't work. So maybe we're just not meant to have kids."

That stopped her. "Not meant to have kids," she repeated slowly. "Not meant by whom? God? Fate? Destiny? You don't even believe in any of those. We make our own destiny, you've said that a hundred times." She stopped talking and turned away, trying to stop her tears, but they came in spite of her resolve. He softened immediately, reaching out to take her hand.

"Honey, I just think it would be good to try to focus on other aspects of our lives. We're pretty lucky in so many ways. We love each other. We have a great marriage. We can make a good life together even if we never have children."

She wiped away the tears with the back of her hand and got up to get a tissue to blow her nose. When she returned, he reached over to stroke her hair and gently pulled her into an embrace. "I love you so much, Marcia. I'm happy now. As we are. Aren't you happy with me?"

She kissed his neck. "You know I am. Of course I am.

But I always wanted us to be a family. And I'm just not ready to give up on that, not yet."

"Would it be so terrible if we did? I mean, giving up isn't always a defeat. Sometimes it's more like just giving in."

"Giving in to what?"

"To reality."

She shrugged, lifted her chin and pursed her lips, a gesture he recognized as her stubborn refusal to hear him. He got up and stretched his legs before pulling the chair out and sitting down again. "We're all raised to think having kids is what couples have to do. There's this myth we're all fed of the perfect happy family," he said. "It's a portrait we have in our minds. But it doesn't always turn out that way and when that happens it's like someone erased the two children that were supposed to replace us. We can't help feeling there's something wrong. But it's not always so wonderful. Think of Nick and Sarah—really, Marcia, does their life seem so enviable?"

She couldn't help smiling just a little thinking of the chaos she'd noticed the last time she'd visited their friends.

Encouraged, he went on, "Their apartment is cramped. The couch is stained. There are toys all over—you can't walk through the living room without crunching some plastic action figure underfoot. The kids can be cute, but they also scream and cry and have tantrums when they don't get what they want. Nick says it's almost impossible to work at home. It takes so long to put the kids to bed that Sarah says she usually just goes straight to sleep when they do. No more wine and cheese before dinner as they tell each other about their day. And that's a couple with normal kids. What if there are problems?"

Marcia seemed to be listening so he continued.

"And think of Ben and Kathy. They decided not to have kids and they're living an incredible life. They have money for anything they want. They have an amazing apartment filled with designer furniture and antiques. They have elegant dinner parties using their wedding silver and china, and the place always looks beautiful. She dresses like a fashion model. They do things together and fill their lives with activities and travel and fun."

Marcia gave a desultory shrug. "Their life just seems so empty and shallow and narcissistic," she said. "I can't believe they chose it. It makes me so mad that they had the ability to have a family and turned it down. Did you know she got pregnant?"

Jeff frowned; she hadn't been listening after all, he realized.

"Well, she did. And she had an abortion," Marcia said, ignoring Jeff's expression. "And I, who want it so much, can't get pregnant. It's not fair."

He raised his voice in frustration. "I know. It's not fair. But we've tried everything. Maybe it's time to start accepting it."

"We haven't tried everything. That's my point."

"I've tried everything I'm going to try, Marcia. That's *my* point."

There was no reason to continue. She got up and walked to their bedroom without saying another word.

She slammed the door, just in case he hadn't realized how mad she was. As she changed into her nightgown and brushed her teeth she resolved to do more research and convince him. This wasn't over. Not by a long shot.

3

The next day Marcia got to work early. She was surprised to see her assistant already at her computer.

"Good morning," Julie said brightly. "You're early. Want some coffee?"

"You know I do. Thank you. Have you already had some?"

"Yes. I've been here for a while."

"Why so early, Julie? I feel like I'm overworking you."

"No. I just wanted to finish up my report on the manuscript you gave me before the day got too busy."

Marcia smiled. She remembered her days as an assistant editor and her own efforts to move up in the hierarchy.

"There's no rush on that. What do you think so far?"

"I like it," Julie said. "I'll have the report finished soon."

Julie disappeared down the hallway and returned with a steaming cup of coffee. Marcia thanked her and asked her to do a search for titles of some books written about surrogacy. Then she spent several hours online looking up articles on the subject. She found a wealth of information. There was even a support group for surrogate parents called Organization of Parents Through Surrogacy on whose website she found inspiring success stories and many of the resource she needed. She read a first-person article in *The New York Times* on two kinds of surrogacy. There was the traditional type as was done with Mary Beth Whitehead, where the surrogate's egg is fertilized by the prospective father, and gestational surrogacy, where the surrogate bears a baby who grew from the egg and sperm of the intended parents. As she'd told Jeff, it was clear from the article that many more people chose gestational surrogacy. She couldn't find any mention of how many surrogates changed their minds, so she called one of the agencies for that information. A secretary assured her that was rarely a problem anymore and promised to e-mail her more information. Minutes later, a fact sheet arrived in her mailbox stating that the law was clear: in the case of gestational surrogacy, the genetic parents had precedence. The agency claimed that because of their excellent psychological profiling, they had never, in ten years, had a single case in which the birth mother had changed her mind.

Marcia had closed her office door. An hour after lunch Julie knocked and, as was her habit, entered without waiting for a reply. Marcia looked up, slightly guiltily, since she'd done nothing but read about surrogacy since she had arrived at work.

"Did you get a chance to look at the Olsen manuscript?" Julie asked.

"Not yet. What did you think?"

"Here's my report," she said, placing it on Marcia's desk. "The text is a little rough, but I think it would work if it were edited. I think it shows a lot of potential."

Marcia knew that Julie was eager to bring in something that would be published.

"Do you think we should buy it?"

"I'd love to, Marcia. I think it could really be commercial."

Maria looked thoughtful. "Okay, then," she said at last. "But don't go higher than twenty thousand for the advance."

"You mean I can buy it even though you haven't even read it yet?"

Marcia smiled. She liked Julie. "You've been here for two years. You have a good eye. Go ahead. Good luck."

Julie thanked her profusely and rushed out the door.

Marcia returned to her computer. She was looking up the cost for the surrogacy. The *Times* article was written eight years ago so prices were probably higher now, but even then they were shockingly expensive. She learned that surrogacy was unregulated federally and laws varied by state. There was a list of states where prospective parents were advised to proceed with caution or not at all, and New York, where it was explicitly illegal, was one of them. She'd have to look elsewhere. California seemed to be one of the most liberal states in terms of its surrogacy policies and had the advantage of being far enough away so it would discourage any long-term relationship with the birth mother. She made a note to specify California when she asked the agency for surrogate candidates.

Even though she was prepared, the price was a shock— more than $100,000 by the time fees were added for lawyers, insurance, psychologists, labs, hospitals, and agencies charged with finding the appropriate birth mother. It wasn't clear how much went directly to the birth mother, but Marcia feared the sum wouldn't be enough to balance the enormity of her contribution. The price seemed to eliminate the option of surrogacy. But she couldn't stop thinking about it and she knew that if everything else felt right, she and Jeff would find the money somehow. They had savings, though not enough. But they both had good jobs—they could borrow the balance. It was comforting to learn that there was an entire surrogacy support system, an industry, really, engaged in steering people through the laws and complications and problems. She still felt uncertain about the moral implications. The niggling feeling remained that it was wrong, that however she looked at it she would feel as though she were buying a baby and exploiting a less fortunate woman. The idea of paying someone to go through pregnancy and delivery for her remained distasteful, and if she still felt that way, she couldn't imagine how she could ever convince Jeff. She continued reading. She was hoping to find someone with the same reservations who had navigated these moral shoals and was rewarded with a child.

Julie walked in again. "I'm really sorry to bother you, Marcia, but they're all in the conference room waiting for you. What should I tell them?"

Marcia had been so absorbed she'd forgotten the afternoon conference. It was her job to fire up the sales force about the books she had commissioned so they would be able to sell them to the bookstores and, especially, the online distributors like Amazon. She turned off her computer, riffled through her papers for her notes and rushed to the conference room. She knew she couldn't keep doing this. She was arriving late and ill-prepared to an important meeting. She didn't get to be a senior editor in a major publishing house with that kind of behavior, and she knew too how fragile the business was these days, and how easy it would be to replace her.

She muddled her way through the meeting, neither disgracing nor distinguishing herself, and returned to her office. This time she locked the door. She went back online and found the *Times* article again. She wanted to know what came next. Let's say she contacted the agency or a lawyer and said she was interested; how would they find the surrogate? She read that the client would receive profiles of surrogates in different states. She would be presented with statements from each candidate detailing her life, her ambitions and her reasons for wanting the job. The reporter who had written the story had gone through the process herself and chronicled what she experienced. Marcia was surprised to learn how many applicants there were to be surrogates, and how much they seemed to want to do it. They came from all over the country and many walks of life. They had to be in good health and agree to being monitored during their pregnancy and to maintain good nutrition. While most were struggling economically, none was impoverished. All said they were applying for altruistic reasons, though of course several admitted that the extra money would help. It made Marcia wonder.

Maybe it was condescending to assume the surrogates were being exploited. Maybe it really was a bargain struck by two families that benefited each of them. She wanted to believe that, and the article made a good case for it. Her impulse was to rush home and share everything she'd learned with Jeff but she held back. She knew he thought the matter was settled and she was quietly dealing with it. But she told herself she was just trying to educate herself. She didn't quite admit, even to herself, that she was determined to go ahead. It was now a question of conquering his objections, and keeping her own reservations at bay.

4

A week passed and Marcia continued to read about surrogacy. She had contacted several agencies trying to decide which was best and had even been put in touch with a few past clients who were happy to talk about their experience. She kept her activity from Jeff, but her unusual restraint and secrecy erected a barrier between them, and their conversation felt strained and formal. Now they were in the car, driving north to their country house in Woodstock. It was a glorious Saturday morning. The dogwood and cherry blossoms were all in bloom and the oaks and aspens were just pushing forth their tiny pale green buds. Here and there the canary-yellow forsythia bushes leapt out from the surrounding green. If ever there was a season of hope, she thought, it was this.

"Look at that beautiful tree," she said. "I think it's a

magnolia. I love them, even though they bloom for such a short time."

He didn't respond directly, but said, "I was thinking we should take a few days off and take a trip. Maybe we should drive to Montreal. We could stay in a great hotel and see the sights. You could practice your French."

"Thanks. I really do appreciate that offer," she said quickly. "But I can't. There's a lot going on at work."

They were both silent for a few miles. Jeff turned on the radio.

"Classical or rock?" he asked.

"I don't care. Whatever you want."

He switched it off. "Marcia, you have to try."

"I am trying," she said.

They pulled off the highway and headed toward their house, stopping at the outdoor market for supplies. They were expecting guests for dinner, a woman Marcia had met in this same market a few years back while both were squeezing avocados to test their ripeness. They had started talking, and it turned out the woman, Grace Zilman, worked in publicity for Random House and her husband, Mike, was a doctor with a practice on the Upper East Side. Their apartment was just across the park from Marcia and Jeff's. The women had indulged in the obligatory jokes about the difference between East Siders and West Siders, Marcia asking if she would need a passport to visit them. They both laughed, even though they'd heard that same joke dozens of times. Marcia liked her immediately and had invited the Zilmans to dinner the following weekend. At that point, she and Jeff had been spending weekends in Woodstock for almost seven years, yet knew few people in the area. Because they both had demanding full-time jobs, they tended to leave the city late Friday and return Sunday, departing early enough to avoid the mad Sunday traffic jam as other weekenders headed home. They often invited friends from the city to come with them, almost always a welcome invitation for those without a refuge in the countryside. But she and Jeff had also wanted to get to know more people in the community.

Grace and Marcia found they had a lot in common. They both worked in publishing, both cared about theater, good food and good books, and were both avid readers of *The New York Times*. Luckily their husbands seemed to like each other too, and the couples began to make occasional dates in the city as well as share dinners together in Woodstock. They particularly liked to find out-of-the-way restaurants in the different ethnic neighborhoods New York City was so rich in, enjoying both the food and the cultural diversity. They had even joined a couples book group in the city that met once a month and saw each other most weekends in the country. But all that had come to an abrupt halt almost three years ago when Grace gave birth. Busy, sleep-deprived, overwhelmed, Grace and Mike had dropped first out of the book club, then stopped dinner and theater dates, and had only recently resumed regular trips to the country. Having learned they were coming this weekend, Marcia had invited them for dinner and was delighted when Grace accepted.

Dinner was planned for seven with drinks on the back

porch at six. Grace and Mike arrived at seven-thirty, flustered and apologetic. Stephie, their nearly three-year-old, had apparently objected to the babysitter. She started crying just as they were leaving and threw herself on the ground screaming and kicking as they closed the door. Mike thought they should keep going, teach her that such behavior wasn't profitable. But Grace simply couldn't bring herself to do it, much to the relief of the twenty-year-old babysitter, who looked nearly as upset as Grace. It took about half an hour to calm her down, finally accomplished by relenting on the no-more-television rule and allowing her to watch *Dora the Explorer* as her parents quietly crept out.

Marcia and Jeff reassured them that it didn't matter what time they arrived and the group settled down on the back porch. The sun was low in the sky, surrounded by a spreading aura of pink and fuchsia. Jeff served drinks and they all gazed appreciatively at the view. "What a beautiful spot," Grace said, visibly relaxing.

"It definitely is," Mike agreed. "We had an exhausting day. Stephie woke up at two and couldn't go back to sleep in her own room so she crawled in between us."

Grace shook her head and laughed. "Her feet were on my side," she said. "You know how these kids are. They can't sleep in a straight line. It's kind of equal-opportunity discomfort—that way none of us can sleep.

"But eventually we got a few hours and first thing this morning, we all went to a petting zoo so she could touch the sheep and the rabbits," Grace added. "Then there was a birthday party and then home and her dinner and bath and then the tantrum before we left. She is having some serious separation issues, but the doctors say it's all age appropriate." She drained her glass. "Anyway, you can imagine how much we are enjoying this."

"I'm so glad," Marcia said. "Can I get you another?"

"No, I'd better not," Grace said reluctantly. "I may be up again tonight and I don't want to be hungover." Jeff held up his empty glass. "I wouldn't mind more," he said, "if you're going in." Marcia left to refill his glass and Grace followed her.

Jeff turned to Mike. "How's it going? We miss you guys."

"I know. We feel the same. But it's been tough to make time." He took a long swig of his drink. "It's been a tough transition all around. You know, kids all day in my practice and then making sure I have some time with Stephie when I get home, there's just not much time for . . . well, you know." He shrugged. A slight, uncomfortable pause followed. "How's the law business?" he asked.

"The same. We never run out of business."

"I heard a quote about lawyers the other day and I thought of you."

"You never run out of lawyer jokes either."

"You don't mind, do you?"

"Nah. Shoot."

"Well, this one was something like, 'In every legal transaction there is a moment when money hangs in the air, suspended between two parties. It is that moment that the clever lawyer makes his own.' I think it was Shakespeare."

Jeff smiled. "I doubt it. But it's pretty good."

In the kitchen, Marcia asked Grace how her job was going.

"It's fine. I like the hours. I don't do book readings or interviews anymore. I specialize in online publicity. I work while I'm there but I'm free when I go home and I can leave every day at six. That gives me more time with Stephie. And actually, I'll probably be going on leave soon. I'm expecting another baby in the fall."

Marcia tried hard to smile. "Congratulations."

"I love those months at home after the baby is born. And this time, I'll have a better idea how to handle things. Last time, I was pretty nervous. But Mike took paternity leave for two weeks and that helped."

Marcia couldn't think of anything to say.

"What about you, Marcia? Do you two have any plans for kids?"

"I don't know. Maybe."

Marcia picked up a knife and busied herself slicing vegetables for the coq au vin. She poured another vodka for Jeff and handed it to Grace. "Would you mind taking this out? I need to get this going. I'll be out in a minute."

When she called them to the table twenty minutes later, after finding enough to do in the kitchen so she didn't have to reappear right away, they seemed to be deep in conversation.

Grace looked at her sympathetically as she sat down.

"Jeff's been telling us about your problems getting pregnant," Grace said. "I'm so sorry."

Marcia turned toward Jeff. Two scotches or not, he felt
the heat of her glare and knew he had made a mistake.
Mike caught the look and stared at his plate.

"This looks delicious," he said, glancing nervously at
his wife, who barreled on, oblivious.

"He says you tried everything, but, I was wondering,
have you thought of surrogacy? I have a friend who just
brought home a beautiful baby girl from a surrogate in
Tennessee."

Jeff stiffened. There was an awkward silence.

"Grace, honey, maybe Marcia doesn't want to talk
about this. It's kind of private."

"I'm sorry," Jeff said to Marcia, clearly nervous. "I
should never have—"

Marcia got up abruptly and walked briskly back to the
kitchen, her jaw tight. The kitchen was a large, loft-like
room, separated from the dining area by a granite-topped
counter. No curtains adorned the floor-to-ceiling windows so she could clearly see the full moon casting a soft
light in the night sky as she prepared the vegetables. The
effect was soothing as she tried to calm down. Jeff's telling these people whom she hadn't even seen for months
their most intimate disappointment was a huge betrayal.
But she realized she might be able to use their support
in her ongoing argument with Jeff. She heated the asparagus and arranged it on a serving platter, adding
lemon slices and a few drops of melted butter. She could
hear her guests turn to less sensitive subjects. Grace was
describing how amazed she and Mike were at the com-
petitive challenge of getting a three-year-old into nursery

school in New York City. She came from Madison, Wisconsin, where you simply signed your kid up. The only challenge was having enough money to pay tuition. But in New York, the schools started testing kids at three to see if they measured up. Stephie had frozen at the interview and didn't interact with the adults at all. They'd asked her to string beads and she balked, picking up another toy instead. "I mean, she'd been stringing beads since she was two," Grace said. "She was bored by it."

Marcia took the bread out of the oven, placed it in the breadbasket and picked up the asparagus platter, which she passed around. Grace was talking about people in Woodstock who refused to vaccinate their children. Grace felt they were putting all children at risk. Mike said that as a pediatrician he had been asked to appear as an expert witness in the case of an immune-compromised boy who had caught measles from a child in his nursery school class who had not been vaccinated. The unvaccinated child had recovered, but this boy had died and the parents were suing the family and the school.

They all expressed their outrage, both at the parents who refused vaccinations and the school for not insisting. "Will you do it?" Marcia asked Mike.

"I will. And I'm very sympathetic to the family, of course. But I'm not sure if they'll win."

The conversation segued into other interesting cases. "Remember Mary Beth Whitehead?" Mike said. "The surrogate mother who wouldn't give up the baby?"

There was a tense silence and he seemed embarrassed, remembering this was a sensitive subject. He looked nervously at his wife and they all looked at Marcia. She held both hands up in protest. "Please, I'm so sorry to have made you uncomfortable. I know you were being kind, Grace. It just took me by surprise, that's all. It doesn't mean surrogacy is a taboo subject. Actually, now that you've been inducted into our private life, I might as well confess that I've been trying to get Jeff to agree to look into it with me."

Now it was Jeff's turn to abruptly leave the table. He returned with the salt and pepper.

"That's a wonderful idea," Grace said. "Aside from the friend I mentioned earlier, I also know someone in L.A. who had three children through surrogates and it worked out fabulously. I think it all depends on finding the right surrogate. But you can; there are women who really want to do it and agencies to help you locate them." She looked at Jeff, who had just sat down. "Why do you have to be convinced?"

"I don't know," he said, "it just feels wrong."

"How so?" Mike asked.

"It feels exploitive," Jeff answered. It annoyed Marcia that he kept saying that when she knew his real opposition was the fact that it wasn't "normal" in his view, or traditional.

"I'm not so sure," Mike countered. "Maybe some women really like being able to do it. I think there's basic altruism, but it must also feel good that they can do something these rich women can't."

"And think of the power these surrogates have," Grace added. "For nine months, how they eat, what they drink, how they behave, suddenly becomes vitally important to a group of wealthy people who never thought twice about them before."

"Well, that might be," Jeff said. Before anyone could say more, he got up and opened the door to the deck.

"Let's step out for a minute," Marcia said. "It's such a beautiful night."

They all made their way outside. The sky was cloudless and the constellations stood out clearly. At first Grace and Mike couldn't make them out, but Marcia knew them all and described them, until, slowly at first and then with a sudden flash of recognition, the others could see them. "First you find Polaris, the night star," Marcia said, explaining how it was the brightest. Then she pointed out the Big and Little Dippers because they were the easiest, and finally Orion, the Hunter; Ursa Major, the bear.

A cool breeze stirred the air and Mike put his arm around Grace's shoulders as she slid hers around his waist.

"This is beautiful," Mike said, "but I'm afraid we have to get home. You know the drill—we'll have to pay the babysitter, take her home and try to get some sleep before Stephie gets up early tomorrow."

Marcia and Jeff led them back into the house, where they collected their things and said good night. Afterward, Marcia suggested they leave the dishes for the next morning and Jeff gratefully agreed. She put the butter and other perishables in the fridge, and he went around the house turning off lights and locking doors. She put on her nightgown and got into bed.

"I hope I didn't ruin tonight," he said as he joined her. "I'm really sorry. You did a good job of covering it, but I know you were upset."

"I got over it."

"So, we're okay?"

She smiled as she leaned over to kiss him on the cheek, the warmest gesture she'd made in a week. "Yeah. Of course. I just felt embarrassed. I mean, we were just starting to reconnect."

"Did you do that with Grace?"

"I don't know. She's different. Did you notice that from the moment they arrived, their one topic of conversation was their child?"

"I did. People with kids always think everyone is as interested in them as they are. Especially her. That's all she could talk about; it's like the rest of her mind has totally turned off."

"I won't be like that if we have kids, don't worry. But if we don't have kids, something like that is going to keep happening, Jeff. We'll always be the couple listening to stories about other people's children. It will never get easier."

"Maybe we'll just have to make other friends."

She settled into her pillow. "I haven't given up yet," she murmured. "But I'm falling asleep. Let's turn off the light."

He reached up and switched it off, then leaned over and kissed her lightly on the mouth. "We'll figure it out. I love you."

"Me too," she murmured.

She turned to get into her sleep position, lying on her side with her back to him. Her mind was racing and she knew she wouldn't sleep. "Good night," she said.

"Good night." He turned over too. In a few minutes she could hear the deep, regular breathing that indicated sleep, and a few minutes after that it was confirmed by loud snoring. She lay awake thinking well into the night.

5

Marcia awoke early. Her bed faced a picture window through which she could see the woods and, beyond them, the mountains. Well, she thought as she admired them, not high mountains, not like the Rockies or Mount Rainier, but high enough for her and beautiful in the morning light. She tiptoed out of bed to put on the coffee. She didn't want to wake Jeff because this early morning solitude was important to her. She loved watching the cardinals and finches stop by the bird feeder, scattering husks on the ground in their enthusiasm as they pecked greedily at the seeds. She often enjoyed watching the hummingbirds, furiously beating their little wings as they drank the pink sugared water in their own feeder a few feet away, but today they were absent. She brewed the coffee and took her cup onto the back porch. It was a little chilly so she wrapped a shawl around her and luxuriated in the stillness of the morning. She thought about the previous night and wondered if the discussion had made an impact on Jeff. He'd had a chance to hear other people say surrogacy was a good idea and tell about friends who had done it. All in all the conversation had made surrogacy seem less controversial, less strange, and that, she knew, would be important to him. She returned to the house and refilled her cup. She heard stirring in the bedroom so she stood at the door and asked Jeff if he was ready for coffee. He was, so she brought it to him. He smiled his thanks.

"You're up early," he said.

"Yes. It's a lovely day. I so enjoy these morning hours when we don't have to rush off to work and we have time together." She crept back into bed beside him, propping herself up on pillows. "And it's so beautiful here. I love the city, but we're lucky we have this too."

"I know," he said. "This is the kind of thing I was talking about the other day. Imagine how different it would be if we had a kid. We'd miss all this quiet private time together."

She smiled. "Yes, we would. But we'd have it again someday and we'd have so much more. It would be worth it."

"Maybe."

He stretched, then sipped his coffee. "Remember what we were talking about last night?" His voice was amused, teasing. "I noticed you were less angry I confided in them when they approved so much of surrogacy. Did you plan that somehow?"

"No, but I was grateful. I hope you listened to what they were saying."

"I heard them," he answered, noncommittal.

"They had friends who'd done it three times. And no one backed out and they said it was a big success. That could be our story too. If we went ahead with this, we could still be parents, Jeff."

"Whoa. I didn't mean to open up that subject again," he said good-naturedly. She snuggled up next to him.

"If we ever did have a baby, I'd want him to have your thick, unruly black hair and your deep brown eyes. I'd want him to be tall like you are and inherit that cleft in your chin," she said. "But I wouldn't mind leaving out your resistance to the modern world."

He grinned and played along. "I'm an old-world kind of guy. I thought that's what you liked about me. And if we'd been able to conceive the old-fashioned way, I'd have wanted our daughter to be stubborn and compulsive like you. Then you'd see what a hero I am for putting up with you all these years."

"Hey!"

He laughed. "And I'd have wanted her to inherit your beautiful hands, and your long brown straight hair and hazel eyes," he said. "That's why I don't want to adopt. I don't want some stranger's short curly hair, however pretty it might be."

"You don't inherit long hair," she said, laughing too. "You just let it grow.

"Whatever.

"Remember that famous Bernard Shaw quote?" he

asked, clearly ready to move on. "He was at a party sitting next to a beautiful actress. She turned to him and said, 'Mr. Shaw, we should have a baby together. With your brains and my looks, it would be a triumph.'

"'Ah, madam,' he answered without skipping a beat. 'But what if it had your brains and my looks?'"

She laughed again. "We'd have fun trying to figure out what the baby inherited from whom," she said.

"I wish it could have happened, honey. I know how much you wanted it. But you're okay, right?"

"Yeah. I'm okay. Sort of."

The rest of the day passed happily. They went for a bike ride and stopped in town for lunch. At home, Jeff read the paper and puttered around the house and garden while Marcia worked on a manuscript she was editing. On the way back to the city, they bought a basket of apples at the farm market and some fresh eggs from a neighbor who kept chickens. Surrogacy didn't come up again, but she felt she'd brought him a long way toward agreeing to it and she decided she would register with the agency and tell them she was ready to see applications.

6

The first thing that attracted Marcia to the woman who would become her surrogate was her name: Eve. It was perfect. Eve, the mother of us all, would be the birth mother of her child, she thought. Wouldn't that be appropriate? She had slogged through dozens of applications with slightly discouraging results. While there was something good about most of them, there was something wrong with most of them too. She couldn't put her finger on it, but she felt she had to go by instinct, and her instinct told her that she had not yet found the right person. One seemed excellent—a stay-at-home mother of four whose husband was recently laid off and who needed money to support her family until he found another job. *I don't have a job or a career*, she wrote. *But one thing I know how to do is push out babies and I'd be happy to do that for someone else for a change.* She sounded clear-headed and even had a sense of humor, but she lived in New Jersey, much too close if there was to be little chance of contact after the birth. Another said outright that she needed the money and that was her main reason for applying. While Marcia appreciated the honesty, she recoiled from the cold, business-like tone and doubted the woman, who had not had her own child, had a full appreciation of how her emotions might factor in. Another applicant waxed on poetically about wanting to give joy to others. Her application was well written and movingly expressed, but Marcia feared she was a romantic who might find the reality of bearing and then relinquishing a baby traumatic. Eve's application, however, stood out. She seemed realistic and able to balance a sense of service with her own need. She was a widowed mother of a ten-year-old boy whom, she wrote, was the joy and purpose of her life. She had a limited education and worked as a housekeeper in a nursing home in Los Angeles, far enough away, Marcia thought, to discourage any impulse for contact after the baby was born.

She read the application several times, especially the essay, which read: *I want to give my boy a better life. He has nobody but me in this world and I want to put away something for him. He's a good boy and he is smart, but our neighborhood is rough. I want him to go to a decent school. I want to live where there is not so much drugs and gangs.* In response to the question of whether she thought she would mind giving up the child and whether she would want an ongoing relationship with the family, she answered:

*I liked being pregnant. I had no problem. I won't mind
doing it again. I want to give this feeling of love I have for my
boy to someone else. I want to see a woman who thought she
could never have a baby smile the first time she looks at her
child and knows her life will never be the same. But I do not
want to carry my own baby. It must be the egg of the baby's
future mother. And I don't never want to see the mother or
father or baby ever again after. I will do this. I'll do it right.
But it will end when the baby is born.*

She was exactly what Marcia had been looking for. Of
course she had to meet her and see if they got along, but
this was the first application that felt like a distinct possibility. The woman sounded strong, sure of what she
wanted, nobody's dupe. She seemed smart too, regardless of her minimal education. Marcia briefly considered
going to L.A. to meet Eve before talking to Jeff, but she
quickly rejected that idea. She was ready to present her
case to her reluctant husband and then, if all went well,
he would come to L.A. with her and they would go
through every additional stage of this life-changing
adventure together: the choice of the surrogate, the
development of the fetus (she would fly there every month
for doctor appointments, she resolved) and the birth.
She could already picture sharing the ultrasound photos
of the baby in utero, and choosing names together and
decorating the nursery. But she was getting ahead of
herself. Tonight she would read Eve's application to Jeff.
She returned to the manuscript on her desk, a quasi-
historical novel that fabricated a love life for Jane Austen.
It wasn't easy to concentrate. She tried several times,

before calling Julie and asking her to take a look at it. It would have had to be very good to engage her attention at this particular moment and, frankly, she thought impatiently, it wasn't. Maybe that was a good way to judge a book's commercial appeal: Did it grab you when you were obsessively involved with something else?

She packed up the rejected applications, put them in a file cabinet in her bottom drawer. It was already eleven and she hadn't done much work yet, though she had been up till one the night before, reading the new novel of an author she had great hopes for. She had made notes all over the manuscript and now called Julie in to dictate an editorial letter. Julie arrived carrying two cups of coffee, and handed one to Marcia before sitting down on the black upholstered chair across from Marcia's.

"Have you seen the sales figures on the adoption book? They're awesome," Julie said.

Marcia smiled. "Julie, please, you work in a literary establishment, don't say 'awesome.'"

Julie colored slightly. "I'm sorry. I just was excited because it's doing so well and I know it was one you particularly championed."

"I'm joking, Julie. Even about this being a literary establishment. Our fiction is usually more what I like to call 'faux literature.' But now and then . . . when we're lucky, we get a commercial success that's also a good book. I'm very pleased. In fact, I've been thinking about commissioning a surrogacy book. What do you think?"

"Fiction or nonfiction?"

"Either, if it's good. Why don't you see what's around

or what you can suggest to the right author. If you bring in something promising, you can edit it."

Julie beamed and Marcia began dictating the letter. After that there were the e-mails and calls to return, agents to mollify or bargain with, and meetings to attend. The work distracted her and she didn't start worrying again until she was walking from the subway to her apartment. She had a clear idea of what she wanted to happen and she was nervous about achieving it, going over in her mind what would be the best way to recruit Jeff.

He was already home when she arrived. He'd had an afternoon meeting that ended later than expected, so instead of going back to the office, he had come straight home. He suggested they go out for dinner and she readily agreed. They walked arm-in-arm to Broadway, heading for their favorite restaurant where, in spite of its popularity, they could usually get a table. Today was no different. Dave, the maître d', met them with an effusive greeting and, shaking his head at how busy they were, checked his reservation list. He assured them that hard as it was, he could probably do something for them, as Jeff slipped him $20. When they were seated, Jeff ordered a vodka martini and Marcia asked for a glass of Pino Grigio. She wasn't much of a drinker, but she reached for it and took a deep swig. Jeff smiled affectionately. "Don't drink it too fast, honey. You know how quickly it goes to your head."

She smiled back. "Yeah, I know. It's usually enough for me to just smell the cork, right? Cheap date." Their eyes met in appreciation of their old joke. She felt ready to tell him what was on her mind.

Like most scenes set up in someone's imagination beforehand, this one didn't go exactly as planned. After the first course arrived, she couldn't hold back her excitement a moment longer. She launched into a long explanation of how her thinking about surrogacy had developed and changed after their dinner in Woodstock, how she had researched the subject and found how often it worked successfully, how she had read dozens of stories and was now convinced that, when the surrogate was chosen correctly, the process had great benefits for both families. She had contacted an agency, she told him, she had studied applications ("Applications, Jeff. I mean, they seek out these opportunities. These women aren't victims, they are lining up to do this.") and finally had found one she thought would be perfect and would obviate all his fears about it. Did he want to see what the woman wrote? She reached into her briefcase and took out Eve's application and thumbed through it, looking for the essay, but not looking up at him. If she had, she would have noticed that he appeared surprised and disturbed. He had let her tell the whole story without a single interruption but now he said softly but firmly, "No. Wait, Marcia. We have things to talk about."

He had stopped eating and now pushed his plate to the side. "I thought you had finally come around," he said. "I mean, I knew you were still disappointed about not having a baby and I knew that day in Woodstock was a setback, but you seemed okay. I mean, we even joked about it together. I believed you were facing reality and realizing that we were just not meant to be parents. I don't understand how you could let me think that when all this was going on."

She put the essay on the table and looked at him in disbelief. "How could I know what you were thinking? I never joked about it. I didn't imagine you would think I would just let go of something this big just like that, without even telling you."

"You were planning and plotting to do something you knew I was against without even telling me."

She reached for his hand and covered it with her own. He didn't withdraw it. "No, darling, no, that wasn't it. I just didn't want . . . no, I just *wanted* to come to you with all the facts, with my own mind satisfied, before I brought you into it. I never meant to deceive you. I love you. This is for both of us. All I want is for us to do this together, both of us ready for this great moment in our life, and I knew you were more reluctant than me so I wanted to have some answers for you. Please don't feel betrayed. It's the opposite. I promise." Her eyes were moist with tears she was trying not to shed but he could see them and it was impossible to deny the strength of her feeling or her sincerity. He squeezed her hand and patted it before withdrawing his own, and he seemed calmer.

"Okay, okay. It just took me by surprise." He called over the waiter and ordered another vodka and another Pino Grigio for Marcia. She looked so sad.

"Another *moment parfait* ruined—right?" he asked softly.

"No. This is different." When they first met and early in their relationship, they had talked about enjoying beautiful times together, perfect moments that they seemed to fall into so naturally that the reality matched their most romantic fantasy. Later, when they would argue or disagree about something, one of them would accuse the other of ruining a perfect moment and, somehow, probably because Marcia was studying French at the time, they started referring to it in French, a button each could press without succumbing to a full apology. "Remember our *moments parfaits*?" one of them would ask, and usually, especially when the actual disagreement was solved, it would be enough to bridge the gap.

"I know it is," he said. "Please, show me the essay."

In the end, she prevailed. Although he was disturbed by the high cost, he resigned himself to the necessity of taking it on if all his other reservations could be satisfied. He was mollified by Eve's strong desire not to continue any relationship with them or the baby after the delivery, and he agreed in principle to keep investigating surrogacy as a solution. He even agreed to accompany Marcia to L.A. to meet Eve.

Later that night, as Marcia was brushing her teeth, it struck her that Jeff was not only ambivalent about the surrogacy, he was ambivalent about having children at all. She also knew that for her, the latter outcome would mean she would always feel this ache, this hole inside her. She felt a wave of immense gratitude that he was willing, against his own inclinations, to go along with this for her. And she was sure that once they had the baby, he would love it as much as she would. He would be grateful that she pushed so hard to make it happen. She rinsed her toothbrush, swallowed her nighttime vitamins and climbed into bed, snuggling up against him. He turned and pulled her to him. They made love without the need for it to produce anything other than their mutual enjoyment. And it was good.

7

Eve Russo lived in Los Angeles's East Side, a neighborhood that Marcia discovered was more than 96 percent Hispanic. This surprised her because Eve was Caucasian, of Italian-Irish extraction. But like most of the people who lived in East L.A., Eve was poor and everyone knew where to find the poor side of town. She had moved to this neighborhood with her Mexican husband, Jorge, and had stayed after he'd left, bringing up their son, Danny, alone.

Jorge had loved East L.A., where legal immigrants from Mexico and other countries in Latin America mingled with the many illegals. Known to outsiders as a section of violent gangs, drugs and rampant crime, it was home to the people who lived there who filled it with their missed culture and delicious Hispanic food. The bodegas and *mercados* in the neighborhood transported patrons, at least in their imaginations, to the streets of

Antigua or Mexico City. Here shoppers could find
delicacies they loved from their home countries—pigs'
feet, empanadas, *líuidas*, burritos, pan dulce, mixed in
with the sugary American products they favored. Jorge
relented when Eve insisted they give their baby son an
American name, but he wanted Danny to be part of his
Hispanic culture and just living where they did accomplished that. Eve liked it at first too. Even though her
mom was Irish way back and her dad said he was Ital-
ian, neither had any ties to those countries anymore and
were pretty much homogenized American. Jorge and
his world were foreign and exotic, and she appreciated
and encouraged Danny's dual heritage. She learned
Spanish and made sure Danny spoke it too, even continuing to use it occasionally at home after Jorge disappeared. But as her boy grew, Eve began to understand
the downside of the neighborhood. She worried con-
stantly about how to protect him from drugs and crime.
This made her ambitious and she was working on her
GRE to finish high school, hoping to graduate from
housekeeper at the care home to nurse's aide. Sometimes
she even dreamed of studying to become a nurse. That
wouldn't have been so far-fetched if she hadn't run off
with Jorge years before. Her father was a construction
worker. Her mother worked at Walmart. She was their
only child and they wanted her to go to school and make
something of herself. But after she met Jorge they went
crazy, she often said. They forbade her from seeing him,
just because he was Mexican (and in the country illegally),
she bitterly told her friends. Finally, she got pregnant, ran

off to California with him and married him on her eighteenth birthday. She wanted to reconcile with her parents,
she'd tried a few times, but they wouldn't speak to her.
She figured they'd come around eventually, but three
years later, it was too late. A car accident ended both their
lives. Eve was alone.

By the time Marcia and Jeff had made arrangements
to meet her and landed at LAX, Eve and her ten-year-
old son were living alone together in their own two-room
apartment down the street from a market that sold the
Hispanic food Eve had learned to prepare and Danny
loved. Marcia and Jeff took a taxi to the address she had
sent them and noticed how the neighborhood deterio-
rated as they got closer. The houses were smaller, the
yards, when they existed, less cared for. Eve and her son
lived in a shabby two-story building that housed four
apartments. It was Saturday, usually a working day for
Eve, but she called in sick. Eve's job paid minimum wage
but she found she could scrape by doing overtime and
working two shifts twice a week and one on Saturday.
Since public transportation was almost nonexistent, she
needed a car and couldn't afford one—even one as old
and beat-up as the one she'd managed to procure—
without the extra work.

Marcia rang the bell, but it didn't work, so she knocked
on the door. When Eve answered, Marcia nervously extended her hand. Eve took it awkwardly and smiled shyly
at her. They entered and the women silently examined
each other. Eve saw a tall, stylish woman with hazel eyes
that seemed both anxious and kind. She had long chestnut

hair that was swept up on the back of her head and was wearing a navy and white dress with a matching jacket. She looked to be around thirty, even though Eve knew she was actually thirty-nine. Eve also saw that the woman was rich, so wealthy she could afford to pay more than $100,000 to have this baby. She had smooth skin, few lines and a strong body. Her soft white hands had never scrubbed floors. She probably goes to a gym to work out, Eve thought. She doesn't have to worry about having enough money to take care of this kid she wants so much. She didn't look too closely at Jeff except to note that he was tall and well dressed. Her husband comes with her, she thought. He helps her. No wonder she has no wrinkles.

Marcia was looking and appraising too. She saw a thin pretty woman with long blond hair pulled into a pony-tail and straight bangs. She looked more like a girl of eighteen than a woman of twenty-nine and was wearing clean, khaki pants and a short-sleeved yellow flowered blouse. Her home was bare—only a couch and a table with three unmatched chairs in the first room and two twin beds and two dressers in the second. But everything was spotless. A bat and glove lay on the floor in the living room, and a small *Star Wars* Legos set was on the dresser in the bedroom. Apart from that, Marcia didn't see any toys or games. There were no bookcases. A kid's backpack was on the floor near the door, and some note-books and a few baseball cards lay on the table.

After greeting each other, Eve presented her son, a short, black-haired boy with large round dark eyes, high cheekbones and smooth light brown skin, clearly

inherited from his father. He was wearing a Dodgers
T-shirt that had been washed many times and a pair of
jeans. "This is Danny," Eve said proudly. Danny mumbled
hello, looking embarrassed.

Eve offered them coffee and they accepted. Danny
took an iPod from his backpack and disappeared into the
other room. Ah, thought Marcia. He doesn't need other
toys. He plays with that instead. She was determined to
strictly limit the "device time" for her child, having read
several articles about how harmful too much screen time
could be for young children.

It was a little awkward at first. No one seemed to know
how to begin or what to say. "I see your son likes baseball," Marcia began.

"Yes. He loves it," Eve said, nodding. "He wants to play
all the time. He's good too. He got on the travel team. But
I have to buy the uniform. It's expensive." She shrugged.
"Everything is expensive. That's why I want to do this."

Jeff said, "But you obviously care so much for your
son. Won't it be hard to give your baby away after it's
born?"

Eve's eyes flashed and her face colored slightly. She
stared straight at him. "I would never give my baby away.
Never." She turned away and spoke more softly. "This is
not my baby. This is your baby. I will eat right and take
care of myself and give you a healthy baby but otherwise,
this baby is nothing to me."

Marcia was a bit taken aback by the ferocity of her response. "Eve, is it all for the money? I mean, do you
have any other feelings about it we should know?"

Eve shrugged. She looked straight at them, directing her remarks to both of them. "Look, you seem like nice people. I'll be happy to do this for you, to give you this gift. But if you ask me would I do it for free, the answer is no."

Marcia shook her head vehemently. "No. Of course I wouldn't ask you to do it for free. I think your attitude is perfect and it's what my husband wants too. After the birth, we will go home and you will go back to your life."

Eve leaned forward. "I want to put some money away for my son. He has no one else to help him. My parents are dead, his father is gone, no sisters, no brothers, no aunts, no uncles. Just me. I must do what I can. I will try to have enough to rent a place in another neighborhood where there are better schools, nicer people, not so much drugs and gangs. This will help me."

Jeff shifted in his chair. Marcia glanced at him, then looked back at Eve. "I'm so sorry about your family. What happened to his father?"

Eve shrugged. She walked to the bedroom, closed the door, returned to the table and lowered her voice. "He was Mexican—Danny looks just like him. He got to Phoenix, where I used to live, with a smuggler. You understand? He didn't have papers. But he had ambition. He showed up at my high school one day and, well, we ended up together. But his mom got sick when Danny was still a little kid and he wanted to see her so he went back." She looked down and pursed her lips. "Look, there's no point talking about it. He died."

Jeff squeezed Marcia's arm. He was uncomfortable.

She joined Eve at the table and, reaching out, took Eve's hand in solidarity. "I'm so sorry."

Eve withdrew her hand gently but resolutely. "Then choose me," she said. "Give me a strong seed and I will grow a strong baby. And pay me."

"How much of the money we pay the agency goes to you?" Jeff asked, suddenly back in his comfort zone.

"I don't know what you pay them. They told me I'd get thirty thousand dollars."

"We will add another fifteen thousand, if all goes well," Marcia blurted, "if we work together to make this baby healthy." Jeff looked at her as though she'd lost her mind. "That will give you forty-five thousand. You can save some and have money for a better apartment and a security payment too."

Eve was stunned and, sensing Jeff's reluctance, she spoke directly to Marcia. "I've been trying to save for this and I have some put away. But it's hard. Just when I think I'll soon have enough, something happens. Two months ago, Danny needed to have four teeth pulled. It cost three thousand dollars. That was all I had managed to save."

"Don't you have health insurance?" Jeff asked.

She laughed and met his eyes. "I have it. But it doesn't pay for this."

Marcia stood up and Jeff followed. "I hope this will be enough to make a difference for you. I know you understand the difference you will make in our lives."

"I know. Then you have decided?"

Jeff looked unsure. Marcia looked at him beseechingly

and he put his arm around her and nodded. Marcia was overjoyed. "Yes, definitely. It's you. And if it's okay with you, I'd like to help you choose a doctor and come to your monthly checkups so it feels more as if the baby is mine."

"I'm good with that," Eve said, smiling. She stood and embraced Marcia. "Thank you, Mrs. . . . I don't remember your last name but I'm very happy."

"It's Naiman, Marcia Naiman, but please, call me Marcia. I'm glad you're happy about it. I am too, pleased and excited. We'll be seeing a lot of each other in the next nine months."

Eve turned to call Danny, but Marcia reached out and touched her arm. "How will you explain this to him?"

"I'll tell him the truth. He's a smart boy. He will understand."

She called and Danny came. "They're leaving now," she said.

Danny nodded. "Bye," he said, looking at the floor.

"Bye, Danny," Marcia said. "It was nice meeting you."

Jeff patted him awkwardly on the head. "Bye, Dan. See you soon."

They told Eve they would tell the agency they had chosen their surrogate and find out what the next step was.

When they were alone together, Marcia was euphoric. Jeff gave her a moment to express her joy but he couldn't resist saying what was on his mind. "What the hell did you do in there? You offered her fifteen thousand dollars more than she asked. Are you out of your mind? We have to take out an equity loan for the rest of the money and you just added fifteen thousand dollars more?"

She looked a little sheepish, but not apologetic. "I know it's a lot, but when I was researching this I saw that many surrogates are paid between twenty-five and fifty thousand dollars. I think the agency was short-changing her. We can add a little more to the loan. It won't make that big a difference to us each month and it will change her life. It will mean she will be extra willing to eat the proper diet and go to the right doctor and share everything with me. It will be good for us and for her. This is a racket for the agency. She doesn't get enough. It's up to us to make it fair. I mean, won't you feel better if the birth of our child also means that her child will have better prospects? I know I will."

He gave her a half smile and put his arm around her. She was impulsive, generous, enthusiastic, all the qualities he fell in love with, but sometimes, for those very same reasons, she was exasperating.

8

In the months that followed, Marcia and Eve found an obstetrician and as soon as the pregnancy was viable, they started monthly visits. Marcia read everything she could find about pregnancy and prenatal care and shared it with Eve, who promised she was eating nutritious meals, taking her prenatal vitamins and not drinking or smoking. In the fourth month they discovered, to Marcia's delight and Jeff's panic, that Eve was carrying twins, a boy and a girl. Marcia carried a copy of the ultrasound photo in her wallet and showed it to her friends. She was working hard because she wanted to accomplish a lot before the twins were born, when she planned to take six months off. But sometimes, in the middle of reading a manuscript or returning from a meeting, she would take a break, ask Julie to bring her a cup of coffee, and pull out the ultrasound photo to stare at. She could see that one twin had a high forehead and the other seemed to have a slightly bigger nose. Was that possible or just the angle of the photo? She didn't know. She didn't care, really, but she liked imagining what they would look like, be like. She didn't mention this to Jeff because the idea that they would soon have two crying, hungry, needy babies in the house made him anxious and she was trying to give him time to get used to it.

She concentrated on the pregnancy and wondered if they should switch to a physician who specialized in high-risk deliveries. But Eve was happy with her doctor and resisted change. The doctor himself told Marcia that a high-risk specialist was not needed in this case, so she relented. But she worried about the possibility of the babies being premature and she insisted that Eve stop work in her eighth month so she could rest and take care of herself. Since Marcia and Jeff had agreed to make up Eve's lost salary, and since her company agreed to the time off, Eve went along with it.

Usually, Eve scheduled her prenatal visits on a Monday. Marcia would take a plane Sunday morning and spend the day with Eve and her son. It enabled her to monitor the way Eve lived. An unintended but pleasant consequence was that she and Eve found that in spite of their huge cultural, educational and class differences, they had enough in common to become friends. It wasn't just that they shared this pregnancy, although clearly that was part of it. The excitement, the utrasounds, the first detection of the heartbeat, the first kick, all these were experienced together largely because of Eve's gen-

erosity, her ability to understand how much Marcia
wanted to be a part of the pregnancy and how Eve could
satisfy that desire. But they spent so much time together
that soon they also spoke of other things. At first it was
Eve who wanted to talk. She seemed hungry for a friend
and confided stories about her childhood, her regret
over her parents, her love of her son, her desire to become a nurse and some of the problems at her job.
Marcia would listen and try to advise her, much as she
did her assistant, Julie, and little by little, she began to
feel protective of her.

Once, when Marcia came for the monthly visit to
the obstetrician, she offered to pick Eve up at the care
home after work to drive her to the appointment. When
she arrived, Eve wasn't ready. A colleague came out to
meet Marcia. "Eve said she's really sorry, but she can't
come right now. Please wait."

"But we have an appointment with the doctor," Marcia said. "How long will it be?"

The colleague laughed. "Oh God, I don't know. Sometimes it's really quick and sometimes it seems to take
forever, but Eve won't go till it works."

Marcia frowned, annoyed. "Till what works?"

"Mrs. Thomisson. She's the lady with really bad de-
mentia. Sometimes she just starts crying and moaning
and rocking and nobody can do nothing for her. Unless
they give her a shot of something and the doctor isn't always here to order that. So the psychologists come. The
social workers. They all don't know what to do. Mostly
the nurses just leave her alone until she gives up and stops

on her own. But Eve can't stand to hear her like that. And she can calm her. She just goes in and does her magic and after a while Mrs. Thomisson quiets down."

Marcia thanked her and sat down, amazed. Thirty minutes later, Eve came out, rushing through the lobby, apologizing profusely.

"Did you calm her down?" Marcia asked.

"What? Oh yeah. I sang to her." She smiled. " 'Michael Row the Boat Ashore'; for some reason that always works."

Marcia frowned, startled.

"Why that one?"

"I don't know. Danny learned it at school and I tried it once and it worked. It's old. Maybe she heard it when she was a young girl."

Marcia had a flash of remembering singing that song with her own mother when Marcia was about seven years old—before her mother got so sick and everything changed. After the sickness set in, whenever her mother would have a seizure, Marcia would sing that to her, hoping to bring her back, but was never sure it mattered.

Eve's ambition and compassion were more than Marcia had expected, and she soon found herself wanting to help her change her life. She spent hours at home looking on the Internet for programs that would allow Eve to study nursing while working at her job and then pass the information on to Eve, urging her to follow up. She'd ask her every time she visited how Mrs. Thomisson was doing, and when one day Eve told her with tears in her eyes that Mrs. Thomisson had died, Marcia choked up too.

This was not a development that pleased Jeff. He wanted things to go smoothly, of course, and amicably, but he didn't want attachments that might be likely to continue after his children were born. One day in Eve's fifth month of pregnancy, Marcia told him another of her "Eve stories." "She saw a new resident coming into the home bent down so badly with osteoporosis that she could look only at the floor," Marcia recounted. "She was just coming out to meet me but first she ran up to this lady, bent down very low so that her face looked right into the face of the woman, actually made eye contact with her, and smiled so sweetly and said, 'Hello. You look beautiful today.' And then she kind of sprinted on. That's how she is. She is really special. I feel like we're lucky to know her."

"Yeah," Jeff said, but he didn't look happy. He waited a minute or two and then, with worry lines creasing his face, he said, "Honey, you're getting so close to her. I hope that isn't going to be a problem. You know we agreed we aren't going to stay in touch after the baby is born. Will you be okay with that?"

She reassured him, though that thought had occurred to her too and she wasn't at all sure how it would work out. Still, she assumed she'd be so busy being a real mother after the twins came that her maternal feelings for Eve would diminish. And Eve had wanted the separation too, so maybe their relationship would fade naturally. Still, it continued to grow and both enjoyed it. They'd hang out together during the monthly visits when Marcia would take Eve and Danny out for dinner, or accompany

Eve to her doctor's appointment. Over time, they grew even closer. They admired each other. Although Eve barely had time to read, she knew education was the key to success and she was in awe of Marcia's executive position in the world of books. And Marcia was impressed by Eve's kindness and empathy, which reminded her of her own years of caring for her mother. She valued Eve's ambition, her determination to carve out a better life for herself and her son against punishing odds.

Marcia also came to like Danny, the source of all of Eve's hopes and plans. Eve worked so many hours, she wasn't around much to supervise him, but she was proud of how independent he was. He did his homework every night and left it for her on the kitchen table. She'd look it over when she got home, even the two nights a week she did a double shift and didn't arrive home until eleven. She didn't check it for accuracy—he already knew the subjects as well or better than she did—but she liked to see his neat hand, the papers lined up on the table, ready for her signature, which the teacher required. When she wasn't there, she'd leave his dinner out for him, or money to go to the *mercado* for an empanada. Marcia dropped by the market with him once. It was bustling, with stalls of fresh fruit and vegetables and staples of Hispanic cooking. Danny knew the vendors—he must go there often, she thought—and also ran into neighbors whom he greeted politely. One of her visits fell a week after his eleventh birthday and she brought him a book about the history of baseball for a present. She could tell he wasn't thrilled with it, but he thanked her politely. She tried, as she had on other occasions, to start a conversation with him, but it was difficult. He was shy and polite but distant, a little suspicious. She noticed that with his mother, he was boisterous and affectionate, full of stories about his day. When it came to his mother's pregnancy, however, he was clearly not interested. Once, when Marcia was visiting, one of the twins (or maybe both of them) started to kick. "Come, Danny," his mother called. "Put your hand on my stomach. They are moving around inside me."

Danny made a face and picked up his iPod. "That's gross," he said, slipping into the bedroom and closing the door.

"He doesn't like me to be pregnant," Eve said.

"Maybe it's because he knows the babies aren't going to stay. That they're not his."

Eve looked thoughtful. "Yeah. Maybe. I think I look funny to his friends. He doesn't know how to explain why I got babies inside me but no father around. He told some of them we were selling them and said he was taking offers." She laughed. "The parents got all upset. I got mad and told him to stop talking so much. He stormed off. It'll be better after we go back to normal."

Marcia nodded. "I know. We are all waiting for that day."

Jeff came with Marcia for one of the last visits to the doctor, a month before the due date, which was June 10. He stayed in the waiting room when the two women went in and was relieved when they told him everything looked good. There were about four weeks to go, and the doctor was hopeful the babies would go to term, unusual for twins. In fact, he said, he didn't want the pregnancy to go past term and would induce labor if the twins didn't come on their own by the due date. They had a plan, though they recognized it was tentative. If they were going to induce, Marcia and Jeff would arrive a day earlier. Marcia would go into the delivery room with Eve, and she and Jeff would stay with Danny a day or two, until Eve came home from the hospital.

After the doctor visit, they picked up Danny after school and drove to a park. Jeff parked the car a few blocks away and they all walked together. Danny brought his glove and ball, and Marcia encouraged Jeff to play catch with him.

"I'm not dressed for it," he said.

"You're fine. You're wearing slacks and a shirt. It doesn't matter. It's just catch."

"Isn't it too hot for catch?" he asked.

"I guess they're used to it in Los Angeles," she said.

He frowned, but he got up and threw the ball to Danny. Danny missed but he ran for it, and the two moved away and continued playing. Marcia smiled, imagining Jeff playing ball with their own children one day. She and Eve watched them for a while.

"Eve, what happened to Danny's father?" Marcia asked gently.

Eve shrugged. "He died."

"I know. But how?"

"He was illegal, you know? He went home to see his mother and stayed for her funeral. He thought he could just pay the smuggler and come in again the same way he did the first time. But I don't know. Something happened. Everyone told me he left Mexico but he never showed up here. Then one day the police came. They said they found a dead guy in the desert. It was his DNA. They think he hurt his foot and couldn't keep up and the smugglers just left him there. It was hard." She rubbed her eyes and turned away. A few seconds passed. "Anyway," she said more brightly, "things are getting better now."

They looked back at Jeff and Danny but they were no longer playing catch. Danny had thrown his glove and ball on the ground and was running toward home, his shoulders slumped, his head down. "Danny, *que pasa?*" Eve called after him. Marcia had noticed that Eve, true to Jorge's wishes, had tried to maintain the connection to his Mexican heritage, even by occasionally saying a few words to him in Spanish. When she shouted after him, he slowed down but kept walking. "You come back here and pick those up right away or I will leave them and you know you won't get new ones," Eve shouted. Danny stopped and without looking at her ran back and sulkily picked up the bat and glove. "I wanna go home, okay, Ma?"

"Yeah, okay. What happened?"

"Nothin'. I just don't wanna play no more." Marcia noticed that he was purposely using street grammar when he usually spoke perfectly.

Jeff had reached them by now and they all headed to the car. Jeff and Marcia lagged behind.

"What was that about?" Marcia asked.

"Nothing. I threw an easy ball a little high. He just had to jump for it but he was too lazy so he missed. I told him he should have caught it and he got mad, threw his glove down and walked away. Not even a thank-you."

"He's just a kid. He probably felt bad he missed it and then you hurt his feelings. Forget it."

"I already have."

"He doesn't have a father to play ball with him, Jeff. He doesn't know how to behave. Be nice."

"I'm nice. But in a few more weeks, I'll be buying a baseball glove for my own little boy and all this will be behind us."

She smiled and put her arm through his, hugging it as they walked. "I know. I can hardly wait. You know, you might be buying that baseball glove for your little girl too."

Eve walked ahead of them, trying to catch up with her son, who was charging toward the car. She had grown very big and her body swayed back and forth as she walked. It was hot and she was panting. Sweat dripped down the sides of her face. Marcia quickened her pace to catch up with her. She put her hand on Eve's arm to slow her down. "Don't rush like that, Eve. It's too hot."

Eve slowed. "I want to catch up with Danny."

"I'll do it. You walk slowly. You'll see him at the car."

Jeff walked with Eve, and Marcia ran ahead. She saw Danny a block away and called for him to stop, but he just kept running. He was quiet and sullen when they reached the car, and when they arrived home, he was the first to run in. He was already in the bedroom with the door slammed by the time they entered the apartment. Eve went in after him, and Jeff and Marcia, hanging back uncomfortably in the living room, heard his voice, whining and angry and then tearful, followed by Eve's, soft and comforting, soothing him, until he calmed down.

9

They got the call at two in the morning a week later. Although she'd been sleeping, Marcia picked up on the first ring, immediately fearing some calamity. "These kids of yours, they don't wanna wait," Eve said, her voice faint on the other end of a scratchy line.

"Eve. Are you okay?"

"Yeah, yeah. Don't worry. I'm having a little trouble breathing 'cause these babies are pressing on my lungs but I'm fine. My water broke so I'm on my way to the hospital. I'll call you after I see the doctor." She hung up.

Marcia shook Jeff, who was still sleeping. "Wake up. It's begun. Her water broke. She's already left for the hospital. We have to get ready to go."

Labor had begun earlier than expected, but the doctor had reassured them during the last visit that Eve had already passed the time when prematurity would be dangerous. Although it would be better if the babies had gone to term, Marcia knew that would have been unusual for twins. Not waiting for Jeff, who had turned over and put the pillow over his head—she wasn't even sure he had been awake enough to hear her—she used her cell phone to check flights and was relieved to see they could get on a direct one to LAX at 8:00 A.M. Her bag was packed— she had taken care of that just last week—so she brushed her teeth and threw her cosmetic bag into her suitcase. They'd need to be at the airport by seven so they'd have to leave the house at six, she calculated, realizing that she could sleep a few more hours. But she knew there was little chance of that.

Her thoughts raced around the last-minute preparations she had made. She silently checked them off in her mind. She had the newborn diapers, the receiving blankets, the onesies in pink, yellow and blue. She walked to the nursery and stood in the doorway, taking it all in. She noted how still the apartment was, how perfectly quiet, maybe for the last time. Once the babies were there, she thought, their presence would fill the place, even when they were asleep. She looked approvingly at the two white cribs, neatly made up with the bunny-print sheets, one in pink, the other in blue. She had stocked the room with everything they would need, at least at the beginning. She and Jeff had pasted stickers on the walls next to the cribs—rainbows and bunnies and fairies and ballet dancers on one wall, basketball hoops and soccer balls and racing cars and robots on the other. "This is pretty sexist," Jeff had said as they peeled the ballet dancers off the backing and pressed them on the wall near the pink bunny sheets. "Unless we put the boy in this crib and the girl in the other." He was joking, but she knew he was right. This was how she had always imagined it, though, so she didn't let it worry her too much. She told herself that she was flexible and if their kids developed differently, so be it. She'd adapt. In the meantime, she would just assume her daughter would be somewhat like her, and she had loved fairies and magic and ballet as a child. Her eyes moved to the corner of the room where Jeff had just yesterday put together the Duvalier glider she'd bought to sit in while she fed the babies. She and Jeff would both be using it, she thought, one of the advantages of her inability to nurse. It would give him a chance to share the nurturing right from the start. She smiled. She had thought of everything. She fired off an e-mail to Julie telling her the day had arrived and setting in motion the work plan she had composed for her absence. She was ready.

Now she just had to get there in time to help Eve during the delivery. She had trained for this, taking breathing lessons with Eve during her last three visits. "I already know how to breathe," Eve had said dismissively, when Marcia had suggested they register for the class. "I know," she'd answered. "And I know you've been through all this before with Danny. But it might still make it easier for you and it would be very special for me," she'd pleaded, and Eve, good-natured as she was, agreed.

Marcia's phone rang again, and she quickly answered. "Eve?"

"Yeah. I'm at the hospital in this fancy private room, like you arranged. Don't worry. I'm fine. Labor hasn't started. I think your kids want to wait for their mommy. The doctor said he'd try not to induce till you're here. When are you coming?"

"The plane leaves at eight this morning. We'll be there around ten your time, I hope. How's Danny? Is he home alone?"

"I got my neighbor to look in on him and I left him a note so he knows where I am when he wakes up. He knows how to get himself off to school in the morning on his own."

"Is he even a little bit excited?"

Eve paused. "I wouldn't say he's excited. But he's glad it's almost over."

"Do you think he should come to the hospital?"

"No. Definitely not. I'll be back with him tomorrow. You ready for this, Marcia?"

"You know I am. Thank you. Thank you so much."

"Nah. Thank *you*. From me and from Danny too. Only, he doesn't know it yet."

When Marcia walked back into their bedroom, Jeff was still soundly sleeping and she didn't wake him. He'd be getting up in the middle of the night soon enough, she thought. Let him have this last peaceful night. She had hired a baby nurse to help them and she made a note to tell her she would have to start sooner than planned. She climbed back into bed next to Jeff and watched him sleep. He inhaled, and a deep snore escaped him. His lips puffed out and vibrated as he exhaled, and he turned over to settle more comfortably. She couldn't sleep, but she could rest, she thought, closing her eyes. Suddenly they sprung open. She sat up abruptly and set her phone alarm—just in case . . .

It woke both of them at five-thirty. They got to the airport in plenty of time and the plane trip, though tense, was uneventful.

When they arrived at the hospital, Jeff bought a coffee and that morning's *New York Times* and *Wall Street Journal* at the shop in the lobby while Marcia rushed ahead to the maternity floor. "Stay in the waiting room," she suggested. "I'll give you updates when I can." She hurried to the nurses' station on the fourth floor, identified herself and was ushered into the labor room to join Eve. As she entered, she saw that Eve's face was contorted in pain and she was gripping the sides of the bed. She was clearly in the midst of a powerful contraction and Marcia rushed to her side. "I'm here, Eve. I'm sorry I wasn't here when it started." Eve reached for Marcia's hand, gritted her teeth and groaned. "Don't tense up, Eve," Marcia reminded her. "Remember the panting. Try to do it. One, two, three, four. One, two, three, four," she repeated, emphasizing the first beat, as they had been taught. Eve tried to follow. She gave one last breath as the contraction subsided. Marcia wiped the perspiration from her brow.

"I'm glad you're here. Where's the picture?" Eve whispered.

They had been told to bring something for Eve to stare at during the contractions to help focus her concentration on the breathing technique, and Danny had made her a picture they had practiced with. It was composed of different-colored concentric circles, the bull's-eye a bright orange. Marcia thought they would need to use these techniques for only a short time because Eve would have an epidural as soon as the labor was established, but for some reason she didn't completely understand, Eve was adamant about rejecting the epidural. She'd heard of someone, she said, who'd gotten paralyzed after a spinal and no matter how many times Marcia and the doctors told her that wasn't a real possibility, she still refused. That meant she insisted on having the babies without any anesthetic, just as she had had Danny.

Grateful she had remembered it (she had stuffed it in her bag right before leaving), Marcia retrieved the crumpled picture, smoothed it out and taped it to the wall in Eve's direct sight line. In less than three minutes, Eve's body tensed again. "Breathe," Marcia coaxed.

"I want to push."

"No. Don't. Try not to do anything until the doctor comes."

"I can't hold it. I have to push. It's coming."

Marcia ran down the hallway where she found the nurse and told her the babies were about to appear. The nurse looked skeptical, but she followed Marcia into the room and examined Eve. Suddenly, she moved faster. She paged the doctor who arrived just in time. After a quick examination, he said, "Okay, Eve, it's time. Push. Give it everything you've got."

Eve pushed. Her face flushed, and every muscle in her body seemed to tense. She grunted, she moaned, and suddenly, there it was, a baby. The doctor cut the umbilical cord and handed the baby over to a nurse. "It's the girl," he said. Eve gasped, a short intake of breath and a hoarse sound, and the doctor turned his attention back to her. There was still another baby to come. Marcia was staring at the nurse ministering to the baby girl. "Why isn't she crying?" Marcia asked. "I didn't hear her cry." A bell rang, bringing two more doctors. One took the baby from the nurses while the other bent over Eve. They were talking softly, in whispers. Marcia couldn't hear what they were saying. "What's going on?" she begged. Her voice sounded very loud. One of the doctors looked up for a second and turned to the nurse. "Get her out of here," he ordered.

Jeff looked up expectantly as Marcia entered the waiting room. He rose and started to smile as she approached, until he saw her face. "What happened?" he asked. "What's wrong?"

"I don't know," she answered, reaching for his hand. "Something is wrong with the baby. They made me leave."

"How do you know something is wrong?"

"I just know, Jeff," she snapped but then recovered herself and took a deep breath. "Our little girl was born first. She didn't cry. The nurses worked on her for what seemed like a long time but there was still no sound. Then some other doctors came in and I think they were trying to revive her."

"What about our son?"

Marcia tried to hold back her tears but the panic in her voice was uncontrolled. "I don't know. I don't know anything."

Jeff put his arm around her and felt her body go limp against his. "Let's not get too upset yet, sweetheart," he said, but his voice betrayed his own uncertainty. "Twin births are always difficult. She's probably fine now."

He sat down and she sat heavily next to him, together, but lost in their own thoughts. After a few minutes he got up and approached the nurse at the reception desk, asking if there was any news about Eve Russo who was in the delivery room. The nurse shook her head sympathetically, and Jeff returned to his seat.

He feared the worst and dared not say so. The truth was he had never thought this surrogacy idea was a good one. Of course he had wanted children, but he understood that you can't always get what you want. But Marcia had become obsessed. If his idea was that maybe some things were not meant to be, Marcia's was that anything was possible by the sheer force of her will. When Marcia wanted something this much, she was relentless, Jeff reflected. So they had moved forward, step by step. Her enthusiasm was so infectious, he had almost forgotten that the whole thing was a bad idea, fraught with dangers. He had worried again when he learned Eve was pregnant with twins. But Marcia convinced him it would work out. After all, she'd said, this wasn't Eve's first delivery. She'd had an easy time with Danny, no reason to think this would be different. Thousands of people were doing this, Eve had insisted. What could go wrong? And now, maybe something had.

Marcia's thoughts were all about what she had just witnessed, trying to put together what happened in a way that didn't result in a bad outcome. She had seen the look on the nurse's face and the doctor's urgent response. She had sensed the tension in the room. Those images haunted her. Why didn't they come to tell them what was happening? She bit her nails, a habit she'd been trying to overcome since adolescence.

It was almost an hour before a pale, serious Dr. Jensen walked into the waiting room and beckoned to Jeff and Marcia. Marcia had gotten to know and like Eve's doctor during the eight months of appointments and she saw that his normally friendly expression was grim. He led them to a small office and invited them to sit on the couch. But they remained standing, huddled together, their hands intertwined. When he started to speak, Marcia heard the strain in his voice even before she processed the words, and she knew.

"I'm very sorry to tell you this," he said, "but your daughter didn't make it. We tried everything we could for a long time, but we were unable to revive her." Marcia drew in her breath sharply. Jeff squeezed her hand ever tighter. "Didn't make it?" Marcia's first reaction was anger. *"Didn't make it?"* Like it was something the baby did wrong. She concentrated on fighting back the suffocating wave of pain. Her baby was gone. Even before she entered their lives, she was ripped away. A series of images flooded her mind: the pink bunnies, the wall stickers, the blanket edged with lace she had spent way too much for. What would she do with them? Oh, how stupid, why think of that? She turned away. When Jeff put his arm around her, she could feel the tightening of the sinews in his arm, hear his breathing, knew his own disappointment and pain, and it was too much for her. She let herself go and started to cry in deep heaving sobs. Dr. Jensen paused. He offered her a glass of water. He asked if she wanted a sedative. He seemed so distraught that even Marcia felt a moment of pity for him. He seemed to be about to add something, but Jeff spoke first. His voice was shaky.

"And our son?"

Dr. Jensen permitted himself a small, relieved smile. "You have a healthy little boy. He will have to temporarily stay in an incubator, but you will be able to take him home in a week or so. But there's something—"

"Thank God for that," Jeff interrupted him.

Marcia nodded slowly. "When can we see him?" she asked.

"We are settling him in now," the doctor answered. "You can view him soon, but you won't be able to hold him for a few hours."

She was deeply relieved about her son, but she couldn't stop the wave of grief and she struggled to come up from under it. She clung to Jeff, who alone could share her pain. She thought of her mother—not because she could turn to her in her grief; her mother had been dead since she was eighteen—but because she wished there was another woman who loved her whom she could talk to. Her

father, long remarried, was far away. She thought about
Eve, whom she knew would be devastated. After all, these
were Eve's babies too. Marcia had read everything she
could get her hands on about childbirth and she knew
about the fierce emotions pregnancy creates. Yes, it was
Marcia's egg and Jeff's sperm, but it was Eve who carried
the twins. It was her body that changed, her breasts that
swelled and ached, her sleep that was disrupted by her
nausea, her discomfort. It was Eve who felt the first signs
of quickening when the baby stirred and Eve who placed
her hand on her belly and knew there was life under it,
life that grew and thrived because of her. And it was Eve
whose body produced the hormones and chemicals that
must have filled her with protective impulses as surely as
they swelled her breasts with milk. This terrible, profound loss belonged to both of them. She needed Eve
right now even more than she needed Jeff.

Dr. Jensen cleared his throat and swallowed. "There's
something else," he said.

"Poor Eve," Marcia said, ignoring him. "She must be
so upset. Is she awake? Does she know what happened?
I have to go to her."

The doctor raised his voice. "There is something else,"
he repeated firmly. Marcia could see a slight quiver in his
throat as he swallowed. He put his hand on Marcia's arm
and looked searchingly at Jeff, who now stood next to
Marcia, his arm around her shoulder. Dr. Jensen reverted to the relative comfort of formality. "Eve had a
pulmonary embolism during the delivery. There was
nothing to prepare us for this, no reason to expect it.

We did everything we could, but we were not successful. I'm so sorry."

Jeff got it right away. He seemed to reel backward, releasing Marcia for a second and taking a step to balance himself. But Marcia seemed confused.

"What do you mean? How is she? How long does she have to stay here? When can I see her?"

The doctor looked down. Surely this was the hardest part of his job. He looked helplessly at them both and took a deep breath. Marcia looked stunned. Jeff took her in his arms and pulled her close before leading her toward the couch, where she refused to sit. "A blockage in her lungs, Marcia," he said gently, holding her steady. "She's dead."

10

Jeff paled and looked at Marcia, holding her even tighter for support.

Marcia continued to stand and stare at the doctor. At first, she uttered only one word. "What?" she asked in a confused whisper. Surely she had misheard. Jeff had gotten it wrong. This couldn't be happening. Then she turned angrily to Jeff. "Why do you say that, Jeff? What's wrong with you?" Her voice percolated with fury. "The doctor said she had an embolism. He didn't say she died. Why do you say such a terrible thing?" She turned to the doctor, shaken, disoriented. "Right, Doctor? She's going to be okay, right?"

The doctor sighed and took her arm, urging her again to sit down and easing her onto the couch. He held her arm a moment longer, sliding his hand to her wrist, starting to check her pulse, but she pushed him away angrily.

"You don't need to examine me, for Christ's sake," she barked. "You need to answer my question."

The doctor nodded. "Yes, I'm sorry. Listen, Marcia, you just heard emotionally devastating news and you're in shock. You're pale, your heart is beating very fast and you're overwhelmed. This is normal. I understand. But you need to try to calm down and take deep breaths slowly in and out." He took a few to show her how but she just stared at him as though she still didn't understand. "I'm so sorry, but your husband was right. Eve passed away on the delivery table."

She didn't move except to change the direction of her stare to the wall, hearing but not hearing, removed. She spoke softly, as if to herself, "This is all my fault." She looked at Jeff. "Can you ever forgive me? Can anyone ever forgive me?"

Jeff hugged her, smoothed her hair, rubbed her back. "It isn't your fault. You had no way of knowing any of this would happen." He turned to the doctor. "Please, tell her."

"Of course it's not your fault, Marcia. As I said, the trauma of this double loss has thrown your body into a state of mild shock and one of the symptoms of that is feelings of guilt, disorientation, disbelief. But you had nothing to do with this." He paused. "Would you like me to give you something to help you?"

"No," she said, shaking her head. "I want to feel what I feel. My baby and my friend deserve at least that much."

Her heart rate was slowing down, she could feel it, just as she felt the reality of what had happened sink into her consciousness. She looked up and saw Jeff's anxious, grieved look and the doctor hovering, waiting to see if he was needed. She took a few deep breaths, as he had suggested, then squeezed Jeff's hand and looked at the doctor. "I'm okay," she said, struggling to emerge from a fog of confused emotions. "Thank you. I'm sorry for the way I behaved."

"No. Not at all. Completely normal," Dr. Jensen said quickly. "I'm going to leave you two alone for a while now. You can stay here as long as you need to."

Soon after he left a nurse knocked on the door and opened it without waiting for a response. She asked gently if they would like to see their baby, but they both were too dazed to answer. Clearly uncomfortable, the nurse told them where the preemie ward was and expressed her condolences before turning to go. At the door, she turned back. "I can only imagine what you're feeling. But you have a healthy baby boy to take care of. Go to see him, try to take some comfort from him." They nodded mechanically. She told them they could remain in the office until they were ready. They stared after her, neither of them moving or knowing what to do next. Finally, Jeff helped Marcia to her feet and together, they made their way to the preemie ward to view their baby.

They stood outside the glass window staring at the tiny forms in their enclosed glass bassinets, most hooked up to wires and machines. It didn't seem real, but they scanned the room looking for the crib with their name. They didn't find it but they saw one that said Russo, Eve's name. Marcia winced. Even though they had arranged all the surrogacy papers in advance, the legal transition wouldn't be official for a few more days. Marcia pressed her face against the glass, straining to see the baby. He was so small. So fragile. Marcia felt a pressure in her chest, like a hand squeezing her heart. He has lots of black hair, like Jeff's, she thought. She had black hair too, she thought with a stab of pain. But already her image of her baby girl was fading—they had whisked her away so quickly, she had barely seen her. Now she and Jeff continued to stare at their son. They watched his chest move with each breath, with life. Tears flowed down Marcia's cheeks. Jeff felt weak; he reached out for Marcia, this time to steady himself. A passing nurse noticed them and asked if they'd like to sit down somewhere, but Marcia shook her head. "No," she said. "We'll go now and come back later." She wiped her tears away, squeezed Jeff's hand and turned to leave. Jeff accompanied her into the elevator, holding his arm tightly around her shoulders. They took a taxi straight to their hotel. When they got there, they climbed out slowly, moving as though they were walking through water, and in that dazed state they finally arrived in their room, where they sat heavily on the bed, looking at each other, utterly lost.

This was the one outcome they had never considered. They had worried that Eve would change her mind when the babies were born. They had fretted over how Danny would react. Would he think the twins were his siblings and be angry that his mother was giving them away? But it had never occurred to them that Eve might die. They had never heard of that. Surely that was something that didn't happen anymore, Marcia thought. Not today. Not in America. Not in a big modern hospital in Los Angeles. And yet the unthinkable had occurred. They had a new baby and, it suddenly hit her with new force, Eve's son had lost his mother.

"We have to adopt him," Marcia blurted.

Jeff blanched. "What? Who?"

"Danny," she answered impatiently, walking to the mini-fridge to get a bottle of cold water. "Who else? Eve's son."

"Wait a minute," Jeff said sharply, responding quickly, intuitively. He knew he had snapped at her and he knew he shouldn't have, but he couldn't help it. "We can't do that, Marcia."

She whipped around to face him.

"What are you saying? We have no choice. His father died years ago. Eve was his only family. She's gone because of us. We have an obligation here to try to set things right."

"She had an embolism, Marcia. That wasn't our fault. This is shock, like the doctor said, blaming yourself, us."

"That's ridiculous. She wouldn't have had that embolism if she wasn't trying to deliver our twins."

"You don't know that. People die suddenly, they have aneurysms and embolisms they never suspected, it might have happened without us."

"But it didn't."

He took her hand in his and lowered his voice. "Honey, listen, we can find out more about Danny's family. Maybe there are grandparents. Maybe there's an aunt or an uncle. We can send money every month. He'll be better off with his own family."

Marcia pulled her hand away. She made a point of checking her watch. It was 2:00 P.M. She spoke slowly.

"I wish he had his own family. I wish to God he did. But he doesn't. All he has is us."

"We'll help him. I agree, we owe him. But we are not his family, Marcia. That was the agreement. No contact after the birth."

"That was before. That was if he still had his mother. Everything is different now."

"We need some time to think of a solution," Jeff said.

"All I know is that he'll get off the school bus in about an hour. He'll let himself into his apartment and wait to hear how his mom is and when she'll be home. Someone has to meet him and tell him that his mother is dead."

Jeff stood and began pacing. She turned her face up to him. He saw how red and swollen her eyes were. "So maybe you should be the one to do that, Jeff. You seem so sure of what's right."

Jeff took a deep breath. "I need to get some air. I won't be long."

When he was gone, Marcia sat on the bed, staring at the wall. Her mind raced through the series of events that had brought them here, to this hotel room, to this awful moment. She remembered their fears that this surrogacy was a kind of exploitation, the feeling that they were benefiting from Eve's poverty. But she remembered that Eve herself had talked them out of that. She had said that this would help her as much as it would them, that her only concern was Danny, whom she loved more than anything in the world. After all, Eve maintained, she was a single mother. She had no family, no one to help her. She wanted to give things to Danny that her salary as an aide in a nursing home would never provide. The $45,000 this surrogacy would pay was more than she could imagine saving in any other way. She was determined to put it away for Danny. Maybe even for college, she'd say shyly. They allowed themselves to be convinced this was as good for her as it was for them because they wanted it so much, Marcia thought. Or *she* did, she acknowledged.

She couldn't believe this had happened. She had done everything right. The papers were signed. The check had been written. The handover was set to happen as soon as the babies were born. She went over their most recent conversations in her mind. Eve had reaffirmed that she didn't even want to see the twins and though Marcia had been a tiny bit hurt, she knew it was what they had initially agreed upon. And she knew too that Jeff had been relieved. He had worried repeatedly that Marcia and Eve would insist on entering into a lifelong relationship— photographs, updates, holidays together, God forbid, he'd said. Marcia had always denied that would happen, but the two women had bonded so much during the pregnancy, he didn't really believe her. She remembered with a flash of resentment how Jeff had tried to discourage their friendship, emphasizing that they had nothing in common other than the twins. She knew he was wrong. She had found, to her surprise, that she and Eve had a lot in common, but it didn't change things, at least for

Eve. She was adamant about what she wanted. No strings. No entitlement. No future relationship. The babies would belong to Jeff and Marcia. Eve and Danny would go on with their lives, just a little bit more financially secure.

Well, now everything was different.

She checked her watch. It was almost time for Danny to come home. Jeff had disappeared. She would have to tell Danny herself. She went into the bathroom. She looked in the mirror and saw her grief-ravaged face. She ached for her dead baby. Who did she look like? What would she have been like? She splashed cold water on her face and toweled it dry. She rubbed so hard it irritated her skin and that felt good, somehow. When she emerged, Jeff had returned and was sitting on the bed. He got up quickly and stood in front of her. His manner was firm but seemingly rational.

"I'm sorry, babe. I really am. I can't see it your way. I'm looking into the future and seeing the ways that adopting a ten year-old boy whom we hardly even know and is probably a pretty screwed up kid will fuck up our lives. I just never signed on for this."

"Eleven years old," she said softly.

"What?"

"He's eleven now." She paused. "Eve never signed on for this either." Her voice softened further. "She was my friend, Jeff. I really cared about her. She loved him so much. I know this won't be easy, but we will never feel right if we abandon him."

"We won't do that, of course. We'll try to find family and if that isn't possible, we'll find good foster parents.

We'll send money, we'll subsidize him. If he wants to go to college someday, we could even help him pay for it."

She didn't answer.

"We'd keep in touch," he continued, trying to come up with a suggestion that would convince her. "Maybe he could even come for a summer sometime."

Marcia shook her head sadly. "It isn't enough, Jeff. Money alone can't solve this. Look, things don't always work out the way we want. People adopt kids who turn out badly, but they can't give them back. They give birth to babies with such serious problems that they spend their whole lives trying to take care of them and worrying about what will happen when they die." She put her arms around him and buried her head in his chest. "Or their baby dies at birth, like ours just did. They go on. We will go on. But it can't be by leaving this boy behind. Not Eve's son. I can't do it. I just can't."

He held her, awkwardly caressing her. "Look, maybe we're both in shock. We've had a terrible blow. We can't make any reasonable decisions now. So maybe we don't need to talk about adoption yet, but if they let us, I suppose we could take him home until we find a better solution."

She hugged him tighter. "Yes. Thank you. Yes." She tried to stop herself from crying, and sniffled a few times, reaching into her bag for a tissue. "But what do you mean if they let us? I don't think there's anyone who cares enough to stop us."

"The authorities. Child Services. You can't just take a child who is not related to you out of state."

"I think Eve made a will. She was always worried about

what would become of Danny if anything ever happened to her and she asked if we'd be his guardians. I know we should have talked to you about it, but it was so far-fetched I just said yes."

He stiffened. "Did you sign anything?"

She bit her lip. "No, but I gave her my word. I promised."

"Jesus, Marcia." He shook his head in exasperation.

"I'm sorry, Jeff. I never in a million years thought anything like this could happen." She looked at her watch and stood up. "But we've got to go. I don't know how we're going to do this, but we have to tell Danny what happened."

Jeff followed her out the door. "And our son?" he said suddenly. "How do you think this will affect him?"

She was at the door and she turned to face him. "I think he will grow up knowing his parents did the right thing and didn't run away from their obligations. I think he'll be proud." She paused. "And he'll have a big brother. Maybe they'll grow up to love each other."

"I never said they'd grow up together, Marcia. This is just temporary."

She nodded. "Day by day," she said. "For now, we have to get Danny. Will you come with me?"

"Of course. We'll go together. We'll need to consult with someone when we get home," he said, almost to himself. "Maybe a psychologist to help you get rid of some of the guilt you're carrying."

She stopped short. "To help *me*?" She hid her indignation as best she could. "Yes. I will definitely need help dealing with this grief for our baby and for Eve, we both will. But we'll also need some help for Danny, that's for sure. And some guidance about how to deal with a grieving child." They walked together to the taxi stand outside the hotel. "We should have gone in," she said.

"Where?"

"To the preemie ward. We should have insisted on holding him."

"We can't take any chances, Marcia. We have to listen to what the doctors say. We'll go back right after this."

She thought of her little son, alone in an incubator when, if things had gone as expected, they would have been with both of their babies, cuddling them and happily making the final choice of names. She looked at Jeff. His face was set and taut and his eyes as sad as her own. She took his hand.

"What are you thinking?" she asked tenderly.

"I'm thinking of our son. He doesn't even have a name."

"Our poor little boy!" she said. "His world is already filled with so much sorrow. None of the names we thought of sound right now. I don't know what to call him."

"Don't worry, Marcia. We can't settle everything at once. One thing at a time."

They hailed a cab and climbed in.

"Maybe we should call him Job," Marcia said.

Jeff frowned. "No. That's not a great role model. That would mean this tragedy is only the first."

"Job was tested, but he was loved by God."

"God had a strange way of showing it. I'd rather He just ignored us from here on out."

"Okay, then how about Griffin?"

"Griffin? Where did that come from?"

"I found it in a baby book."

"What does it mean?"

"It means 'strong.'"

"Griffin," Jeff repeated, trying it out. "Strong. Yeah. I like that. He'll need to be."

11

THREE MONTHS LATER

It was much harder than she thought it would be. Of course she didn't expect things to be easy. Everyone told her that having a baby changes your life, but those are just words until one day you realize you and your husband and your relationship, that thing that is not you and not him but something else that you have worked hard to create, is not what it was before. The sudden flood of responsibilities, the lack of sleep, the need, the constant need that you have to fill—no one really explained it all, or maybe she just never thought about how totally selfless you have to be, at least at the beginning. She never said she minded. She wanted this. She was ready for it. But for the first two months, she learned, you are giving, giving, just giving, and the baby doesn't give back. He doesn't even smile in response to you yet, but later— she knew because everyone told her—when he does, it is very gratifying. She was aware that some people claim their babies smiled at them when they were two weeks old, but they were just imagining it, she was sure. Sometimes you see a little movement of the baby's lips that looks just like a smile, she admitted, but it doesn't seem to be connecting to you, not a social smile, just a response to something inside the baby itself. "I don't know," she said to Jeff. "Maybe it's gas." She told him that she made that comment to one of the other mothers at the pediatrician's office and the woman looked at her pityingly. "Either she thought my baby had something wrong with him, or that I did and I didn't measure up as a mother," she said, laughing. "That woman was just so sure her baby was smiling directly at her. But I'm just as sure that baby wasn't and I don't think Griffin has yet either and no mother could love her baby as much as I love Griffin."

And she did love Griffin. She held his naked body next to her breast after she fed him sometimes, skin to skin, as she had read helped build bonding, and couldn't imagine loving him more. She had heard that if she took hormones and pumped her breasts she could actually stimulate them to produce milk even though she hadn't given birth, and she had briefly considered doing this. But in the end she decided not to. Jeff, who always objected when she suggested anything that wasn't natural, had already come pretty far by going along with the surrogacy and, especially after everything that had happened, she didn't want to push him further. She also worried both about what effect the extra hormones would have on her health long-term and whether she would ever produce enough to satisfy Griffin's growing need. Once she made the decision, she wondered if without nursing and especially without the experience of giving birth, it might take longer for her to bond, but from the first moment she held him in her arms and gave him the bottle, she knew she didn't have to worry. He'd lock his eyes onto hers as he fed, making little groaning, gurgling noises, and she was hooked.

But after the first few days, he sometimes squirmed and pulled away sharply while she fed him, starting to cry and then frantically rooting around until she put the nipple back in his mouth. It soon became clear that crying would not be an unusual occurrence. Griffin seemed to cry most of the time. He had colic, the doctor said. His little body seemed wracked with pain. It was tempting to think that maybe he was crying for his dead sister, that he was lonely for the companion he'd had in the womb. But she didn't really believe that and she didn't want to think that way. The doctors said it was his stomach or an immature nervous system and she concentrated on that. He woke every two hours to eat and then cried almost nonstop until the next feeding. He'd fall asleep about half an hour before it was time to feed him again and then he'd wake with a short sharp cry that grew louder and more insistent until she offered him the bottle. When he finished, she would try every way she had read or heard of to burp and comfort him, and sometimes she would be successful. But as soon as she lowered him into his crib, he started to cry. She couldn't bear to hear his cry—he was so tiny, so helpless. So she'd pick him up and rock him and try to find a way to soothe him. But nothing helped for long. She sat in the glider holding him, hearing his screams, feeling inadequate, a baby book open to "Why does the baby cry?" She never found out. The only thing that worked at all was movement. If she'd put him in the baby carriage and rock it hard, he sometimes quieted. But the best solution was the car. This wasn't too bad during the day, but it soon developed that his worst episodes would occur in the middle of the night.

"It would be three in the morning," she'd tell friends when they came to visit, and they would listen openmouthed, "and I'd bundle him up and walk across the street to the garage, put him in the car seat and drive around till he fell asleep. The guys who worked there got used to me—this crazy lady and her screaming baby. But it was amazing. As soon as I turned the key and the engine turned over, he'd stop crying. I knew this really was nuts in a way, but the thing is, it stopped that incessant screaming and as soon as it stopped I felt better. Sometimes, after driving randomly for a while, after he was asleep, I'd pull over in front of the garage and try to get up the nerve to take him home without waking him. But often, as soon as I stopped the car, he'd start crying again. Finally, I'd come home, exhausted. Maybe by then he'd really fall asleep for a few hours, if I was lucky. The next time he needed to eat, I'd feed him and then wake Jeff and ask him to rock him until he fell asleep."

"I was wondering when you'd mention Jeff," Grace had

said. She and Grace had become close since that fateful dinner in Woodstock when Grace had suggested surrogacy. "Why isn't he helping you more?"

"He wanted to help. He'd have done more if I'd asked him, but he didn't have paternity leave. I had a few months off."

"Have you considered letting him cry for a while? Some people think that's the only way to beat this. It's sleep training."

"Did you do that with Stephie?"

Grace laughed. "What do you think?"

"I think you didn't."

"Yeah. Well, you're right."

"Even if I ever do decide to do that, it wouldn't be now, when he's so little and clearly suffering from colic. That's inhuman."

Julie came to visit several times, filling her in on office gossip and asking for instructions and advice. Marcia enjoyed her visits and regaled her with the by now stock stories of her motherhood trials, which she had polished practically to performance art. "You're not encouraging me to have a baby," Julie said with a nervous laugh. Marcia smiled. "I know, I'm sorry. But it's not an issue right now, right? By the time it is, you'll be ready for it." She took out a box of homemade chocolate chip cookies one of her friends had brought and offered it to her. Julie took one.

"That's delicious," she said.

"I know. I'm trying to get rid of them before I eat them all."

Julie finished and reached for a second.

"Were you ready for it?" she asked.

"Ready for what?"

"All this," Julie said, gesturing to Griffin, who was asleep in the swing, and all the baby equipment and paraphernalia that had invaded the living room.

Marcia didn't answer right away.

"Yeah. I was," she said thoughtfully. "But not all of it."

She could have handled Griffin's first colicky months, difficult as they were. But the part she didn't confide to Julie, though Julie knew the story, was the stress of everything else she had to deal with. She was trying to cope with the grief over losing her little girl, the guilt and sadness over losing Eve, and the silent, sullen presence of eleven-year-old Danny, filled with rage and confusion and pain and not knowing how or to whom to release it. When Jeff complained that no one ever told him how hard it would be, she told him it wasn't the same for everyone. "Some people are luckier than others," she'd said. "Some people have babies who eat and sleep and rarely cry at all. But I already knew that my life as a mother, our life as parents, wasn't going to be lucky. I mean, look how it started. Our job is to change our luck, to make our own luck, not to count on fate because fate has kind of messed things up right from the beginning."

She obsessed over how things might have been. Maybe if they had gone to a doctor who specialized in high-risk pregnancies. Maybe if Eve had gone to the hospital earlier. Maybe if she had checked Eve's health records before engaging her. Maybe if Griffin had been an easier baby. Maybe if Jeff had been more flexible. Her mind stayed with that last thought. The worst problem she faced with Danny was the way he affected Jeff.

They had enrolled him in the Claremont School soon after they arrived back in New York. It was a small private school that specialized in children who had not "thrived" in their first schools. In practice this meant kids who had behavior problems or struggled to keep up with the work, who would benefit from more attention, smaller class size and specialized teaching. Danny had not been in the lower half of his class in his L.A. public school—he was an above-average student—but the tests he was given in New York put him behind others his age and it was clear he would need additional help. They had returned in June, and the school suggested he attend summer school to help his transition, which Marcia was grateful for. Jeff wanted him to join the local public school, which had a pretty good reputation, but Marcia felt that at least during the transition period he should get more individual attention. His academic deficits could be fixed, the teachers assured her, but she saw that his unhappiness was harder to repair.

The summer session was relaxed—part school, part summer camp—with only a few kids participating, and Danny didn't seem to run into too many problems. Marcia was pretty taken up with being a new mother so she didn't have much time to pay attention to his state of mind, and although Danny was still overwhelmed by the changes in his life, grieving and not interacting much, everyone seemed to understand and cut him a great deal of slack. By September, more was expected of him. When Marcia took him in on the first day of school, he barely looked up to acknowledge the teacher whose class he would be in. He stared at the floor but his manner appeared more sullen than shy and the teacher picked up on it right away. "There are three empty seats in the back, Danny," she said. "Which one would you like to take?"

"None of them," he said. She chose for him and Marcia left. She asked to speak to the guidance counselor, but no one was available without an appointment. When he came home from school on that first day, Marcia was waiting with brownies and hot chocolate to ask him how it went. But he went straight to his room and slammed the door. When Jeff came home and she called Danny for dinner, he said he had a stomachache and wasn't hungry. She got up to go to him but he had locked the door.

"Danny, open the door. We don't lock doors in this house."

Danny didn't answer. Marcia looked helplessly at Jeff, who joined her in front of Danny's room.

"Open the door," Jeff said in his most authoritative voice. There was no reply.

"Danny, we can't allow you to keep this door locked. If you don't open it, I will unscrew the doorknob and let myself in. And you will be in big trouble."

They could hear the lock click open. When they entered, Danny was sitting on his bed. "I just don't feel good. Can't you just go away?"

Jeff went back to the table, but Marcia sat down on the

chair near the bed. "I know you need some alone time, and that's fine. We just want to be sure you're all right. You can't lock the door when you want to be alone, but if you just tell us you need some time, we won't bother you, okay?"

He didn't answer.

"Does your stomach still hurt?"

"No."

"Are you hungry?"

"No."

"Do you want me to give you some space now?"

"Yeah."

She patted his knee and left the room.

A few days later, he came home with a black eye and a note from the principal that he had been in a fight on the playground. Danny wouldn't tell her what had happened. When Jeff came home that night, she tried to engage him in finding a strategy to help Danny.

"I think he needs a firm hand. He's never had discipline. He's been left free to do whatever he wants, and in a crisis like this, regular rules that never vary and have to be followed might help," he said.

"Eve didn't ignore him, Jeff. She worked a lot to support him, but he knew what was expected of him. He's had a huge loss. I think he needs comfort not strictness."

"I think that kind of coddling will just make him worse."

They agreed to disagree while they looked for a therapist who could advise them. Marcia believed that what would help Danny most would be if Jeff could be the father Danny never had. But Jeff's understanding of this role was contrary to hers and opposite to the loving attention he showered on Griffin. He never really tried to reach Danny. He flinched at every example of Danny's unhappiness, his poor adjustment, his fights at school. When they got called in a few weeks later because Danny was caught cheating on a test, Jeff came down hard on him, taking away his weekend movie (a treat Marcia had instituted) and sending him to his room after lecturing him not just about cheating but about his belligerence to the teachers and his sullenness at home. Marcia watched unhappily as Danny submitted, shifted uneasily and fought to control his tears. It seemed to Marcia that Jeff was always haranguing him, and the result, she thought, was making him more guarded, less reachable. She fretted, she complained, but she was helpless to change things. Jeff made strict rules and insisted Danny follow them: homework as soon as he came home, no television during the week.

The new regime didn't seem to work, however. Although Danny was sent to his room to do his homework as soon as he came home, the teachers called and sent home notes to report that he rarely completed it. Marcia started insisting that he give it to her first, and she went over it with him to see if he needed help and signed, where the teacher indicated, to show she had checked it. Part of Jeff's strategy included his insistence that Danny eat everything on his plate whether or not he liked it or was hungry. When Danny balked at a food he didn't like—spinach, for example—Jeff made him stay at the table, even after he and Marcia left it, until he forced it down. He demanded that Danny go to his room to get ready for bed at seven-thirty—very early for an eleven year old boy who wasn't at all tired at that time and was used to setting his own bedtime. Marcia told Jeff that it would be good to have some time to be together as a family, but he said he needed that time for himself, for them, without Danny around. "He can read in his room for an hour before he goes to sleep," he said. "It will be good for him—improve his reading level." When she tried to tell him it made him feel rejected, he dismissed it as unreasonable. He seemed to think all Danny needed was structure and discipline.

But that wasn't true. What Danny needed was love and Jeff just couldn't love him.

12

Danny came home from school and slammed his back-pack on the kitchen table, a gesture he'd been asked repeatedly not to do. He knew Jeff made a big deal over that kind of thing. He was supposed to put it on the bench near the door and hang his jacket on the rack. He paused briefly, thinking he'd better do what Jeff wanted so he didn't get in trouble again, but instead he took off his jacket and let it drop on the floor near the table. He'd had a terrible day at school. It was almost six months since he'd moved to New York and his new school was as bad as he thought it would be. He still didn't have any friends. The teacher was really lame and he couldn't stand the other kids. No one, not one of them, had noticed him at first, no one said hello or asked him who he was or where he came from or anything. Not that he wanted them to. They were a bunch of idiots. At his school the kids were much cooler and he always sat with a group of his friends at lunch. He'd just get his food on a tray and go straight to the table and the kids would be there already or come later and they sat together every single day. If a new kid came in the teachers always brought him over to some new table and told the kids that was his place at lunch from then on, so he had somewhere to go. At lunch in this new school, he couldn't find a place to sit. The kids took up all the tables and even if there was room at one, it felt weird to just barge in, and if they saw you walk in their direction, no one moved over or anything. Anyway, he couldn't just go over and sit down next to someone he didn't even know. He tried to go outside the first day and eat in the playground, but of course they wouldn't let him. One of the older boys had made fun of him, said something about his mother not teaching him right, so he swung at him. He knew it was important to let them know right off he wasn't afraid. But then the kid hit him back and the teacher pulled them apart and told Marcia and Jeff.

But that wasn't the worst part. The worst part was at the beginning, when he first got there. Everyone was staring at him when he walked into the classroom and that dumb teacher introduced him. He couldn't believe how bad that was. She said right then in front of everyone that his mother had died and everyone should be nice to him. That was so awful, but it still wasn't the worst part. That was when he couldn't stop himself from crying after she said it. He didn't sob or anything stupid like that, but he knew his face was getting wet and he sniffled like a baby and couldn't do anything to stop himself. Everyone looked at him. His face got hot even now as he pictured it. He didn't want to think about it.

Then he remembered that he was wrong about no one talking to him, because one of the girls did. She was one of the pretty ones too. She had long brown hair and glasses. She came over afterward. He could see her eyes through the glasses and they were so big, he thought the glass must have made them look bigger than they were. He could tell they were all soft with pity and she said she was sorry about his mother. Like it was her fault. He figured he might cry again, so he just walked away and she didn't talk to him again but he saw her talking to her friends and they all looked at him, whispering.

I hate her and all of them, he thought. I hate it here. Except for Griff. My mom gave birth to him so that makes him my brother, whatever they say. Whatever Jeff says, really. He's the one who likes to say he isn't really my brother. Whatever that means. Well, he's the closest thing to a brother I have.

He walked into the kitchen to get a snack and found the brownies Marcia had baked on the kitchen counter with a note: *Danny, we're at the park. Come join us. Here's a snack I made for you. Love, Marcia.* Marcia was always trying to be nice but it made him uncomfortable. He fought liking her because if she hadn't showed up, he would still have his mother. He knew that somehow this whole thing was Marcia's fault. She'd be going back to work soon, he thought, and that would be better. He wouldn't have to talk to her when he came home from school.

Maybe she wouldn't even know when he came home. But what good would that do? He didn't know where to go and he didn't have any friends to hang out with. If he could just go back to L.A. and live in his old place. He was almost twelve years old. He didn't need to have people watching him. He could live at home and go to school and hang out with his friends. Manolo, who lived next door with his wife and baby girl, would look out for him if he needed him, he figured. They always helped his mother.

He stared at the brownies and at the note Marcia had left, then crumpled it in his fist and threw it away. He stood staring at the trash and then, hardly knowing what he was doing, he retrieved the note and tore it into tiny pieces, which he dropped on the floor. He took a bite of the brownie and then threw that down too, and stomped on it, grinding the pieces into the floor. He started to cry. He could feel the rage swelling in his chest. He heaved and sobbed but it didn't provide relief. He looked around the kitchen wildly. He opened the food pantry and suddenly swept all the jars onto the floor. The glass crashed against the slate and splattered sticky honey and red jam and dill pickles at his feet. That felt a little better so he did it again; this time he threw down opened boxes of cereal, rice, sugar, flour, watching their contents spill out in piles and lumps and thin trickles. But he wasn't done yet. He found a can of whipped cream and sprayed it everywhere he could, the cabinets, the floor, the refrigerator. For just a few seconds after that he felt some relief. He could feel his heart, which had been beating hard in his ears, slow down a little. Then he ran out of the apartment and turned west toward Riverside Park, far from the spot in Central Park where he knew Marcia would be. He felt bad about Marcia. Even though he couldn't forgive her he could see how hard she tried. She'd have to clean it all up and she'd be real upset. She'd be mad. He ought to go back anyway, he thought. She'd be worried. Maybe he could try to clean it before she came back, but he knew there wouldn't be enough time. No, it was finished, he thought. He could never go back there now. They'd probably be glad if they never saw him again.

He wanted his mom. He wanted her so bad he couldn't stand it. Why did she have to do that anyway? She said she did it for the money, for him. He didn't want the money. He wanted his mom. Didn't she know she might die? How could she take a chance like that? How could she leave him? He felt the rage return, his chest swelled with it, his eyes smarted. He picked up a rock and threw it as far as he could. Then he picked up another and threw it even farther. He kept throwing rocks, one after another, until his arm hurt. For the first time he felt really mad at his mother. None of this would have happened if she hadn't been so stupid. I hate her, he thought. He threw another rock. Then he sat down on the park bench and started to cry, heaving with sobs. He looked up, guilty, sure his mother had heard him, could hear him now. "I'm sorry, Ma," he cried. "I didn't mean it. I love you."

13

When Marcia returned home she found the kitchen as Danny had left it. Her first reaction wasn't anger or even confusion. It was fear. She looked at the kitchen clock over the oven. It was four-thirty. She had to clean this up before Jeff got home at six-thirty. He couldn't know Danny had done this. First, she looked for the boy, walking from room to room, calling his name. When she didn't find him, she figured he'd run out ashamed of himself and would come back when he cooled down. She didn't like him wandering around the city alone—he'd never done that before—but she wasn't really worried. Danny was used to taking care of himself, and she was pretty sure he'd be back in a few minutes. She put Griffin in the infant swing and wound it up. He laughed happily when it started to sway back and forth. This should entertain him for fifteen minutes, she thought, as she stared at the mess, trying to decide where to start. She picked up the shattered glass, used paper towels to absorb the spills, swept and washed the floor, sponged the cabinets and refrigerator. When she was half done, Griffin began to cry and she wound up the swing again, hoping for another fifteen minutes. Time was passing, he would need to be fed soon, and she had to finish cleaning first. She attacked the mess with new urgency. Griffin started to cry before she was done. She wound up the swing again, but it didn't work this time; he was hungry. She let him cry for five more minutes while she continued cleaning and then took him in her arms and sat in the glider chair she had bought what seemed like years ago, when she was happily preparing for motherhood. He latched on to the bottle hungrily, he had begun lately to hold the bottle with his hands while she fed him, and she tried to relax. But more than an hour had passed and Danny still wasn't home and she began to worry. What had happened? Why had he done this? He was obviously more deeply disturbed than she had realized and she had to do better figuring out how to help him. He'd been seeing a therapist twice a week. She wondered if he opened up to him. But most of all, where was he?

She changed Griffin's diaper, put him on a blanket on the floor outside the kitchen, gave him some toys and returned to cleaning up. He's over his colic now, thank God, she thought, and she smiled at how happy he seemed, beaming up at her while he shook his rattle and then tried to roll over. She kept looking at the clock, worried

that Jeff would walk in before she was done. Jeff had
very little patience with Danny, she thought wearily. He
would use this as another argument for sending him
away. She couldn't let that happen.

By the time Jeff came home, the kitchen was clean
and Marcia had just finished giving Griffin his bath.
By now, she had stopped worrying about Jeff and was
seriously worried about Danny. She imagined every
frightening scenario that could befall an eleven-year-
old boy alone in New York City as night fell. Jeff had
gone straight to Griffin. He'd picked him up and played
with him, barely saying hello to Marcia and not asking
about Danny at all. She'd been too busy to make anything for dinner so when Jeff finally handed Griffin
back to her and said how hungry he was, she answered
that she hadn't had time to prepare anything and suggested they order in.

"Jesus, Marcia. Even if you didn't have time to cook,
couldn't you have called in an order by now? I just picked
up a sandwich for lunch and I'm really hungry."

She walked to the drawer where they kept the menus
and took a few out, handing them to him. He looked at
her in surprise.

"I'm sorry," she said. "But it's not like I do nothing all
day. I've been busy. I've got two kids to take care of."

He ignored that and went in to the bedroom to change
out of his suit. She looked out the window, hoping to
see Danny returning. She called the doorman to see if
maybe by some wild chance he'd come in and was just
hanging out downstairs, afraid to come home. But he

wasn't anywhere. She knew she had to tell Jeff and they had to get help.

She put Griffin in his crib, gave him his pacifier, sang him one verse of "Hush Little Baby," and wound up his musical mobile. She dimmed the lights and walked out and, luckily, Griffin fell asleep quickly. Jeff had returned to the kitchen. He was on the phone and he put his hand over the mouthpiece as he called to her.

"Do you want pizza? That would probably be the fastest."

"Sure," she said. "Just plain cheese." She waited for him to order and hang up. Then she said, "Jeff, Danny isn't here."

Jeff was looking through the mail. He barely looked up. "Oh? Where is he?"

"I don't know. He's gone. He wasn't here when I got home from the park with Griff. I'm worried."

He had opened a letter and was glancing at it. "He's probably at a friend's house," he said absentmindedly. "Did he leave a note or anything?"

"No, Jeff. What friend's house? He doesn't have any friends. I think he was upset and he just left. Please put that letter down and listen to me. Danny is not here. It's late and it's getting dark out and I'm worried. I think we need to call the police."

Jeff looked up. "Shit. What now?" he said. "He probably got in trouble at school again. Maybe he got into another fight. Maybe he thought his teacher called us again and he's afraid to come home. He's probably wandering around working up his courage."

"For four hours? It's almost seven. I'm going to call the police," Marcia said.

"Hold on. Maybe I should go out and look for him first. Maybe he's hanging around nearby."

"You can try that but just for ten minutes. If you don't find him, I'm going to get help."

"I'm going to kill that kid when I get hold of him," Jeff said, putting on his coat.

"Maybe if you didn't talk like that, he wouldn't run away," she shouted after him. But she knew why Danny had run away. The door slammed.

Griffin started to cry and Marcia went to him. He had lost his pacifier and she didn't see it in the crib. Thinking he had thrown it over the edge, she glanced at the floor, then got on her hands and knees and felt under the crib, where she found it. She put it back in his mouth. He grabbed it greedily, sucking hard, and then more slowly as he settled back down. She tried to think where Danny might have gone but couldn't come up with anywhere. There was their neighbor upstairs who was always friendly to him, she thought, but she couldn't imagine Danny hiding out in her apartment. She considered that he might have a friend at school she didn't know about. Maybe he lived nearby and Danny went over to his house. She hoped he had, he was such a lonely child. But she doubted it. If that had happened, wouldn't the kid's mother have called by now? She didn't know how to follow up on that anyway; she wouldn't have any idea who the kid might be or how to get in touch with him. But the police would know how to track him down, she thought.

Time passed excruciatingly slowly as she waited for Jeff to return, worried, not really believing there was any chance he would find Danny.

The phone rang and she ran to answer it, picking it up eagerly. But it wasn't Jeff, it was the doorman, telling her the pizza was on its way upstairs. When it arrived, she dug into her bag for a tip and carried the box to the kitchen counter.

She felt a little queasy and wondered if she might be hungry, so she opened the box and took out a piece of pizza. She took a bite. It made her feel worse, so she abandoned it. She sat at the kitchen table, then rose and walked around the apartment nervously. Where was Jeff? It was already way more than the ten minutes she had allotted to his search. She decided she wouldn't wait for him anymore and was just about to pick up the phone to call the police when it rang sharply, startling her. It was the doorman, telling her that Danny and a policeman were on their way up.

A policeman! She didn't know whether to be relieved or alarmed. She managed to feel both, though the relief edged in first. He was okay, no one had hurt him, no one had kidnapped him. But the alarm followed soon after. Why a policeman? What had he done? And then the relief again—at least Jeff was still gone.

The bell rang and, full of dread, she opened the door. Danny stood there, his head down, his eyes scrutinizing the floor as if something incredibly interesting was on it, refusing to look at her. Her heart turned over at the sight of him and she reached for him and tried to pull him close, to reassure him, but he wiggled away from her, his body tense. "It's okay, Danny," she said. "Whatever it was, it's okay."

She invited the police officer in and asked him what had happened.

"Nothing, ma'am. I just noticed this kid wandering around on Broadway around five o'clock and when I came back at seven he was still there. It was getting dark and I wondered if he was lost. I tried to ask him, but he ran away when I approached. So I just watched him for a while. He went into the Stop and Shop on Ninety-second Street and stayed a long time, so I went in after him."

Her dread increased. "Oh, I'm sorry. If he took something, please, let me pay for it, let me talk to him. He's had a really rough time lately."

The policeman laughed. "No, ma'am. He didn't take anything. That's what I thought he might do, but he didn't. He walked up and down the aisles like he was deciding what to get. Finally he bought himself a Snickers bar."

She looked confused. "Then I don't understand. Why are you here?"

"I realized he wasn't going home and thought something might be wrong. He's kind of young, but we get a lot of runaways so I asked him where he lived."

Marcia looked at Danny, who still hadn't raised his eyes. "Danny, were you running away?" she asked softly.

He didn't answer.

"Thank you for bringing him home, Officer," Marcia

said. "I'll talk to him." She turned to Danny. "Are you hungry? We have pizza." He just shook his head. He stood around awkwardly, not seeming to know what was expected of him. Marcia said another thank-you to the policeman, who left, saying he was glad he could help. After closing the door, she turned to Danny again. "Listen, Danny, I think I know why you stayed away, but I didn't tell Jeff about the kitchen. And it's okay. I cleaned it up. Don't mention it when you see him. I'll tell him something to make it okay that you came home so late. Don't worry about it."

He nodded without lifting his eyes from the floor. "Can I go to my room now?"

"Sure. But are you sure you don't want a piece of pizza?"

"Yeah." He walked to his room and closed the door.

Marcia called Jeff's cell phone. He picked it up on the second ring. "No luck," he said.

"He's home. It was nothing. I forgot he told me he was doing homework with some kids in his class. Everything's fine. I'm sorry," she said.

"Jesus, Marcia." He hung up. An hour passed before he came home.

She knew he was mad and assumed he was either walking it off or had stopped to get himself a better dinner. She walked to Danny's room and paused outside his door, trying to think of the best approach. She knocked. He didn't answer, so she opened the door a crack and asked if she could come in. He was sitting on his bed. He still didn't answer but she pushed the door open and walked in. His eyes were red and he looked like he'd been crying, but he got up when she entered and moved to his desk. She sat on his bed.

"Danny, you're not in trouble. I know how bad you feel. You must have been really angry to do what you did in the kitchen and it might help if we could talk about it."

He looked down and sniffled. He wiped his nose with his hand.

"Do you want to tell me what happened?"

"Nothing happened. I need to do my homework."

"Danny, something happened. Do you want to tell me why you did that to the kitchen?"

His eyes filled with tears. "I don't know," he mumbled. He looked at her and lowered his voice even more, almost to a whisper. "I'm sorry. I'm really sorry. I don't know what happened. Maybe there's something wrong with me."

"I don't think there's anything serious wrong with you. But I do think you're very unhappy. Sometimes people just flip and do something they wouldn't ordinarily do. Sometimes, life is just too hard and they let go."

"Yeah," he said. "Crazy people."

"You're not crazy, Danny. Just very sad and very angry and we know why and we know you have a right to be. We're going to find a way to help you, I promise. Do you talk about your feelings with your therapist?"

He just shrugged.

"Okay. That's between you and him. But you know, we care about you, we're responsible for you, and when you don't come home and it's getting late and dark, we worry about you. You have to think about us too. You need to come home where it's safe."

"I didn't think it would be safe," he murmured, looking at the floor.

"What?"

"Nothing."

"It can be dangerous in New York City. Can you tell me where you were all day? What did you do?"

"I didn't do nothing," he said. "I went to the park. Then I was looking for the market."

"What market?"

"Like at home. The *mercado*. You saw it. I used to go there after school sometimes when Ma was late from work. She said it was okay. But I couldn't find one. Not even a bodega. Everything's different here."

Marcia knew exactly what he was referring to. She remembered how Danny used to go to the market to buy himself an empanada or a treat with his allowance, how he'd meet friends sometimes, or neighbors, and how he knew everyone. That's all he was doing. Looking for something comforting and familiar. She understood how lonely he felt and her heart hurt for him. She reprimanded herself for not having thought to get some of the food he used to eat at home. "Please, Danny, come on out and get something to eat. A chocolate bar isn't enough."

"I'm not hungry."

"I know. But eat something anyway. Please."

He took a deep breath and walked into the kitchen.

Jeff had come in and was making himself a cup of tea. He nodded at Danny. "I was out looking for you," he said.

"I told him you were doing your homework with some kids in your class, but I had forgotten," Marcia said, laughing. "There was nothing to be worried about after all."

"How did you get home from school?" Jeff asked.

"On the bus," Marcia said quickly. "He went to a kid's apartment a few blocks away and then just walked home after."

"Well, did you get it all done?" Jeff asked Danny.

Danny looked at Marcia.

"I asked you a question," Jeff said. "It's polite to answer."

"Yeah," Danny muttered.

"He got it all done, Jeff. Now he's going to eat something. Can I get something for you?"

"No," Jeff answered. "I grabbed a bite at the corner."

Danny finished his pizza and brought the plate to the sink. He looked at Marcia again.

"Thanks, Danny," she said. "You can go back to your room now if you want to."

He left and she turned to Jeff. "It's so tense between you two. Can't you try, Jeff?" The teakettle whistled and Jeff quickly picked it up and poured the boiling water into his cup.

"I asked him if he finished his homework. You saw, he didn't answer. What am I supposed to do?"

"You're supposed to act like you like him. What would you do if Griffin was that age and you came home from

work? What would you say to him? What do you think
your tone would sound like?"

Jeff added honey to his tea and stirred it. "I'll never
be able to talk to him like I'll talk to Griff," he said.
"That's asking too much. He's a sullen kid and he doesn't
appreciate anything we do for him. I'm trying to do the
right thing here, Marcia, but you're asking too much."

Marcia nodded. She followed him into the living room
and sat next to him on the couch. She put her arms
around him and murmured into his ear, "I know you're
trying. I guess I just want you to try a little harder."

He smiled. She thought it was a twisted sort of smile,
a smile that said he had had enough of these conversations. He disentangled himself from her arms and got up
to turn on the TV. She sank bank into the cushions.
They both heard a sharp cry from Griffin's room and
shared a look. "I'll go," she said. Griffin had lost his pacifier again so she found it, put it back in his mouth and
tiptoed out as he fell back asleep. She was tired, so she
went to their bedroom and got ready for bed.

After changing into her nightgown and brushing her
teeth, she stopped in front of Danny's room and knocked.
He didn't answer, so she spoke through the closed door.
"I just wanted to say good night, Danny."

"Good night," he answered. She hesitated, wondering
whether she should try again to talk to him, but decided
against it. She returned to her bedroom and slipped into
bed but her mind was whirling and she couldn't sleep. Finally, she got up and walked back to the living room,
where Jeff was still watching television.

"Jeff, we've talked about family therapy," she said. "Every time I mention it, you say sure but not now. But it's time to do it. His individual therapy isn't enough. And I think we'd all benefit from it."

He didn't answer, which she took as agreement. She resolved to set up an appointment as soon as possible.

14

Marcia's six-month maternity leave was coming to an end. It had seemed like a long time at the beginning, when lack of sleep and constant demands blurred day and night and often left her in a daze. But now that it was over, it seemed too soon and arrangements had to be made. Luckily, Colleen, a colleague at work, no longer needed her full-time nanny and she gave a glowing recommendation for a Guatemalan woman named Berta Hernandez. Marcia interviewed and quickly hired her. That circumstance relieved a huge pressure because she didn't need to go through the task of checking references, and no matter how good they were, worrying about what went on when she wasn't there. Colleen vouched for this woman who had been with her for fifteen years, and Marcia liked and trusted Coleen. She also felt calmed because Danny was in the house. Jeff found this surprising, since

Danny's presence never seemed a positive addition to him, but Marcia tried to explain that Danny would see how Berta was with Griffin and report back. She was also hopeful that a Spanish-speaking housekeeper would make Danny feel more comfortable when he missed his old neighborhood, and less isolated.

Marcia was torn about going back to work. She was bound so closely to Griffin, to his cycle of eating and sleeping, which lately was more and more interspersed with periods of alertness and play, that she found it hard to imagine leaving him for so many hours each day. As a senior editor she had been able to arrange her schedule so that she could work at home two days a week at the beginning, and that helped her make the transition. But it was also true that part of her yearned to be back at her desk in her quiet, organized office, reading and editing manuscripts, going to meetings and lunching with clients and associates. Just thinking about it made her smile. Work problems that before seemed troublesome now seemed relatively minor. And she was convinced that Griffin would be fine with Berta. She had asked the woman to come in for a few days while she was still at home so she could teach her Griffin's schedule and observe her interactions with him. Berta had arrived with a baby book about farm animals and the sounds they each make. She said a pleasant hello and then went straight to Griffin, talking to him and holding out her arms for him. He flashed a big smile and leaned toward her. Marcia was delighted to see how competently she took over.

The only problem was Danny. She explained to Berta that she would be responsible for him too, that he needed to be home after school and do his homework, and Berta would be expected to monitor his behavior. Danny didn't seem to take to her, however. He resented her telling him what to do, seeming to think he was too old for a baby-sitter, and refused to answer her in Spanish when she used it to address him. Worse, Berta showered affection on Griffin while speaking abruptly and dismissively to Danny. Danny responded in kind, and Marcia worried that his intransigence and downright rudeness to Berta would make her quit. She tried to think of ways to min-imize the time Danny was with her. Danny's therapist thought Danny resented Berta simply because she was another person telling him what to do and that the rela-tionship might get better with time. He suggested en-couraging Danny to join group activities at school as a way to make some friends. So, for his own good, as well as the household's, Marcia encouraged him to come up with an after-school activity that he would like, but so far, he'd turned down every suggestion. Did he want to do sports? Maybe baseball, Marcia suggested—she knew he loved it in L.A. and was good at it. Jeff loved baseball too; he was a devoted Yankees fan. Maybe they would share that passion, she thought hopefully.

One night after dinner she prodded Jeff to broach the subject. They were sitting at the dinner table and, as usual, Jeff and Marcia were carrying the conversation, trying occasionally to bring in Danny, who answered, if he answered at all, in monosyllables. Marcia brought the conversation around to the upcoming baseball season, which would start in the spring.

"Your mother told me how much you love baseball, Danny," Marcia said. "Maybe you'd like to play on weekends with the town team in Woodstock. You'd miss the practice sessions during the week up there, but we could get you into some program in the city where you could practice a few times a week. What do you say?" Danny didn't answer.

"Danny, Marcia asked you a question," Jeff said.

"I don't want to," he mumbled.

"I thought that was your favorite thing," Marcia prodded.

"Not anymore."

"What team do you like?" Jeff asked.

Danny shrugged.

"I asked you what team you liked," Jeff snapped.

"The Dodgers," Danny muttered.

"Yeah. I get that. But you're a New Yorker now. Time to switch to the Yankees."

Danny looked up and for the first time his face looked animated. "I don't like the Yankees. My ma said the Yankees don't need fans. They win all the time. She said you gotta root for the guys who don't always win, 'cause they need you more. I like the Mets."

"The Mets? Man, they are such losers."

"They made it to the World Series."

"Yeah, and they lost."

Danny's face flushed. "Yeah, but they *made* it. They weren't as good but they worked hard and they made it.

The Yankees, they think they can do anything but they suck."

Marcia broke in. "Anyway, Danny, I'm talking about you. You need to get some exercise. You have to choose. If it's not baseball, then soccer or basketball. I'd really like you to do a team sport."

Danny didn't answer and, for the time being, she let the subject drop. But she told Berta that she would have to count on taking him to some activity as soon as they worked out which one.

"What about the after-school clubs at school?" Marcia asked Danny another time. "Is there anything that sounds like fun?"

Danny just shrugged.

Jeff left most of the arrangements to Marcia but the day Marcia returned to work, he pulled Berta over after Marcia left and told her that he didn't want her to leave Griffin alone with Danny. She was surprised. "You think the boy would hurt him? He seems to like him."

"I don't know what to think, but I don't want to take any chances."

She nodded.

The transition went smoothly and within a week, Marcia was well installed back at work and Berta was managing the household. On the two days Marcia worked at home she would break at lunchtime and take Griffin for a walk in the park or play with him on the living room floor. Then she'd go back to her reading and break again when Danny came home. She'd try to engage him about his day, though with little success, and she'd sit with him to be sure he finished his homework. There were tense dinners with Jeff, but she tried to tell herself they were getting better, though there was little evidence of that. Still, all seemed to be going relatively smoothly, until the third week when she got home to find out that the school had called about a problem with Danny. She was asked to make an appointment to speak to the science teacher at her earliest convenience.

She had just taken off her coat when Berta presented her with the message. Danny was in the kitchen drinking a Coke. He wasn't allowed soft drinks and they didn't keep them in the house, so he must have bought it himself with his allowance. Marcia walked over to him, took the can of Coke from his hand and poured it out in the sink. "What's this about, Danny?" she asked.

"I just wanted it. I paid for it with my allowance. I always drank it at home." He was indignant.

"Not the Coke. Why does the science teacher want to see me?"

"I don't know."

"Try to imagine." She was losing her patience, taking up her time with this nonsense when she hadn't even seen Griffin yet.

"Mommy's here," Berta sang out as she carried Griffin into the room. Marcia broke off her conversation with Danny to go to him, smiling and cooing as he held out his pudgy little arms to her and she took him greedily into her own.

Danny took the opportunity to disappear into his

room, but it didn't work. Marcia handed Griffin back to Berta and followed him in.

"It isn't fair," he said.

She sat on his bed. "Okay. So tell me what happened. If it isn't fair, I'll take your part. But what happened?"

His eyes filled with tears, but he stopped himself from crying. "I knocked over the science table. Everything broke."

You mean by accident?"

"Kind of."

"So tell me exactly what happened."

"John Rochman brought in this kit where you make a volcano and we all did it. It was really cool. Everyone did something. But when it was my turn, he, like, moved the thing I was supposed to put in farther away so I couldn't reach it. And when I tried, he moved it again when the teacher wasn't looking. And then a few of the kids looked at each other and laughed and every time I tried to get it one of them moved it further away and they kept passing it around."

"That's mean. So then what happened?"

"When it got back to John, he did it again so I pushed him hard in the chest and grabbed it. He fell down and I fell forward and the whole thing fell off the table and broke." He wiped his eyes, which were full, though not dripping. "It wasn't my fault. It's not fair but I'm the one who got in trouble."

"She reached for him and pulled him to her, wanting to protect him from all the things that seemed set on hurting him. But he wriggled away.

"Danny, did you tell the teacher what happened?"

"Nah. What's the good? She won't believe me."

"But I believe you, Danny. And I will tell her."

"No, then everyone will hate me."

"We'll see. We'll work it out. Just trust me, okay?"

He nodded and wiped his nose with his shirt.

"Not with that. Use a tissue."

He picked up a rubber ball and turned it round and round in his hands. "What about Jeff?"

She rubbed her lip with her finger for a second, thinking. "We'll have to tell him. But maybe after I talk to the teacher. It's okay. It's not your fault. You shouldn't have pushed that boy, but they all provoked you. Jeff will understand. You have to learn to use your words instead of your hands when you want to solve a problem."

"What do you mean?"

"I mean, you should have told him, told them all, to stop and if they didn't you should have told the teacher."

He bounced the ball against the wall and caught it. Then did it again.

"No balls inside," she said.

"If you do that you're a snitch. Nothing is worse than that."

"Nothing is worse than hitting or punching someone." She looked at her watch. Berta would be leaving soon. "We'll talk more later," she said as she walked to the door.

"Marcia," he called as she started to leave. She stopped and turned toward him.

"I can't go back there. I ran away after the volcano broke. I can't see them again."

She sighed. She seemed to be doing that more and more lately. "You mean you ran out of the school?"

"Yeah."

"It's far away. How did you get home?"

"The cop."

"What?"

"The cop. The same one. He saw me and I told him what happened. He took me home."

"He did? How?"

"In the cop car. I sat up front right next to him. It was pretty cool."

"Danny, you can't just leave the school whenever you want. They're responsible for you. That's against all their rules. I wonder why Berta didn't tell me this right away."

"She doesn't know. He dropped me downstairs. He told me to tell you what happened. But I can't go back there."

"You have to go," she said softly. "And you have to apologize. I'll go with you. It will be okay. It will be hard at first, but then it will be fine. You'll see." She left the room and took Griffin from Berta, who already had her coat on, ready to leave.

In his room, Danny sat heavily on his bed. "It won't be fine," he said. "It won't ever be fine." He picked up the ball and threw it once, hard, at the wall.

15

Fall turned to winter. There was time for the leaves in Central Park and in Woodstock to turn yellow and orange and red, time for them to fade to brown and crinkle and fall into heaps that Jeff raked and blew into neat piles and then grumbled when the neighborhood kids jumped into them, time for those same trees to bend and groan under the weight of the snow, time for the lawn in Woodstock to lie buried, looking like a frozen seascape marked only by the tiny hooves of passing deer, and time for the streets in New York City to turn to yellow slush pounded by the boots of thousands of people hurrying from one place to another. But there wasn't time enough for Danny to adjust to living with them.

Jeff claimed they had done everything they could. They had all seen a family therapist a few times until Jeff felt it was useless and expensive and refused to continue.

Although Danny went alone once a week, he still didn't seem to have any friends, his grades didn't improve, and his silence and withdrawal at home only increased. Even in this special school, he was behind others in his grade, so the teachers suggested it would be easier for him to repeat fifth grade and made his return to the school contingent on his doing that. This humiliated him, Marcia realized, but she didn't have a choice. She understood that he was bigger and stronger than the kids in his class but while he was behind them in math and reading, he was way advanced in independence and self-reliance. He also was accustomed to behaviors these private school children had never seen. Their problems were mostly confined to talking back to teachers or not doing homework. Danny's were different. He knew how to fight and he didn't hesitate to use his fists to settle disagreements or avenge hurt feelings. When she tried to explain to him that he couldn't do that, he viewed her as well-meaning but naive. The world in which he had grown up taught him that was how people got respect.

A few days after Christmas break, Marcia received a call from the principal. He asked that she and Jeff come in for a conference. She feared the worst and she wasn't wrong. The principal admitted they couldn't handle Danny. He didn't seem to be learning, he didn't turn in his homework, he was sullen and rude to the teachers, he failed tests, he fought during recess, he sat alone and isolated at lunch, he was destructive.

"How is he destructive?" she asked.

He pointed to the incident with the science table.

"I explained that. I spoke to Mrs. Mullin and I thought she understood. It was an accident. He was being bullied. You ought to be calling in the parents of those children who provoked him."

"That was a complicated case. Perhaps others were also to blame in that instance but it isn't the only example."

"You say he sits alone and isolated at lunch. He's so young—just eleven years old. He came in to the class late without knowing anyone. Aren't they too young to be choosing where they sit? Has anyone tried to help him integrate?"

"We have tried, Mrs. Naiman, I assure you. We encourage the children to be inclusive and to be independent. I acknowledge that we failed with Danny. We knew there would be problems given the background he came from and his recent trauma," the principal said, "but we hoped together we could overcome them. At this point, I'm afraid, we're forced to recognize that our hopes were not realized. He is disruptive to the other children. Their parents complain that he is displaying the very behavior they sent their kids to a selective school to avoid."

"He's a child who has suffered a terrible loss. Can't you please give him another chance?"

Jeff hadn't said anything. Now he chimed in. "Marcia never gives up," he said, apologetically. It sounded condescending, but she let it pass. Still, it bothered her that he couldn't find it in him to defend Danny, to fight for him, even a little. It made her feel even more responsible for Danny because she saw that she was the only advocate he had.

"He does do his homework. I know he does," she said. "I often sit with him when he does it and I check it and make sure he puts it into his book bag. So if you don't get it, he somehow isn't feeling safe enough to hand it in."

"Maybe he wants to fail," Jeff said. "Maybe this is exactly what he's been hoping for."

Marcia was annoyed at his response in front of the principal, viewing it as a betrayal, not just of Danny but of her. "But surely as educators, as people who care for children, you can help us turn this around," she said. "He's probably insecure about his ability. But he's smart. He did very well at his old school when his mother was alive. A lot of what you are seeing is the result of grief."

The principal shifted uncomfortably. "That actually supports my point. Perhaps he did well there because the standards were different. He would be happier in a school where the academic level and background of the other kids would vary more and he could find his own place."

Jeff agreed. Marcia didn't. But it didn't matter. It had already been decided and the upshot was that the school had given up on him. The principal agreed to keep him for the balance of the school year with the understanding that he would go to another school for sixth grade.

"If he improves, if you see a difference by the end of the year, will you reconsider?" Marcia asked.

"Yes, but frankly, I think it's unlikely," the principal answered.

As they left the building Marcia and Jeff didn't look at or speak to one another. When they got home, Marcia went into their bedroom and closed the door. She sat on their bed feeling sad and worried and wishing for Jeff, the old Jeff, she thought, the one before all this, who could share this disappointment and help fix it instead of acting as another obstruction. He opened the door and walked over to her, sitting down next to her and speaking softly, "Honey, I know how you feel. You've tried so hard to make this work. But we're spending more than forty thousand dollars a year for him to go to a school he hates and where no one likes him. Maybe it's time to try something else."

She sighed and put her hand in his, feeling guilty for her thoughts before he'd come in. "You're right. We have no choice. I'll do the research and see if there's a charter school he could go to. I'll talk to his therapist. Maybe he'll have some advice. But you know, Jeff, this isn't the whole picture. He's having a rough time adjusting and he's not responding to them in school, but there is more to him than that."

"He's not responding to us that well either," Jeff said.

She shrugged. "I don't know. That's getting better." She paused, wondering whether to say what was on her mind. Finally she said it with an apologetic smile, to soften it. "He's scared of you."

"How is he going to learn how to act if I don't teach him?" Jeff asked, irritated.

That was the reaction she had expected, but she pushed on, knowing she was treading on dangerous ground. "I know, honey. I think it's important that you teach him, but maybe not right now. I mean, he knew pretty well how to act before. Eve taught him. It's not that he doesn't know. It's that he can't act better. He's too full of anger and hurt. His behavior is just crying out for help, for attention of the right kind. I think he just needs more encouragement, more understanding."

Jeff rolled his eyes. They'd been over this ground before and his opinion hadn't changed. "Marcia, it's great that you think love is the answer to everything, but it isn't. Look at us. We're tense and arguing and resentful half the time. Love isn't even the answer for us."

"Love isn't the answer for *us*?" She repeated. "Wait a minute. What does that mean? I know we've disagreed about Danny but it hasn't changed my feelings for you. Has it changed yours for me? For Griff?"

"No, of course not," he said, getting up. He straightened his pants, smoothing out the wrinkles. "I didn't mean that. I meant even though we love each other, it hasn't stopped us from having arguments. It's kind of gotten in the way and interfered with our relationship with Griff, don't you think, Marcia? When was the last time we just enjoyed being at home together? It's always so tense."

"I know. I'm sorry. I think it's temporary. Please, honey, hang in there with me. I know we can make this work. Danny and Griffin love each other. Danny is never happier than when he's with him. He runs in to see him first thing when he comes home from school and Griff's face lights up when he sees him. I've started asking Danny to help out a little—to make him feel like he's needed, like he's part of the family."

Jeff had walked out of the bedroom, collecting items

he needed as he walked—he was in a rush to get back to work—and Marcia was following him as she talked. Now he turned around sharply and stopped walking. "Don't let him help too much, Marcia."

"What do you mean?"

"I mean, don't let Danny do things with Griffin when you're not in the room. I've already spoken to Berta about it. He's a troubled kid. I don't know what he'd do."

She laughed incredulously. "I can't believe you said that. I mean, do you honestly think Danny would ever in a million years hurt Griffin? He loves him. And Danny is not a bad kid."

"No. Every eleven-year-old kicks over the science table at school; every kid comes home, goes straight to his room, only comes out when he's forced to and then sits at dinner without saying a word."

"I admit all that. But every kid hasn't lost his mother in this awful way."

He softened, reaching out to her.

"You want this so much you're not seeing clearly. But Danny is an angry kid and angry kids do scary things."

"Jeff, he's a little kid. He's not some pathological teenager. We know what he was before, a good kid on the neighborhood baseball team. It's not even a year after his mother's death. He's grieving. That's normal. And he doesn't come out of his room because he knows you don't want him around, honey. He feels it. I feel it too."

"We do everything we can to make it up to him. Why is he still so angry?"

She put her hand on his arm and spoke as gently as

she could. "He blames us for killing his mother." She shrugged. "It's pretty straightforward."

He shook his head stubbornly. "He'll blame Griffin too. He'll realize it was giving birth to him that killed her."

"No. It was an embolism that killed her. You reminded me of that. Now it's my turn to remind you."

"You think he'll make those fine distinctions? Look, I can't have this conversation now. I've got to go." He walked out and she followed him into the hallway.

"This is ridiculous," she said. "You're really beginning to sound paranoid."

"Just do what I ask, will you?" he insisted. "It's not asking that much." He stepped into the elevator.

"Okay," she said as the door closed.

16

Marcia took the rest of the day off. She had meant to work for a few hours and then spend some quality time with Griffin. She had read essays advocating "quality time," claiming that it was even better than always being around because it meant less "wasted time." But more and more she saw this as a theoretical balm to working mothers who felt guilty about being away from their babies for long hours. She was thinking of commissioning a book that reported on psychological studies on this question. Her own opinion was that "quality time" meant "quantity time," because no one could mandate when Griffin would say his first word or take his first step or, when older, share a picture he had made or confess a troubling thought. Those kinds of interactions often happened on the fly to mothers who just were around a lot. Still, this realization didn't mean she wanted to quit her job. She loved working and they needed the income. She just didn't like fooling herself with bromides. She could live with knowing she'd miss some things in her son's development, as long as her absence didn't hurt him, which she believed it didn't. She read a news story online about research showing that children of working mothers actually did better in some ways than children of mothers who stayed at home and, delighted, she forwarded it to all her friends. Still, she vowed to do her best to be there as much as possible.

That was the plan for today. However, after that last confrontation with Jeff, she couldn't stop thinking about him and Danny and wondering what, if anything, she could do about their relationship. She blamed herself as well as Jeff. She recognized that she hadn't spent enough time specifically trying to help Danny integrate into his new life. And she had neglected Jeff, she admitted to herself, thinking pretty exclusively about Griffin's needs and Danny's problems and ignoring her husband. She took a spiral notebook and a pen out of her desk and brought it into the kitchen. She plugged in the electric tea kettle, chose a ginger tea bag from the ten boxes of assorted teas she kept in the closet, added some honey and poured the boiling water into her favorite porcelain cup—she'd picked up the idea that tea must be drunk only from a porcelain cup from an English author she had worked with. She waited for the mixture to turn just the right color and when it did, she stirred and brought it close to her nose, inhaling and luxuriating in its aroma. She sat, took a sip and put the cup on the table, then drew a line down the middle of the first page in her notebook. On one side of the line she wrote, "Things to do for Danny," and on the other: "Things to do for Jeff." She began with Jeff:

1) Prepare some nice meals.

Right, she thought. I'll start next week. I'll make barley soup and lentil salad. He loves those. And I can give Berta a menu for the days I'm at work—no more pizza delivery for a while. She didn't mind being responsible for their meals since she was home two days a week and Jeff was a terrible cook. Besides, he always did the dishes, a job she disliked.

2) Ask Berta to baby-sit once a week and go out for dinner or to a movie.

That was a pretty obvious fix, she thought. "Date night" after a new baby. They had just let that slide.

3) Invite friends over.

Actually, they didn't have that many mutual friends anymore, she thought. Their jobs, the baby, the added responsibilities of Danny, had taken all the free time they had and many of the people they used to see had dropped out of their lives. Marcia had always been the person who kept their social life going and she had been preoccupied. She would have to make some calls, she resolved.

    4) *Flirt with him sometimes. Ask him about his day.*
       Really want to know. Try to act interested. Try to be
       interested.

She paused. There was one more resolution that came quickly to mind but she resisted writing it down. She picked up the pen again. After the last item, she skipped two lines and scrawled:

    5) *Make love.*

She felt uncomfortable writing this, though she recognized how remiss she'd been on that score. The truth was, she had hardly ever wanted to make love since she'd come home from L.A. At first she blamed it on the loss they had suffered, then on the lack of sleep and finally on going back to work, but as time went by and as her sexual urge didn't return, she began to think there might be a more serious problem. It wasn't as though she wasn't still attracted to Jeff. She was, but she was also distant from him, even angry at him a lot of the time, disappointed that he wasn't more accepting of Danny. On the whole, she thought, it was worse than his not helping Danny to assimilate; he actually seemed to be preventing it. Not deliberately, of course. But by demanding so much of him, by not relating to him, he made every day more tense than it might have been.

She thought about the times Jeff had reached for her when they were in bed and the series of excuses she had offered. "I can't. I'm too tired." "Not tonight, honey, I think I'm getting a cold." "I had a terrible day. I need to get some sleep." Even the classic and obvious "I have a headache." Then one time, unexpectedly, she had felt her body soften, her pulse quicken when he put his arm around her and gently bent to kiss her. She turned toward him, pushing herself close and winding her legs around his. They had barely gotten started—and she was actually beginning to remember how much she enjoyed this—their naked bodies touching, his hands on her breasts, his mouth on hers—when Griffin started to cry. It was just a little cry at first, but she stiffened, and wanted to go to him. "Wait," Jeff had said. "Maybe he'll settle." She waited, but instead of settling, he cried louder. Danny woke up and they could hear him plodding into Griffin's room, sleepily talking to him as he entered.

"It's okay, buddy," he said, copying words he'd heard Jeff use. "I got you."

Now it was Jeff's turn to stiffen. He hurled his legs over the edge of the bed and stood up, grabbing for his robe, which was folded on the easy chair.

"It's okay," Marcia said. "Let him help. It's good for both of them."

But Jeff ignored her. He walked briskly into the room and took Griffin, who had quieted in Danny's arms, into his own. "You can go back to bed, Danny," he said. "You have school tomorrow." He brought Griffin to Marcia in the kitchen. She was already warming a bottle for him in hopes it would soothe him back to sleep. Her pediatrician had told her she didn't need to warm the milk anymore, but it just felt kinder to her than giving it to him from the refrigerator. By the time she had fed him and put him back in his crib, whatever sexual spark had ignited between them had fizzled out. They both had turned away from each other and fallen asleep, back to back.

She stared at her page of resolutions briefly, then got up and rummaged in her desk until she found a thick red pencil she sometimes used for editing notes. Returning to the kitchen table, she looked at her list again. Then she underlined the last entry two times.

She turned to Danny's column and was about to write, but Berta came into the kitchen holding Griffin, and when he saw her, his face lit up with such a happy smile that she could stay away from him no longer. She put her pen down and closed her notebook, determined to return to it later.

"Hello, my beautiful boy," she said in that slight sing-song voice she used when she spoke to him. Jeff had objected the first time he heard it—it sounded phony to him, or sappy or something like that, she never really understood his objection, but basically he clearly didn't like what he thought of as "baby talk." Then she had read an article claiming that research into young infants revealed they were much more responsive to higher pitches and singsong intonations. The writer, a developmental psychologist, theorized that this was the reason most people naturally spoke that way when addressing an infant. She showed the article to Jeff and while he never spoke in that inflected, high-pitched way himself, he stopped objecting when she did.

She took Griffin in her arms. "I'll take him for a while," she told Berta. She brought him into the living room and held him on her lap, talking to him, handing him toys, which he grasped in his pudgy little hands, shaking them, and of course putting them in his mouth. She sang "Itsy Bitsy Spider" to him, and he rewarded her with a smile. Then she changed his diaper, dressed him in a warmer outfit and put him in his stroller for a walk. It was a bright, crisp day, and she headed for the park, stopping to look in shop windows as she wended her way to the playground, where she sat on a bench watching the toddlers while Griffin dozed. When he awoke, she pushed him in the baby swing for a bit. It was a new one, built on a slant with a headrest, so it was just right for a baby his age. He loved it, just as he did the one they had at home, and it amused them both for a good fifteen minutes. When he got restless, she lifted him out and strapped him back in his stroller for the walk home. It was almost three-thirty, and she thought Danny might be home.

She was having a cup of tea in the kitchen when she heard a noise at the door, so assuming it was Danny, she walked into the hallway to greet him. He burst into the room, happily laughing and chatting to a boy at his side. She hadn't seen him so animated since before his mother died. He stopped short when he saw Marcia. "Oh, I didn't think you were here," he mumbled, suddenly uncomfortable. He looked at the boy with him and shrugged, embarrassed.

"I had a meeting at your school so I decided to take

the rest of the day off. But who is this?" Marcia asked, smiling.

"Raul." Danny spoke so quietly now it was hard to hear him.

"Hi, Raul. Welcome. I'm Marcia."

"Hi," Raul said. "Could I use the bathroom?"

"Sure." She pointed to the guest bathroom in the hallway and he went in.

"Why didn't you tell me you were bringing home a friend? Did Berta know?"

"No. It wasn't like that. We were on the bus playing Minecraft on his iPad. We wanted to finish the game so he came over. I'm sorry."

"No need to be sorry. It's good."

Raul came back. He was looking around as he passed the living room with its high ceiling, silk curtains and baby grand piano. "Wow. This is a big place," he said. She smiled at him. He was about Danny's height with the same black hair, but Danny's was straight and Raul's was curly and longer and his skin a shade darker. They are both handsome boys, she thought.

"You guys must be hungry. Why don't you come into the kitchen? I made some Rice Krispie treats. Danny, show Raul where they are and offer him some milk."

Neither boy wanted milk but they both accepted a glass of water, and together they devoured half the tray of treats. Marcia followed them and invited them to sit at the kitchen table but Danny ate standing up, shifting from leg to leg.

"Are you in the same class?" she asked them.

"Yeah," Danny answered. "Can we go to my room now?"

"Sure. Just one thing. Raul, do you need to call your mother so she won't worry?"

"No. I told her this morning I was coming here."

"Really?" She looked at Danny, who looked at the floor, registering that she had caught him in a lie.

"How are you getting home?" she asked Raul.

"My mom is picking me up at five," he said.

"And does she know where we live?"

"Yeah. I told her."

Marcia nodded. There was an uncomfortable pause. "Well," she said, in as bright a voice as she could muster, "go and play, then. Have fun."

At five o'clock the doorman called to say that Raul's mother had arrived. Marcia and Danny accompanied him downstairs to meet her. She was a slight, short woman with long black hair, large brown eyes and the same attractive brown skin tone as her son. She was wearing black jeans and a dark purple car coat and carried a large brown canvas bag on her shoulder. She introduced herself as Maria Ramiro and thanked Marcia for entertaining Raul.

"It's a pleasure," Marcia answered. She stared at her. She didn't look like one of the mothers from their expensive private school. She also looked slightly familiar. "Excuse me for staring," Marcia said, "I keep thinking I know you from somewhere but I can't place where."

"I work in this building sometimes," Maria said. She looked straight at Marcia. Was there a slight defensive tone in her voice? Marcia wasn't sure. "For the Duncans," she added with a slight Spanish accent.

"Oh, right. That must be it. We must have passed each other in the elevator." Of course, Marcia thought. That's why she doesn't look like the other mothers. She's a housekeeper here. Raul is probably on scholarship.

"They seem to like each other," Maria said, gesturing at the boys, who were huddled over Raul's iPad on the couch in the lobby.

"Yes. I'm glad. Danny just started this year and he doesn't have many friends yet."

"I heard what happened to him. I'm sorry."

"Thank you. The best thing for him is a nice friend like your son."

"They speak to each other in Spanish sometimes. I hope you don't mind."

"Mind? No. I'm delighted. We don't know Spanish and I'm sure it makes Danny more comfortable to speak it sometimes."

Maria nodded knowingly. "Well, we have to go. Raul still has homework for tomorrow."

"Yes, of course. It was nice to meet you."

"For me too." She called Raul and they walked toward the door.

"Put on your coat," she told him. "It's very cold outside." He obeyed immediately and they left together.

Marcia put her arm around Danny as they waited for the elevator. "He seems like a very nice boy," she said. She felt him stiffen, but he didn't pull away. "He's my best friend," he said.

"That's great, Danny." She paused. "You know you don't have to invite him when you think I'm not home. I'm happy for you to have a friend over. And you can go to his house if he invites you. But I just would like you to tell me, okay?"

Danny nodded. "I'm sorry."

"It's okay. I understand. But do we have a deal?"

Danny smiled. "Yeah. For sure. Thanks."

She had meant to speak to Danny today about having to find a new school for next year but she couldn't bear to have that conversation now. He finally had made a friend and this would mean starting all over again. It seemed so cruel. She wondered if she should appeal to the principal one more time, but didn't think it would do much good. She decided to wait before telling Danny, let the friendship and his confidence grow; maybe that would improve his behavior at school. Maybe the teachers would notice and suggest giving him another chance. It was so clear that Raul's Spanish roots, his familiarity with the language, meant a lot to Danny. She had heard them in Danny's room, laughing together, talking a kind of Spanglish, selecting words from each language. She also heard them playing Minecraft together. She resolved to speak to Jeff about allowing Danny more leeway with electronic devices. She would like to buy him his own iPad for his birthday, which was coming up in a month. Or maybe an iPhone. The iPod he had in L.A. had somehow gotten lost in the move and he'd been too shy to ask for another, she figured. One of those devices would be good for him, she thought, a pathway to connect him to friends. They could set limits on how much he was allowed to use it without prohibiting it completely.

As she bustled around the kitchen checking the stew Berta had prepared, washing the lettuce, making the salad dressing, she felt happier and more optimistic than she had in a long time. She had been worried about how to celebrate Danny's upcoming birthday. She had thought he didn't have even one friend he could invite to a party or out for a pizza and cake. Now he had someone. She felt a pang of hurt for him when she remembered that he called Raul his best friend, when she knew Raul was his only one.

She told Danny to start his homework and asked Berta to give Griffin his bath as she set the table. Forgetting her earlier disagreement with Jeff, she was excited for him to come home. Not only did she want to start implementing her resolutions, she could hardly wait to share the news about Raul. As she walked back to the kitchen to get some wine, she glanced in the hallway mirror and realized with a scowl that if she was going to be flirtatious with her husband again, she probably needed to comb her hair. She was in the bathroom putting on some makeup when the phone rang.

"Marcia?" It was Jeff. She started to tell him she had some good news for a change but he cut her off.

"I'm really sorry, but I can't get home for dinner. Something's come up at the office."

"What?"

"I have a dinner for work and it will go late. Don't wait up."

"What came up? I mean, you didn't know this before you left today?"

"No. I said it just came up." His voice was testy, impatient. "I have to go, Marcia. I'll see you in the morning." He hung up and she stood at the phone, puzzled and disappointed. Berta came in carrying Griffin, clean and sweet-smelling and ready for bed. She handed him to Marcia and retrieved her coat from the closet. "See you tomorrow," she said. "Bye-bye, Griffie." Marcia took him in her arms and hugged him. She carried him into his room, read him *Goodnight Moon*, wound up his mobile, gave him his pacifier and put him in his crib. He watched the mobile intently and made cooing noises. Relieved he wasn't crying, she tiptoed out. She walked back into the dining room and removed Jeff's place setting from the table. Danny came in. "Did you finish your homework?" she asked.

"Yeah. It's all done. How come there's only two plates?" he asked. "There's three of us."

"Not tonight," she said. "It's just us."

17

It seemed to her as though fate was always against them. Just when Danny made his first friend and she had reason to hope this would help his adjustment, just when she had made resolutions aimed at easing the tensions between her and Jeff, Jeff had landed a big international case that kept him working way past dinner most nights and even on some weekends. When he mentioned that he would have to do some additional traveling back and forth to California on some weekends for the foreseeable future, she was bereft. She tried to tell him how she felt but he took it as a criticism and thus a provocation.

"Are you going to turn this into another problem?" he asked angrily. "I mean, this case could take care of us for years, it could pay for Griffin's college tuition." He paused. "And if that doesn't mean anything to you, how's this? It could pay for Danny's education too. That ought to make it all right with you."

She flinched. "Jesus, Jeff, why would you say something like that?"

He looked away. "I'll get the coffee," he said.

In accordance with her resolution to show more interest in his work, she tried to ask him about it, but he told her it was complicated and boring and would take too long to explain. Something about a new international airline. She didn't press him because he obviously wasn't interested in sharing the details and frankly, she was not very interested in hearing them. She had been proud of her resolutions aimed at repairing the trouble between them and now had little opportunity to implement them. Her table was set for two more frequently than ever, and while it had the advantage of much less tension at dinner, it left the situation between her and Jeff, and Jeff and Danny, more fraught than ever.

One rare Friday when Jeff announced he didn't have to work that weekend, she suggested they go to Woodstock. They hadn't been in a long time and they used to be so happy there, she said. He agreed and they packed up the car and left that afternoon. She awoke early the next morning. Griffin, miraculously, was still asleep and Danny hadn't stirred either, as far as she could tell. Jeff was reading the morning paper on his iPad and sipping a cup of coffee. "Good morning," she said, indulging in a luxurious stretch. He mumbled a greeting and returned to his reading. In the old days, she thought, he'd have reached out and touched her. She'd always loved that, as if he was reassuring himself she was still there. Maybe he'd have even gotten up to pour her a coffee, she thought, remembering when he did that every day. No more.

It was early February and the trees outside their window were heavy with snow, many of the boughs drooping under the weight. Marcia stared at the scene disconsolately. Soon she would bustle around making breakfast, but the distance between them had lengthened and she felt very much alone. For the first time in her adult life she was at a complete loss about how to fix things. No ideas, no optimistic plans on how to work on the problem. She didn't even really understand it. Why was Jeff so hostile? She had tried everything on her list, as best she could in the time she had with him, and although sometimes things got better for a few days, he never really came around. Danny was a barrier between them that she couldn't cross. They had resumed making love but unlike that period in her life that she had come to think of as "Before Los Angeles," she always had to initiate it and he didn't always go along. Now it was he who had a headache or was too busy or worried or preoccupied. She consoled herself with the thought that sex was always supposed to be difficult to reestablish with a new baby in the house, but still, it added to her general malaise.

The only bright spot was Jeff's obvious delight in Griffin. He would rush to him as soon as he came in and try to make up for all the time he was away by playing exclusively with him when he was at home. This was great, she thought, but the downside was that he had even less time for her and no time for Danny, no time to see how much better Danny seemed, how much more adjusted he was now that he had a friend. He had no time or interest in hearing stories about Raul and how Danny sometimes did his homework without supervision and had asked for guitar lessons. He did look up when she mentioned the guitar, however, pointing out that his own guitar was expensive and he didn't want Danny using it. "Get him a beginner's acoustic guitar," he said, "and see how he does." She was fine with that.

Raul was key, she thought. He came over many days after school and the boys often did homework together. She always had a special snack for them and on the days she was home, she sometimes joined in their conversation. Because Raul liked to chat, she found out much more about what their school day was like from him than she did from Danny. It was Raul who told her about the school's book fair. Delighted it was on an at-home day, she went to it and bought Danny some books as well as a few baby books for Griffin. It was also Raul who mentioned that Danny was working on the class play. Danny had shot him a warning look, but it was too late; Marcia learned that he was going to help make some of the scenery. Once she came into the living room and overheard a conversation they were having before they saw her.

"Your mom is really cool," Raul had said.

Danny had whirled around. "She's not my mom," he'd said sharply.

"Oh, sorry."

"But she's okay," Danny added. And Marcia thought

that was definite progress. She was beginning to know him. It was like looking at him through increasingly sharp lenses, his personality slowly, surely coming into focus. When they sat at dinner together, he'd tell her about the backdrop he was helping to construct for *The Sound of Music* and how lame the girl was who played Maria. Or he'd complain about his math homework but mention proudly that he got a seventy-five on the latest quiz, his best grade since he'd arrived at the school. Or he'd tell how he and Raul couldn't stop laughing at lunch and he'd laughed so hard his apple juice had come running out through his nose. She invited Raul to come to Woodstock with them one weekend, but his mother wasn't comfortable letting him go. Marcia was considering inviting his mother too, but when she checked that out with Jeff, his response was predictable but disappointing. "Save that for a weekend I'm working, okay?" he said with a laugh.

At first Raul always came to Danny's house for play dates. But after a while, he got a much-wished-for invitation to Raul's house. Raul lived in Queens, a fifty-minute subway ride. Raul was allowed to take the train on his own, something Danny had not yet been permitted to try. His father, Juan, was at home with Raul's baby sister, Teresa. Maria was usually working. Raul told Danny that his dad used to work in construction but he hurt his hip over a year ago and couldn't do it anymore. Now he stayed home and his mom was the one who worked cleaning houses. Raul seemed ashamed that his dad didn't work.

"Nah," Danny said. "You're lucky you have a dad. And anyway, your mom would have to pay someone to take care of Teresa if your dad didn't, so it works out, right?"

"Yeah."

Raul had an older half-brother named Julio, Juan's son from a different mother, he said, but he didn't live with them. "My mom doesn't like him so much," Raul said. "She says he was really smart, he did really good in high school and could have got a scholarship but then he dropped out right before graduation. Now he's twenty-five and she says he doesn't have a real job. I mean, he does have a job—he lives in his own place and every-thing—but my mom doesn't want me to be like him."

"What's his job?"

"He says he gets people to pay what they owe."

"So what's wrong with that?"

"I don't know. My mom doesn't like it. But he's really cool."

"Could I meet him?"

"Maybe. She doesn't usually let him come around unless she's there, though."

Some days Maria was home, but that wasn't as much fun. With Juan, they could just play the whole time Danny was there. They could go out and walk around or watch TV and play video games. Danny loved it. But when Maria was home, they had to do their homework first and then play Legos or Monopoly or Uno. It was as bad as going to Danny's house, where Berta was under strict instructions to watch them like a hawk. A couple of times when Juan was home and Maria was at work,

Julio was there. He'd play video games with them. Once they heard Julio in the other room fighting with his dad, asking for money. But usually, he'd just hang out with them. He'd even go out with them. He told them how when he was their age, he'd go out with his friends and they were really good at taking stuff from stores. "You just put it under your shirt when no one is looking," he said. "It can't be too bulky, of course. Then you don't just leave. You walk around awhile, look at things and then buy something cheap on your way out." Then he took them into the toy store and bought them both a small set of *Star Wars* Legos. They were nervous, but they didn't see him put anything under his shirt, so they thought he'd just been kidding. When they got a few blocks away, he reached into the back of his pants and pulled out a bigger set.

"You gotta share this," Julio said. "Now I gotta go." He winked at Raul and walked off.

"I told you he was cool," Raul said, when Julio left. "Don't tell my mom he was here."

"I won't." Danny was conflicted. He did think Julio was cool, but he understood what the adults he knew would think. He wasn't worried about Marcia or Jeff— he didn't care that much what they thought. But he worried because he knew his mom would be crying if she thought he was hanging out with someone who stole things.

"We could get in trouble," he said. "I mean, if he got caught and we were with him, we'd be in big trouble."

Raul shrugged. "He won't get caught."

Somehow, time passed, the way it does when there is a baby in the house. Life fell into a pattern that was less than perfect but repetitive and exhausting enough so that there was little time even to think about how to change things. Marcia had never gone back to her resolutions about Danny, because the problems with him were no longer foremost in her mind. Danny had become very helpful with Griffin. They adored each other— Griffin would smile and laugh and hold out his arms to him whenever Danny came home, and Danny would pick him up and play with him without being asked. If Griffin was crying and Danny was home, Danny would get to him before either Marcia or Berta, but never when Jeff was home. He knew, without being told, what the prohibitions were. It touched her to see the bond between the boys and she tried many times to share that with Jeff, but he was so unbelieving and unresponsive that finally, she just stopped telling him. He kept pressing her to make other arrangements for the boy. He even offered to send him to boarding school, but she put him off saying Danny was too young. Maybe high school, she'd said, in two or three more years. She had started to make inquiries about charter schools, but there had been no more complaints or calls from his current school and she was beginning to hope that maybe they would allow him to continue where he was.

Danny's twelfth birthday was coming up and she decided to throw him a party and buy him his own iPad. She knew Jeff was against this, but he was so clearly un-interested in Danny that she didn't think she needed to clear it with him. She knew Danny would be thrilled. She asked him if he'd like to have a party. He shrugged and said he didn't really want to, but she tried to persuade him. He seemed uncomfortable but finally he said he only wanted Raul, and she agreed. She ordered a birthday cake in the shape of a baseball field and put little plastic baseball players around it (she wanted to reignite his interest in the sport and had had some success since Raul was an avid Mets fan). The party was on a Saturday, and she invited Raul and his mother for cake and ice cream at three o'clock. Jeff went in to work in the morning and she begged him to come home in time to celebrate with them. He surprised her by saying he would.

After Jeff left, she blew up balloons and decorated the dining room with streams of crepe paper. Danny helped. They put Griffin in his high chair with a few toys and he watched happily, banging a spoon against the tray. At one, after lunch, he refused his bottle and started fussing, so she put him down for a nap. She had been up late the night before working on a manuscript so she was exhausted. "I'm going to lie down for just half an hour," she told Danny. "Please wake me if Griffin gets up."

She went into her bedroom and laid down, falling asleep almost immediately.

Griffin started to cry about fifteen minutes later. Danny picked him up, but Griffin wasn't mollified and kept crying. Danny changed his diaper, but he still complained, so he brought him into the kitchen and sat him in his high chair, thinking he might want his bottle. He had never given him a bottle on his own, but he had seen

Marcia do it a hundred times and he was sure he could do it without having to wake her. He gave Griffin some toy plastic keys to distract him. Danny took Griffin's formula out of the refrigerator and poured it into the bottle. Then, feeling proud of himself for remembering this, he took out a saucepan, ran some water into it and put it on the stove. He let it boil and when he saw the bubbles, he turned it off and put the bottle in it to warm. Then he took the bottle out of the boiling water and gave it to Griffin.

Marcia woke up to the sound of piercing screams. She jumped out of bed and ran into the kitchen to see Griffin wailing in Danny's arms and Danny holding him, bouncing up and down, helplessly trying to comfort him, his eyes wide with fear. Before she could grab Griffin or find out what had happened, Jeff walked in the front door, ran to Griffin and grabbed him from Danny's arms. "Get the fuck out of here," he said, pushing Danny away. "What happened?" he thundered, scaring Griffin and making him cry harder. Danny stood at the door, his mouth agape, tears running down his face.

"Danny, what happened?" Marcia asked.

"I don't know," Danny said between sobs.

"You have to tell us what happened so we know how to help him, Danny."

"He was hungry. I didn't do anything bad. I did what you do. I just warmed the bottle and gave it to him and he started to scream."

"Shit, he burned his throat," Jeff said. "Call an ambulance."

It turned out to be less severe than they feared. The formula hadn't stayed long enough in the boiling water to really scald him, but it hurt his throat, which was red but not seriously injured. He had stopped crying by the time they got to the hospital, and the doctor told them to feed him lots of ice cream, so he was back at home two hours later, happily eating a dish of vanilla ice cream that Marcia had bought for Danny's party. The party, however, was called off. She had called Raul's mother from the hospital and told her what had happened. When they got home she barely registered that the decorations she had hung were torn down, the balloons busted and the crepe paper all over the floor. Danny came running out of his room.

"Is Griff okay?"

"Yes, he's fine. Don't worry," Marcia said.

Jeff was carrying Griffin and when Danny ran over to see him, Jeff hugged Griffin tighter and pushed past him. Danny looked helplessly at Marcia.

"I didn't want to hurt him. I'm sorry." He sniffed hard. She reached for him and he put his arms around her waist. "I didn't mean it. I didn't mean it."

"I know, Danny. Shhh. I know. And he's fine. He's just got a little sore throat, that's all. But why didn't you wake me? I told you to wake me when he woke up."

"I thought I could help. You said you were tired."

Marcia nodded. Her heart felt as if it would break.

"It's okay. You didn't know. You just aren't old enough to take care of him on your own yet, that's all. You know that now, right, Danny? You must never try to take care of him yourself, okay?" He nodded. She noticed, as if for the first time, that the decorations were all scattered on the floor. "What happened here?"

"I don't want a party. I don't want anything."

"I'm sorry, Danny. I had to call Raul and tell him not to come." She walked to the hall closet and retrieved a brightly wrapped package. "But here's your present. Why don't you take it in your room and play with it while I talk to Jeff?"

Danny drew his breath in and looked nervously down the hallway toward Griffin's room. He didn't reach for the present.

"It's okay. I'll handle it. Take the present and go into your room and we'll talk later, okay? That's the best thing to do right now." She took a tissue from the box on the table and tried to wipe his eyes.

"I'm okay," he said, flinching. "I'm not crying."

"I know. Go on, now."

He slowly reached for the package and then walked quickly into his room and closed the door.

She slipped into Griffin's room. Jeff had put him down for a nap and he was settling in. He was in his favorite sleep position, one pacifier in his mouth, one next to him and a third tucked under his tummy, the plastic rim protruding slightly. Jeff was sitting in the chair watching him. She approached him and put her hand on his shoulder, but he pulled away. She wasn't surprised. She was already girding herself for the onslaught she knew was imminent, though she had hoped that their shared relief that Griffin was okay would bring them together. He seemed about to say something, but she put her finger to her mouth to hush him and beckoned him to follow her out of the room. She walked to the kitchen, put some water on for coffee and sat at the table. Jeff didn't sit and refused her offer of coffee. Instead, he poured himself a Scotch and turned to her.

"I thought we agreed that Danny was never to be left alone with Griffin," he began, his voice tight with barely controlled fury.

She stiffened. "I didn't leave him alone. I took a short nap."

"Really? That's your explanation? You aren't concerned that your baby was just scalded by an angry kid who happens to live with us? You're not worried about what else he might get up to?"

She didn't answer right away, but stood and walked to the drawer in which they kept the first aid kit and non-prescription medicines. Shaking three Advil out of the jar, she washed them down at the same time with a sip of water. "Look, Jeff, you're not in court and I'm not going to be cross-examined. Of course I'm 'concerned,' as you put it, so please don't be such an asshole. I was as worried and upset as you were and I'm as relieved as you are now that it wasn't more serious. We dodged a bullet. I wish it hadn't happened. I wish Danny hadn't tried to help and made a mistake. But if you'd been around here you'd know that this wasn't the malicious act of an angry kid. He wanted to help, to do the right thing. He used the judgment of a twelve-year-old and screwed up and he knows to never take it upon himself to do anything like that again. He is as guilty and sorry as any boy could be. And thank God, Griffin is fine. So lighten up, okay? We've all been through enough today."

Jeff sat down heavily. "I want him out of here, Marcia. I don't feel safe with him here."

"You're overreacting. You are completely off base. You don't know him. You are rarely here when he is, but I am. I have dinner with him every night. I have met his friend and his friend's mother. I help him with his homework. And I know that you haven't given him a chance from the start, but I'm not going to give up on him."

He was shaking his head as she was speaking and finally, he looked straight at her. "Will you promise me, I mean without exception, promise me that he will never be alone with Griffin again, not while you nap, not while you run to the store for five minutes, never?"

She met his gaze. "How about when I'm in the bathroom? Would that be okay?"

"If it's fast."

She poured the coffee but it had cooled, so she put the cup in the microwave.

"I promise," she said in a softer voice. "But I'd really love it if you would try to see how they are together, Jeff. There's really love there, on both sides. Danny is heartbroken about this. Imagine how he feels. And today is his birthday. I cancelled his party. Maybe we can all have dinner together. We can eat that birthday cake I ordered, and maybe you can see what I'm talking about."

"I can't. I have to get back to the office."

She didn't respond. She just sat at the table, sipping

her coffee slowly and staring ahead of her. He sat next to her, reaching out tentatively to put his hand on her arm. She didn't move away. "I was so scared," he said.

"I know. Me too." She patted his hand and got up. "I'm going to check on Griffin."

He hesitated. "I'll go with you but then I have to get back."

"Yeah, I know. Go ahead."

They stood at Griffin's crib, looking down at him peacefully sleeping. As they re-entered the hallway, Jeff asked, "How old is he today? Twelve?"

"Yeah. Twelve."

"Maybe I should go say happy birthday."

She was overcome with gratitude. "That would be great, Jeff. It will mean so much to him."

He walked to Danny's door and knocked, then opened it without waiting for an answer. She listened, but she didn't hear him say anything. Instead, she heard the door close sharply. Jeff met her in the kitchen. "Did you say he was heartbroken? Yeah. Really. He was sitting on his bed playing a game on a goddamn iPad. I don't even know where he got it."

"It was his birthday present," she said sadly. "I gave it to him."

He shrugged and shook his head. "Don't wait up for me," he said before walking out the door.

18

Julie stood at the door of Marcia's office, weighed down by a seven-hundred-page manuscript that had to be cut by three hundred pages.

"It's impossible," she said. "This guy never met a fact he didn't love."

Marcia laughed. "I know. But he's also brilliant. And stubborn, so I admit you have your hands full."

"Tell me about it," Julie said, indicating her full arms.

"I didn't just mean with that heavy manuscript."

"I know, I know. And I'm about to dig in," she said. "The problem isn't only suggesting the cuts, it's persuading him to make them. No one told me you have to be a diplomat as well as an editor for this job."

"Well, now you know," Marcia said. "It turns out you have to be a diplomat for almost any job."

"Anyway, I stopped by to tell you that Jeff called three

times and just called again.
back."

"Damn. I forgot. I've bee

call right now."

"Should I close your door?

"No. That's okay."

When Julie disappeared, lu
own office (recently awarded wh
ciate editor based on Marcia's ent ___uc recommendation) Marcia picked up the phone. She wondered why
Julie asked if she should close the door. Did she think
they needed privacy? Had anyone been hearing the phone
arguments she'd been having with Jeff, even though she
thought she'd been so careful to disguise them? It seemed
like they were at each other all the time these days, and
not just about Danny, and their arguments had become
just as much about the tone as the substance of their conversations. It was as if the general goodwill that had always accompanied their relationship had been lost, and
without it, even the most innocent remark became a
problem. "You look tired," she had said to him this morning, and he had taken it as an insult.

"Yeah, well, I *am* tired, Marcia," he'd said, "I'm trying to earn enough money to support this family."

"You don't do that alone," she had replied, "I work
too," and then both had eaten breakfast in silence and
gone off to work with a bad taste in their mouths. Their
phone calls were no better. But they didn't shout. It wasn't
likely Julie or anyone in the office had picked up on the
tension, was it? It also occurred to Marcia that she might

as careful as she should have in her con-
with Grace Zilman. Ever since Grace had sug-
surrogacy at that now seemingly long ago dinner
Woodstock, she and Marcia had grown close. It had
been Grace whom Marcia had talked to during Eve's
pregnancy and Grace whom she cried to about everything that happened after the birth. Marcia often took
a break from work to call her to discuss the problems
she was having with Danny and with Jeff. Grace always counseled patience but also supported Marcia in
her refusal to give up on Danny. Could Julie have overheard some of these discussions? She dismissed that
idea, thinking too much of Julie to believe her capable
of eavesdropping. Julie was simply being polite, Marcia
concluded. She was getting paranoid.

She picked up the phone to return Jeff's call. The
phone rang three times before his secretary picked up
and Marcia waited a few minutes to be put through to
him. He'd continued his punishing work schedule, skipping dinner at home regularly and going in most Satur-
days. They had planned to both be home tonight and she
wondered if he had called to beg off again. But when he
picked up, his voice lacked the guilty apology it held when
he was about to cancel their plans.

"Marcia, guess who's in town?"

"A new client you have to have dinner with?" she said.

"Guess again," he said dryly.

"I'm really busy, Jeff, so just tell me."

"It's Charlie Posner," he said, referring to Marcia's

first college boyfriend who had become their mutual close friend. "He's here for just one night and he wants to have dinner. Can you get Berta to stay late?" It was odd, she thought. Jeff had gotten as close to Charlie as she was. Sometimes she thought they were even closer, though she still had a special bond with Charlie and with his wife, Eden, who had been one of her roommates. The Posners had moved to San Francisco, where Eden worked as a midwife, and he'd gotten a job with a tech investment firm—a long way from the student activist he'd been when she'd known him. Marcia loved teasing him about his rise to a member of the establishment, which both pleased and embarrassed him. They texted and spoke from time to time, but were no longer an everyday presence in each other's lives. Charlie and Jeff, however, were often in touch, talking business or just having a beer together whenever one was in the other's town.

She hesitated. "I, uh, was kind of looking forward to a family meal for a change tonight," she said.

"Sweetheart, it's Charlie. We haven't seen him in a year. He's leaving tomorrow. Don't you want to see him?"

It sounded strange. He hadn't called her sweetheart in a while and it made her want to cooperate. And she did like Charlie. "Yeah, of course," she said in a warmer voice. "Maybe you should invite him to dinner at our place."

There was a long pause. "Well," Jeff said, "if it was just us and Griff, I'd love to do that."

"I don't understand."

"You know how tense it is with Danny. Besides, I want to fill him in and I can't do that with Danny around."

There was a pause during which she squelched the angry reply that first came to her mind. "Okay. I'll call Berta," she said, the warmth replaced by a brittle efficiency. "Where should we go?"

"I'll try Primola. I'll text you. Seven okay?"

"Yeah."

She got the text and arrived at Primola early. Charlie was having a drink at the bar and she joined him.

"Hi, beautiful," he said.

She smiled. Same old bullshit but she liked it. "Hi," she said. They leaned in and kissed briefly on the lips, a little less than romantic, a little more than platonic.

"Everything good?"

"Sure. Everything's great."

"You look amazing. Motherhood must be good for you. What are you drinking?"

"Pino Grigio."

"It's reassuring how you never change."

"I change. How's Eden?"

"She's okay, I guess."

"You guess?"

"Look, I was going to wait for Jeff for this, but what the hell. We're having problems."

"Who isn't having problems?"

"No, I mean it. We're going to try separating for a while to see if it helps."

"What? I didn't see that coming." Marcia felt disturbed. The Posners had gotten married a year before she and Jeff did and they always seemed like a perfectly matched couple. "I can't believe it. I just talked to Eden last month and she didn't say a word. I'm so sorry."

"We agreed to keep it secret until we made a decision," he said. Silence followed as neither could think of the right thing to say.

"I should have married you, you know. I always said that," he joked, trying to lighten the mood.

She looked at him and shook her head. It was a bad joke, under the circumstances. With his boyish looks and athlete's build, Charlie Posner was as handsome as ever. He and Marcia had maintained a completely harmless flirtatious relationship over the years. It would never go anywhere, but both enjoyed the game. This time, however, it was inappropriate and awkward and she was about to tell him so, but just at that moment she caught sight of Jeff pushing his way toward the bar. He stopped and gave her a kiss on the cheek, then grabbed Charlie's hand.

"Hey man, great to see you," Charlie said.

Marcia got up to tell the maître d' they were all there and he led them to a table. Marcia and Charlie took their drinks with them, and Jeff ordered a vodka tonic and an expensive bottle of Beaujolais. "Don't worry," he said as the waiter brought it to the table. "I'm paying." The restaurant was noisy and the acoustics were bad but Marcia quickly let Jeff know what Charlie had told her. Jeff was shocked.

"I can't believe it," he said. "You two were so tight."

"Do you want to tell us what happened?" Marcia asked.

"She wants to have a baby. I told her from day one I would never want that and she agreed, but now her goddamn clock is ticking and she says she won't be happy without it."

"Don't do something like that just to make her happy," Jeff jumped in. "Believe me, that's a mistake."

Marcia stared at him. "Really? Was Griffin a mistake?"

"Look, I love being Griffin's father. I love Griffin. But shit, of course it was a mistake. Look what happened."

"Nobody could have predicted that," Charlie said. "That wasn't a mistake. That was a terrible accident."

"Yeah. And I'm still paying for it."

Marcia took a long swig of her drink. She spit out her words, "You're paying for it? You son of a bitch." She turned to Charlie.

"Actually, we have another kid," Marcia said. "That's who Jeff is referring to. You know the story. We have a twelve-year-old adopted son."

"He's not adopted," Jeff said quickly.

"No. You're right. He's not. Not yet." A silence followed.

"Anyway," Marcia said, taking a deep breath and attempting to turn the conversation back to Charlie. "You couldn't give in on this, Charlie? Jeff and I have problems over Danny but he loves Griffin. You might surprise yourself. Did she leave you because of this?"

"No. I left her. I couldn't be responsible for her unhappiness and I couldn't give her what she wanted. I absolutely don't see me with a baby."

"How about a twelve-year-old kid?" Jeff asked, laughing. "We could give you Danny."

"That's just not funny," Marcia snapped.

"No, there's nothing funny about Danny." Jeff called the waiter over and ordered another round of drinks.

"Where is Eden now?" Marcia asked, trying hard not to keep rising to the bait Jeff continued to dangle.

"She's at home. Her sister came. I'm in an apartment."

"Do you think you might work it out?"

"I don't know. Maybe. But what's going on with you two?"

Marcia shifted her position. "Look, Danny is dealing with a lot. He's having troubles at school. He doesn't have a lot of friends. He's still mad and confused about his mother. But he's slowly getting better and becoming adjusted. The one who can't seem to bend or adjust is Jeff. He just doesn't want him around."

Jeff bristled. "You can see that it's all my fault, right, Charlie? Poor Danny. He fights so much at school, the expensive private school I agreed to pay for, by the way, that he's going to be expelled from; he barely speaks to me and when he does he's sullen, he gets brought home by the police, he 'accidentally' gives Griffin a bottle of boiling milk and we're lucky as hell there was no serious damage to the baby's throat, but it's all my fault." He had finished his second vodka tonic by now and was on his third glass of wine and Marcia knew further discussion would be useless. She repressed her anger and tried to make her tone conciliatory. "Let's not bore Charlie with our problems, he's got plenty of his own. In fact, let's not talk about anybody's problems."

"What's left?"

"How about those Mets?" Jeff said, laughing, an old joke among them whenever the conversation got tense.

They all laughed. Jeff asked what time Charlie was leaving the next day and he said he was taking a late flight. Marcia suggested he come over for brunch. If it was a good day, they could all go to Central Park and take a walk.

"I'd like you to meet Griffin," she said. "He'll make you change your mind about babies."

Especially if you can have them naturally," Jeff added. It was more bait, but she didn't rise to it, though she wanted to.

"I don't think we've made an afternoon with our family seem that enticing," she said, her voice like ice. It warmed when she turned to Charlie. "But I would love you to come, Charlie. I'd like you to meet *both* kids."

"Sure. What time should I get there?"

"What time do you have to leave for the airport?"

"Probably around four."

"Great. Come at eleven. I'll make pancakes."

"Done."

Griffin was on his best behavior when Charlie arrived. He was all smiles and gurgles and babbles, some of which definitely sounded like "Mama."

"He loves his mom," Charlie said, smiling.

"Actually, it turns out that the *M* sound is easier to say than the *D* sound," Jeff said. "Almost all babies say 'Mama' before they can say 'Dada.'"

"Right," Marcia said. "It has nothing to do with the fact that you are hardly ever here when he's awake."

"I wonder how you'd like living with two kids on just your salary," Jeff snapped.

"Let's go for a walk," Charlie offered, clearly uncomfortable.

Danny had been polite at lunch, although as usual, when Jeff was around, he barely spoke and seemed restless, tapping his heels and jiggling his knee until Jeff ordered him to sit up straight and be still. He didn't want to join them at the park, but Marcia insisted, so he came.

"Why don't you bring your glove and baseball?" Marcia suggested.

They decided to go to Central Park instead of Riverside, even though it was a little farther away. Jeff carried Griffin in a backpack and Marcia pushed the stroller in case they wanted to change later. Danny lagged behind and Jeff kept telling him to walk faster. They passed a playground and Marcia asked Danny if he wanted to go in for a bit, but he curled his lip in disdain. "That's for little kids," he said. When they got to the sailboat pond, he dawdled a bit, interested in the remote-controlled toy sailboats and watching people manipulate them. "They don't have motors," Marcia said. "You have to actually know sailing principles and make use of the wind." Jeff kept walking, but Charlie was intrigued.

"Wait up, Jeff. Hey, Danny, want to sail one with me?"

"I don't know how," Danny said, looking down.

"Me neither. We can try to figure it out together. You in?"

Danny shrugged.

"Yes or no?"

Danny didn't answer but he walked over to the rental booth with Charlie and they spent the next half hour trying to position the boat so it would catch the wind and sail across the pond. At first Danny just watched, but little by little he got involved, and when Charlie offered him the controls he took them eagerly, joining in a discussion of the best sailing strategy. They weren't very successful, especially compared to another boy whose father, they learned, was a sailing instructor in Montauk, but they did manage to get it going a few times. Marcia looked gratefully at Charlie, thinking how different it would be if Jeff could bring himself to behave that way with Danny. Even Jeff seemed chastened. After they returned the boats, he offered to put Griffin in the stroller and play catch with Danny, but Danny said he had a lot of homework and asked if he could just go home. Jeff tried to share a "see what I mean" look with Charlie but Charlie wasn't looking his way. Jeff shrugged and said, sure, Danny could go home, so Danny turned to leave. Marcia reminded him to say goodbye and thank you to Charlie, and he dutifully did. She asked if he had his key, which he didn't, so she gave him hers. After he left, Charlie looked at his watch and said it was time for him to go too. Jeff said he needed to go into the office for a few hours so the men shook hands and said their goodbyes. Marcia didn't object. It had gotten to the point where it was easier when Jeff wasn't there. She helped take Griffin out of the backpack and put him in the stroller, and

Jeff took off on his own since Marcia said she'd stay a bit longer in the park.

She was sad to say goodbye to Charlie. This was the first family day they had spent in a long time and he was central to it. She also felt that she should have tried to talk to him more about his marital problem. It had segued so quickly into the trouble between her and Jeff, they had just glided past Charlie and Eden.

"Do you have ten more minutes?" she asked.

"Yeah. I think so. Why? What's up?"

"I thought maybe we could walk together for a bit."

"You going to tell me how to fix my marriage?"

"No. As you can see from mine, I have no idea how to fix a marriage. I was just going to tell you how much I hope you can work things out. I know an outsider never knows what's really going on in another marriage, but I always thought you two were good for each other."

"I thought so too." He shrugged. "Look, it's not a done deal. We've got plenty to work on and we know it. Maybe it's just a rough patch and we'll get through it. Don't worry about us. But I'm worried about you."

She seemed surprised. "No. I don't think there's anything to worry about—long-term, I mean. I know things are tense now, but we're going to work it out. I mean, we're not talking about anything drastic. If we could just come to an agreement about Danny, everything would be okay."

"I hope you're right. But I'm not so sure you can come to an agreement about Danny. Is there any way you would bend on that? How about boarding school?"

"We've talked about it. He only just turned twelve and he's behind a year at school. It would still be another two or maybe even three years before that could happen. And Charlie, his mom died in this dramatic way, he's still adjusting to a drastically different life; it would be a second abandonment, a cruel act, to send him away now."

"It can't be good for him to realize that he's the cause of the trouble between you and Jeff. It can't feel good to know how Jeff feels about him."

"I know. I try to tell Jeff. He's not a bad person, you know that. He wouldn't purposely hurt a child. But he feels threatened somehow. I honestly don't understand it."

"I've never seen him take against someone like that," Charlie said. "It's almost like he blames him for what happened. It's screwed up, but it's almost like he's jealous of him. I think Danny isn't the only one who was traumatized by what happened. Maybe you need to get Jeff some help."

"I've tried. He went a few times and then refused." She reached into her bag to get some Advil and swallowed two without water. "Look, I can't manage my job and these kids and him too. He has to step up to the plate. I'm feeling pretty much like a single mother lately."

"Yeah. What's up with that?"

"What do you mean?"

"Why does he spend so much time in the office?"

"You should understand that more than I. Do you think it's too much?"

"A bit."

"I wish you'd tell him that."

He looked uncomfortable. She noticed and blurted a thought she'd had before but had tried to convince herself to reject. "You don't think he's cheating, do you, Charlie? I mean, did he say anything?"

"No. Nothing."

"Would you tell me?"

"You know I would. He's probably just working too hard. Maybe he's using it as an excuse to stay away because life isn't as much fun at home lately."

"It isn't as much fun for me either," she muttered angrily. She wasn't at all sure Charlie would tell her if he knew.

"I don't know. But if I were you, and I was worried, I'd ask him." He looked at his watch. "I really have to go now or I'll miss my plane." He gave her a hurried hug. "I'll stay in touch. Good luck."

"Yeah, good luck to you too."

19

The weeks passed and although there was little change in Jeff's attitude or in the tension at home, there were no new dramatic episodes with Danny. Marcia had convinced herself that he was doing better. But it wasn't as if all Danny's problems had evaporated. He could still be sullen and uncommunicative at home, and he still had trouble at school. Having a friend made him happier but he still had problems controlling himself. When a math teacher forced him to stay after school in detention for throwing food across the room during lunch period, he claimed it was unfair. He told her he was just trading another kid a banana for an apple. The other kid was in the front row and he was in the back, they weren't allowed to get up without permission and the teacher had stepped out of the room for a minute. She came in just as the banana whizzed across the room, accidentally hitting another boy in the head. Danny joined the rest of the class in laughing, but the boy started to cry—"like a baby," Danny spat out derisively—and the teacher sent Danny to the principal's office. He would have to do detention for a week, she told him, her face flushing red with anger. He looked at Joe Scelfo, the kid he had tried to trade with, hoping he'd support him, but Joe didn't look back, staring fixedly at his desk. "It's always my fault here," Danny mumbled, suddenly feeling his eyes tear up and fighting hard not to shame himself by crying. "I didn't do nothing bad."

"Leave now, Danny," Mrs. Woolf had said in her most authoritative voice.

"Stupid fucking bitch," Danny hurled at her as he grabbed his books and lunch box and headed for the door.

She heard him, of course. Everyone did.

"What did you say?"

He didn't answer.

"I'm talking to you. Do you hear me?"

"Yes."

"Then answer me. What did you say?"

"Nothin'."

She wrote something on a piece of paper and put it in an envelope, licking it sealed. "Give this to the principal," she said. She turned back to the class.

"Now, who was able to solve the extra-credit problem in the homework?" she asked in a cheerful voice that everyone in the class knew was fake.

Danny didn't go to the principal's office. He left the school and wandered around the streets for a while, warming up by stopping in shops where he looked so conspicuous—a gangly twelve-year-old kid alone during school hours—that he was watched carefully. Finally, not knowing what else to do, he went back to school. He was seen and sent immediately to the principal's office. His detention was three weeks instead of one—an extra two weeks for the rude words he had hurled at his teacher and for leaving the school without permission.

The story of his outburst didn't remain in his classroom. Word spread and soon it was the main topic of conversation among groups of kids huddled in the school yard during recess and among parents who congregated at the pickup point. Danny could hear the whispers, the voices that trailed off as he approached, just as he could feel people pointing at him or looking up from their conversations to indicate he was nearby, or stopping talking as soon as he approached. The worst part, however, was that the principal called Marcia, and because, as Marcia believed, luck had deserted their family, she was at work and Jeff was going in late that day so he took the call and called Marcia immediately after.

The incident was another arrow in Jeff's quiver, or at least that's how Marcia saw it. Danny wasn't a problem they could work on together; it was her against him, and every time Danny did something wrong, Jeff used it as ammunition. She almost believed he was glad Danny was getting in trouble because it proved his point. The upshot of this last incident was depressing. She no longer had hope for a reversal of Danny's expulsion. He would have to leave the school and she had to look for the best replacement she could find. She was disappointed in, even angry, at his therapist. Danny had been going to him every week since he'd arrived and he still didn't have enough self-control to hold back insulting curse words to his teacher or stop himself from barging out of school just because he was angry. She called to make an appointment to talk to the therapist directly. She hoped he would squeeze her in later that same day. She was lucky—he had a cancellation and told her to come right over.

They called him Dr. Benson, but he wasn't really a doctor. He wasn't even a psychologist, which she would have preferred; those doctors were way too expensive. Dr. Benson was a clinical social worker who specialized in children and families, and though Marcia thought he wasn't really up to a case as difficult and complicated as Danny's, he was the best they could afford. One of the problems with Jeff's refusal to actually adopt Danny was that he was not eligible for their health insurance, and every appointment, whether with the social worker or with a doctor when he needed one, had to be paid for out of their own pockets. Marcia left work early and headed to his office.

Dr. Benson's practice was on West Ninety-eighth Street in a walk-up brownstone on the third floor. She entered the small waiting room, sat on the cracked fake-leather couch and waited for Dr. Benson to call her in. Another woman sat in a faded side chair, looking nervous. Marcia nodded and smiled at her, and she nodded back. Marcia looked for a magazine to get her mind off how worried she was, but could only find that day's *New York Times*,

which she had already read. Further searching revealed
a pile of *People* magazines, which she read only in doctors' offices. A story about Angelina Jolie and Brad Pitt
caught her eye—reading about those two was her particular guilty pleasure—and she picked it up and leafed
through it. A few minutes later, Dr. Benson entered
from his inner office accompanied by a girl of about ten
years old. The girl walked to the door without so much
as glancing at the woman but they were obviously together because the woman hastily gathered her things
and followed the girl out, calling to her to wait up. The
doctor asked Marcia to wait for a few minutes and withdrew, returning shortly and asking her to come in.

She got right to the point, explaining what had been
happening and expressing her concerns about Danny.
Dr. Benson was understanding but unapologetic. He
explained what she already knew—this was a difficult,
traumatic situation and would take time to resolve. He
asked if there was anything going on at home that
he should know about. That was the way in which the
conversation passed from Danny to Marcia and Jeff.
Dr. Benson suggested it would be best if Jeff would resume family counseling, but she explained that he was
unwilling and lately unable to do that because of time
constraints.

"Look, Marcia, Danny was the child of a single mother.
A boy his age really needs a male figure in his life, a
kind of same-sex model for him to identify with and feel
accepted by. This would have been a problem for Eve if
she had lived, but not a difficult one. Most people handle

this with family friends or uncles or teachers who become, excuse the word, 'surrogates.'" He smiled, pleased with himself.

Marcia gave a weak smile back.

"But now he is an orphan so his needs are even more pronounced. There's not just a missing father figure, there's a hostile one and that is a much more serious problem. On top of that, he's angry and he isn't quite sure where to direct it. But he knows that all this would not have happened to him if you and Jeff had never come into his life. He doesn't blame Griffin, fortunately, because he knows Griffin came from his mother and Griff is his last tangible connection to her. He is slowly coming to trust you. But he knows Jeff doesn't like him, doesn't want him and is uncomfortable with him, and when he behaves wildly or impulsively or angrily, it often comes from the combination of all those elements."

"I understand that," she said quietly. "But what I can't understand is where Jeff is coming from. Why is he so dead set against him?"

"You know what he expressed to both of us in this office. This was not the life he signed on for, he says. He never even wanted a continuing relationship with Eve and he certainly doesn't want to be a father to a twelve-year-old boy he thinks is disturbed."

"But that's so selfish, so inflexible. I never saw that in him before."

"I think he's jealous of your affection and attention to Danny, jealous in a way he doesn't even understand or acknowledge. And because he knows that being jealous of a kid is wrong, he's overreacting about the possible bad effect Danny could have on Griffin. And just as Danny hangs on to Griffin as the symbolic connection he can maintain with his mother, Jeff, in some deep unaware way, conflates Danny with all the bad luck you two have had. He looks for ways to reject him and, unfortunately, he finds them."

"Well, that's just crazy and unacceptable. How can we fix something like that?"

"With a long time in therapy. He needs to see and accept it first and then he needs to want to change it. I don't see either of those happening if he won't even come in to talk."

Her shoulders sagged and she closed her eyes and took a deep breath. "You're right. So what should I do?"

"I can't tell you that."

She frowned.

"I don't mean because it wouldn't be therapeutically correct, Marcia. I mean I don't know. You have to work it out with Jeff."

She was about to thank him and get up to go, but she hesitated.

"Was there something else?" he asked.

"Well, there is something I'd like to ask you," she said. "But I need you to be completely honest."

He bristled. "I'm always honest," he replied crisply. "That's my job."

"I'm sorry. I just wanted to emphasize how important your answer is. I don't even really know exactly how to ask this."

He waited.

"I guess I want to know if you think Danny is worth it. I mean, that sounds awful. Of course he is but what I mean is, will things get better? Will he get better? Am I fighting with my husband and creating a terrible atmosphere for my son and maybe even risking my marriage because I feel guilty in a lost cause, or is it Jeff who is unreasonable? I guess I want you to tell me I'm doing the right thing."

He seemed to be gathering his thoughts in the silence that followed. Sometimes silence served to prod Marcia to say more, but this time, she waited for him to speak.

"Look, Marcia, I can't totally answer all those questions. Do I think you feel guilty and are acting partially out of guilt? Yes. Do I think Jeff is being unreasonable? Partly. But do I think Danny is a lost cause? No. Definitely not. Only you can decide what helping him is worth to you. But, if you can pull it off with Jeff, I would urge you not to give up on him. Remember how Danny was at the beginning? He still has problems, of course, but he's doing better. It's a long, slow process but there is undeniable improvement. His friendship with Raul is helping him a lot. Everyone needs a friend—some people have many, but having even one friend who likes you and whom you like is very important, as you know. For a kid like Danny, it could have been anyone. But he picked a really nice kid, from what I hear."

"Yeah. I'm grateful for small favors."

"It's not small, Marcia. That's my point."

"I guess that's what I needed to hear. Thank you."

She gathered her bag and coat and said goodbye. On the way out she checked her messages. Jeff had called to say that he had cancelled an important meeting and decided to come home that evening to handle the "Danny situation." This didn't augur well for her or for Danny, and she wanted to be there before Jeff arrived. She hurried home.

20

She made it home in good time. She stopped first to see Griffin, fresh from his bath in his blue bunny pajamas. He stretched his pudgy arms out to her and she gratefully embraced him and inhaled his sweet scent. How innocent he is, how trusting, she thought. Danny had been like this, she was sure. She could imagine Eve as infatuated with him as she was with Griffin, as protective, as fierce. Somehow, she had to provide at least some of that for Eve's boy. She asked Berta if she could stay, telling her what had happened. They both knew how angry Jeff would be and Marcia expected an unpleasant scene.

"It would be good if you could take Griffin into his room and play with him after Jeff sees him, and then read him a book and put him to sleep. Hopefully he'll go right down but if he doesn't, please stay with him until he does."

"Of course."

"Where is Danny?"

"In his room."

She knocked and then entered. It had become clear to Danny that the adult knock on his door was an announcement rather than a request for permission to enter, so he was ready. He had been playing a game on his iPad, which he wasn't supposed to use during the school week, and he hurriedly stashed it under his pillow. He sat on his bed, looking sheepish. Before she could ask what had happened, he apologized, at least for the way he spoke to his teacher.

"I know you're sorry, Danny. But it's not enough to be sorry after. You have to learn to control yourself. Everyone has those feelings sometimes, but it's important to know when and how you can express them."

He nodded. "Does Jeff know?"

"Yes. He's coming home early tonight. I think he wants to talk to you."

"Can't you just tell him I'm sorry?"

"No. You have to tell him."

"He won't believe me."

"If you mean it, he'll believe you."

She heard the outer door open and went out to meet Jeff.

She was expecting a storm, but he surprised her by seeming unusually calm. He didn't let Danny off the hook, but he didn't, at least at first, drive it in deeper. Instead, without even stopping to see Griffin, he called

Danny into the living room. The boy arrived hesitantly, with a mixture of fear and bravado. His face was set, as though ready for an explosion, and though at first his eyes were cast downward, they soon met Jeff's with something like defiance, or maybe, Marcia thought, pride. Jeff told him what the teacher had said and that he would now have to stay after school for three weeks doing his homework and extra assignments. Danny already knew this, but he didn't say anything.

"Do you have anything to say to me?" Jeff asked.

Marcia looked at Danny pleadingly.

"I'm sorry," he said, in the tone kids use when they aren't.

"I hope you really are," Jeff said sternly, clearly irritated. And then, just when she thought the worst was over, Jeff threw a verbal grenade. "You know because of this behavior and many more like it since you've been at the school, you won't be allowed to continue there next year. There are consequences. It's not enough to say you're sorry. You have to mean it and that means changing your behavior."

Marcia was stunned. They had agreed to tell him together, at the right time, after they had found another school, hoping to make the new school sound exciting to try to soften the blow. Now Jeff had done the adult version of what Danny had done, she thought. Jeff was angry so he impulsively reached out to hurt him.

Danny didn't react visibly. His face showed no emotion. He just asked, "When?"

"Next year. After the summer," Marcia said quickly. "So you still have a few more months there. But then you'll start in a new place. We're just trying to pick the best one now. It will be more like your old school."

"You mean easier, right?"

"Maybe a little. But bigger, more kids, you'll see."

"Will Raul come?"

"No, Danny. But you'll still be his friend and you'll still see each other."

"Could I go finish my homework?"

"Sure."

She could barely control her anger until he left. Then she turned to Jeff, "How could you do that? We had discussed this."

"It just pissed me off the way he said he was sorry, like he's said it a hundred times and never meant it. Does he think we're idiots?"

She couldn't answer. She knew it would just lead to another row that circled around the same issue and was never resolved.

"Look, I have an idea. That's what I really wanted to talk to you about," Jeff said. He opened his briefcase and took out some glossy brochures. She was confused. At first she was touched—she thought he was trying to arrange a vacation for them. Maybe it was a romantic place and he thought if they went together they could patch up some of the bad feeling between them. She reached out and glanced down at one of the brochures, the hint of a smile on her lips. It was from a place called the Glen. A picture of a large farmhouse surrounded by fields and the woods beyond was featured on the front page. Maybe he was thinking of a vacation for all of them. She looked at him, puzzled.

"What's this?"

"It's a therapeutic community for disturbed teenagers," he said. "It's perfect for kids like Danny. I don't think it would be too expensive. I'm pretty sure we could get some financial aid, given his situation. He could live there and maybe they could straighten him out."

Her first reaction was intense disappointment: this was just another plan to get rid of Danny. She was annoyed at herself for her first reaction; she should have known better. But she picked up the brochure and scanned it. It was in Utah. The kids lived under strict rules, worked on the farm, lived in dorms, had group therapy and went to school. The text asked: *Are you at your wits' end? Has your teenager run away, taken drugs, been expelled from school, behaved violently, resisted all efforts to straighten out? Come to the Glen, where trained professionals will do the job for you.*

"This sounds like something out of Dickens," she said. "I mean, first of all, Danny isn't a teenager. Second, he's not nearly this bad. He's never run away or taken drugs."

"He's run away from school."

"Temporarily. That's not the same thing. He always comes home."

"So far."

"And he certainly doesn't take drugs."

"Not yet."

"Jesus, Jeff. You want to send him to a therapeutic community for stuff he might do but hasn't done?"

"I want to send him because I think he needs it."

"He's trying, Jeff. In spite of everything you are doing to make it harder. And he has had some success. He's with a therapist who believes he just needs more time and more nurturing."

She couldn't miss Jeff's gesture of impatience and frustration. "Yeah. That therapist is completely disinterested, right? More time, more nurturing and more therapy sessions with him at a hundred bucks an hour."

"He's a really good man, Jeff. He has plenty of patients. He doesn't need Danny." She paused and tried to calm things down. "Look, maybe if things are rough in two years we will need to consider something like this. But not now. And not a place that's so far away. We couldn't even visit him often."

"This may not be your decision, Marcia. I admit that this is what I want, but not just for me. It's a famous place with a great reputation and I honestly think this is right for him, but if you refuse, we will have to come up with another solution. I can't go on like this anymore. I'm uncomfortable in my own home."

"You're hardly here anyway," she shot back.

"Did you ever ask yourself why that is?"

They stopped talking as they heard Berta pass through the hallway on her way to the kitchen. She was probably getting a bottle for Griffin.

"Listen to what I'm saying, Marcia. I mean it," Jeff said when they heard the door to the kitchen close.

"Oh Jesus, Jeff. Please don't make this a choice between you and him."

"I think it may come down to that." He walked to the door. "And the sad thing is I'm not sure who you'll pick." He put on his coat. "Think about it. I'm going to take a walk."

"Don't leave," she called after him. "Let's try to talk this out."

"We talk and talk and can't come to a conclusion. It's no good." He closed the door behind him.

She watched him leave and then sank heavily into the living room couch. She glanced again at the brochure but she didn't want to think about it. She knew she wouldn't let Danny go there, not yet. Just today the therapist had said not to give up on him and this felt like it would be doing just that. How would he feel to be rejected, abandoned, sent to a place he'd regard as a prison? She couldn't believe Jeff meant what he'd threatened. He was just speaking in anger and frustration, she thought. He would take that back when he calmed down. She hoped Danny hadn't heard anything, and she peeked into his room. It was a mess—he'd obviously thrown his things around and he was on his iPad again without permission. She allowed him to e-mail with Raul and she hoped that's what he was doing. Maybe it would comfort him. She wondered if he ever used the Internet for browsing on unacceptable sites. She knew she had to check up on him, but didn't have the heart to do it now.

Marcia opened the door to Griffin's room and walked

in. Berta had come back and was sitting in the chair by
the crib holding him on her lap and giving him a bottle.
Marcia whispered that it was okay for Berta to leave and
took over with Griffin. He looked up at her, locking eyes
as he sucked, and she gazed back at him, completely absorbed in him until she had a sudden thought. What
would happen if Jeff left? What would that do to Griffin? He was so young and already he would be the child
of a broken marriage. She didn't even think about how
she would feel. Her feelings about Jeff were so confused.
It seemed like whatever love she had for him existed more
in her memory than in her life. Day to day there was only
worry and anger. But did that mean she no longer loved
him? She didn't know. She didn't want to think about it.

Griffin finished and was sucking air, so she gently
withdrew the bottle from him. He was drowsy, almost
asleep, so she was able to put him into his crib, wind up
his mobile, give him his pile of pacifiers and tiptoe out
of the room. There was a part of her that wondered, use-
lessly, whether they had done the right thing from the
beginning. Usually she pushed that thought away but it
surfaced from time to time. Grace had asked her if she
ever regretted the surrogacy. She had answered that of
course she regretted what had happened, if she had
known she wouldn't have done it, but how could she ever
regret Griffin? He was the one uncomplicated joy of her
life.

She had work to do and she sat at her desk, trying to
distract herself with the manuscript she needed to edit,
but she wasn't doing a good job of it. Finally, she gave up

and got ready for bed. She turned on the TV to pass the time bingeing on reruns of *The Good Wife* until Jeff returned, but when he hadn't come back two hours later, she started to worry, seriously considering the possibility that he might have actually meant what he said. She walked back into the living room, picked up the brochures, took them back to bed with her and started reading them.

21

She fell asleep before he came home and was dimly aware when he slipped in beside her, but too sleepy to check the time. In that semi-awake state she reverted to behavior more reminiscent of their former closeness; she reached out to touch him, curling up closer, brushing his arm with her lips before falling into a deeper sleep. In the morning, they spoke little. She awoke early, picked Griffin up at his first cry and had already brewed the coffee, fed the baby his bottle and placed him in his high chair when she heard Jeff's alarm go off. She put some Cheerios on Griffin's tray and darted into Danny's room to be sure he was up and getting ready.

"I'm making scrambled eggs," she said. "That okay?"

Danny nodded, gathering his books and stuffing them into his backpack. He was wearing jeans and a hooded sweatshirt, which was not acceptable dress for school.

"You know you can't wear that," she said, irritated. "Please change into your uniform."

"A lot of the kids do it," he argued, his voice sullen.

"I don't believe you," she answered. "Anyone who doesn't wear the school uniform gets points against them and sent home."

"Well, Raul does it sometimes."

"That's absurd, Danny. Please don't lie to me. Raul's mother would never let him."

"It doesn't matter anyway. They already threw me out," he said defiantly.

"They could make you leave now instead of at the end of the term," she answered. "Then what would we do?"

He shrugged with that casual indifference to the future so common in adolescents. "Just change your clothes right now," she said in her firmest voice, trying to control her temper. "I don't have the time for this."

She poked her head into the bathroom and shouted loud enough for Jeff to hear her over the shower. "Scrambled eggs okay?"

"No thanks. I have a breakfast meeting," he shouted back.

He stopped in the kitchen to give Griffin a kiss before he left, ignoring Danny and barely looking at Marcia. She walked into the hallway with him when he stopped to get his coat. "Now it's a breakfast meeting. Between breakfast, lunch and dinner meetings, I sometimes wonder why you bother to come home at all," she said.

He put on his coat and opened the door. "Sometimes I wonder the same thing," he said as he left.

She didn't have time to parse that last comment and, though it upset her, tried to brush it off. Today was a workday for her too, so she hurried Danny out the door, handing him his lunch money. She put some scrambled eggs on Griffin's tray, talking to him in as cheerful a voice as she could muster as she wolfed down some eggs herself, followed by a third mug of coffee. When Berta arrived a few minutes later, she handed Griffin over and rushed into the shower. When she emerged, she tore around her room, choosing her outfit, searching for a lost shoe, which turned out to be under the bed, collecting her papers, checking to be sure she had her wallet and MetroCard. Finally she said goodbye to Berta, kissed Griffin and went to the closet for her coat. She looked herself over quickly in the hall mirror and decided she looked as acceptable as she was going to that day. While waiting for the elevator, she fished around in her bag nervously, double-checking her essentials, looking for her reading glasses and thinking, not for the first time, that she had to stop using such big bags because she could never find anything in them. Finally, her fingers closed on her glasses case. But she soon discovered her glasses weren't in it, so she let go the elevator, which had just arrived, and returned to the apartment to find them. They were on the floor near her bed—she must have put them there before she fell asleep last night. She noticed her phone on the dresser and gratefully grabbed that too. She had thought she'd already taken it, but this was such a chaotic morning, she must have been mistaken.

She got to work in time for the morning meeting.

Julie brought her a cup of coffee, her fourth since awakening, so she was beginning to feel a little wired. Afterward, in her office, she started to write the final page of an editorial letter she knew would not go over well with the author and paused to think of a tactful way to say he needed to restructure several of the chapters. As she was concentrating, she heard the familiar ping of a text coming in on her cell phone. She was going to ignore it, but it was followed by a second ping and she worried it might be about Griffin so she retrieved it from her bag and checked the message. *Good morning, sweetheart,* she read.

Who was this? The text identifier didn't help. *Ilana.* Who was Ilana? As she stared in confusion, another text popped up. *My cat jumped up on the bed and woke me in the middle of the night. I reached over for you but you were gone. I think he was looking for you too. He misses you. So do I.*

She could feel her heart pounding in her ears. She turned over the phone and noted that the back cover was transparent, not solid gray like hers. This was Jeff's phone. He must have forgotten it this morning and she'd picked it up by mistake. She just kept staring at the text. Another popped up—an emoticon of a heart. She looked up as Julie knocked and then popped her head in. "Do you have a minute?" Julie asked. "I'd like to go over some questions with you on the Fullerton manuscript."

"Not now," Marcia snapped. "Julie, don't keep walking in on me, for God's sake. The door's there for a reason. Knock on it."

Surprised, Julie was flustered. "Oh, I'm so sorry, Marcia. I knocked but I thought you didn't hear."

"Well, wait for an answer next time. I'm busy right now."

She was sorry she'd snapped as soon as Julie backed away and closed the door, but she hadn't been able to control herself. She looked back at the phone; no new message popped up. She pushed it away as if it burned her fingers and closed her eyes, trying to process what she'd just learned. Then she reached for it again and answered the text.

This is Marcia. Jeff's wife. I'll be sure to give him your message. She pressed SEND. She pushed it away again and picked up her landline, punching in Jeff's office number. Her heart was still pounding but she felt resolute when Karen, Jeff's secretary, answered.

Trying to make her voice sound as natural as possible, she asked Karen to please tell Jeff she wanted to speak to him.

"Hi, Marcia," Karen said, "I'm really sorry but he's in a meeting. I'll tell him to call you as soon as he's out."

"No. Please interrupt him. Tell him it's me and it's urgent and I need him right away."

"Okay," Karen said, her voice unsure.

She was gone for about five minutes. When she returned she was apologetic. "I'm really sorry," Karen repeated nervously, "but he says he'll call when the meeting ends."

Marcia replied with barely contained fury. "Just tell him that if he doesn't come to the goddamn phone right now, I'll come over to his office and interrupt his meeting in person."

Another few minutes passed. Marcia could imagine how embarrassed he was, how he would have to apologize and excuse himself. How he'd storm over to the phone. She wondered if he suspected. Did he know he'd left his phone behind? Did he worry that she'd seen it? She looked at it, lying on the desk, full of damning, hurtful information, information she both wanted and didn't want to know. Her mouth felt dry. She heard him pick up the phone and thank Karen.

"Marcia, what the hell is the matter with you? What is so goddamn important?"

"I just have a message for you," she answered as evenly as she could. "I thought it couldn't wait. Ilana's cat misses you. Apparently he was disappointed you were no longer in Ilana's bed this morning."

There was a silence. Probably seconds, but it felt like minutes.

"You have my phone?" he asked softly.

"Yes. I told you we should change the cases so they weren't so easily confused."

"I can explain."

"Really? I'd almost like to hear what you come up with. But actually, I don't think so, Jeff. Please don't try. Don't feed me some lawyer's lies. Just tell me what's going on." She felt her eyes tear up, a weakness she couldn't allow. Not if she didn't want to fall apart completely.

"Now? On the phone?"

"No. Let's both leave the office and go home."

"Maybe not home. Berta is there. Griffin. Danny."

"Danny is at school."

"Let's meet in the park."

"Where?"

"The Sixty-third Street entrance." Jeff's office was just a few blocks away from Marcia's on East Forty-eighth Street, so she knew they could both get there fairly soon.

"Okay," she said. "I'll leave now."

She wished she had something to stop her heart from pounding. She wanted to think clearly before she confronted him. What did she want out of it? She tried to think calmly. The first question she needed answered before she could begin to think of where she wanted to go from here was how far his affair had gone. Was he in love with this woman? Did he want to make a life with her? A fist of anxiety twisted in her gut. She feared what might lie ahead, the specter of divorce, lawyers, loneliness, Griffin growing up in a broken home, custody arrangements, Danny . . . Danny, whose arrival in their lives precipitated all this. She wanted to avoid all that, to keep their marriage going even if it wasn't perfect, to remind Jeff of what they were before, even to find a compromise if she had to about Danny if that made the difference. But she was caught in a maelstrom of emotions: fears, hopes, anger, rage and deep despair. When she thought of the lies, the so-called meetings, the weekends with the "client," the missed dinners, the utter betrayal, it galled her. More than that, it hurt her, maddened her, filled her with fantasies of revenge. But she had to admit that on some level she had suspected it; that's why she had asked Charlie if he knew anything. She hadn't wanted to see what was right in front of her; she had lied to herself, protected herself, hoping it would go away. She thought Charlie had probably known too and her cheeks flushed with humiliation and shame.

She arrived at their meeting place full of these contradictory passions.

The park was nearly deserted at this hour. She was surprised by the force of the wind when she reached Sixty-third and Fifth Avenue, but she pulled her hood tighter and the wind seemed to die down as she entered the park. The weather mirrored her mood. The sun was masked by the sky, which was the color of lead. Dry brown leaves, their edges brittle, huddled in little piles under scraggly bushes. Occasionally whipped up by a gust of wind, they'd land in jagged pieces on the frozen ground.

She saw Jeff right away, bundled in his black parka and sheepskin hat, a red and blue striped scarf pulled tight around his neck. He was walking toward her and even before he reached her she could see that he looked ashamed, his shoulders hunched over, his step tentative. She knew him so well, she thought, but apparently not well enough.

"Marcia. I'm sorry. I don't know what else to say. I'm so sorry."

She took a deep breath and looked straight at him. "I just want to know one thing before we say anything else," she said. "Are you in love with her?"

He too took a deep breath. His shoulders collapsed even more. "It's ridiculous to talk here," he said. "Let's go get a cup of coffee."

Her mind was reeling. He hadn't answered her question. Was that because he wanted to find a way to tell her

the bad news or because it was complicated and he wanted
to explain? Whatever the reason, it wasn't the resounding
no she had hoped for and expected. She nodded stiffly.
They found a luncheonette on Seventieth and Lexington and chose a booth in the back. Some time was taken
up as they both peeled off their heavy coats, stuffed their
gloves in their pockets and their hats in their sleeves.
They sat facing each other and ordered coffee, still without talking. She waited. He looked at the table briefly,
then up at her.

"Listen, Marcia, you know things have not been good
between us for a while," he began.

"Do you love her?"

"I don't think so."

"You don't *think* so?" She pressed her lips together.
"What do you *think* you need to help you decide?" Her
voice was colder than her hands, which were still sting-
ing as the heat thawed them.

"I mean I still love you, Marcia."

"You have a funny way of showing it."

"I might say the same to you."

"How? Have you gotten any text messages from any
of my lovers recently?"

"Stop being such a bitch. That's not going to help."

"It helps me."

"Marcia, there is more than one way to betray someone you love."

"You ought to know. How many of them have you
tried?"

"Stop it."

"You stop it. You're trying to say this is my fault somehow. You said you were sorry but it doesn't sound like it. It sounds like you feel justified." She looked at him, feeling sad and vulnerable. "I don't understand, Jeff. How could you do this? How can you talk to me like this? How can you hurt me like this?" She struggled to keep her voice from breaking. She brushed away the tears that had started to drip down her cheek and turned her face toward the wall so no one would see.

He reached for her hand reflexively, the way he would if she'd been hurt by someone or something else, but she pulled it away. "I am sorry," he said. "I don't want to hurt you. I want us to fix this."

She sniffled. "How can we fix it if you don't even know if you love her?"

"I don't know anything anymore. I know I don't love her like I love you, like I've always loved you. But lately, since . . ."

"Since Griffin?"

"Since Danny. You know, Marcia. We've been on opposite sides of this from the beginning. And coming home became a trial instead of a pleasure. I begged you to do something about it, something that might have helped us and him too but you wouldn't listen. Then I met Ilana and she—"

At the mention of her name the anger Marcia had felt when she read the texts returned. Her voice hardened with sarcasm.

"Wait, let me guess. You met Ilana. She's a single woman or maybe divorced. She has no children, though we know she has a cat she's devoted to. She has a spotless little apartment somewhere. Maybe she has flowers in every room, especially when she's expecting you, and scented candles, right? She'd have time for that because she wouldn't have a household to manage and a baby to take care of as well as a demanding job and a husband who works all the time. Maybe she even gets a full night's sleep once in a while. Does she cook gourmet organic meals for you? I get it. I really do. No baby crying. No unhappy preadolescent orphan hanging around. No stressed wife trying to balance her marriage, her motherhood and her conscience. In fact, obviously, you aren't troubled by conscience at all."

"Hold on. You paint me as such a villain. Is it such a surprise I liked being around someone who likes me?"

She stared at him, surprised and saddened, her fury temporarily expended, like air whizzing out of a balloon. "I like you, Jeff," she said softly. "I love you. And I know how hard it's been at home. But how did we let ourselves get so far apart that you could do something like this?" She paused and looked away. Her mouth was dry. "Do you want a divorce?"

"What? No. No, of course not. I want a family, our family. But just our family."

The air rushed back in. "I presume that means without Danny. So who do you mean? You, me, Griffin and Ilana?"

He pursed his lips and shook his head. "It's hopeless talking to you when you're like this. Of course I don't mean Ilana. I'll stop seeing her. I'll come home. We can go to a marriage counselor, if you think that will help. But it has to be without Danny. I can't live with him."

"You said you didn't know if you loved her."

"I didn't mean that."

She didn't answer.

"Marcia? What do you say?"

She rubbed her eyes, then looked at him. "How long have you been with her?"

"I don't know. A few months."

"A few months? I mean, this is March. Griff isn't even a year old yet. So when did this start? When did it get so bad that you figured it was okay to break your vows to me and lie and cheat and sneak around? I'm just wondering what your threshold for unendurable discomfort is. A month? Two?"

His jaw tightened. "You're too angry to have this conversation now. Maybe we should talk tonight when you've had some time to calm down and think it over. I have to get back to work." He started to gather his belongings.

"Don't come home tonight." She said it impulsively, out of anger, but once said, she couldn't take it back, didn't want to. "You can't live with Danny? Well, after this, I'm not sure I can live with you."

"Marcia, don't do this."

"I didn't do it, Jeff. You did. Won't you even take responsibility for that?"

22

Marcia had insisted that Danny wear his school uniform, but she couldn't control how he wore it. As soon as he arrived at school he pulled out his shirt, threw his school blazer into his locker and went looking for Raul. He didn't see him in the school yard, the hallway or the bathroom and the class bell had already rung, so he slipped into his seat in his homeroom hoping to catch up with him there. Raul was in his usual place in the third row. He looked particularly neat today—Danny was surprised to see his shirt tucked in, his blazer buttoned and his hair cut short. Raul saw him come in but didn't nod at him and Danny was puzzled as he took his seat. The teacher was going over the week's schedule, announcing that auditions were going to be held on Thursday for the school choir. Danny's mouth curled into a sneer. The choir! They never sang anything worth listening to.

They performed kid songs, stuff he'd heard when he was eight, and oldies that the teachers liked. Why didn't they do something cool like form a rock band? He didn't play any instrument well enough, so he couldn't be in it, but it would be fun to hear them. He balled up a piece of paper and pitched it at Raul's head to get his attention, but Raul ignored it. What was with him? He tore a piece of paper out of his notebook and scribbled a note: *Hey, what's up? Gotta talk.* He folded the paper into a small packet and handed it to Joey Fontana, who sat next to him. He didn't even have to say pass it to Raul, because Raul was the only person Danny ever sent notes to, and Joey and everyone else in class knew that. Joey passed it to Dawn, who sat in the row ahead of him, and Dawn gave it to Harlan and finally it reached Raul. Danny watched as Raul took it and put it in his pocket without reading it. Danny couldn't figure out what was going on.

When class ended, Danny walked up to Raul as they filed out of the room.

Raul looked uncomfortable and upset. His eyes kept flicking around, not settling on Danny but looking beyond him.

"What's up?" Danny asked. "You okay?"

"No. My ma heard about what happened."

"What happened?"

"I mean here. With you."

"Oh yeah. I gotta talk to you about that. They're throwing me out of school."

"I know. My ma says I can't hang out with you anymore.

I'm on scholarship. She thinks I'll get in trouble if they see me with you. She thinks you're a bad influence."

Danny didn't know what to say. He hadn't expected this but now that he heard it, he felt stupid not to have known. Why wouldn't it happen? Everyone he cared about disappeared. Now it was Raul's turn.

"You gonna listen?"

"I gotta."

"So you can't come over to my house anymore?"

"No. And you can't come to mine."

"But we can sit together at lunch, right?"

Raul looked miserable. "No. I can't. I promised. I gotta find another place to sit."

Danny bit his lip. "So how are we gonna see each other? What are we gonna do?"

"I don't know."

"Maybe we can, like, say we're staying for choir and hang out instead."

"I can't. I promised my ma." The bell rang, announcing five minutes till the next class. "I gotta go. I'm really sorry."

Raul hurried off.

Danny got through the rest of the morning somehow. He couldn't concentrate and he was lucky no teacher called on him for an answer. He just kept thinking about how unfair everything was. He saw Raul in every class and at recess but he couldn't approach him, couldn't hang out with him, couldn't even talk to him. When he tried to catch his eye, like they always did before when something was funny or someone said something stupid, Raul looked away. When lunchtime came and he walked into the lunchroom and saw Raul sitting at another table with a bunch of kids Danny didn't even like, his hurt turned to anger. He ran out of the lunchroom, out of the school, onto the street. What difference did it make? He was going to be thrown out of the school anyway. What more could they do to him? So maybe they'd make him leave now instead of in September, so what? It might be better. Then he wouldn't have to see Raul every day. Raul was such a mama's boy, Danny thought bitterly. He listened to everything she said. He could see how Raul couldn't invite him over, but he could have still sat with him at school. They could have worked out a way. But Raul didn't want to. As soon as there was a little trouble he just caved.

He wanted to go home and play with Griffin—that always made him feel better. Griffin laughed at everything. And he was always so happy to see Danny—his whole face would light up when Danny came in. But Marcia was home today and she'd ask why he wasn't at school. Maybe he could tell her it was a half day. But she'd probably find out. He thought about going to see Dr. Benson but he didn't have an appointment. It was cold and he had left school without his coat and without his subway pass. He thought about going back to get them but it was too embarrassing, so, hugging himself for warmth, he started walking. The Claremont School was a good eighty blocks from Marcia and Jeff's apartment (he still thought of it that way even though Marcia kept encouraging him to think of it as his home). He wasn't going to be able to walk eighty blocks without a coat. He couldn't take the subway because he didn't have his pass, but maybe he could just sneak in. He was a little afraid to do that—he'd heard you got in big trouble if you got caught, but he didn't know what else he could do, and he couldn't really imagine any trouble bigger than the one he was already in. He wished he had a cell phone like almost everyone else in his school. Then he could have called someone. But who could he have called? Maybe in the end he could have called Marcia and she'd help him. But there was no point in imagining. He didn't have a phone.

He walked a few more blocks and ducked into a kids' clothing store to warm up. He looked at the winter jackets covetously. He found his size and tried one on. It felt so nice and warm. What if he walked out wearing it? he wondered. Would they notice? He spotted a saleslady watching him and hoped she hadn't noticed the name of his school emblazoned on the sweater of his uniform. When he walked over to the mirror in the dressing room to see how the jacket looked, a salesman followed him, so he knew he'd better not risk taking it. He pretended to look at a few more jackets and finally, warmer than when he'd entered, he hung up the jacket and left the store. He headed for the nearest subway station.

It was empty—just the guy in the booth selling Metro-Cards, no one on the platform. He stood staring at the turnstile for a while, trying to figure out his chances of sneaking in. A train thundered in, disgorging a few passengers. One old man on crutches was trying to push open the exit gate instead of using the turnstile, but was having trouble with his crutches. Danny ran over as if to help and held the door for him. The guy smiled his thanks and Danny slipped in behind him, moving quickly down the platform and out of view. Another train stopped and Danny ran into the open door. When it closed and the train rumbled on, he breathed a sigh of relief and sat down. He was trembling a little. He'd been scared but now he was exhilarated. He felt proud—he'd pulled it off. His mother always told him to use his head and he had. He didn't need Raul or anyone. But then he saw the cop.

It was the same one who had brought him home that day that already felt so long ago. He was walking through the train like he was looking for someone and when he entered Danny's car, he stopped.

"Hello, Danny," he said.

He remembered his name. That wasn't good. "Hello," Danny said, still hoping this was just a weird coincidence.

"I saw that maneuver at the station. You know it's illegal to jump a turnstile, don't you?"

"I didn't jump it."

"No, you sneaked in the gate. I saw you. You know the law on this? Anyone who doesn't pay the fare gets taken to the police station, fingerprinted and charged with a crime."

They had reached Danny's stop at Eighty-sixth Street and the cop told him to come with him. They left the train. Danny talked fast.

"Please don't do that. Please," he begged. "I just didn't

have my coat and I was cold and I didn't have my pass. But I have a pass. It just wasn't with me."

"Where was it?"

"At school."

"And why aren't you at school?"

Danny didn't answer.

"Do you want to tell me at the police station?"

"No. I . . ." He was thinking fast trying to come up with a lie, but he knew it was useless. "I had some trouble and I left. I didn't take my stuff."

"Should we go back to school and you show me your pass?"

"Oh please, don't make me go back there. Everyone will know. They already hate me there."

"Why do they hate you?"

His eyes filled with tears. "I don't know," he said simply.

"Is your mother home?"

"She's not my mother," he mumbled.

"Okay, let's go to school then."

"No," he shouted. "She's like my stepmother. She's home today. She can tell you I have a pass. She bought it for me. Please, let's go there."

Marcia was shocked to open the door to a shivering Danny without a coat or hat and standing next to the same policeman who had brought him home before. What had he done now? Danny was so relieved to be home, to be out of the cold and to see Marcia's worried but friendly face that he impulsively threw his arms around her waist and gave her an awkward hug. It was the first time he'd done this. She tried to hug him back but he had already pulled away, looking embarrassed. She invited the policeman in and offered him a cup of coffee, which he accepted. She made a cup of hot chocolate for Danny and they sat in the kitchen as Danny told both what had happened.

"The school called to say he had left," Marcia told the officer. "I was afraid something like this would happen. His teacher said she thought he had a fight with his best friend. That would have upset him very much and I'm afraid he has trouble controlling his impulse to run away when things upset him." She turned to Danny. "Is that what happened, Danny? Did you and Raul have a fight?"

Danny looked down, trying to keep tears from his eyes. He nodded.

"I'm sorry, Danny. I know how you must feel. Do you want to tell us what it was about?"

He shook his head vigorously. She turned to the policeman and shrugged. "It's hard for him to express his feelings; you know how it is with kids. But he sees a therapist and hopefully he will talk to him." The policeman nodded thoughtfully. "I want to thank you for bringing him home," she continued. "We're having problems but he's not a bad kid. He doesn't always have the best judgment, but he's twelve years old and has a lot to deal with."

"He keeps insisting you're not his mother. Is he a foster kid?"

"Sort of. His parents are both dead. His mother was a friend of mine and died recently. She wanted me to take care of him if anything ever happened to her."

The officer drained his cup and stood up. "Look, I'm the cop on the beat here. I don't see anything good coming from hauling him downtown for riding the subway illegally, especially since he tells me he has a pass. Is that right?"

"Yes, of course. He goes to the Claremont School. All the kids have one."

He turned to Danny. "That's three times you ran away from something instead of facing it. This time you made two bad choices—running away and sneaking into the subway. Three times is usually an out. I'm letting it go this time, but think before you run next time." He got up, accepted Marcia's profuse gratitude and left.

"You're a lucky boy, Danny. Another cop and this could have gone very differently. Do you understand?"

"Yeah." He was looking down. "Where's Griff?"

"In his room, napping. He'll be up soon."

"Can I go see?"

"No, you might wake him."

Danny bit his thumbnail, a new habit she'd noticed lately, but she didn't try to stop him this time. "I'm sorry," he said.

"I know."

"Are you going to tell Jeff?"

"No. But I don't know if the school called him. I hope not."

"He hates me enough already."

"He doesn't hate you, Danny. But it's true that he and I are having some problems."

"I know. It's all my fault."

"It isn't. There's a lot you're too young to understand."

They heard Griffin stirring in his bedroom. He wasn't crying to be picked up yet, just gurgling and babbling to himself. Danny looked beseechingly at Marcia and she smiled. "Sure. Go get him."

She was at her desk trying to work when Jeff barged in. Obviously, he had heard.

"Where is he?" he demanded as he entered the kitchen.

Just then Danny entered, carrying Griffin, who was ready for his snack.

Jeff grabbed the baby so forcefully that he started to cry. "I don't want you carrying Griffin," he shouted. "What the hell did you do? You left school without permission. The school called the police and found out you had snuck onto the subway. A local store reported you were trying to steal a coat but ran out when you were observed." He looked at Marcia, handing her Griffin, who was howling. "What will it take, Marcia?"

She took Griffin to comfort him and put him in his high chair with a bottle. "Danny? Were you trying to steal a jacket?"

"No. I swear. I tried it on just to warm up. Then I took it off and left."

"What are you doing here, Jeff?"

"I live here, remember?"

"I already told you, you can't live here and there too."

"And I already told you I have no intention of living there. But this isn't about that."

"Danny," Marcia said. "Jeff and I need to talk. Please

go to your room and close the door. You can play games on your iPad."

Looking miserable, Danny obeyed.

After he was gone, she closed the kitchen door and put some Cheerios out for Griffin, who was now finished with his bottle and banging it against the tray.

"Look, we can't have this conversation now with Danny in the other room and Griffin here," she said. "Let's just try to calm down."

"I want you to agree to find another place for Danny to live."

"We haven't even decided if you're going to be living here," she answered.

"I've decided."

"Well, it's not a unilateral decision, Jeff."

"Marcia, you aren't hearing me. I think Danny is a bad influence on Griffin, I think it makes him unsafe. And if I leave here, I won't go alone."

"What? What the hell does that mean?"

"I'll go to court if I have to."

"Court? Have we gotten there so fast? You mean you do want a divorce?"

"I don't. I already told you that. But if you won't let me stay, if you won't agree to find a solution to Danny, if I can't protect my son in any other way, I'll go to court."

"For what? What will you go to court for?"

"I'll sue you for custody of Griffin."

23

His ear pressed to the tiny crack he had left in his bedroom door, Danny heard everything. Not that hearing was difficult, they were shouting half the time and then, remembering he was there, lowering their voices until their emotions overcame them again and he could hear the volume rise. He didn't know the whole story, of course, but he knew what he most feared: Jeff was going to take Griffin away, not just from Marcia but from him. More than that, it was all happening because of him. He wouldn't have to be a genius to know how Jeff felt about him, Danny thought. Jeff hated him and he didn't want him to have anything to do with Griffin. Marcia had been standing up for him all this time and now she'd lose. Jeff was a lawyer, Danny thought. What did Marcia know about how to fight him? Jeff could do whatever he wanted. And pretty soon Marcia would give in to him. All she had to do was agree to send Danny away and Jeff wouldn't be able to do anything to her. Of course she'd do it. She'd do anything for her own kid, who wouldn't? His felt a pang as he remembered his own mother. For the first time he thought about what she had tried to do as something she had done for him. He'd known she'd always said that, of course. But he started to think how sick she was at first when she was pregnant and how slowly she walked as her stomach got bigger and how she did all that and wasn't even going to keep the baby. It was all for him, to move into a better house, to go to a better school. But that flash of gratitude was replaced almost instantly with bitterness. So look, Ma, he thought sadly. Here I am living in a better neighborhood and going to a better school and I don't have you. And that's why I can't learn anything and I fight with everyone, and I'm getting kicked out because you made me good and now you're not here and I'm bad.

He looked around at his room, the Legos and games Marcia had bought him, his iPad. He clenched his teeth, trying to be brave, but he felt more like a condemned man on his walk to the death chamber. He'd seen a show about something like that. A kid's parents died and he was supposed to go live with a really mean aunt so he ran away and there was this scene where he just looked around at his room and his toys and you just knew how he felt. That's what Danny felt now. He didn't know where they'd send him but he knew it wouldn't be good. He didn't want to go. He thought about calling Dr. Benson, but it didn't feel right. The only person he wanted to see, the only person who would understand was Raul, and Raul wasn't speaking to him. He pulled out his iPad and texted him. *Need you real bad. Can you meet me?*

A few minutes passed in which he stared at his iPad, willing it to signal that a text had arrived. And then it did.

sorry about today. ma is working. come over?

He was so grateful he could barely answer. *yeah. be there*, he texted.

But how would he get out? Marcia would never let him go. Raul lived too far away so she wouldn't let him go there. Besides, she thought they'd had a fight. But she didn't know what he did at school. Maybe he could use that. He walked into the kitchen. Marcia was on the phone. She was hunched over at the kitchen table with a cup of coffee, the phone pressed tightly against her ear, talking softly—probably so he wouldn't hear, he thought. She looked terrible. Her face was pale and her eyes were red. He felt sorry for her. It's all my fault, he thought again, sadly. He remembered how she'd tried to help him and how ungrateful he'd been, how he kept doing bad things and never told her anything he was feeling. How he had lied to her and was going to lie again. He shrugged it off. It was too late now. He had to get to Raul's house.

"Marcia, I gotta go out," he said.

She had barely noticed him when he entered the room, but looked up when he spoke.

"Have to go out?" she asked mechanically, covering the mouthpiece with her hand.

"Sorry. I have to go to Ron's house about the home-work."

"Who's Ron? Where does he live?"

"He's a kid in my class. We're supposed to do a project together. He lives on Sixty-fifth Street on the East Side."

"You can call him to get it when I get off the phone," she said.

"No. We have to do it together. I'll get in trouble if I don't show up." He held his breath. He'd never out-and-out lied to Marcia before and he was afraid she'd know. And he didn't have his pass. He would need her to give him some money. But he was counting on Marcia being distracted because she was upset, and he was right. She nodded absently and waved him away as she returned to her phone call.

"Grace? I'm sorry," he heard her say. "So what do you think I should do?"

"I'm sorry, Marcia. I don't have my pass. I need some money." He held his breath. This might stop her. But she just frowned impatiently and reached behind her for her purse.

"Hang on one more minute, okay?" she said into the phone. She threw her wallet over to him. He opened it. She had three $20 bills. He held up one of them, with a helpless shrug.

"It's okay. Take that. Bring me change. Don't stay late. And don't interrupt me again." She turned back to the phone. "I hate to bother you at work with this, Grace, but I don't know what to do," he heard her say as he slipped out the door.

He was a little nervous about going on his own, but also excited. He knew how to get to Raul's house from school but he wasn't sure of the route from his apartment. He remembered it was the F train to Queens, and he knew he could get that if he got to the East Side. He walked through Central Park and found the subway station at Sixty-third Street and Lexington Avenue. From there, he knew the way. Twenty minutes later, he was proudly knocking on Raul's door. It was answered by Julio, Raul's stepbrother.

"Hey kid," he said. Danny was surprised. It was bad enough that Raul had agreed to go against his mother's instructions and hang out with him. He was also never supposed to let Julio in the house when she wasn't there. Raul came out of his room and greeted him with a smile. Danny looked around nervously. "When's your ma coming home?"

"Not till six. She's at work, I told you."

"What about your dad?"

"He's out too. He took Teresa to the doctor."

"How come? She sick?"

"Nah. Just a checkup."

"How come you didn't talk to me at school but it's okay for me to come over?"

Raul shrugged. "I changed my mind."

Julio laughed. "Tell him what I told you," he said.

"He said you don't do that to your friends," Raul said quietly, looking down like he was ashamed.

Danny looked gratefully at Julio He wanted to hug him, but he didn't dare. Julio was the first person other than Marcia, the first guy, to look out for him since his mother died. Manolo, who lived next door, used to do that sometimes, but he was part of his past life. He tried to say thank you, but Julio brushed it off. Instead, Julio lit a cigarette, offering one to Raul and one to him. He was shocked to see Raul take it and light up. He seemed to know what to do with it too. Danny shook his head. He just wanted to tell them what had happened and ask what he should do.

"They'll probably put you in foster care," Julio said. "You don't want that, man. It'd be better to live on the street. I could probably find something for you to do to make some money." Danny's eyes grew wider. He was scared. He figured Jeff could really do that to him, just put him in foster care and never look back, but he didn't think Marcia would let him. He imagined what his mother would think if he lived on the street and worked for Julio. "Marica won't let them do that," he said.

"Oh yeah? Wait till he takes away her baby. She'll do anything to keep her own kid. She don't care about you."

"Don't they always give kids to the mothers?" Raul asked. "That's what I saw on TV."

"Yeah, but this dude is a lawyer. He can work the system," Julio said.

"He thinks I want to hurt Griffin. How can I show him I don't? I would never hurt him."

"You can't show him, man. He thinks you're a bad kid and you're gonna make Griffin bad."

"I'm not, I won't." He was starting to cry.

"Don't worry, kid." Julio laughed. "I'm pretty good at

convincing people of things. Maybe I should take a crack at him."

Danny knew what that meant. He'd learned how Julio got people to pay his debts from a *Law & Order* episode he'd seen on TV. He knew that was why Raul's mother didn't want him around Raul. It suddenly hit Danny that she was afraid of Julio the same way Jeff was afraid of him. This wasn't making Danny feel any better. He was beginning to regret having come. He understood that his one chance of staying with Griffin was for Marcia to win. If he was good, if he didn't get into any more trouble, maybe Jeff would back off. Maybe the judge would see that Danny loved Griff, that he wasn't going to do anything to hurt him.

"No. Julio," he said in a panic. "Please don't do that."

"Don't worry," Julio laughed again, "I'm just kidding." He fist-bumped both boys and said he had to go. Before he did he tore a piece of lined paper out of Raul's school notebook and wrote his cell phone number on it. "If you need help call me," he said to Danny. "Don't want my little brother's friend living on the street alone."

Danny folded the page and put it in the zippered compartment of his backpack. Then, suddenly, he was in a rush to get home. But Marcia might ask to see what he'd done. "Raul, I need the homework for today."

"Wanna do it together?"

"Yeah. I told Marcia I was working on a project with Ron so she'd let me go out. She'd never have let me come all the way here this late on my own. What could I say it was?"

"I don't know."

"Think."

"Maybe we could, like, give each other quizzes and mark them. We did that in school a couple of times, remember?"

"Yeah. That's good. Maybe science."

"Yeah. Okay. We could do it on today's homework."

They sat at the kitchen table and worked out the details, finishing the next day's homework while they were at it. Before he left, Danny asked him if now they could sit together at lunch again.

"Nah, I can't," Raul said. "The teachers would see and tell my ma. We gotta do this like a secret." Danny nodded. He got it. "Okay." He left, walking to the subway and retracing his route until he got home.

Marcia was cooking dinner in the kitchen. She looked stressed but a little better and her eyes weren't red anymore. She greeted him and asked if he had any trouble getting to his friend's house. He said no and carefully counted out the change for her twenty and put it on the table. She smiled. "You're getting to know your way around. I'm proud of you."

He swallowed. "Thanks." Griffin was in his high chair. He laughed when he saw Danny and stretched out his arms to him. Danny looked at Marcia.

"Don't pick him up," she said. "I'm just giving him dinner. Did you get your project done?"

"Yeah."

"Well, good. You can show it to me after dinner." Good thing he'd done it, he thought. He started to walk

to his room to put away his backpack but stopped half-
way down the hall and returned to the kitchen. He stood
in the doorway.

"Marcia?

"Yeah."

"Am I . . . no, nothin'. I wanna go wash my hands."

"Sure. Go on."

He'd heard her fighting with Jeff, she thought, though
she didn't know how much he had taken in. She wanted
to reassure him but she didn't know how. She'd spent the
afternoon talking to Grace and making appointments,
one for a divorce lawyer Grace had recommended, another with Dr. Benson. Her stomach was in knots and
she was still finding it hard to believe this was all happening. She was consumed with protecting Griffin, but
her maternal instinct extended to Danny too and she was
worried about how this would turn out.

"He's scared," she murmured to herself, draining the
spaghetti she had cooked for their dinner. "But what can
I do? I'm scared too."

24

It amazed her how quickly her mind adapted to her new circumstances. By the next morning, she had already noticed that words like "divorce," "custody," "lawyer," "child support," "alimony," words that belonged to strangers, or unlucky friends or movies or books, suddenly had become her personal vocabulary. It also surprised her how ignorant she was. She had no idea what her rights were or where to start. She was so shocked that Jeff, who in her view should be begging for forgiveness, was instead threatening her in such an ugly way. Sue her for custody of Griffin? Was he kidding? Her anger overcame her despair. How dare he? But that thought was quickly followed by another. *Could* he? Were Danny's problems at home and at school really enough to convince a judge that he would hurt Griffin or even be a bad influence on him? She needed advice and she needed it fast. Not just the advice the therapist could give, she thought. She needed a lawyer. She had a few friends who had been through divorces, though she hadn't seen much of them in the past year. The first person she thought of was Marian, her college roommate for her first three years, who lived in Brooklyn.

Marian had lived with Collin, her steady boyfriend, during her senior year. They seemed a perfect match and everyone assumed they'd marry. When they did, right after graduation, Marcia was maid of honor. Their first child, Jared, was born just seven months after the ceremony and their second, Lizzie, came two years later. They asked Marcia to be godmother to Jared. She tried to explain that she was a poor choice for that particular role because she wasn't religious, but Marian smiled and said, "Neither am I. You know that. I just want him to have a special relationship with you, like an aunt."

"You want me to be the maiden aunt?" she'd joked.

"Well, for now. Until you get married. Then you can just be the crotchety one."

"Okay. I accept. I'm honored. Thank you."

She'd seen a lot of the family and always remembered both children's birthdays as well as adding them to her family gift list for Christmas and Chanukah. When she decided to marry Jeff, Marian was the first friend she told. They saw less of each other once Marcia married, however. She was busy with her job and her new husband, and Marian was overwhelmed with the obligations of work, a husband who travelled a lot and two young children. But they did still occasionally invite each other to dinner. Sometimes Marian and Collin would get a babysitter and they'd all go out to a concert or a show together, but the couple was so consumed with parenthood that their conversation consisted almost exclusively about their children's triumphs and disappointments—mostly triumphs; the disappointments were usually with others: teachers, schools, parents of playmates. As Marcia tried and failed to get pregnant, she couldn't help feeling envious and that led to feeling critical of Marian's apparent lack of other interests, as well as her insensitivity to Marcia's infertility. They had started to drift apart. By the time Marcia decided to try surrogacy, she and Marian were more cordial than close. Marcia was still invited and still attended the children's lavish birthday parties, and she considered Marian her friend, but they rarely phoned each other just to chat, as they had in the old days. Marcia did tell her what she was doing with Eve, but Marian, while encouraging and excited for her, had her own problems by then. She told Marcia that she and Collin had separated and were planning to divorce. The news shocked and saddened Marcia. It also made her realize how distant she had become from Marian—she hadn't even known they were having serious problems. She tried to support her through the divorce, calling her more often and spending time on the phone listening to her anger and despair. And Marian had tried to reciprocate, asking questions about Eve, the pregnancy and how Jeff was reacting. But Marcia was closer to Grace at that point and tended to confide more in her about anything having to do with the surrogacy, and

Marian was so unhappy, she didn't reach out as much as she might. When the tragedy happened, Marcia relied more on Grace than on Marian, who was involved by then in a fierce custody battle with Collin, which she eventually won.

Now Marcia needed her expertise. She decided to call her at work and set a date to see her. She looked up the number on her phone and was relieved when Marian herself answered.

"Hey, Marian, it's Marcia. What happened to your secretary?"

"She's getting coffee. I'm glad to hear from you. How are you?"

"Not great. I don't want to bother you at work, but I need to talk to you pretty urgently."

"Yeah, of course. Let's make a date. Just tell me quickly what's up."

"I need the name of a divorce lawyer."

"For you and Jeff?"

"Yeah."

"Oh God. I'm so sorry. Listen, the kids are with Collin tonight. Why don't I just come over after work?"

Relief flooded in. "Would you, Marian?" She felt herself tearing up. "That would be so good. I don't know what to do."

"I know. I know just what you're feeling. I'll leave early. I can get there by five-thirty."

"I don't know how to thank you."

"Don't thank me. See you later."

"But wait. I think it would be better if we met at the

restaurant down the block—I don't want Danny to hear us. I can ask Berta to stay late tonight."

"Whatever you want," Marian answered. "Where is it?"

"It's right around the corner near my building, on Broadway. I'll text the address."

"Okay. I'll be there."

Somehow Marcia got through the rest of the day. She was supposed to be at the office but had called in sick and said she'd work at home. Danny had gotten up early, dressed and taken his own breakfast, some Cheerios and milk, by the time she came into the kitchen to brew her coffee. She looked at him questioningly.

"I'm ready for school," he said.

She shook her head. "It doesn't work that way, Danny. You left without permission. The school heard that a policeman stopped you. You were accused of canvassing a store to steal a jacket. You don't just clean up and arrive for school like nothing happened. I'm not sure you'll ever be allowed back in that school."

He sat down heavily on a kitchen chair, his legs spread wide, his shoulders slumped. He shrugged. "So what do I do? Where do I go?"

He sounded so helpless, so like the child he was that she softened. "I don't know. But we'll find out. I'll talk to the principal and if he won't let you back, we'll just have to start at the public school earlier than we planned. You'll be okay." She was bustling around the kitchen as she talked, preparing breakfast for Griffin.

"Are you going to send me home?"

"What do you mean?"

"I mean back to L.A."

She stopped scrambling the eggs, shocked and saddened by the question. She turned to face him.

"Of course not. This is your home now, Danny."

"I know. But where do I go if I can't stay here?"

"You'll be okay, Danny. I don't know what exactly is going to happen yet, but I won't let anything bad happen to you. Can you trust me on that?" She sat next to him and took his hands in hers and he didn't pull away. But he didn't answer either.

"Since you've come here, I've tried hard to never let you down, Danny, and I promise I never will. You have to trust me."

He nodded briskly without looking at her.

"Now, here are some eggs. Eat them and then you can go play on your iPad or build with your Legos or something." She smiled at him. "You might even try reading one of the books I bought you."

"Those eggs are for Griffin. I had cereal."

"Okay. Then you can go."

When he left, she covered her face with her hands and rubbed her eyes. She heard Griffin stirring and went to get him. By the time Berta arrived, Marcia had changed and fed him, and Danny had come out of his room to see him. They were happily playing on the living room floor. Marcia had showered and was dressing when Berta knocked on her bedroom door to tell her that a call had come from the principal's office. His secretary left a message for Marcia to come over as soon as possible. She knew this must be his final expulsion, but she had to play it out. She told Berta to be sure Danny stayed at home until she got back and she left.

She had been right. Her meeting was brief and to the point. Danny was out. He had forfeited his right to stay until the end of the school year. The principal suggested she contact the neighborhood public school, which was obligated to take him, and they would forward his records when she told them he was registered. He was sorry. He continued to talk but she had stopped listening and finally she left. She had a brief impulse to call Jeff, but what would be the point of that? Instead, she hailed a cab and headed for the neighborhood school. She had already done some research for September and she had entered the lottery for a charter school, hoping he could get into the Success Academy on West Eighty-fourth Street, but it was too late for that now. Maybe he could transfer in September, she thought, if he was lucky enough to get in. The cab stopped in front of an unprepossessing building, one of the large redbrick structures built early in the last century that still housed several of New York's public schools. Inside, the linoleum floors were polished to a high gloss and the walls were covered with the brightly colored artwork of the students. She didn't stop to admire them, though she noticed that many were good. She found the right office, told the receptionist why she was there and was given some forms to fill out. She'd have to return them with Danny's birth certificate, proof of residence and health records, she was told, and he'd be in. No interviews, no tests, no recommendations required. She said a silent thank-you to the New York public school system. He could start the next day. She was so relieved. At least that was settled.

She asked if she could look around and was told she could. A secretary in the front office suggested that Marcia bring Danny in that very day so they could both see the school together. Marcia loved that idea. She called Danny at home, told him where the school was located, and asked him to meet her in front of the building. "Look nice," she reminded him. "We're going to visit your new school." She asked if he could find it by himself and he assured her he could. He was proud that she suggested he come on his own and didn't offer to pick him up. It was a short walk away, and easy to figure out the route, so it wasn't long before he showed up in front of the building and hesitantly walked inside. Marcia was waiting near the door and greeted him. He had dressed in jeans and a blue turtleneck she had given him. He looked fine, and she realized how relieved he must be to not wear the Claremont school uniform. She showed him into the office of the secretary who had volunteered to accompany them. He looked nervous but resolute, and she was impressed at his bravery.

Danny would be entering sixth grade so they were taken to see his classroom. The first thing that struck her was the diversity of the students. It was a large class, maybe thirty kids instead of the fourteen in his class at Claremont, but they were all colors and ethnicities. There was a wide array of dress styles, but most of the kids were wearing comfortable clothes, much like the way Danny was dressed. The teacher was an elderly African-American woman who looked to be in her sixties. She nodded pleasantly as they entered and listened as the secretary explained that Danny would be joining the class. Smiling warmly at them, the teacher indicated a few empty seats in the back, and continued talking to her students. Marcia observed them. Some turned full around to stare at Danny. Some listened attentively to the teacher. Some whispered to each other. Some passed notes. Some looked like they were daydreaming. Some were engaging with the teacher in a lively discussion about Ellis Island. The teacher explained how immigrants used to have to pass through there to be processed before being allowed into the United States. She emphasized that America had always been a country of immigrants who had made many contributions to the nation. She asked how many of the students had parents who had come to the U.S. as immigrants. A few hesitated and looked a little nervous, but many hands shot up. Marcia glanced at Danny, wondering if this subject would upset him but he was leaning forward, listening, interested. Then the teacher asked how many were immigrants themselves and a few tentatively raised their hands. Maybe this would be better for Danny, she thought. Maybe he'd fit in. After a few more minutes, the secretary led them out and the teacher stopped briefly to tell Danny she looked forward to seeing him in class the next day. Marcia felt optimistic when they left.

"What did you think?" she asked Danny.

"It was okay," he said. He shrugged. "I didn't know if

I should raise my hand when she asked if anyone's parents came here as immigrants. I mean, my dad did, but then he went back and he never made it back again and anyway he wasn't legal."

"I don't think all the kids who raised their hands have parents who are legal either," she answered. She paused "I was thinking the teacher seemed pretty nice," she continued.

He nodded. He didn't look so nervous anymore.

"Are you hungry?" she asked. He was, so they stopped at a luncheonette and she ordered a tuna fish sandwich and a cup of coffee for herself and a burger and fries for him. He seemed uncomfortable and she found it hard to make conversation, but she could tell that at least his first impression of his new school wasn't negative.

In her concern for Danny, she had stopped obsessing over Jeff, however briefly, but now her mind circled back to Jeff and centered on herself: her loss, her anger, her fear. She had made an appointment to see Dr. Benson and she started to think about what she wanted to discuss with him. She asked Danny if he wanted her to go home with him before she went out to do some errands, but he insisted he'd prefer to go alone, so she allowed it.

An hour later she sat in Dr. Benson's office. After listening to her relate the latest developments, he said, "It seems to me that you are trying to separate you and Jeff and what's going on with your marriage from Danny and what's going on with him," he said. "But you can't separate them. They're linked."

She uncrossed her legs and leaned toward him, shifting

forward in her seat and planting both feet firmly in front of her. "I know they are, at least partially. But it's more than that. It's that Jeff isn't who I thought he was. I've lost so much respect for him in so many ways. He's weak, he's deceitful, he's lacking in compassion. Now he threatens me with divorce, suing me for custody of Griffin, for God's sake, just to get his way, to get rid of Danny, a child who lost so much and has so little." She shook her head, making her hair swing over her face, and then brushed it away. "To make that helpless boy his enemy." She paused and waited for the enormity of this to sink in. "I mean, what's wrong with him? How could I have been so mistaken in him? In a way that's what bothers me the most. That I could have chosen so badly, could have been so stupid."

"He might argue that fighting to protect Griffin isn't weakness but strength."

"Protect him from what?" she exploded. "That's my point. Protect him from some specter he invented. Surely not from a twelve-year-old boy who loves Griffin, who would do anything for him."

"I see how angry you are, Marcia," he said. "So before we go on, I want to ask you a question. What do you want to happen here? Do you want to divorce Jeff, work out a custody arrangement? Or, as bad as you now say he is, do you want to repair your marriage?"

"Only if it can be repaired. I can forgive his affair. I hate it, but I can overcome it if he renounces her and recommits to his family. But if he continues this persecution of Danny, I can't go on. If I have to fight him, I will. I just don't know if he has any chance of carrying through on his threat to sue for custody."

"For that, you need a lawyer. My job is to help you define for yourself what you want and what is the best outcome for Danny."

"Well, what is the best outcome for him? It can't be good for him to feel this hostility and suspicion."

"No. Nor to think he is the cause of the problems between you and Jeff, the reason for your divorce and unhappiness."

She couldn't sit still a moment longer. She got up apologetically, but he didn't seem to mind, and paced around the room before she spoke. "So what do I do?" she asked. "What is the solution to all this?"

"Do you want to try again with Jeff?"

"I don't know. Maybe. I somehow can't believe the Jeff I fell in love with isn't in there somewhere. It's like he's been taken over by someone else."

"That's not an uncommon feeling when people are estranged. He's probably feeling the same way about you."

She stiffened. "Well, you've heard the whole story. What do you think I should do?"

"I think it might be a good idea to send Danny to summer camp in July. It would give you and Jeff a chance to work this out on your own. You might find a way to reignite some of your old feelings for each other. And it would be good for Danny to get away from all this as well. I could recommend several camps that specialize in children who are struggling and need a break."

"Are they therapeutic camps? I mean, are there doctors and psychologists on the staff?"

"Yes. But the one I like best has the main goal of giving the boys a happy summer. Sometimes that's the best therapy there is."

She shrugged. "Well, right now, Jeff isn't even living at home. I don't know where he is. Maybe he's moved in with his girlfriend. And it's March. There would be three more months before camp started. I don't know what we'd do until then and he didn't sound like he was ready to negotiate." She sat down again, dejected. "Maybe it's hopeless and I should just get a lawyer."

"I think that's something you should do in any case. And the sooner the better."

She nodded. That was a subject she would take up with Marian.

25

Marian arrived at five-thirty sharp, a surprise because Marian was one of those people who is habitually late. At school her friends referred to real time and "Marian time," which was like a clock that always ran a predictable half hour slow. She hadn't changed in all the years Marcia had known her. She had gained a few pounds since Marcia had seen her last but she still didn't wear any makeup, and her olive skin was as smooth and flawless as ever. Her early arrival was the first sign that Marian viewed this problem, quite correctly, in Marcia's view, as of the first order, needing the emergency services of a dedicated old friend. There were many other indications of how seriously Marian took the news. First there was her compassionate, longer-than-usual hug and her head-shaking and virtual hand-wringing. Then there was the fact that she called over the waiter and ordered wine even before she took off her coat. Finally, when both women, glasses in hand, had taken their first sips, Marian leaned forward.

"So what happened? I can't believe he'd do this to you after everything you went through. Did that bastard have an affair?"

Marcia gave a little smile. Before knowing anything about what had happened, Marian automatically blamed Jeff. Marcia knew this was not only support, it was generalizing from Marian's own experience, but it felt good anyway, even though it made Marcia a bit uncomfortable. This was new to her, this victim status, and she had too much pride to take much pleasure in it. Still, she was grateful. Marian's support couldn't change things, Marcia knew. But it could and did make her feel a bit better, just like in her childhood when her mother used to kiss the place she hurt and tell her that the kiss made the pain go away. It didn't, but in some magical way, it did.

Marcia tried to fill her in on the problems and tensions that had torn at their marriage since Eve died. She tried to explain that Jeff did genuinely seem to love Griffin, but completely misunderstood and refused to accept Danny. "The bottom line is that Jeff has threatened to sue me for custody of Griffin," Marcia said with a deep sigh. "I have to talk to a lawyer. I hoped you could recommend the one you used."

"Yes, of course, She's terrific. But she's expensive. You have no idea how much money it costs to get out of a marriage, unless you both agree on the terms of the divorce."

"I'm not sure it will come to that, but I need some advice. I'd like to make an appointment for a consultation."

"Wait a sec." Marian reached into her bag and fished around until she retrieved her iPhone. When she found the information she was looking for, she sent it to Marcia. "Her name is Gloria Stein. I just sent you her contact numbers. Call her right now and tell her we're friends. She's busy but I'm sure she'll try to see you as soon as she can."

Marcia thanked her, but didn't move. The enormity of what she'd just asked for had hit her hard.

"Wait a minute," Marian said, noticing her friend's distress. "Why don't *I* call Gloria? I might be able to get through to her directly."

A few minutes later, Marian was on the phone with Gloria Stein and had secured an appointment for Marcia the next day.

"Marian, you're amazing. How did you do that? I thought you said she was so busy."

"She is . . . Do you remember how complicated my divorce was? It cost a fortune and most of it went straight into the Hermès pocketbook of Gloria Stein. She owes me."

"Well, apparently, she knows it."

"She's probably seeing dollar signs arranged in a halo around your head. But don't worry. She's honest too. She'll tell you if he has a case."

They talked a little more, about Marian's life post-divorce, about the kids, about their jobs, and finally Marian looked at her watch and said she had to go home to relieve the nanny. Marcia was a little late too, so they exchanged hugs, promised to see and speak to each other more often, and said good-bye.

The next day, after sending Danny off to his new school with a hot breakfast and encouraging words, Marcia went to work. Her appointment with Gloria Stein was during her lunch break and she hoped to get a lot done before she left. She made a few calls, caught up on her messages and attended a sales meeting, and before she knew it, it was time to go. Just as she was putting on her coat, her cell phone rang. She glanced at it. Jeff. She hesitated, but picked it up.

"Yes?" she began, her voice cold.

"Marcia, I'd like to come by tonight. We need to talk."

"I think we talked enough. In fact, I'm just on my way to see a divorce lawyer to go over what you said the last time we had a talk."

"A divorce lawyer?" He seemed taken aback, even shocked. "Why?"

Now it was her turn to be shocked. "Why? Don't you remember our last conversation? You threatened to take Griffin away from me. You threatened to sue for custody."

"Oh shit. I was angry. I hadn't thought things through. I didn't mean it."

"I think you did."

His voice hardened. "You can't tell me what I meant or didn't mean, Marcia."

She sighed. "Listen, I don't have time for your lawyer's voice. I have to meet her in half an hour. Come over tonight if you want to see Griffin, and if there's anything to say, we can talk then."

"Of course there's something to—" She hung up before he could finish.

She could tell that Gloria Stein was as expensive as Marian had reported just by seeing her office. On the top floor of a modern steel and glass Park Avenue office building with expansive views of the New York skyline, the office screamed "money." The waiting room was decorated with Danish modern furniture and featured lush beige carpets, on which Marcia didn't see one stain, and an original Botero on one wall, immediately recognizable by the full-figured women it portrayed. On the opposite wall were framed photographs of African wildlife, one striking series of a lioness stalking a wildebeest, followed by a shot of the kill and then one of the lion devouring her dead prey. A none-too-subtle visual parallel of the work of a hotshot divorce lawyer, Marcia thought. It made her uncomfortable, even a little sad.

When she was ushered into Gloria's office, she was met by a thin, tall woman in a Chanel suit with very short, chic black hair, small gold hoop earrings and enough makeup for a fashion runway. She was sharp featured and angular and her lips glistened with unblotted lipstick, giving her a contradictory air of aggressive elegance. She strode across the room, shook hands with Marcia and took a seat at her desk, indicating a black leather chair across from her for Marcia. The lawyer got right down to business, listening carefully to Marcia's description of everything she thought relevant up to and including Jeff's threat to sue for custody of Griffin.

Gloria didn't waste time with her response. "He doesn't have a case," she said. "Not with what you told me. You don't take a baby from his mother because his adopted brother had a few problems at school. You say he's a lawyer, and I'm sure he knows that. He's just trying to bully you."

"We haven't actually adopted Danny yet," Marcia said. "I want to, but Jeff always puts it off."

"That doesn't matter. As things stand now there is no case and you don't need me unless you intend to pursue a divorce. But you should know that as Griffin's father, your husband will have a great deal of access to him, even if you become the custodial parent. If he wants to share custody, he will likely succeed in that. But that is simply the usual procedure in cases like yours. It has nothing to do with . . . what is the name of the boy?"

"Danny."

"Yes, sorry. It has nothing to do with Danny or your husband's belief that the boy is or could be a serious negative influence." She waited for Marcia to respond, but Marcia, relieved, sat still, processing what she'd just heard. She had the feeling Gloria thought she was wasting her time.

"Do you want to proceed with a divorce?"

Marcia hesitated. "I don't know. Not yet."

Gloria nodded, pushed her chair back and stood up. "Then we are finished for today. If you change your mind, make an appointment to see me and we will take it from there." They shook hands, Marcia thanked her and turned to go. She could feel Gloria Stein watching her as she walked to the door so she lifted her chin and stood up straighter.

Danny was home by the time she arrived and she asked him how his first day went. He said the kids were much nicer than at Claremont and the work looked easier so he thought it was pretty good. He was always hard to read and reluctant to share his feelings, so she couldn't judge how sincere he was, but he seemed more upbeat than usual, so she accepted his answer and hoped for the best.

Jeff arrived before dinner. Griffin's face broke into a joyful smile when he saw him and he lifted his arms to be picked up. "Hey, buddy," Jeff said, grinning and lifting him high into the air. Griffin laughed and Jeff threw him up and caught him, a game Griff loved and Marcia hated, but she held her tongue. Jeff asked if he could feed him dinner and take over the bedtime ritual, and Marcia said he could. Danny hung back as soon as he saw Jeff. He said a shy hello, looking at the floor, and then retreated to his own room. Marcia called him back to the kitchen and served him his dinner while Jeff was giving Griffin a bath and getting him ready for bed. Danny said he wasn't hungry, but he wolfed down the spaghetti and meatballs she'd made, gulped a glass of orange juice and, claiming he had homework, asked if he could go to his room. She knew he was uncomfortable with Jeff around, so she said yes. She didn't sit down to dinner herself, taking bites and tastes while she cooked and finishing what was left

on Danny's plate. She cleaned up the dishes, brewed a
pot of coffee and went to see how Griffin was doing.
She stood in the doorway of Griff's room and watched
Jeff sitting with him in the rocking chair, reading *Pat
the Bunny*. She felt an overwhelming sadness as memories of how all this was meant to be swept over her. After
Jeff put Griffin in his crib, Marcia wound up the musical mobile, arranged his pacifiers around him, handing
him one, which he popped into his mouth. Watching
this, as if they didn't remember for that moment that
they were alienated from each other, Jeff and Marcia
caught each other's eye and smiled proudly. The moment
passed as soon as they tiptoed out, however. Marcia
paused outside the bedroom door waiting for the howls
of protest, but they didn't come. Griff must have really
been tired.

In the living room she offered Jeff coffee but he asked
for a scotch and she poured herself a glass of wine. How
could it be, she wondered, after so long and so much love
that they could be so estranged? Finally he spoke.

"So, did you go to see a divorce lawyer today?"

"Yes."

"Is that really what you want?"

"You make it sound like I initiated it."

"I haven't been to a divorce lawyer."

"No, but you threatened to sue me for custody of my
son."

"Our son. And you knew I just said that out of anger."

"I didn't know that. I don't know you as well as I
thought I did."

"What does that mean?"

"I think it's clear."

"So what did she say?"

"She said you have no case and I don't have to worry."

He finished his scotch and poured himself another.

"Look, I came here on a peace mission. I want us to try again. I'll come home and we'll do our best to work things out."

She was considering whether she thought they could when he added, "I mean, we owe that to Griffin."

She stiffened. "What about us? Don't we owe it to us?"

"Yes, of course. That's a given."

"How is it a given if you aren't even faithful to our marriage?"

He looked exasperated. "Marcia, what are we talking about? Is this about your anger because of what I said last time or about Ilana or Danny or what?"

He had raised his voice and she looked nervously toward Danny's room, hoping he couldn't hear. "Please lower your voice. It's about all of it. To start with, we can't try again unless you and Danny try again. I spoke to Dr. Benson today. He suggested we send him to a special therapeutic camp he can recommend for the summer. He said it would be good for him and for us too; it would give us a chance to try to reestablish our relationship without the constant tension. But you'd have to be willing to wait until the summer—that's three full months—and make an effort to be nice to him during the time he's here. Could you do that?"

"I don't honestly know. I was hoping you'd be willing

to send him to a boarding school I heard about. Did you read the brochures I left here?"

Her disappointment was keen. She shrugged. "Yeah. I'm not ready for that step."

No one spoke. Then he took a deep breath and let the air out through his mouth. He said, "All right. I'll give it a try." His tone was skeptical.

"I don't think it will work if that's your attitude, Jeff."

"I said I'd try. What more do you want?"

"I want you to mean it."

"I mean it, goddamnit."

"Please don't talk so loud. I don't want him to hear. And you know, we haven't even really discussed this Ilana thing. I mean, you're acting like that was nothing. But you lied to me, you slept with another woman, you betrayed me. How do I forget that? How do I go on from there?"

She fought back tears. That was the last thing she wanted to do now, show weakness. She didn't want to beg him to apologize. She wanted him to do it on his own and then plead with her to accept.

He looked away, like he was concentrating on something in the corner of the room. "There are all kinds of betrayals," he said.

"What?"

He looked back at her. "You heard me. You pushed me away. You chose Danny over me. You knew how I felt but you insisted on taking him and keeping him no matter what he did or how he behaved or how much he disrespected me."

She was stunned. Her voice was cold. "So you're saying it was okay what you did? That it was actually my fault?"

"Shit, that sounds terrible. I don't mean that. But I think in a way that's what I felt. I guess it was kind of my excuse, my self-justification. I'm not saying it's right. I shouldn't have done it. I'm sorry."

His words were sorry but his tone wasn't. He could have come to her. He could have reached for her. He could have put his arms around her and reassured her that he loved her, that he never loved Ilana. She might have accepted that, but he didn't.

"You don't sound sorry," she said quietly, exerting great self-control. She took a while to answer, thinking very intensely before she did. Finally she nodded and pursed her lips together. "Okay," she said. "Come back. You try harder with Danny and I'll try hard to forget what you did and how you justified it. As you say, we owe it to Griffin."

He winced. She got up and started to leave the room. At the doorway, she turned. "Will you stay here tonight?"

"I'd like to. I have to check out of the hotel and pick up my stuff, but I'll come back."

"Have you told her you're doing this?"

"I told her she and I were through, so what I do doesn't concern her anymore."

She bit her upper lip. "You can't sleep in our bedroom."

"Yes, that's what I figured." She could feel his anger. She wasn't sorry.

"It's going to take me a while to get over this. You can't have expected there would be no consequences."

That faraway look came over his face again. "Fine," he said. "I'll sleep in the guest room."

She nodded, irritated. How did he manage to construe this so that he was the victim? she wondered bitterly as she turned to go. He stayed in the living room after she left and finished his scotch. Then he picked up his coat and slipped out quietly, closing the door behind him.

26

Marcia hadn't wanted Danny to hear her conversation with Jeff, but he did, and not by accident. He knew something important was happening and, as before, he cracked open his bedroom door just a little, so they wouldn't notice. He stood by the door, his ear to the opening. Of course he didn't hear it all, but he knew by the time Jeff left that Jeff and Marcia had narrowly avoided a divorce, at least for the time being. Jeff was coming back and Marcia had made him promise to be nicer to him. That provided little relief. He didn't care if Jeff was nice to him—he knew they would never like each other and Jeff would never trust him. Mostly he hoped Jeff would just ignore him. But he worried about the camp Marcia mentioned. He didn't want to go away, not even for the summer and especially not to some camp Dr. Benson recommended. He'd heard of those places for

"special" kids and he knew perfectly well what they meant
by "special." Anyway, it would mean he'd be away from
Griffin for the whole summer and around a bunch of
weird kids he didn't know and wouldn't like. Maybe Griff
wouldn't even remember him when he came back. And
it would give Jeff time to turn Marcia against him.

He was upset and, as always when he was unhappy, he
wanted to talk to Raul. He couldn't get out of the house
right then, he knew. But he remembered that the teacher
had said tomorrow was early dismissal because the teachers had a meeting or something like that. He had carried
home that note for Marcia, reading it first, of course, in
case it was something about him. But it was just a notice
that everyone got. He was so relieved he smiled through
his fears and started to hatch a plan. He could meet Raul
when Claremont kids got out at 2:45. Marcia would be at
work and he'd tell Berta he had to stay late at school for
extra math help. If he was careful, no one would know.

The next day it all seemed to work out exactly as he
had hoped. He got out of school at twelve-thirty and had
to hang around for a couple of hours until Claremont's
dismissal. He knew because of what happened last time
that he'd better not pay a visit to any stores, so he just
stopped at a newsstand and bought a Spider-Man comic
book and then checked his change and realized he still
had enough for a Coke so he stopped at a deli on the
corner and took a seat at the counter. He ordered a Coke,
which he drank slowly while he read his comic book.
Then he went to Central Park and walked around for a
while before taking the subway to Claremont, arriving a

few minutes before dismissal. He waited in front until he heard the last bell and then crossed the street and watched from a safe distance—he didn't want to run into anyone he knew—as the kids started to trickle out. First he saw the young ones with their teachers looking for the parents or nannies who picked them up, then the older ones, who came out on their own. He ducked behind a truck when he noticed a bunch of kids from his old class, but there was still no sign of Raul and he shifted impatiently, peering into the group. Some of the kids formed into smaller groups, talking and laughing before they drifted away. It was getting late, but Raul didn't come out. Danny waited and waited until the last kid had left and still no Raul. It hadn't occurred to him that Raul might be absent. Maybe he was home sick. He didn't know what to do. He wanted to go to Raul's house but what if Raul's mother was there? That would be just his luck. He didn't think she'd be home because he knew she worked almost every day, so he decided he would take the train to Raul's house and try to figure it out when he got there.

He was lucky. He was on the corner, walking toward Raul's building, when he saw Julio coming down the stairs, two steps at a time. If Julio was there then Raul's mother wasn't, that's for sure, Danny thought. The boys idolized Julio; he was cool and grown-up and had a faint whiff of danger about him. Just hanging out with him made them feel brave and rebellious. Danny waved to him as he got closer and Julio stopped. He didn't smile or fist-bump like he usually did. He just stopped and stared for a minute. Something about him didn't look right. His shoulders were slumped and his face looked darker, like he was mad about something. That's how he acted too, like he was mad. He didn't even say hello. He couldn't be mad at him, Danny thought, he didn't do anything—he'd just got there. Maybe he was mad at Raul. Or maybe he's mad because I'm not supposed to be here, Danny thought, worried. He wondered if he should run away, but decided that would be bad.

"Hi, Julio," he said tentatively, feeling shy around him for the first time.

Julio didn't answer at first. He looked around nervously. A woman passed, pulling a grocery cart. Otherwise the street was empty.

"Is Raul home?"

"Yeah. The little bastard is home."

Scared, Danny put his head down and started to walk toward the steps.

"Wait up," Julio said. His grimace faded and he forced a tight smile. "Listen, kid, you gotta do somethin' for me."

Danny stopped short and turned to him. Julio approached closer and spoke in a hoarse whisper.

"This is a secret, you got it? You can't tell nobody, not even Raul. Think you can handle that?"

Danny nodded, flattered.

"Remember when Raul didn't wanna hang with you because his mama told him not to? What did I say? You remember? I said friends gotta look out for each other."

Danny nodded again, slowly.

"So, we're friends, right?"

"Yeah, I guess."

Julio looked around nervously again, and seeing a man in a black down jacket walking a dog he waited till he passed. Then Julio pulled a small cardboard box closed with masking tape out of his backpack. "Quick, put this in your backpack," he said. Danny hesitated.

"Do it," Julio ordered. "Fast."

Confused and scared, Danny obeyed.

"I'll get it from you in a few days. Hide it in your house. Someplace cool where no one goes but you, got it?"

"But how will I—"

"I'll find you. Don't show nobody. Don't tell nobody. You gotta show me you understand."

Danny nodded. Julio was even talking different than usual. It made him sound tougher, scarier.

"Say it. Say 'I understand.'"

"I understand," Danny whispered, trying really hard not to cry.

"Now go home and put it away."

"But I want to see Raul. I gotta talk to him."

"Not today, kid. Today you go home and do like I told you." His voice was hard, scary.

Danny knew this wasn't right. He knew it was probably really bad and he could get in a lot of trouble. But he didn't know what to do and he didn't have anyone except Raul whom he felt he could ask. And now Julio wasn't even letting him talk to Raul. Julio took a $20 bill from his pocket and stuffed it into Danny's hand. "Don't take the subway. Take a cab and get off a block away from

your house. Then walk home and hide it in the best place
you can find." He stared at him for a minute. His voice
got softer when he said, "And after, when I pick it up, I'll
take you and your buddy Raul someplace cool, okay? You
can make some money too. It's just a few days. You'll hear
from me." He turned and walked toward the subway, his
hands in his pockets, taking long strides.

Danny stood frozen after Julio left. Then he started
to walk toward the corner but when he saw Julio disappear into the subway he turned back and ran to Raul's
house. He banged on the door and Raul's father answered.
Danny didn't expect this and he worried that he'd be
thrown out, but his father just glanced at him and turned
back inside. "Raul," he shouted, "it's for you." By the
time he and Raul were alone in Raul's room Danny had
almost forgotten the reason he'd come in the first place.
Now he wanted to talk about Julio. After begging Raul
to swear he wouldn't ever tell Julio that he was there, he
told Raul everything that had just happened. Raul just
shrugged.

"Yeah. He tried to get me to hide it here but no way.
My ma finds everything. I told him but he got mad."

"What's in the box anyway? Did he tell you?"

"Nah. But I know it's something my ma wouldn't like
and neither would the cops. So hide it good."

Danny paused. He reached into his backpack and took
it out. The boys looked at the sealed box and at each other,
scared and excited at the same time.

"Should we open it?" Raul asked, reaching for it.

"I don't know. What if Julio finds out?"

"How could he find out?"

"I don't know. I don't want to." Danny grabbed the box and stuffed it back into his backpack. "I better do like he said."

Danny figured he had no choice. He started to think where he could hide it and then he remembered why he'd come to see Raul. It didn't seem so bad to be going to camp anymore. It would get him away from Julio. He wouldn't know where he was. Still, he told Raul about Marcia and Jeff and how Jeff did something that made Marcia want to divorce him but she said he could stay if he was nicer to Danny.

"What did he do? Did he screw another woman?"

Danny's eyes widened. He knew that word, of course, the kids bandied it about all the time, but he'd never thought of it in relation to Marcia and Jeff. He tried not to sound shocked. "I dunno. I don't think he'd do *that*."

"Why not? That's what my uncle did. My aunt found out and he got in a lot of trouble 'cause he hit her."

"Who? The other girl?"

"No, stupid. My aunt. She called the police."

"I don't think that happened."

"I swear."

"No. I mean with Marcia and Jeff. Anyway, what should I do?"

"I don't know. You better go home and hide that box. That's the first thing."

Danny bit his lip, stood up and grabbed his coat.

"Yeah. See ya."

He decided not to take a cab and waste all that money.

He might need it, he figured. So he took the subway like he always did, thinking the whole time about where he could hide Julio's package. He got out at Ninety-sixth Street and was walking toward his house when he saw the cop on the corner, the one who had three times taken him home. He tried to turn around quickly to avoid him, but he'd been seen.

"Hey, kid, Danny, how you doin'?"

He stopped and turned to face him. He tried to smile and look casual but he was nervous and it showed. "I'm good," he answered. "Just on my way home." He waved and started to walk toward his apartment building.

The cop looked at his watch. "School out late?" He sounded friendly but Danny thought he was suspicious. Danny looked at his watch. It was four-thirty. At normal dismissal, he would have gotten home an hour earlier. "Nah," he replied. "I had to stay late."

"How come? Detention?"

"No," Danny said quickly. "I just needed help in math."

"Ah, well, that's good. Never be afraid to ask for help."

"Yeah. Thanks."

The cop reached toward him and Danny froze, but he was just putting his hand on his shoulder. "Well, be good," he said as he squeezed it. "See you around."

The cop turned and sauntered jauntily down the street, and Danny walked as fast as he could to his house. He didn't want to think about it but he couldn't help imagining what might have happened if the cop had looked in his backpack. He would have found the box.

Julio would have been really mad. Danny was scared. He didn't even know what was in the box but no one would believe him, he thought. He pictured Jeff yelling at him. He pictured Marcia crying. He pictured his mother up in heaven feeling so sad, and his eyes filled with tears. He put his hands in his pockets and felt the twenty-dollar bill. He should have taken the cab, like Julio said. Well, he didn't but he was okay, he thought. He had made it so far. Now he had to get into the house and hide the box someplace good.

He entered the apartment quietly but Berta and Griffin were right near the front door and saw him immediately. Griffin squealed with delight and held his arms out, but this time Danny just gave him a half smile and kept walking to his room.

"What's the matter with you?" Berta shouted after him. "Hang up your coat."

He sped up.

"You had a bad day?" Berta asked, almost sympathetically.

"Nah," he mumbled. "I just got a lot of homework to do."

"That's a first," Berta huffed to Griffin, sitting him in a playpen with a pile of his toys. "Come get a snack," Berta shouted. "It's in the kitchen."

"I'm not hungry," Danny answered, also shouting from behind his closed door.

This caused Berta to walk to his bedroom and open the door. "Do you feel okay?" she asked.

He had just taken off his backpack and thrown his coat

on the bed. He was looking around his room trying to find a spot that no one would clean or look in. He was startled by the door opening and he jumped.

Berta laughed. "You look like you saw a ghost. It's just me."

"This is *my* room," he yelled, furious. "You're supposed to knock. Even Marcia knocks. She said you're supposed to knock too. I'm gonna tell."

"Okay, okay," she said in a huff, leaving the room. "I thought you was sick."

"Close the door," he shouted after her. And when she didn't, he slammed it tight himself.

Berta returned to Griffin and picked him up. "He like a teenager now," she grumbled. "Like we didn't have enough troubles in this house."

Danny looked wildly around the room. He wished he had a lock on his door. He'd asked Marcia if he could but she said no. No one had locks on any door in the house except Marcia and Jeff, for their bedroom, and they practically never used it. He took his desk chair and propped it against the door under the handle like he'd seen on TV. Then he surveyed the room. He couldn't use the closet or the dresser because Berta or Marcia were always going in there for one thing or another. He couldn't just put it under his bed because Berta sometimes vacuumed there. He looked at the closet a second time. There was a top shelf which no one used—it had some cardboard boxes of clothes that didn't fit him anymore and some stuff he took when he'd left his home, including some pictures of him and his mom when he was little. He considered that for a minute. No one would look there but him. No one cared about that stuff but him. He took the desk chair from the door and dragged it over to the closet, stood on it and pulled down the biggest cardboard box. It was heavier than he expected and when he dropped it the contents spilled on the floor. He glanced nervously at the door and quickly picked everything up and threw it back in the box, then placed the box on his bed and started looking through it. He hadn't really been able to bring himself to look at any of these things before and his heart was beating fast. He pulled out a tin box from the bottom and opened it. There it was, right on top, his mother, staring up at him after all this time. She was smiling, looking at the camera. He remembered taking that picture. She had bought him one of those disposable cameras and he was fooling around with it, he remembered. It was just before Marcia and Jeff ruined his life, he thought, before he'd ever heard of them or Claremont or Raul. He felt a physical burn in his chest and he recognized it. It was the bad sadness. The kind he'd had almost all the time the first few months after his mom died. He didn't want to look anymore. He had the weird feeling that his mom was watching him and was disappointed so he quickly put the cover back on the tin box. Then he took the box Julio had given him out of his backpack. It was kind of heavy, he realized, and he shook it to try to figure out what it was, but nothing moved inside. He pushed aside his old baseball jersey and his old cleats that didn't fit him anymore, lifted the tin box and put Julio's box at the very bottom. Then he stuffed everything else back around it and, struggling with the weight, he managed after a few tries to put it back on top of his closet. Satisfied, he moved the chair back to his desk and lay on his bed. He didn't feel better. He felt scared and he thought he would go on feeling scared every minute of every day until Julio took that box away.

27

The first night Jeff moved back into their apartment, he brought her two dozen long-stemmed roses. It was a sign of how little she forgave him that she secretly scorned them. She preferred peonies. Or daffodils, she thought wistfully, remembering again the time Charlie, her first college boyfriend, had picked wildflowers and wrapped them in paper towels for her. Roses were so generic, she thought, so 1950s, so reminiscent of some cheesy movie about a romantic gesture from a repentant husband. The memory of Charlie brought a sweet smile to her lips and she pretended it was in gratitude for the roses. She swept the flowers into her arms and carried them to the kitchen, where she cut all the stems at a diagonal and placed them in lukewarm water in her favorite vase. She noticed that, as usual, they had no scent and, still awash in memories, she thought of the roses that grew in her family's garden when she was a child, before her mother's illness changed everything. Her mother prided herself on the perfect blooms of red and yellow, and Marcia still recalled how she would play amid the sweet scent they emitted. She sometimes went close to them to inhale deeper, and even though she was careful, and even though her mother always shouted from the back porch for her to watch out for the thorns, she always pricked herself and drew back sharply, sucking the drop of blood from her wounded finger. What happened to that scent? she asked herself as she bent again, inhaled and smelled nothing. Gone. Like so many things. She wondered if this was how it would be from now on with Jeff—a marriage that looked like a marriage the way these lifeless, odorless roses looked like roses but was false at the core, full of little lies and hypocrisies with few real intimacies.

She had decided to try to stay with him simply because it was easier—she couldn't face a court battle over Griffin, a bitter divorce, a rehashing in court of their lives together, ordained times when she could and couldn't see her own child. And she wanted to protect Danny, whom she feared would come off badly in a legal battle. This way, if she could just get over her anger and jealousy, she might be able to salvage something that at least resembled a family, even if it wasn't the marriage she once thought she had.

He came up behind her and put his arms around her, and her body stiffened involuntarily. He had to have noticed, but he didn't react. "I'm sorry I missed dinner tonight, but that won't happen again. I'll be here and we can have family dinners most of the time now," he said. She smiled again, sadly, this time.

"That will be great," she said. But what she thought was, Too little, too late.

But she had decided to move forward and that, she realized, meant trying very hard not to look back. He had given up Ilana, but he had never really renounced her. By seeking to justify his affair, to attribute it to Danny and her unswerving loyalty to keeping him rather than compromising in some way that Jeff too could have found satisfying, he ended up not sounding very sorry for what she viewed as an almost unforgivable transgression. He had broken his vows to her, he had lied and cheated, and although when she chastised him in her mind, she always said it was the lies and her subsequent lack of trust that were the worst, she knew that wasn't true, not really. The worst was that he had wanted another woman and he had acted on it. She tried not to picture him with her, flirting first in that way she knew so well—did he tease her and make her laugh at herself the way he did when they first met? She tried not to imagine the intimacy that preceded the sex, the kissing and touching and finally the two of them in bed together. Some of those nights he had come home after he'd just been with Ilana. How had he felt, crawling into bed with his wife, still smelling of his girlfriend, to have lain next to her, even made love to her sometimes, as though they were still married? Married. The word had meaning for her way beyond the legal ceremony and she knew it did for him as well. Or she knew it used to. Or he just said those things and didn't mean

them. That was part of the fallout of this affair; she didn't
know what to believe, what was real, what she could trust.
It made her question not only their future but their past.
They had discussed their ideas of marriage early on when
they talked about whether they would take that step together, tighten their bond willingly and formally. It was
a decision to enter into a sexual intimacy so exclusive it
meant that each of them agreed to give up all others in
order to maintain it, and so deep that they were each
willing to promise it would last forever. "In sickness and
in health, till death do us part"—those weren't just old-
fashioned words to her. She didn't want to write her own
ceremony, as many of her friends did; she wanted to say
those ancient words, make those sacred promises. And
she meant them, even during her anger at him over
Danny, even when he hardly came home at night and
when he did they were tense and unhappy. She always
thought it was temporary. This hostility wasn't real, it
wasn't "them," it would change if she just held on. So
when he had that affair, when he allowed another woman
to invade that delicate space they had built together, she
needed more than his agreeing to stop doing it. She
needed true repentance and she didn't think he felt that.

But she was going to try to move forward anyway and
see if she could make it work. She felt nervous the first
time they sat down to dinner together again as a family.
She could tell Danny did too—he returned to the reti-
cent, shy boy he'd been at the beginning, barely looking
up from his plate and speaking only when he was spoken
to. Jeff tried to engage him, she could see.

"So, Danny, how do you like your new school?" he asked him.

"It's good," Danny mumbled.

"How is it different from Claremont?"

"Danny shrugged. "I don't know."

She stiffened, expecting Jeff to show annoyance, but he didn't.

"Yeah, it's hard to say, right? But I meant, is the work harder or easier?"

Danny shrugged again. "Easier."

Marcia sliced into the silence that followed. "What about the other kids? Do you miss Raul a lot?"

Danny stiffened. Were they trying to trick him? "Yeah," he answered.

"Maybe I should call his mother and try to arrange a time for you to get together. Maybe now that you're not in the same school she'll feel better about your seeing each other sometimes. Would you like that?"

"No, that's okay."

"Maybe it would be better not to," Jeff said. "I mean, it will just make separating harder. He needs to make new friends. Right, Danny?"

Danny nodded uneasily. "I have a lot of homework tonight," he said. "Could I go do it?"

"Are you done eating? There's a nice dessert tonight. Brownies and ice cream. Are you sure you don't want to wait?" Marcia asked.

"Nah, that's okay. Thanks."

"Well, sure, then. Go ahead," Marcia said.

It wasn't a perfect family dinner, but it was better than

she'd seen before and better than she'd feared. It was clear that Jeff was trying.

The next day Jeff was the one to get Griffin out of his crib in the morning. Marcia cooked a hot breakfast for everyone. Danny was late coming to the table and Marcia started to go to his room to hurry him up. "That's okay. I'll get him," Jeff said. Marcia worried how that would go, but there didn't seem to be a problem. They all sat down to breakfast. Marcia had made scrambled eggs, which she knew was Jeff's preference. "I know you don't like them, Danny," she said, when she saw Danny's face. "I'm making you some oatmeal."

"He should eat what the family eats," Jeff said. "He doesn't need a private chef."

"It's okay, Jeff," she snapped. "This is how we do it." He didn't answer. She served the oatmeal and Danny barely ate it, which Jeff noticed. Danny looked at the kitchen clock and grabbed his coat and backpack and rushed to the door, shouting goodbye as he left. When he was gone there was a moment's silence. Griffin started to cry—he always cried when Danny left—and Marcia lifted him from his high chair and wiped his face. "That's okay, Griff, he'll be back," she crooned. "Soon Berta will be here and you'll go to the park."

Jeff poured himself another cup of coffee. "Listen, Marcia, I didn't say that about breakfast to be a dick. If you want me to have a relationship with him, you've got to let me have a say too. I'd have said the same thing if Griffin was older and you were cooking separate meals for him."

They heard Berta at the door. "Where's my boy?" she cooed as she came into the kitchen and took Griffin in her arms. He didn't seem to mind. He was happy to see her, flashing a big smile, putting his arms out and leaning toward her. This always produced a mixed reaction in Marcia. She was happy he truly seemed to love Berta but she was also just a little bit jealous that he was so willing to leave her arms without a backward glance. Berta left, taking Griffin to his room to get dressed while engaging in a nonstop monologue about what she had planned for them to do that day.

"You're right," Marcia said, pouring another cup of coffee and offering it to Jeff. He shook his head, so she kept it for herself. "I'm just not used to that kind of involvement from you. It's a transition. I'm sorry." She paused. "But I don't mind making him a bowl of instant oatmeal if he hates scrambled eggs."

"Isn't he old enough to make it himself if it's different from what you are cooking for the rest of the family? Wouldn't that be good for him?"

"Maybe," she said. "We can try that."

They finished their coffee and busied themselves getting showered and dressed. They left the building together and waved goodbye at the corner. She walked to the subway deep in thought. He'd been back home for less than twenty-four hours, she thought, and so far it wasn't too bad. She should have felt encouraged but she felt sad. She was grateful they were both trying so hard but dejected that their relationship had devolved into good intentions and cautious attempts at civility when it used to seem so easy, so natural. As she stood on the train—it was crowded this morning and she couldn't get a seat—she forced her attention back to the workday ahead of her and thought that there might be a book in this, the whole area of making do in a relationship, the subtle change from infatuation to love to adaptation and then what? To tolerance, she thought. To patience. To trying, through goodwill and effort, to fit the occasional round peg through the square hole, and when it didn't work, not throwing away the whole puzzle. She even knew to whom she would suggest this topic—Brynn Godson, a lively thirty-year-old writer who'd had a big success five years earlier with a book on young couples and alternate lifestyles. Brynn had gotten married three years ago and might be the perfect person to investigate this subject. Marcia became more enthusiastic about this idea as she considered it and placed a call to the author after she settled into her office. Brynn liked the project immediately.

"But you make it sound like it's all downhill," Brynn said. "Maybe at the end in successful marriages, the puzzle is a little malleable. The round peg squares off a little and the square holes get slightly rounded, and it fits, and when that friction ends, when they stop trying to fit that one peg into that one hole, there's time to explore all the other things that might fit into that box. Maybe that's what people mean when they say the love changes but it doesn't die, it deepens."

"I knew you'd be the right person for this," Marcia said, laughing. She loved this about Brynn—her tendency to run with a metaphor even if sometimes she crashed into the nearest wall. "That's a great idea," she said, "but we've probably taken the round-peg thing about as far as we can. Anyway, think about it, will you?"

"No problem," Brynn replied. "I've already begun."

28

Jeff suggested they go to Woodstock for the weekend. Marcia wasn't sure she was ready. Woodstock was special for them. They had bought the house there early in their marriage and had been close and carefree there. She remembered that they had revisited the idea of surrogacy at their dinner table when Grace suggested it. The tension that conversation had produced seemed so benign these days, especially since they had ultimately decided to follow Grace's advice. The house and the town would bring back so many memories, and Marcia feared it would make her sad to return to the place with everything the same except them. But in the spirit of trying to make their arrangement work, she agreed.

It was a beautiful March day. The sun was high and piercingly bright, and the air, although cold, was clear and dry. They drove up the long driveway to their house in silence. A light breeze stirred a few brown leaves that had piled up around the rocks and in the crevices of the stone pathway. It had snowed a few days before but most of the snow had melted, though there were a few brush-strokes of white on their front steps and on the branches of the trees most shaded from the sun. They unloaded the car, lifting out Griffin's car seat first. Marcia opened the front door. Danny was right behind her. She put Griffin's seat on the floor in the living room and asked Danny to go back to the car and see what he could carry in while she went from room to room turning up the thermostats. She glanced over her shoulder to see him skulking slowly toward the car and wondered if there was something wrong. The house was cold and she moved Griffin away from the window and covered him with an extra blanket. Then she went to the woodpile on the back porch and carried in some logs. By the time Jeff and Danny had unloaded the car she had a fire dancing in the stone fireplace and had taken Griffin out of his chair. She was holding him in front of the fire, delighted at his fas-cination with the light, when she heard Danny and Jeff at the door. She could hear them arguing as they entered.

"It's not that heavy, Danny. It's just a bag of groceries."

"But it's got a lot of heavy things in it. Why do I have to carry the one with the milk in it? That's the worst one."

"I'm pretty sure you can handle it. Haven't you ever helped carry groceries before?"

"No. In the city you don't have to. I don't know why we have to come here."

"Because it's our house and we like it."

"I'm twelve. Why can't I just stay home in New York?"

"Because you're twelve."

Danny stomped into the house without wiping his feet on the doormat and slammed the package down on the table.

"Danny, there are eggs in that bag," Jeff shouted. "I bet you broke every one."

Marcia handed Griffin to Jeff and walked over to the table, where she opened the egg container. Two of the eggs were broken. She frowned at Danny and shook her head. She looked quizzically at Jeff. He shrugged his shoulders. Neither knew why Danny was acting like this.

She had invited Grace and Mike for dinner that night, and she called Grace to tell her they'd arrived and to confirm the time. She bustled around the house putting away groceries as Jeff played with Griffin. Danny hung around watching, shifting from foot to foot, a bored look on his face that Marcia found annoying. "Danny, why don't you help me put these away?"

He went through some of the motions, but slowly and rebelliously, making it clear this was a huge imposition. She'd never seen him like this before.

"Danny, are you all right?"

"Yeah. Fine."

"Are you angry at something?"

"No." He slammed down the orange juice container he was holding. "Why can't you just leave me alone?"

She stopped unloading the groceries and stared at him. "Can I please just go out?" he asked.

"Yeah. Go."

He slammed the door when he left. She searched her mind for something that could explain this behavior. He was screaming for attention, she thought, even negative attention was clearly better than nothing to him right now. Why? Was this a cry for help or just the real beginning of adolescence, and was this what they had in store for them from now on? Or was it simply that Jeff was back and he was happier and more comfortable with him gone? She continued putting away the groceries, deep in thought. She heard Griffin laughing and one of his toys squeaking repeatedly, and looked up to see that Jeff had put him into the fenced-off area in the living room surrounded by his toys. Glancing out the window, she spotted Jeff outside playing catch with Danny. She felt a rush of gratitude and hope. There was no doubt he was trying. Even now, with Danny worse than he'd been before, Jeff was making an effort to engage him.

The rest of the day went more smoothly. Danny seemed less sulky by the time he came inside, his cheeks flushed from the cold, his hands stiff because he hadn't worn a coat or gloves. The weather had been crazy— this felt more like February than March. He asked if he could watch TV and she said yes before Jeff could say no. "There's a game on later," Jeff said. "You interested?"

Danny seemed surprised. "Yeah."

She hadn't known him to watch basketball before, so she knew he must have agreed because he welcomed doing something with Jeff. Again she felt a surge of hope.

Jeff walked up to her and impulsively put his arm

around her and squeezed her shoulder encouragingly. His hands were cold and she jumped. They laughed and locked eyes. "Thank you," she said. He smiled.

Grace and Mike arrived at six as planned. They were as obsessed with their kids as ever, complaining about Stephie as soon as they walked in. "She is so bright," Grace said, "so she knows just what our weak points are. She says, 'Mommy, why can't I come?' And I say, 'Because this is a grown-up party,' and she says, 'It's not fair. You always go away without me.' And then I feel guilty, and I swear, she knows it and that's why she said it. And the baby fusses when we go because he's not used to the babysitter and Stephie is so mad at us that she doesn't try to console him the way she sometimes does." She smiled, embarrassed.

"Grace, I'm so sorry I didn't invite you all. Of course you could have brought them. Our kids are here." Marcia remembered how jealous she was the first time she heard Grace's litany of stories about her child. It seemed a world away. "Well, let me see that baby of yours," Grace said. Jeff was feeding him while Marcia was putting the finishing touches on the goulash she was cooking. "Oh, he's so adorable," Grace said. "Hi, little guy. I can't wait till you and Petey can have a play date." Marcia called Danny out of the TV room to say hello. He didn't answer and he didn't come. "Maybe he didn't hear me," Marcia said.

"He heard you," Jeff said. "Danny, get out here right now or I'll turn off that television and you won't watch it again today."

Danny emerged.

"You've heard me talk about Grace and Mike," Marcia said. "They'd like to say hello to you."

"Hello," Danny said, not looking up.

"Hi, Danny, how are you doing?"

"Fine," he mumbled, still looking at the floor.

"Do you like your new school?"

"It's okay. Can I go now?"

Marcia nodded. "He's not usually like that," she said apologetically. "Something is bothering him but we don't know what it is."

"He's twelve. It's probably started."

"What?"

"You know what. Adolescence."

She sighed. "Maybe. But I don't think that's it."

It was easier to let him watch television than to insist he join them or read a book. It was easier, when he said he wasn't hungry, to let him take a plate in front of the TV, and that's what she decided to do. She was tired and she just didn't feel like fighting with him. She had been half dreading and half looking forward to this weekend and in particular this dinner, and it was already off to a bad start. She had wanted to act as if everything were back to normal and by acting that way, she hoped to feel it, but the truth was that nothing in her life or relationship either with Danny or with Jeff felt normal. She had brushed off Jeff's fears about Danny as a bad influence on Griffin, but now she wondered. She knew Danny loved Griffin and Griff adored his big brother, but it seemed that there was always some trouble, some tension, some misunderstanding whenever Danny was around. She looked across the table at Jeff and thought he looked handsome. He had one of those youthful faces that make some men look boyish years after their twenties. He said something—she hadn't been listening and now the others were looking at her as if she was supposed to answer.

"I'm sorry. My mind was drifting." She turned to Mike. "What did you say?"

"Jeff was asking when you had to start applying for nursery school for Griffin, and Grace wanted to know whether you were interested in Montessori or Waldorf or something else. She did so much research into this she's the perfect person to advise you."

"Oh right. Yeah. Thanks. But Griff isn't even a year old. I think we have time."

"That's where you're wrong," Grace said with her customary self-assurance. "This is New York City we're talking about. The good schools get booked when the mothers are still pregnant."

Marcia nodded wearily. "Well, I guess I'll have to start thinking about it but I haven't yet." She started to clear the table. Jeff and Grace both jumped up to help, but she stopped them. "It's just a few dishes. It's easier if I do it myself."

She put the dishes in the sink and went into the TV room to see what Danny was up to. He was sitting on the floor in front of the TV watching *Indiana Jones.* "Where did you find that?" she asked. "Did we have the DVD?"

"No. It's on Netflix."

"Do you like it?"

"It's okay."

"Everything's always just okay, Danny. Is anything ever really good?"

He looked up and shrugged. "No."

"What about really bad?"

No answer.

"Danny, did something really bad happen? You can tell me."

"No."

"You mean no, nothing bad happened, or no, you don't feel like you can tell me?"

"Both, I guess," he said.

She wasn't getting anywhere, obviously, and she could see that wouldn't change, at least not in this conversation, so she switched tracks.

"I picked up cider doughnuts and ice cream for dessert. I'm about to serve it. Do you want some?"

He shook his head.

"Damn it, Danny. I'm really losing my patience. I know something's wrong but I can't help you if you won't tell me what it is."

He didn't respond. She turned angrily and walked to the door.

"Okay, I give up. If you want some dessert, come in and I'll make a plate for you. You can finish it in here."

He didn't follow her. She served dessert to everyone and sat back at the table. She was upset so she reported what had happened.

"I really think he needs something stronger than

therapy," Grace said. "They have these therapeutic schools where they have a lot of success straightening kids out."

"He's not a juvenile delinquent, Grace. He's an unhappy boy."

"I think they help with that too."

"Didn't Dr. Benson suggest something like that?" Jeff asked carefully.

"Yes, but for the summer, a camp not a school." She paused. "I've been giving that a lot of thought and I think we may have to try something like that. So now, let's talk about something else, okay?" She wanted to turn the conversation away from kids and problems and toward work and politics, but with Grace that was always a little hard. She still worked, although not full-time, and she claimed she liked her job, but nothing interested her as much as her children—Stephie, now five, and Petey, the baby, who always had some new issue she could talk about: he didn't sleep, he slept too much, he didn't reach some arbitrary developmental milestone that it was clear to Marcia he would meet in a few weeks, but Grace was worried. So Marcia just let the conversation go where the others led, which meant some whispered analysis of Danny's behavior that she suffered in silence, some sympathy for Jeff, some shared anxiety about Danny with Marcia. When they finally said good night, she was glad to see them go.

There hadn't been much wine consumed, and Marcia and Jeff finished the bottle between them. Their problems became less clear, fuzzier around the edges, and Jeff was so handsome and he looked at her in that old way in which she could see how much he wanted her. She looked away, but her cheeks flushed. She wanted him too. She looked at him, pushing the hair out of her eyes. "You're beautiful," he said. She didn't answer and he didn't press her. She asked him about his cases and he told her about one he was having some trouble with. He asked her how her work was going and she told him about the new book she had discussed with Brynn about relationships. They were on the verge of crossing a threshold but neither could take the final step. At last, tired, she got up. Slowly, she started to load the dishwasher. Jeff joined her and they finished the table and counter together. He looked a little unsure of himself and it touched her—he so rarely looked that way.

"Well," he said, stifling a yawn, "I guess it's time to go to bed." He started walking toward the guest room and she walked with him, stopping at the door to the master bedroom.

"Good night," he said.

"Do you want to sleep here?" she asked softly.

"You know I do. But only if you want me to."

"I want you to."

They were tentative, they were considerate, they were gentle with each other, and their lovemaking wasn't what it once was, but they had broken a barrier and they both knew it. She laid in his arms for a few minutes, allowing herself to feel comforted. "I'm falling asleep," he murmured. "I love you."

"I love you too," she whispered almost mechanically, but he was already breathing deeply and she wasn't sure he heard her. They had always ended their lovemaking with those words, she thought. But did she? she wondered. She thought she knew the answer. In spite of everything, she still did.

She couldn't sleep. She was hopeful about Jeff but very worried about Danny. After tossing and turning for a while she got out of bed and tiptoed to his room a few doors down the hall. She could see that the light was off and assuming he was sleeping, she was about to go back to her bedroom when she heard a sound inside his room. She put her ear to the door. He was crying. It was unmistakable. She hesitated only a few seconds and then knocked softly and opened the door. He was lying in bed and buried his head in his pillow when he saw her, trying to stifle his sobs. She sat on his bed. "Danny, please, tell me. Whatever it is, I'll help you. I'll be on your side. Just tell me." She gently removed the pillow and saw his tear-stained face and red eyes.

"I miss my ma," he said. "I need to talk to *her.*" His sobs had subsided but now they returned stronger than before.

"I know you miss her. I know I can never take her place, Danny, but is it so impossible to talk to me instead? I was her friend. She'd want you to talk to me if she wasn't here."

He didn't answer.

"Okay, Danny, if you can't, you can't. But maybe you can still talk to her. You believe in God, don't you? I know your mom took you to church sometimes."

"Yeah."

"So your mom is in heaven and she's watching you. She can hear you. Talk to her. Maybe you'll hear what she says. It will be like a voice inside your head, like your own thoughts."

"You really think she could hear me?"

"Yeah. I do."

He nodded. "I'll try."

She patted his arm and bent down to kiss his cheek.

"Give me a chance one time, Danny. I might be smarter than I look."

He smiled at this and rubbed his eyes. She smiled back. She had lied. She didn't believe his mom could hear him. But if ever there was such a thing as a white lie, she told herself, that was it. It seemed to be what he needed.

29

In the weeks that passed after the family returned from Woodstock, Danny's behavior didn't improve. Marcia was called into school twice to discuss problems he was having: homework not turned in even though she had seen him finish it and put it in his backpack, rudeness to this or that teacher, even missing school without permission. One teacher said he insisted on mimicking everything anyone in the class said, including the teacher. "Stop it now, Danny," the teacher had said.

"Stop it now, Danny," Danny had reiterated, imitating the tone as well as the words.

"I mean it."

"I mean it," he shot back.

"If this doesn't stop this instant I'm sending you to the principal's office."

"If this doesn't stop this instant—" But before he could

finish she had grabbed his arm and physically pulled him out of the classroom. He was growing fast and was bigger and probably stronger than his sixty-year-old teacher, so Marcia was grateful that he hadn't fought back but submitted, at least in that respect, to her authority. But it was clear he was going through some passage that no one understood, and several extra meetings with Dr. Benson didn't get them any further in pinpointing the source of this behavior. She had asked Dr. Benson about camp recommendations and was reading brochures and speaking to the different program directors.

After the mimicking incident at school Marcia asked Danny to sit down in the living room with her for a talk. She chose a more formal room in the hope that he would not feel too comfortable, that he would realize this was serious business. Her tone was not full of compassion and understanding this time. She was both frustrated and furious. "What do you think you are up to, Danny? You told me a few weeks ago that you miss your mother. Do you think it would make her happy to see the way you're acting? She would be ashamed. She would tell you that this is not how she raised you."

"I tried doing what you said. But she didn't answer. Not even in my head like you said."

"Sometimes you have to keep trying."

He looked at the floor, his face angry and disbelieving. She tried again.

"Look, Danny, we were all devastated by your mother's death and especially you, of course, I understand that. But there's one way she still lives—the only way people get to live after they die. And that's through how she is remembered and what she has accomplished. You were her greatest achievement. She was so proud of you and so hopeful for your future. What you're doing now doesn't just hurt you, it hurts her memory. Do you want to do that?"

He sniffed hard. "No." His voice was barely audible and several emotions that she couldn't read played around his face.

"Say it louder. Do you want to do that?"

"*No!*" he screamed. "I don't know what's wrong with me. I can't help myself."

"Okay, then let me help you. Tell me what is bothering you. Do you even know?"

"You can't help me. No one can help me." He ran to his room and slammed the door.

He and Jeff were doing better together, and even under these difficult circumstances Jeff was still trying much harder to get along with Danny. But Marcia still tried to keep Jeff from knowing about many of the infractions Danny was accused of. There was no point in making it more difficult and she thought she was protecting both of them by this course. But Jeff couldn't help seeing the sullen behavior at home and Danny's general alienation and unhappiness. He pressed hard for them to choose the camp and to pick one that lasted for the entire summer break. Dr. Benson supported this and one evening, over dinner, Marcia mentioned it to Danny. She feared he'd be upset, feel rejected, worry that it was a step in getting rid of him, but he surprised her.

"Where is this place?" he asked.

"It's in the country."

"No, but where? Is it Woodstock?"

"No," Jeff said. "The one we think would be best is in Maine. We would go up to visit you and take you out for a lobster dinner. I don't think you ever ate a lobster, did you?"

"No, I've seen it. It looks disgusting."

"Well, we'll see," Marcia said.

"How far away is it?"

"You mean how long does it take to get there?"

"Yeah."

"A long time. Maybe eight or nine hours' drive. But you go in a bus with the other kids and sing songs and tell stories and it's fun," Marcia said.

"Sing songs?" Danny asked with a frown.

"Okay," Marcia said, laughing. "You don't have to sing songs. I just meant it's fun."

After a brief pause Danny responded. "Okay," he said. "That's good. When can I go?"

Marcia was so surprised she didn't answer right away. "July first to August thirtieth," Jeff said. "You come back right before school starts again."

"It doesn't have to be that long," Marcia said. "We can see how you do."

"No, that's good. That's good," Danny repeated.

Jeff looked at her after Danny left to watch TV. "Well, that was a surprise. He wants to go. Much easier than I thought it would be."

"Yeah. Maybe too easy. I don't know why."

"Just don't look a gift horse in the mouth," Jeff said. "This is what he needs and what we need too."

"Yeah . . . Maybe you're right . . ."

The next day was one of Marcia's work-at-home days so she was there when Danny came home from school. He seemed particularly edgy when he arrived, refused a snack, barely said hello to Griffin and went straight to his room. What now? she thought, surmising that he'd probably had another incident at school and was in trouble again. She stood outside his door. "You might as well tell me what happened," she said. "You know I'm going to find out." He didn't answer but he did come to the door and open it. "I didn't do nothing, Marcia," he said.

"Why do you say it like that when I know you know the right way to speak?" she asked. "Is it tougher or do you think it makes you cooler?"

He shrugged.

"I didn't say you did anything, by the way. I just wondered why you seem even more nervous today than usual."

He looked down, his face working as if he was torn between wanting to say something and wanting not to. "I just got nervous because that cop who always comes here was on the corner when I came in. He looked at me funny."

"Did you say hello to him?"

"No."

"So maybe he looked at you because he knows you and he wanted to greet you. These cops are supposed to get to know their neighborhood. He seems like a pretty nice guy. He brought you home three times."

The phone rang. "Hello," Marcia said. "Oh, sure, please send him up."

Danny looked at the door, as though he wanted to run out of it. He looked scared.

"That was the doorman," Marcia said. "There's a cop downstairs who wants to come up. It's probably him."

"Why does he always bother me?" Danny asked, looking nervous.

"He doesn't, he . . . oh, never mind, there's the door."

Danny ran back to his room as Marcia opened the door. Standing there was indeed the same cop who had come three times before. This time, though, he seemed a little uncomfortable and slightly more formal. "May I come in?" he asked.

"Yes, of course, Officer. Please do."

"There was a moment's silence. "Well," Marcia said uncomfortably. "What can I do for you?"

"I'd like to speak to Danny," he said.

Marcia frowned. "Of course, I'll get him. Can you tell me what this is about?"

"I just have a few questions to ask him."

"Has he done something wrong?"

"It's just an investigation we think he may be able to help us with."

"An investigation of what?"

"I think it would be better if I could speak directly to him first."

"He's a minor so I believe you need my permission to talk to him and I need to be present when you do."

"Yes, of course. But he isn't under investigation himself. We just think he might be able to lead us to someone else."

"I don't see how that would be possible. He doesn't know many people. He just goes to school and comes home every day."

"Yes, ma'am, I know. Would you mind if I talked to him for a few minutes?"

She hesitated, still nervous about what this would lead to, but she called Danny and told him someone wanted to speak to him. Her worry increased when he came out of his room. He walked slowly, his shoulders hunched, his gaze everywhere but at them. He looked scared but she had to admit that he also looked guilty. She hoped it was just nervousness at being sought out by a policeman but she had her doubts.

"Danny, this policeman's name is . . . I'm sorry, Officer, I don't know your name."

"It's Kellicut, ma'am. Mick Kellicut."

She nodded. "Officer Kellicut wants to ask you some questions. Is that okay?"

Danny shrugged, still avoiding looking directly at anyone.

"Why don't we sit down?" she asked, leading them into the living room.

Officer Kellicut was tall and wiry, with dark brown hair cut very short, hazel eyes and a slim physique. He was youthful, probably around thirty-two, but looked even younger, and he prided himself on the rapport he was able to develop with the kids on his beat and in his life. "Hey, buddy, how's it goin'?" he said, taking a seat on the wing chair.

"Good."

"I'm glad to hear it. No more problems at school?"

Danny shrugged again.

Marcia waited impatiently for these warm-up pleasantries to end so he'd get to the reason he was there. She was seated next to Danny on the sofa.

"So, Danny, you see much of Raul these days?"

Raul? Marcia thought. Surely he couldn't be in trouble.

"No," Danny said.

"You know now that they're in different schools, they don't have a chance to get together," Marcia offered.

Mick Kellicut nodded. "Yeah, and I hear his mom doesn't allow him to see Danny anymore, right, Danny?"

Marcia stiffened. "I don't think that's true," she said. "They were best friends. Then they had a fight about something but I think they're friends again." She looked at Danny for confirmation but he didn't look up. "We just haven't had a chance to arrange a date for them lately."

"Danny?" Mick prodded. "Didn't you tell your mother?"

"She's not my mother."

"Right. Sorry. Didn't you tell Marcia?"

He just shook his head and kept looking at the floor. He pretty much knew what was coming.

Mick addressed Marcia directly. "I've just come from

talking to Raul's mother," he said. "She was afraid that since Danny got expelled from Claremont a friendship with him would have a bad effect on Raul."

"Well," Marcia said, irritated and insulted on Danny's behalf, "she might have discussed that with me and let me know. That would have been very hard on Danny." She turned to him. "I know that must have hurt your feelings, but I wish you would have told me. I don't think she did the right thing. I know how much you must miss him."

"But Danny saw Raul anyway, right, Danny?"

Danny didn't answer.

"Danny? Did you?" Marcia asked. "It's okay. Just tell the truth."

Very slowly, trapped and seeing no way out, Danny nodded.

"How many times?"

"A few."

"But when? How? How did you even get there?"

Danny was about to answer but the officer interrupted.

"I'm not here about that. You can take that up with him later. But what I want to know is if you ever saw Raul's brother Julio at his house?"

No answer.

"Did you?"

No answer.

"Danny, you have to answer," Marcia said. She turned to the cop. "No one ever told me Raul had a brother. I doubt Danny even knew about that."

"Oh, Danny knew. When Raul's mother was working Julio would come over sometimes—secretly, because he was forbidden to be there when she wasn't—and if Danny was visiting, Julio would hang out with the boys. They did that while Danny was still at Claremont. What I want to know is if Danny saw him again after that."

"Why didn't she allow him to be there without her? Her own son?"

"He's her husband's son, not hers. He'd recently done some time in jail and she wanted to protect Raul from his influence." He turned to Danny. "Listen, Danny, I know you're not a bad kid. And I'm guessing you saw Julio and maybe he made you promise not to tell. But he's in bad trouble and if you don't tell, you'll be in trouble too. When did you see him last?"

"I don't know. A long time ago. I don't remember." He was getting flustered and tears were beginning to cloud his eyes. Marcia moved closer to him and put her arm around him. "Danny, it's okay. Just tell us and you won't be in any trouble."

"Did he threaten you? Did he tell you he'd hurt you if you told anything about him?" the cop asked.

Danny vigorously shook his head. "No."

"Because if he did, we can protect you."

Danny looked at Marcia. His face had taken on a blank expression, the kind he'd had a few times since his mother's death when he was trying with all his might to control his emotions. "I don't know anything, Marcia. I swear. I want to go back to my room."

"If you won't talk to me here, Danny, I'll have to take you down to the police station."

Now Danny let go and began to cry. "I don't want to go to jail. I don't want to go to jail. I didn't do anything."

Marcia squeezed his hand. "You won't go to jail, Danny, don't worry." She stood up and turned to Mick Kellicut. "I think that's enough. You don't have any reason to take him to the police station. He doesn't know anything, he's told you that, and I haven't heard anything to make me think you have any proof to the contrary. I have to ask you to leave."

Kellicut rose. "This guy Julio is dangerous," he said. "You'd all be better off if we found him. We've spoken to Raul and he said they both saw him a few weeks ago and Danny was alone with him for a while. We think he might have given Danny something, asked him to hide something for him. Maybe he can help us."

"He says he can't. I believe him. Please leave."

When he was gone, she turned to Danny. "He may be back, Danny. He's a cop. You can't lie to a cop. It's a crime. So when Jeff comes home we'll need to talk to him and tell him what happened. He's a lawyer, maybe he can give the right advice."

Danny cried harder, his words broken by sobs. "No, please, no, don't tell Jeff." He sniffled. "He'll make me leave. He won't let me live here anymore."

"He won't do that. Haven't you seen how much better things are with him lately?"

Danny's sobs were diminishing. He wiped his eyes. "Yeah," he said uncertainly.

"Okay. So he'll try to help, just like me. But you have to do your part and that means telling us the truth."

Danny took a deep breath and nodded. "I wanna go now. Can I go?"

"Yeah. Go wash your face and try to calm down." She called Jeff while he was out of the room and left a message. "Come home as early as you can tonight, please. We have a . . ." She hesitated, looking for the right word. "We have a situation," she finally said.

30

When Jeff came home, Marcia tried to fill him in as calmly as possible. She knew how excitable he could be, especially on any subject concerning Danny. She recognized and appreciated his recent efforts, but she understood how shaky they were, how easy it would be for him to return to his former prejudices. There's probably a part of him that would be relieved, she thought. He could tell himself he wasn't such a bad guy—he'd tried, after all, but the kid was just beyond help. She knew that while her instinctive reactions were always to give Danny the benefit of the doubt, his were exactly the opposite. In that regard, he didn't disappoint. The idea that a policeman had come to his home to question someone he was responsible for about a criminal investigation worried him and confirmed what he'd been saying about the boy all along. He called Danny, who'd been hiding out in his room claiming he had a lot of homework, into the living room and interrogated him like a hostile witness. Danny approached like a death row convict taking his last walk—his shoulders slumped and his progress infinitesimally slow. It was all Jeff could do to refrain from grabbing him and pulling him into the room. When he finally got there, he stood facing Jeff, his eyes glued to the floor. Jeff told him to sit down and he did. He rested his hands on his knees, which were slightly shaking.

"Okay, Danny, Marcia has told me everything. I know that a police officer came here today because he wanted to question you. The police are looking for a dangerous criminal and they had reason to believe you might have some information that would lead them to him. Marcia told me what the officer asked when he was here. He didn't think you answered truthfully, she said. So now you're going to look me in the eye and tell me what you refused to tell him."

Danny was shaken by this dramatic return to the old Jeff and his hostile suspicions. At first, he was frightened and barely able to look up, let alone look directly at Jeff. "I didn't refuse," he said practically under his breath, still staring at the floor.

"No? Then you told the cop what he wanted to know?"

Danny looked at Marcia. "No."

"So you refused."

"No." He looked at Marcia again. Why wasn't she helping him? "I didn't know."

"Stop looking at Marcia. She can't help you now."

Danny looked down again and in spite of himself, he felt his eyes fill with tears, which shamed him.

"Crying isn't going to help you either," Jeff said.

Danny couldn't stop the tears. "I *know*. *Nothing* helps me. *Nothing ever helps me!*" he screamed between sobs. He started to run out of the room but Jeff grabbed his arm and forced him back.

"Jeff, stop it," Marcia shouted. "You're terrifying him. You don't know what he knows. He's not a god-damn career criminal and you can stop interrogating him like a lawyer setting him up." She put her arm around Danny and led him to the couch. He sobbed into her shoulder until, by sheer force of will, his sobs subsided and he pulled away. "Danny, listen, you could be in real trouble here. I can help you sometimes at school and even here at home," at this she shot an angry look at Jeff, "but if you lie to the police and they find out the truth, I won't be able to help you. Do you understand?"

Danny nodded, taking deep, heaving breaths.

"Try to calm down. It's okay. We want to help you. Jeff wants to help you too, he just doesn't know how." Danny stole a furtive look at Jeff, a look that made it clear that he knew Jeff didn't want to help him, that he believed Jeff just wanted to get rid of him.

"So, tell us. Did Julio say anything to you that might suggest where he went?"

Danny shook his head.

"What did he talk to you about?" Jeff asked.

"I don't remember."

"You need to try," Marcia said.

"He said he helped me when Raul didn't want to be my friend anymore."

"Why didn't Raul want to be your friend?" Jeff jumped in.

"His mother told him he couldn't."

"And Julio told him he shouldn't listen to his mother."

"Yeah. He said that's not what friends do."

"So he reminded you that you owed him, right?"

"No." Danny shook his head vigorously. "He said he was my friend."

"Your friend, right. And did he ask you if you were his friend?"

"Yeah."

"And what did you say?"

"I said yeah."

"And did he ask you to prove it?"

"No."

"Raul told the police Julio was alone with Danny recently. They think maybe he tried to get him to hide something for him," Marcia said. Jeff watched Danny carefully. He saw him swallow and bite his lip and look pleadingly at Marcia.

"He gave you something, didn't he?" Jeff accused sharply.

"No." He shifted in his seat. His right knee bobbed up and down. He didn't know where to look and his eyes darted around the room.

"He told you to hide it for him, didn't he? He told you that's what a friend would do."

Danny didn't answer. The questions were coming fast, one right after the next, giving him no time to think.

"Danny, if what he gave you is illegal and you hid it you are an accomplice, do you understand what that means? It means you are part of his crime, you can go to reform school. He isn't your friend if he asked you to take that kind of chance for him." Danny remained silent. "I'm talking to you, Danny," Jeff said sharply. Do you understand what I'm saying?" Jeff's tone was harsh and he wasn't paying attention to what effect his words were having on Danny, but Marcia was.

She saw that Danny was hunched over, his body jerking and shifting. His knee was bouncing up and down and he didn't seem to know how to control his movements. He was more frightened than he'd ever been but he was still more scared of Julio than he was of Jeff or even of the police.

"Jeff, he's shaking. Stop. He's terrified, can't you see that? Maybe this Julio threatened him."

"Did he?" Jeff asked. "Did he threaten you, Danny?"

Danny lost control. He got up and paced up and down, he was crying again and hitting himself in the face, and finally Marcia tried to stop him but as she approached he accidentally hit her instead of himself. Jeff ran to him and held his arms behind his back. Marcia pushed Jeff violently away. *"Leave him alone!"* she shouted. "Danny, it's okay, it's okay, you can go to your room and try to calm down."

He ran away as fast as he could. She turned to Jeff. "What the hell is the matter with you? He's a child, Jeff.

Do you get that? *He's a child.* You can't treat him like that. It's abusive."

Jeff recoiled. "Abusive?" He looked at her with derision. "That's a little bit of an exaggeration, don't you think?"

"Not that much, actually. And like most abuse, it didn't work. He can't respond when you talk to him like that. It paralyzes him. I think Julio threatened him and he's so scared he can't break his promise not to tell. And he's frightened if he doesn't he'll get arrested and we will abandon him. It's an untenable choice for a twelve-year-old boy. And that's if he actually knows something, if you're right and he did get a package and did hide it, which isn't at all certain."

Jeff seemed to be lost in thought, barely registering what she said. "If he hid it, he must have hidden it here somewhere. I mean, where else? School would be too risky, I think. Anyway, we can start here."

"Start what?"

"A search. We'll take the house apart if we have to. Better us than the police. They can get a warrant if they think it's here."

Marcia covered her face with her hand for a few seconds. It was a futile attempt to withdraw from the madness of the situation, but it did help her to regain some modicum of control. She nodded slowly. "Where should we start?"

"You know him better than I do—where do you think he'd hide something?"

She shrugged. "I don't have any idea. Maybe his room?"

"Wouldn't he know we'd check that out first?"

"I don't know if he'd think it through that much. Maybe he feels safer there than anywhere else in the apartment."

Jeff started to walk down the hallway. "Are you coming?"

"I'd rather not. Does it really need both of us?"

"Probably not." He stopped when he got to Danny's door. Danny was inside, still traumatized, and Jeff didn't relish either forcing him to leave or searching with him there. He walked back to Marcia. "If I were him and trying to hide something I think I might do it in Griffin's room. He would think that would be the last place we'd look."

"Maybe, but I doubt it. There aren't many hiding places in there. Under the crib? In Griff's closet? Where could he put it?"

"I don't know. Maybe under Griffin's mattress."

She shook her head. "Are you suggesting that I wake Griffin up so you can search under his mattress? This is getting ridiculous."

"It was ridiculous the moment you insisted that an eleven-year-old boy from a different culture whom we barely knew join our family," he snapped.

"Oh, please, Jeff." She turned toward the front door. "If you are going to start that again, I'm going out."

"No. I'm sorry. Don't go. Please."

She turned back. "So what now? Can we at least wait

until the morning before we carry on this search? Nothing will be gained by doing it tonight. Let's wait until tomorrow when Berta is here to take care of Griffin and Danny is at school. Can you go in a little late? It's a workday for me, but I don't have any morning meetings and I'll call Julie and tell her I'll be late."

Jeff seemed to be considering her proposal and after a bit, he agreed. She could see him visibly struggle with his emotional impulse to settle this mess instantly and his rational understanding that tomorrow would indeed be a better time. The rational solution won, but at a cost. Without another word, without even looking at Marcia, he entered the bathroom and started getting ready for bed. He didn't say anything else that night, simply went into the guest room, climbed into bed, turned over and fell asleep. Marcia noticed this, of course, but had little inclination to challenge it. She was grateful for the respite and climbed into bed wondering if he had really been able to fall asleep. She doubted she could. She took a minute to marvel bitterly at how he had managed to turn this into anger at her, but telling herself she should have expected it, she tried to sleep.

She tossed fitfully and felt like she had just fallen into an exhausted sleep when Griffin's morning cry awoke her. She didn't hear Jeff going to get him so she dragged herself out of bed and stumbled to his room. She picked him up, trying to speak cheerfully to him in answer to his big smile when he saw her, and started her morning routine. She was feeding Griffin his oatmeal when Jeff joined her in the kitchen. "Good morning," he said, smiling at

Griffin, who banged his spoon on his high-chair tray in reply. "He says, 'Good morning, Daddy,'" she said. At least we're trying, she told herself, trying to find something positive to start the day. She offered Jeff a bowl of oatmeal, which he accepted. Danny had still not appeared, so she cracked the door of his room to see if he was awake. She saw him sprawled on top of his sheets, his blanket on the floor, his pillow tossed aside. He was still dressed in the clothes he wore yesterday, sound asleep. She entered the room sadly, understanding that he'd probably been up most of the night, and shook him gently. "Time to get up, Danny. School today."

"Do I still have to go to school?" he murmured, rubbing his eyes.

"Yes. Of course. You always have to go to school."

"But even if I go to jail?"

She frowned and reached out to touch his arm. "Oh Danny, you're not going to go to jail. But you will need to help us. Maybe you can think about it today and realize you can trust us. And if you do you won't have to worry. No one will hurt you, not Julio and not the police and certainly not us. So get up and get dressed really fast and come in the kitchen for a bite to eat before you leave, okay?"

After Danny left and Berta arrived to take Griffin, Jeff and Marcia looked at each other. "Well, where do we start?" she asked.

"You're going to help?"

"Yeah."

"Let's check Griff's room."

It didn't take long. They searched the closet and the chest of drawers, rummaging under Berta's neatly folded and well-organized assortment of baby clothes for some box that didn't belong there. They lifted Griffin's mattress, but found nothing hidden there either. They even checked the bottom of the diaper pail, emptying the soiled Pampers into a plastic bag to see if anything was hidden on the bottom. Finally, satisfied, they left the room.

"He's clean," Marcia said as they left. "I guess the baby isn't the perp."

"It's not funny, Marcia."

"I know," she said.

Next was Danny's room. It was in greater disorder than usual. Clothes were piled on the floor, the bed was in the same disarray she had seen when she woke him, the towel he'd used that morning was on top of the pile of clothes. They began by picking up each article of clothing. Jeff would toss the ones he picked up aside, while Marcia folded each item and made a pile on the floor. They checked the bed, looked underneath it, picked up parts of the rug that were visible under the desk or in the corners, looked through all the drawers, as they had in Griffin's room, searched the bookshelves and then turned to the closet. They sifted through the dirty clothes and balled-up pieces of paper he had thrown on the floor, Jeff mumbling about what a pig the kid was and Marcia saying he was a typical twelve-year-old in that regard. They searched the closet shelves where he kept games, opening Clue and Scrabble and the few other games he had and looking inside. When they had finished, they glanced upward and saw a sweater thrown on top of the closet on a shelf they couldn't reach. Jeff grabbed hold of the sleeve and pulled it down. Under it, pushed to the back, they could see more clothes and a blanket bunched up. They pulled at it and the pile spilled out, revealing underneath a carton about the size of a small orange crate. Jeff pulled the desk chair over, stood on it and lifted the carton down. Marcia noticed she was holding her breath. She knew this might be it, and she was scared.

They saw right away that the box was full of the treasures of his childhood. Understanding instinctively that it contained his memories, all that he had left of his life with his mother, they both handled everything very carefully. There were photographs of him and Eve, a framed award he'd gotten for good behavior in third grade, a trophy for baseball, a commendation for a science project, drawings he'd done that his mother had saved and he had taken with him when he moved away. On the bottom of the carton in the corner was a smaller box, sealed with masking tape. The tape was applied all over in tight strips. They looked at each other.

"We need to open this," Jeff said. Even he sounded worried.

"I know." She headed out the door. "I'll get the scissors to cut the tape."

Jeff hesitated. "I'm not sure we should," he said. "There might be evidence we'll mess up—prints, DNA, I don't know."

"Maybe it's not that, Jeff. Maybe it's something from his childhood. Something precious he wanted to keep safe."

He looked at her and saw that she knew better, that she was expressing a hope, not a belief.

"Anyway, I think we need to see what it is before we call the police," she said.

He hesitated and then nodded. She retrieved the scissors and he started to cut and unravel the package. When he had peeled off the last piece, they locked eyes one last time. She swallowed. He took a deep breath and opened the box.

"Oh shit," he said.

"Oh no," she cried.

Wrapped loosely in dirty paper, nestled on the bottom of the box, was a small black gun.

31

When Danny left for school that morning, he had no idea where he would go. He stood in front of his building and reviewed his options. He knew he was in big trouble and he knew he had to get some help, but he didn't know where to turn. He thought of Dr. Benson, but he didn't really trust him—he figured that as soon as he'd finished talking to him, whatever he'd revealed would be relayed straight to Marcia before he even closed the door on his way out. He tried to picture his teachers to see if any of them might be sympathetic, even partly on his side. He hadn't had time to build any relationships in his new school and when he pictured those he knew at Claremont, it didn't take long to realize there was no one there he could turn to. He thought of Raul, but knew that would be the first place they'd look for him and besides, he might even run into Julio there. He bit his lip.

He never wanted to see Julio again. He wondered if he should take the package Julio gave him and just drop it in the big garbage can on the corner of his street, but the thought of how mad Julio would be scared him so much he knew that wasn't a good idea. All these thoughts whirled around in his head as he started walking. Before he realized what he was doing he realized he was on his way to school, more out of habit than choice. As he entered the building he felt hopeless, just trying to go through the motions of his normal life, all the while knowing that his life would not be normal ever again. In a few minutes they'd come for him. Maybe the police would arrest him. Would he go to jail? He tried to think what his mother would have told him to do and he knew she'd say to trust Marcia. He was beginning to think he didn't have any other choice.

He was in his social studies class and as he was going over all the possibilities in his mind, he heard snickering. He looked up, confused. Mrs. Huntington was talking to him. She acted like she'd been talking to him for a while.

"I said, where is your homework, Danny? I've asked you three times. I assume you don't have it. Is that right?"

He managed to focus enough to answer. "Oh. No." She stared at him. What did she want him to do? He'd said he didn't have it. "Sorry," he added.

"You're being sorry isn't enough. Why don't you have it?" He couldn't think of an excuse she would accept.

"I don't know."

"That's not an answer," she said.

She was getting mad and the kids were laughing at him. He had to do better but he couldn't. He knew he was in trouble again, but it seemed so mild compared to the trouble he was already in. Okay, he didn't have his homework and he wasn't paying attention in class—maybe she'd keep him after school or send him to the principal but so what, he thought, he had bigger problems. He needed to figure out where to go and what to do to keep out of jail. He didn't look up or respond. Mrs. Huntington was talking to him again.

"Danny, are you with us?" she asked, irritation coating her voice. He could hear the kids in the class whispering.

"You didn't take the trouble to do your homework so I assume you already know the answer to the question it asked. Let's hear it."

He looked up blankly.

"I'd like you to explain why you think the group of current Republican politicians took the name Tea Party. What historical event that we've studied were they basing their name on?"

Danny froze. "I don't know," he mumbled.

"We've been talking and reading about this event for a week. Do you have any ideas?"

"No."

She frowned. "I don't know where you are today, Danny, but it isn't in this classroom." She looked at the girl waving her hand in the second row. "Okay, Tracy, you tell us."

The whole day went more or less like that. He couldn't concentrate on anything but his predicament and the more he thought about it the more hopeless it seemed. He figured he would have to run away, but he didn't know where.

As he was leaving the building after school he was still preoccupied with his worries when he saw a figure in a hoodie across the street. The body was familiar. With a start, he realized it was Julio. Julio was looking the other way and hadn't seen him yet, so Danny ran back into the school, his heart pounding, frantically trying to figure out what to do. There was only one door out and Julio was right there across from it. How could he avoid him? He remembered that there were a few after-school clubs. Maybe he could drop in on one of them and Julio would think he just hadn't come to school that day. He wandered down the hallway trying to think where he should go and ran into Mr. Coles, his gym teacher.

"Hey, Danny. Still here? Are you staying for after-school activities?"

"Yeah."

"Which one?"

"I don't know."

His teacher smiled. "I'm afraid if you haven't signed up for anything, it's too late. You might have to wait till next year."

Danny thought fast. "I just wanted to see what they did in them so I'd know which one," he said.

"Well, what are you interested in?"

Danny said the first thing that popped into his mind. "Baseball."

"No, sorry, Danny. There isn't a baseball club. There's baseball practice, but that's not today. What else?"

"Spanish," Danny said.

"I thought you already speak Spanish."

"Yeah. But I don't ever do it anymore. I don't want to forget."

Mr. Coles smiled approvingly so Danny knew he'd said the right thing.

"Well, that's a good idea," Mr. Coles said. He pointed down the hall. "The last door on the left is the Spanish club. I know Mrs. Rodriguez will be happy to see you."

Danny breathed a deep sigh of relief as he moved on. He wondered if Julio was still there, but he was afraid to look. The longer he took before he left the better, he figured, so he opened the door to the Spanish club and hesitantly walked in.

He managed to delay his departure by an hour, even though it meant trying not to look bored as the rest of the group learned, and often mispronounced, simple Spanish phrases he had learned when he was a baby. By the time the club broke up he felt pretty sure Julio would have given up and gone away. He gathered his books and walked out of the classroom with the rest of the group. When he got to the outside door he hung back and cautiously peeked out. He checked the place he'd seen Julio before, and he wasn't there. He looked right and left and didn't see a trace of him. Feeling marginally reassured, he slipped out with a few other kids and started walking as fast as he could to the bus stop. Half a block away someone walked up to him and put his arm around his shoulder.

"*Hola, amigo,*" Julio said. "Keep walking. Don't turn around."

Danny did as he was told. Julio steered him past the turn to the street that led to his apartment—Danny's heart sank as he left it behind—to a parking garage a few blocks away. He led him down the entry ramp to a corner of the garage. The attendant knew him, and waved. Julio waved back. He looked around quickly. "Listen, I don't have time. I just want to know if you still have the package I gave you."

Danny nodded.

"Have you told anyone about it?"

"No."

"Good. Make sure you keep it a secret. It's important. I don't know how I can protect you if you don't."

Danny swallowed. Should he tell him the cop came looking for him? No, better not. He didn't say anything.

"I gotta go. Keep that package safe. Don't tell no-body nothing, you understand?" Danny wondered why he said it like that. Like in a gangster movie. But he just nodded.

Julio took a hundred-dollar bill out of his pocket and slipped it to Danny. "This is for you. Now go home and keep your mouth shut."

When he left, Danny stood still watching him go. He looked for the attendant to see if he was watching, but he couldn't see him anywhere. He was alone. He stood for a while holding the hundred-dollar bill, crinkling it in his fist. Then he opened it and looked at it. He'd never seen that much money before. He thought about using it to buy a bus ticket somewhere. But where? And what would he do when he got there? Finally, he stuffed the money into his pocket and headed for home. He'd wait for Marcia. Then he'd show her the package and tell her everything. He didn't have a choice.

32

In those first minutes after they discovered the gun, Marcia and Jeff just stared at each other. Then Marcia started to reach into the box, but Jeff stopped her. "Don't touch it," he ordered sharply. She withdrew her hand quickly, as though shocked by an electrical charge. Neither of them said anything else. Then Jeff pulled out his phone and punched in 911.

"No, Jeff, please, don't call the police, let's talk about this first." She tried to pull his arm down but he shook her off and moved away. She continued to tug at his arm. She heard the phone ringing at the police precinct. She talked quickly, urgently, her hand pulling at his sleeve.

"Jeff, I'm not saying you shouldn't do this but please let's decide how," she begged. "Just hang up for a few minutes and hear me out. You can always call when I'm done."

"Police department," she heard through the phone.

Jeff hesitated and then disconnected the call. "I'm listening," he said.

"I know how serious this is. I know we have to report it. I understand that. But maybe instead of calling the precinct and getting some random cop, we could talk to the officer that came here. He knows Danny. He seems like a sympathetic guy."

Jeff took a deep breath. "I don't know what good you think that will do. He will do his duty no matter how sympathetic he is."

"Please, Jeff. I'd like to give Danny this one last chance. He might even be more likely to cooperate if it was someone he knew."

Jeff's voice rose in frustration. "This one last chance? How many chances have you given him? I wish you were as careful about the chances you gave to us, to our marriage, to our family. This whole goddamn experiment, taking a big kid like him from another culture and bringing him here, was crazy to begin with. You wanted it blindly because of your guilt. You think it's because of your responsibility, your kind heart, but you have been willing to sacrifice your family, your own son, to nothing more than your guilty conscience."

She bowed her head and closed her eyes, speaking softly. "You got me, counselor. I admit I felt guilty. I admit I still do." She looked up at him. "Don't you?"

"No. I feel bad about what happened, but I'm not going to let it ruin the rest of my life."

"Jeff, I've said it before and I still believe it. I know

this has come between us, this huge rock we haven't been able to push out of the way. But sometimes life just throws challenges at you, bad things happen and you kind of have to step up to face them."

He rolled his eyes and turned away. That lecture again. Her belief in her moral superiority, her certitude, infuriated him.

"Please don't roll your eyes. This is important."

"I've heard all this before."

"Well, maybe it didn't penetrate. Maybe you need to hear it again. You need to realize that sometimes the nice neat life you planned and thought you were entitled to doesn't pan out. So you do the right thing, the honorable thing, and try to move on. You have to change your dream. Don't you think I've had to do that? Do you really believe this is what I ever imagined or wanted? You think this is my dream? You know it's not. Not even close. But sometimes you get something else in return. I know I was motivated by guilt, especially at first. Then I felt pity—he was so alone and so helpless. But now I feel . . ." She paused, looking for the right word, then she shrugged and gave him a half smile. "I feel love."

"Love?" Jeff's face flushed with anger. "That kid doesn't love you, Marcia. He didn't even trust you enough to tell you the truth about any of this. He put you and me and Griff at risk when he decided to hide a gun in our home. That's how grateful he is for your pity and your love."

This produced a deep sigh, a combination of sadness and frustration.

"I know he doesn't love me," she said softly. "I was talking about my feelings for him."

She paused. He didn't say anything, and she continued, "He's mixed up and he doesn't know what to feel and I'm sure he didn't understand the seriousness of what he was doing. I doubt he even knew what was in that box. Or maybe he did. Maybe that's why he's been so upset and acting out during these past weeks. I don't deny he needs more help than I've been able to give him."

"How do you know that gun wasn't used to shoot someone?"

"I don't. But I believe if it was, he didn't know about it."

He shrugged. "I don't even know that. But even if that's true, he has implicated himself by hiding it." He watched her waiting for an answer, but she was silent. He lowered his voice and spoke more gently. "You really do understand we have to talk to the police, don't you?" he added. "The gun is in our house and we can't get rid of it."

"I understand."

Jeff closed up the box and put it back on the shelf. He paced around the room a bit and then walked toward the door, grabbing his jacket as he left.

"Where are you going?"

"I'm going to look for that cop, this area is his beat. He's always hanging around somewhere nearby."

She had followed him to the door and she reached out to squeeze his hand, but he pulled it away. "Thank you," she said.

Half an hour later, Jeff and Officer Mick Kellicut

walked in. Jeff had obviously already explained the situation to him and he led him to Danny's room. Marcia stood in the doorway, peering anxiously into the room as Jeff took the box from the shelf and handed it over. The officer opened it, glanced at the contents, and closed up the box. "Maybe it's not a real gun?" Marcia asked hopefully.

"No, ma'am. It's real enough. I'll bring it to the lab and see what story it tells us. Have either of you touched it?"

"No," Jeff said quickly.

"Good." He paused, looking thoughtful, and they both wondered what would happen next. "Is Danny at school?" he asked after a while.

"Yes," Marcia said. Then, anxiously, "Are you going to get him from there?"

"No. I don't think I need to drag him out of his classroom. I'll drop off the gun and come back when he's home from school."

Marcia was so glad Jeff had listened to her and not called the precinct. "Will he be arrested?" she asked softly, looking at the floor.

"That depends," the officer answered.

"Really?" she blurted, surprised. She had pictured Danny dragged off to jail. "On what?"

"On what he tells me when I talk to him. And on you."

"On us?" Marcia felt a flash of hope. "We'll do anything we can to help him," she said quickly, talking fast and making some of it up as she went along. "We had already realized he has bad judgment and issues with impulse control and trust. We had decided to send him to a therapeutic community that his therapist suggested, even before this incident. We were going to wait until the end of the school year, but now, of course, we would want to send him immediately." She rushed into her study and came back with the brochure Jeff had brought home, hoping to convince the officer that they could take care of this without legal action against Danny. Mick gave the brochure a cursory look and nodded. "Let's see what he has to say for himself," he said. "I'll do what I can."

"I'm so grateful for the interest you've taken in him," Marcia said. "You know his story, what happened to his mother?"

The officer nodded and walked to the door. "What time does he get home from school today?"

"Around three-thirty or three forty-five," Marcia answered.

"I'll see him then."

After he left, Jeff was the first to speak. "Well, it just might work out a little better than I thought. But he can't protect Julio anymore. I hope he's smart enough to realize that." He looked quizzically at Marcia. "I was surprised to hear we had decided to send him to a therapeutic community. I had this strange idea you had opposed that."

She couldn't resist a small smile. "Thank God you brought that home."

"Are you ready to part with him?"

"I don't think I have a choice. If we're lucky and that cop lets us do this without bringing him in and getting him charged with something, I will count him, count myself, very, very lucky."

Officer Kellicut arrived at three-thirty, but Danny wasn't at home. Marcia offered him coffee, which he accepted, and they waited awkwardly around the kitchen table, making small talk. At 3:45 Marcia mentioned that sometimes the bus was late and the cop just shrugged. Like Marcia, Jeff had taken the day off and he paced around the living room nervously, coming into the kitchen from time to time to apologize for taking up so much of the officer's time. By four he walked briskly into the kitchen again and addressed Marcia. "Do you think he's run away?"

She looked up sharply, angry that he'd suggest that in front of the police officer, even though she had been worrying about the same thing. "Where would he run?" she asked simply.

"Kids don't think that way," Mick said. "Especially a kid who has trouble controlling his impulses, especially a kid who's scared out of his mind."

"I just think there's another explanation. I know this kid. I don't think he'd just take off like that," Marcia insisted. Jeff snorted. Marcia looked at him and spoke softly, confidently, "He may not love me, Jeff, but he loves Griffin. He'll come home."

Jeff impatiently shook his head at her intransigence and walked back to the living room, where he continued to pace. By four-fifteen Mick Kellicut got up to go. "I'm sorry. But you'll have to bring him in when he gets home. I can't wait anymore."

"Please, Officer. Just thirty more minutes. Maybe he stayed for an after-school activity. Some kids do that. That would delay him by at least half an hour."

"Is he signed up for any?"

"I don't know. He might have just recently signed up for one. Or maybe he's reluctant to come home so he's hanging out at school a little longer today. Please give him a little more time." She took his cup and refilled it and offered him a piece of pie, which he refused. She was getting very worried because she knew Danny didn't have any after-school activities and she had run out of other excuses for him. This was their one chance to help him out of this mess and he was ruining it. He seemed to have a talent for hurting himself. She tried to engage Mick in conversation, asking him about his beat and the policy of neighborhood policing that he was engaged in. He answered with his mind obviously on something else, and kept looking at his watch. She was just asking him about what made him choose police work and what his interests had been before he became a cop when the door opened and Danny walked in. The expressions of relief from Marcia and even Jeff were audible. Danny, however, saw the policeman and gasped in dismay. He still had his hand on the doorknob and was about to slam the door and run, but Jeff grabbed him and brought him in.

"Where the hell were you?" Jeff blurted.

"At school."

Mick got up and approached Danny. He asked Marcia and Jeff if he could have a word with him alone. They nodded nervously and left Danny and the cop by themselves in the kitchen. They didn't share a look or say a word to each other. Marcia went into her study and closed the door. Jeff went to the bedroom. Marcia thought it a bad sign that she and Jeff couldn't wait this out together.

Danny sat down nervously across from the cop. He didn't know where to look, so he just stared at his own hands.

"First of all, Danny, you should know we've found the gun."

Danny looked up for a second, his eyes wide, scared and confused. He swallowed.

"What gun?"

"The gun that was in that box you got. The one you hid in your closet. The one you got from Julio, right?"

Danny was too stunned to answer.

"You know this is serious, don't you? You know you could be in a lot of trouble?"

Danny nodded, staring at his hands again, seeming intently absorbed in watching his fingers nervously drumming on the table. His legs were bobbing up and down. He thought about Julio saying that he couldn't protect him if he told anyone about the package. He wondered who Julio needed to protect him from. He had thought the person he should be scared of was Julio. Now Julio was acting like his friend again. He wished he could talk to Raul. He would tell him what to do.

Officer Kellicut reached over to steady him, placing his big freckled hand over Danny's small one. "It can still be okay," he said in a reassuring voice. "I'm going to try to help you but you only have one chance and it depends on your telling me the truth. If you've been threatened, don't worry. I'll protect you. Do you get it?"

Danny pulled his hand away to rub his eyes and nodded again, quick, abrupt movements. He thought of his mother. For the first time he was glad she wasn't there. He knew this would break her heart. He tried to swallow again but his mouth was too dry.

"Okay. So now I want you to tell me everything," Officer Kellicut said. "When did you see him? What did he say? What happened? You understand? Everything."

33

Marcia was in the kitchen feeding Griffin some cottage cheese and apple sauce. Mornings still seemed too quiet and empty without Danny, even though he'd already been gone for a couple of months. She remembered how he'd often be the first to take Griff out of his crib in the morning and how he'd taught him to clap his hands. Afterward, Griff clapped whenever Danny appeared. She shook off the thought. She looked at her watch and saw that she was already behind schedule. She had wanted to get to work early because she had an important meeting at nine-thirty and she wanted to check some figures she had forgotten to take home the night before. Berta had said she'd come in half an hour earlier than usual, but fifteen minutes after the appointed time she still hadn't arrived. This was unusual for Berta and, worried, Marcia had pulled out her list of emergency babysitters when

Berta rushed in, breathless from running all the way from the station three blocks away. She explained that there had been a problem on the subway and they hadn't moved for twenty minutes. She was apologizing and complaining at the same time, telling Marcia that the lights and ventilation had failed, the passengers were crowded together and all in all, New York City was not fit for human habitation. Marcia handed over Griffin, gave him a kiss, grabbed her coat, told Berta how sorry she was that she had to go through all that and rushed out the door.

Her cell phone rang as she hailed a cab—no subway today, especially after Berta's experience—and she glanced at the call waiting. "Caller Unknown" flashed on her screen. That meant the call was probably coming from Children's Village, the therapeutic boarding school where Danny was now living. They had chosen it carefully with Mick Kellicut's approval—he didn't like the Glen because it was too far away and Marcia agreed. Danny was allowed only one call a week and she had spoken to him just yesterday, so her first reaction was alarm and she called the school office from the street before climbing into the cab. "Hey, lady, are you in or out?" the driver asked, annoyed. She climbed in, holding up her hand to ward off the driver's further questions, without giving her destination. She was able to ascertain quickly that nothing bad had occurred. Danny wasn't ill or in trouble, the secretary said, he had just gotten permission to call again to tell her proudly that he was going to play guitar in a school concert the following weekend and ask her to come. Ignoring the driver's irritated scowl, she asked the secretary to tell Danny that of course she'd be there and was very proud of him. She was grateful once again that his school was in Connecticut, just a two-hour drive from the Upper West Side. She hung up and gave the driver her office address, ignoring the honking cars behind them and the driver's angry mutterings in a language she didn't even recognize, let alone understand. As she settled into the backseat and reached over to turn off the annoying television omnipresent in all New York City Yellow Cabs, she thought, as she often did, how good this school seemed to be for Danny. He was a bereaved child in an extraordinary circumstance, and she and Jeff had tried to fix him up with the Band-Aid of weekly therapy, she thought self-critically. She felt foolish and naive when she remembered it. Of course they should have known it wasn't enough. When you added how unprepared he was academically and socially for his new situation, as well as their busy work schedules, the distractions of a new baby and Jeff's hostility to him, it was amazing he hadn't gotten into far worse trouble than he did. She was glad in a way that the problem with Julio brought his confusion and bad judgment to a head. She had a special place in her heart for Mick, the wonderful neighborhood police officer who helped them work out a plan to avoid legal action against Danny. At least Jeff had listened to her, she thought, in those first shocking moments after they found the gun. If he had followed his first impulse and just called the police that day instead of going out to look for Mick, things might have worked out very differently—especially once they picked up Julio and matched the gun to a shooting he was involved in. She shook her head, inadvertently remembering that sad time. Danny had gotten involved with a thug, a guy who beat up people for gangsters, a guy who had gone too far one day and actually killed someone, and she hadn't known anything about it. The fact that he was the brother of a classmate who had become his best friend added to the bizarre nature of that situation. What a close call they'd had.

She wondered if she should ask Jeff if he wanted to come to hear Danny play the guitar but she knew the answer before she made the call. Ever since they had officially separated and Jeff had gotten his own apartment, he was much more honest about his desire to drop out of Danny's life. Still, she thought how good it would be for Danny if Jeff showed even a little interest and she reluctantly punched in his number.

Karen, his secretary, picked up on the third ring.

"Hi, Karen, it's Marcia, is he in yet?"

"Yes. He just arrived."

"Can I speak to him, please?"

"I'll see if he's available."

Was she imagining it, or was his always formal secretary even colder since their separation? Jeff picked up the phone and after a few awkward pleasantries, Marcia asked if he'd be interested in Danny's concert. As she had expected, he begged off, saying he was busy.

"We kind of took him on together, Jeff. Just because we're separated shouldn't mean you just drop completely out of his life," she said.

"We didn't take him on together. You took him on."

There it was again. "Okay, okay. Sorry to bother you." She was about to hang up but he cut in: "Marcia? Wait. How are you?"

"I'm fine. I have to go."

"How is Griff?"

"You just saw him yesterday. His condition hasn't changed. I've really got to go. Goodbye." She disconnected and sat for a little while staring ahead of her. She wasn't thinking, she was processing, in some way, the reality that Jeff was gone, or at least gone from the part of her family that included Danny. Of course she knew that—it was a big part of the reason they'd separated, but that decision hadn't been a permanent one—they spoke of it as a time-out, an intermission, not a finale. But these things have a life of their own and once he rented an apartment and moved his possessions into it, once they set up a visiting schedule for Griffin and often went days without speaking to each other, the temporary began to feel permanent. She wondered fleetingly if they had made the right decision. Maybe if she had tried harder they could still have made it work between them. Maybe with Danny gone, Jeff would have felt less threatened by him. That was the original plan. Once it had been decided that Danny would go to Children's Village, they had both been relieved. Even Marcia had to admit that it was not just that he wasn't going to reform school that calmed her, it was also that the constant pressure of life with him and Jeff was lifted. And Danny was doing well. She had run into Mick Kellicut on her way home a few weeks ago and was happy to be able to report that the teachers and psychologists thought Danny was making a great deal of progress. He hadn't been allowed home on weekends or holidays yet, but soon he would be. At some point they would have to decide how long before he was allowed to move back home.

Unfortunately, her relationship with Jeff hadn't fared as well. She went over in her mind the sequence of events that led to their separation. They had both tried to avoid it—both felt strongly about raising Griffin together and neither wanted the complications and disruptions of two households, but neither of them could get past what had already happened. They had both thought that once Danny was away the space in their relationship that had been taken up with tension and accusations and disappointment would be filled with mutual love of Griffin, family outings, even conversations of the kind they had in the old days, about their work, their friends, their plans, the larger world around them. But it didn't turn out that way. It was true that when Danny was gone a space opened up, but what they hadn't expected is that it stayed that way, just empty space—empty, uncomfortable, awkward space. They tried to fill it with the minutiae of daily life. They gave dinner parties and took Griffin on picnics and pretended they were the couple they once were, the family they had dreamed of becoming, but it was clear to both that they weren't. Jeff seemed to think that Danny's disappearance was permanent and she longed to hear he was coming home. It was like trying to touch each other over a pile of hot coals: they were always fearful of getting burned. Marcia missed Danny. She was sure Griffin missed him. Jeff, it was clearer every day, was nothing but relieved to be rid of him.

But they continued together as if everything would be better. It felt false to her—she knew that they would have a better chance if they were in couples therapy during this sensitive transitional time, but Jeff said he'd had enough dealings with therapy and therapists to last him a lifetime and refused. As always, she thought, he wanted to get back to life as it was and he wasn't willing to put in the work necessary to make that happen. She wanted to talk things through, honestly believing that was the only way for them to heal. She wanted to tell him that she understood some of his complaints, that she had learned something from everything that happened, that she knew she was at fault too and had made him feel relegated to second, even third place after both Griffin and Danny. She wanted to apologize if she had come off as self-righteous and to reveal that, especially at the beginning, though she was loathe to admit it, she had also wished that Danny and all his problems would disappear. She tried to engage Jeff in that conversation several times. One problem was that their time together, when such conversations might occur, was usually at night when Griffin was asleep, they were getting ready for bed and Jeff was wondering whether they would ever make love again. Marcia would respond to his sexual overtures by saying they needed to talk things through before that felt right. Frustrated, angry, his response was either to brush her off and change the subject or to agree so emphatically that she was at fault that she felt he was attacking her and not accepting any of the blame himself. The conversation would deteriorate rapidly and they each would end up feeling misunderstood.

Marcia knew that until they could resume their sexual relationship there was little hope they could ever work things out—Jeff was too hurt and she felt too pressured and guilty. Although she said they had to come to an understanding first and that would lead to intimacy on every level, she didn't know if that was true. What she knew was that she didn't feel desire. It was as if that part of her, the wife, the lover, the sexual partner, had gone to sleep. She wondered if it had died. She had renewed interest in her job and her authors. She was a devoted and passionate mother to Griffin and, from afar, to Danny, following all of his activities and progress, involving herself in the process of his recovery as much as she could. But in spite of taking on some of the blame for their problems, in spite of saying she forgave Jeff's affair, her body simply didn't respond to him anymore. She felt she needed to talk it over with someone and arranged lunch with Marian.

She didn't want to have this conversation in a restaurant so she had invited Marian over on one of the days she was working at home. Jeff hadn't moved out yet, at that point, but the signs of serious trouble were already there and the conversation about a trial separation had begun. She had asked Berta to take Griffin to the park and prepared a chef's salad for lunch, knowing how Marian was always worried about how many carbs she ingested. Marcia was eager to talk to her and had told her in advance how much she needed to have this conversation, so Marian came ready to listen and hopefully to help. She arrived with a bottle of Pino Grigio, their favorite wine, which she held in one hand and waved above her head as she stood in the doorway. Marcia felt relieved as soon as she saw her, a flood of sisterly gratitude that at last she could confess what she felt and be sure she wouldn't be judged or dismissed, counting on the trust and intimacy that are the hallmarks of close friendship between women. Marian came in and the friends hugged.

"Are you okay?" Marian asked.

"Yeah, I guess. Just confused."

"Well, get out the wineglasses and let's get started. But where's Griff? I just want a peek at him first."

Marcia smiled proudly. "I asked Berta to take him to the park so we could really have the apartment to ourselves. I'd love you to see him, though. Maybe they'll be back while you're still here. How long can you stay?"

"I don't know—not that long. Maybe an hour. Should we order in for lunch?"

"No, I made a salad."

They sat down, poured the wine and Marcia brought the salad to the table so they could talk while they ate. She filled her in as best she could, but wanted to focus in on what was bothering her the most.

"The thing is, I can't seem to want to sleep with him.

It's not like he repels me or anything, but that chemistry we had, that desire that seemed to connect us even when other things pulled us apart, is gone."

Marian looked thoughtful. "For him too?"

"I don't think so. He often approaches me and I have to turn away or tell him I'm not ready."

"Is it because of his affair, do you think? Do you think of him with someone else, is that it?"

"No. I think we got past that. It's something else. It's more about me . . . I don't feel like a sexual person anymore." She paused and got up to bring in some coffee. When she returned she poured a second cup for herself and for Marian and put the pot on a placemat in the center of the table. "I don't know. Maybe I'm just tired."

"Look, you have a young baby, a full-time job, a difficult marriage and a foster child who you barely saved from prison. Of course you're tired."

"It's not just that."

"Do you think it's about his attitude toward Danny?"

"Maybe. But the point is, Jeff won't go to therapy with me and he won't even talk about it with me. And I don't think I can get past it without some of that happening."

"Do you want to get past it?"

Marcia looked surprised. "Yes, of course, how can you ask that?"

Marian paused to take a bite of her salad and then a sip of coffee. "Why wouldn't I ask that? Last time we had an emergency meeting you asked me for the name of a divorce lawyer. You've been fighting and struggling since you brought Griffin and Danny home and now you don't want to have sex. Sounds to me like maybe this relationship is over."

Marcia pushed away her plate, looking agitated. "I don't know, I don't want it to be. I still have strong feelings for him, I still see and remember everything I ever loved about him."

Marian took the last bite of her salad. "Is there any dessert?"

"I thought you were avoiding carbs."

"Well, just a little dessert. Like a bite of a cookie or something."

Marcia gave a wan smile. "I'll see what I can dig up," she said. "But what about my problem?"

"I'm thinking."

Marcia cleared the table and came back with a box of English shortbread, her favorite.

"Have you come up with anything?"

"I think you should fake it," Marian said.

"I can't do that."

"Look, you used to have a great sexual relationship and now you're kind of stuck. You're angry and disappointed and it's coming out in an actual physical frigidity."

"I wouldn't say I'm frigid," Marcia said, offended.

"No, you're not. That's not what I'm saying. But I think you're blocked. Maybe if you could force yourself to start, you'd respond and get past this. Right before Collin and I split, I did that hoping it would make things better. I forced myself, and it worked in a way because we still had that chemistry even when everything else was shot. Then, although it didn't save us because I knew I didn't want to be married to him anymore, I woke up sexually. I wanted him even when we were signing the divorce papers. In your case, it might break through your resistance and save the day."

Marcia didn't answer, but as she thought about it, she wasn't sure either that it was good advice or, even if it was, if she'd be capable of carrying it off.

34

It hadn't worked—she couldn't even bring herself to try—and here they were, landed where they had been headed for a long time: living separately, trying to be polite but occasionally sniping at each other, especially if the conversation included anything about Danny. She'd been doing a lot of thinking. The biggest problem, she realized, the biggest barricade they couldn't vault wasn't sex or bad memories or even Danny. It was trust in each other. He didn't trust her to love him enough, she thought. But enough for what? Enough to put him first? Enough to bury her own doubts and obligations and even her sense of right and wrong? She shifted in her seat. Well, I guess I didn't always put him first, she thought. I don't think I should have been asked to. And she didn't trust him to be the person she had believed him to be when they married. That person would have stepped up to the plate for Danny, wouldn't have run to another woman when things got tough. But then maybe that wasn't fair either, she admitted to herself. He was the person he was. It wasn't his fault she'd had an idealized image of him that he never asked for. He had said from the beginning he didn't want to enter into an ongoing family relationship with the surrogate. Hell, he had to be convinced to even agree to the surrogacy.

She asked herself again if she still loved him and this time she couldn't answer, even in the privacy of her own mind. She felt affection for him. She had happy memories of their time together. She wanted him to be well and the thought of anything bad happening to him filled her with dread. She carried around a dull anxiety that she ascribed to a constant sense of loss, loss of him, loss of everything she'd imagined their family would be. But did she miss him? Well, no. Not lately. She missed *them*, what they had, how permanent they seemed, how safe he had once made her feel.

She was doing all this thinking because for the first time in over a year, she had a little free time. She was on a plane on the way to Johannesburg, a twenty-hour flight. She was going to work with a new author who had written a novel she had recently bought for publication. It was an epic masterpiece, Marcia thought, written by a thirty-five-year-old Zulu woman. It spanned four decades in the life of a South African family, from the indignities and oppression of apartheid to the present day. It would, she was sure, create a sensation in the literary world. But it needed some restructuring and editing, and she didn't feel that kind of work could be done without face-to-face conversation. She had asked Jeff if he would fill in at home with Griffin for two weeks. He had agreed to move back to the apartment while she would be gone. Berta would extend her usual hours to allow her to be there all day, every day until Jeff got home from work and all weekend to help him out. She was grateful at how quickly Jeff had agreed.

It was her first long trip away from her baby and she was nervous about it. She wrote long, detailed lists covering everything Griffin might need any time of the day, including information Jeff already knew, like the night-time rituals of reading *Goodnight Moon* and singing "Hush Little Baby." Berta knew pretty much everything Griffin liked or didn't like to eat but Marcia went over the list with her anyway, and left Berta and Jeff copies, which also included the hotel she'd be staying at and its phone number. She'd also have her cell phone, of course, and her computer, and the hotel had wifi, so she assured them and herself that she'd always be in touch. No one had doubted it, though there would be one gap, a four-day retreat she was going on with the author during which there would be no cell phone service and no wifi, so they could work without interruption. Jeff told her this would be fine and she tried to believe him, but it made her nervous. She tried to tell herself not to be neurotic and overprotective and that whatever happened, Jeff (and especially Berta) could handle it. She wasn't worried about Danny. His life at the Children's Village would go on uninterrupted. But she told him she'd be gone, just in case something came

up, and gave the Children's Village all her contact information as well as double-checking to be sure they knew
how to reach Jeff in her absence.

After so much preparation and so much anxiety,
Marcia boarded the plane and ordered a glass of Pinot
Grigio as soon as the stewardess came around to offer
refreshment. She settled into her chair and for the first
time since she'd decided to make the trip, she relaxed. She
could feel her anxiety melt away. She was free. For two
weeks, she would not be responsible for anyone but herself and her work. It was a forgotten pleasure and she felt
grateful for it.

Jeff, on the other hand, was now a single parent and
he was nervous about getting it right. He arranged his
schedule so he could get home by seven every evening,
but that still meant leaving Griffin for nine hours a day
except on weekends unless he could come in late on a few
days. There was no way he could take two days off each
week to work at home, as Marcia did, he thought, but
luckily Griffin loved Berta and she was perfectly capable
of taking on the extra work in Marcia's absence. After a
few days of rushing home as soon as he could get away
and calling every afternoon to make sure everything was
going well at home, he started to feel more confident. He
realized, though, that his job had become more difficult.
Marcia had said that since Griffin was born she had had
to learn to be more efficient at her job with only half her
mind, because the other half was always at home ready
to answer any problem that might arise. She juggled her
daily work obligations with her need to schedule doctor

appointments or figure out who could baby-sit when Berta couldn't or what the grocery or social needs were for her family, all of which she provided. Now, for the first time, Jeff encountered the same problems and he had to admit he wasn't as good at handling them. He couldn't even imagine doing this if Danny had still been at home and he'd had those added duties, and he felt a measure of added respect for Marcia that she had managed so well. As it was, Danny was not his problem anymore.

After Jeff had moved into his own apartment, he rarely even gave Danny a thought, other than when he spoke to Marcia and she brought him up. He tried to dodge those conversations as often as he dodged the responsibility for Danny she tried to foist on him, and he was more or less successful. Now, staying at their family apartment where Danny still had a room though he no longer lived in it, Jeff was often reminded of him. Some of Danny's clothes were still in his closets, his knick-knacks and books and backpack were put neatly away in his room, as if just waiting for his return. Jeff closed Danny's bedroom door and never had cause to open it.

On the Friday of the first week Marcia had been away, Jeff had managed to cancel all his afternoon appointments and come home early. It was a beautiful, sunny day and he wanted to take Griffin to Woodstock for the weekend. He told everyone in his office that he would be unreachable until Monday and he turned off his cell phone, knowing that if Marcia wanted to call, she could use the landline. He did have some paperwork to do but he thought he might be able to get it done at night and

during Griffin's naptimes. Also, he had been a little unsure of himself about taking Griffin on this weekend trip
without Marcia—he'd never done that before—so he
asked Berta if she would be willing to come with them,
and she agreed. He knew he could rely on her to baby-
sit if he needed her.

The weekend went well. Jeff got up with Griffin the
first morning and fed him breakfast (Berta actually prepared it and changed his diaper) before leaving him with
Berta while he did some work and phoned the Zilmans,
inviting them to brunch the following day. Berta took
Griffin out for a walk in the afternoon while Jeff, who
had learned how to cook during the past few months and
fancied himself a burgeoning chef, made a shopping list
for the frittata and sides he intended to prepare as well
as the Bloody Marys he planned to serve. Berta put
Griffin down for his nap while Jeff went to the store to
shop. In this way, including some food preparation when
he returned from the store, Saturday flew by. At seven-
thirty, having put Griffin to bed, following to the letter
his nighttime ritual, Jeff said good night to Berta and
retired to his study, where he buried himself in some
work that required his attention.

The next day Berta helped entertain Griffin while Jeff
put the final touches on his brunch preparations and set
the table. The Zilmans arrived with their two children,
who each wanted a chance to hold Griffin. Petey was too
young, but Grace tried to put him on Stephie's lap while
she sat on the couch. Griffin squirmed away so they all
sat on the floor and played with him, striking the keys

of his xylophone, shaking his maracas, banging on his little toy drum. Jeff couldn't help thinking of Marcia and how she would have enjoyed this. This is what she always wanted, he thought, this family day, these friends whose children would play with our child. He felt a little wistful—it didn't seem like such an ambitious dream, but so far they had both paid a big price for it, and Marcia wasn't even here to enjoy it.

It was Sunday and Jeff didn't want to drive back in heavy traffic so they left around two and were home by four-thirty. Berta took Griffin off to be changed and fed, and Jeff went into his study to check messages. The red light on his phone was blinking, and he picked up the phone. The computer voice announced that he had six messages and he pressed the number 1 key on his phone to listen to them. The first was a sales call and, irritated—he was on the "no call" list and was supposed to be free of these annoyances—he pressed the number 3 to delete it. The second call was made the day before and was from Marcia saying that she was just leaving for her retreat with the author and hoped everything was all right. She said she'd try the landline in Woodstock, but if she had, Jeff thought, they must have missed the call. She reminded him that she wouldn't be reachable for the next few days and sent her love to Griffin. The third call was also made on Saturday. It was from the Children's Village.

"Mr. Naiman, this is Audrey Morgan from the Children's Village. It's urgent that I speak to you."

Jeff frowned and jotted down the number she left. He

was about to hang up and call her back, but thought he'd see what the rest of the messages were. The fourth and fifth calls were from the same number at the Children's Village. Jeff's anxiety grew with each message, as the voice sounded louder and more desperate. The sixth call was from St. Mary's Hospital outside of Bridgeport, Connecticut. "This is Dr. Seth Bernstein calling. It is urgent that you reach me as soon as you can."

Now Jeff knew something terrible had happened. Had there been an accident of some kind? Was Danny hurt or, worse, he thought with a start, did he hurt someone else? He took a quick look at his watch—eight-thirty on Sunday evening. Would the doctor still be there? He didn't know, but he picked up the phone and dialed the number left on voicemail. "Dr. Bernstein here," a brisk voice answered on the first ring. Jeff spoke quickly. "This is Jeff Naiman. I'm returning your call." His voice was tentative; he was not sure what he would hear but feared the worst, and was still not sure what the worst might be.

"Thank you for calling," the doctor said, his voice deep and grave. "Sir, may I ask you if you are in a car at the moment?"

"What? What difference does that make?"

"I need to know if you are driving a vehicle."

This was a surprise and an odd one. What was this about? "No, I'm at home," Jeff answered impatiently. "Why are you calling me?"

"We have bad news. Your son Danny is with us. I'm afraid he is critically ill."

35

Emotions spun around Jeff's mind so fast he couldn't pull out the individual threads. His thoughts mingled and mixed, like the paint in one of the spin-art projects he'd seen at a school fair a long time ago. He's not my son, was the first thought, but it mixed with feelings of surprise, shock, anger and concern. Thoughts like, I've got to tell Marcia, how can I reach her? blended with thoughts like, What did he do, what kind of accident did he have? and, most urgent, Did he hurt anyone else? What Jeff said, as calmly as possible, was, "I'm sorry to hear that. What happened? Was there an accident?"

"No, not an accident. He is very ill. It looks like he has bacterial meningitis, a severe infection of the central nervous system."

"Is the infection under control?"

"No, not yet. He's on strong antibiotics but so far, they

have not been effective." The doctor's voice was formal, uncomfortable. Jeff guessed he hadn't done this too often.

"Listen, I am not his father," Jeff said, distancing himself a bit disingenuously. "His mother and father are dead. But his guardian will want to be with him. She is in South Africa right now on a business trip and is unreachable for the next four days. I'm sure she will return as soon as she learns about this and will go straight to the hospital."

"I don't think you understand." The doctor's voice sounded impatient. "I'll be frank. The boy is in a coma. We don't know if he'll be alive in four days. We're doing everything we can, but his case is very serious."

Jeff was surprised at the tone in the doctor's voice as well as the severity of the situation. He'd heard the word "critical," heard that the antibiotics weren't working yet, but he'd assumed they would work eventually, hadn't really considered the possibility that Danny might die. "But if he's on antibiotics, doesn't that cure meningitis?"

"It usually does, if it is started early enough," the doctor answered. "But five percent of people who contract the disease don't survive it, even with antibiotics, and his case has progressed very rapidly. He is on a breathing machine and we are monitoring him and helping to reduce the pressure buildup in his brain from the infection, but it isn't clear that will work. He may go in and out of consciousness, and someone should be with him if he does."

"Are you sure this is meningitis?"

"Yes, we did a spinal tap when he was admitted to the

emergency room and that confirmed it. We are giving him Vancomycin and Ceftriaxone intravenously–they are extremely strong antibiotics, and now it's about waiting for his own immune system to fight back. I urge you to come as soon as you can. He's a very sick boy and I'm not sure how much time there is."

Jeff paused. Of course he would have to go. "Okay, Doctor. Thank you for keeping me informed. I'll get there as soon as I can. I'll be driving and I can find St. Mary's Hospital. Where do I go once I arrive?"

"He is in the neuro ICU, that's the neurological intensive care unit on the seventh floor."

"Is this in a pediatric hospital or is he in a pediatric ward?"

"No, this is a small general hospital and we don't separate pediatric and adult ICU patients, but we have everything he needs here and I don't suggest moving him in this condition."

Jeff thanked him and stood at the phone for a few seconds after he hung up. I don't believe this, he thought, though he believed it all too well. He understood the gravity of the situation yet he resisted being called upon in this emergency. Everything that happened, from Danny's sadness and sullenness at home in the first months to his trouble with the police to his current critical health problem, reinforced his deep feeling of aversion, his desire to run the other way, his sense that this should not have been his problem, his issue. He knew how selfish those thoughts were and he felt guilty enough for having them that he was able to squash his resistance and make plans to go to the hospital, but he went grudgingly, and wasn't proud of himself for it. It was only a little over a year since his baby daughter, Griffin's twin sister, died, before she was able to take even one breath, and that thought, for some reason, propelled him back to when he was a child and his parents had been in a train accident that left his father with lifelong back problems and chronic debilitating pain. How many times in his life was he going to hear some doctor tell him that he or she had bad news? He threw a few clean shirts and some toiletries into his bag. His father had taught political science in a small college, but after the accident he claimed his back hurt too much to stand for hours, and he sunk into a depression that left him unable to work. A successful lawsuit against the railroad had provided some money but his mother, who had been at home with Jeff, had to get a job to make up the shortfall. She hadn't had a career and the best job she could get was as a saleslady in an upscale dress shop. Life at home was never again as happy or as secure as it had been before, although sometimes Jeff wondered if it had ever been as good as he remembered it, or if that was just a fantasy he'd built up over the years. His strongest memories of his family life were unpleasant dinners in which his father and mother sniped at each other. Although his parents tried to keep their major arguments hidden from their children, he could feel his mother's disappointment with her husband and the trajectory of her life. He believed her death of stomach cancer when he was in college was partly the result of the resentment that had eaten away at her for years.

He told Berta what happened to Danny and asked if she could please stay with Griffin for a day or two while he was gone. She agreed immediately and told him not to worry, however long it took, but he assured her he wouldn't be long. He called Marcia's hotel in Johannesburg, even though he knew she wouldn't be back to it for a few more days. He left a message saying that it was urgent that she call him immediately. As an afterthought, he realized he should tell her the urgency wasn't about Griffin, so he added an addendum to the message saying that Danny was very ill and she needed to come home. He wondered briefly if she would be relieved that it was Danny and not Griffin who was so ill. He knew he was.

As he packed an overnight bag and changed from his jeans and T-shirt into slacks and an oxford shirt and jacket, he thought again about those years after the accident. He tried to remember how old he was at the time of the train crash and quickly did the math to figure it out. It surprised him to realize that he was just eleven when it happened—the same age as Danny was when his mother died and he came to live with them.

As Jeff grabbed his bag and headed for the parking garage, he tried to dismiss this line of thought—he had managed not to think about it for the entire year Danny had been with them except in passing and never as a parallel situation. But now he couldn't stop his thoughts from cascading over him, like a waterfall that held him under as he struggled to come up. Why hadn't he had more sympathy for Danny, especially in the light of his own problems at his age? He didn't know—maybe it was that Danny was so different from him, Jeff never saw a way of identifying with him. Following his father's accident, Jeff had tried to compensate for his problems at home with frantic and productive activity at school. He was relentlessly, if only superficially, cheerful and competent, studious and cooperative, all the qualities that led to success and to a scholarship at Yale, which eventually gave him second and third chances at happiness. Danny, he thought, well, he was different. But who knows, he admitted to himself, maybe another reason he never identified with Danny was that he didn't want to open that particular emotional door.

Anyway, it was too late now. But it struck Jeff how so much of how people behave is layered in from childhood. He thought about Marcia. Her need for a baby and then her devotion to both children were not hard to trace. She had been groomed as a nurturer all her life. Her mother had suffered with various neurological complaints from the time Marcia was seven or eight, he recalled. Marcia had taken care of her and supported her father through her mother's slow deterioration and death. Her father had remarried and moved to London, visiting once a year. From the beginning of their marriage, Jeff mused, Marcia had yearned to be a mother, the kind she had lost when her mother got sick: devoted, competent, protective. He thought it odd that she didn't welcome her freedom for a while, but yearned to return to the nurturing role she'd known most of her life. He wished he could reach her now.

He called his office and explained what happened and

told them he had to be away for a day or two. He re-trieved the car he had parked just a little while before, and, having looked up the hospital's address, entered it into his GPS. The hospital was not far from the Children's Village, which was on the outskirts of Danbury. It would take about two hours to get there. He put the radio on satellite and listened to R&B, turning up the volume to drown out his thoughts for the entire trip.

He found the hospital easily, parked the car and en-tered. A receptionist on the ground floor called Dr. Bern-stein and then directed Jeff to the elevator, which he took, as instructed, to the seventh floor neurological ICU. The receptionist there asked him to stop at the desk and sign in; the doctor would meet him shortly.

The first thing he noticed about Dr. Bernstein was how young he looked. He was not tall, probably only about five-seven, a good four inches shorter than Jeff. He wore wire-rimmed glasses and had a round, soft face and stocky build. He approached Jeff right away and shook his hand. He seemed kind and sympathetic, yet professional. Jeff thought of himself as young at forty-one. But this guy, this expert in whose hands lay Dan-ny's life, couldn't have been more than twenty-eight. Jeff knew it was a common experience for a person who has aged out of childhood and even young adulthood to be surprised by how young his doctor suddenly seems— your image of a doctor, Jeff thought, is formed in your childhood and, until experience teaches you any differ-ent, that image of an older, wiser, expert who knows so much more than you do will most likely remain. It's the equivalent of visiting a house you lived in as a child and finding it so much smaller than you remember. But Jeff was still young enough, and healthy enough, to have not yet experienced that jarring farewell to his youth. Still, he knew enough about hospitals to understand that this young man was probably a resident, still in training, and not the attending physician, who would be more expert.

After greeting each other, Jeff asked if there was anything more he should know, any development in the last two hours since they'd spoken. "I'm afraid not," Dr. Bernstein said, looking at Danny's chart.

"Should I speak to the attending doctor?" Jeff asked.

"She has been to see him already today and we have been over his condition together," the doctor said. "If you would like to talk to her, we can probably arrange it. But maybe you would like to see him first."

"Could you tell me a little more about his condition?" Jeff asked.

"Of course. According to the teacher who brought him in, he had an upper respiratory infection that rapidly became worse. It turned into high fever with an acute headache and neck pain. This is consistent with bacterial meningitis. Unfortunately, they didn't recognize that he needed hospitalization right away. He had already passed into the latter stages of the illness when he came in: he had photophobia—an inability to bear light, along with lethargy, confusion. He was still conscious when he arrived but shortly after he fell into a coma and is now unresponsive."

Jeff was silent. This was worse than he had thought. He

felt a flash of anger at the people in the Children's Village. Why didn't they bring him in right away? When he expressed this to the doctor he was told it was a common problem with meningitis, that it progressed so quickly people often waited too long to come to the hospital.

"We are doing everything we can for him," Dr. Bernstein said. "Shall we go to him now?" Jeff nodded grimly.

They walked down the hall together. Jeff could see that each patient was in a separate room consisting of three walls and a sliding glass door, which faced a central hub. This, he was told, was the nurses' station and the doctor pointed out that the staff could view the patients from the hallway even before entering the room. Each room contained a separate bank of machines and wires. The doctor stopped in front of Room 721. He took a hospital gown and face mask from a shelf, and asked Jeff to put them on. "This is both to protect you from the infection and also to protect him from any germs you may be carrying," he said. "Just be sure to wash your hands every time you enter and leave his bedside. There's a sink and Purell in every room." They stood outside the door and Jeff peered in. He had never seen anything like this before and at first all he could concentrate on was the technology, it looked to him the way he imagined a spaceship. The room was spotlessly clean, with shiny brown linoleum floors that looked freshly waxed and bright fluorescent lighting. He had avoided looking at the small figure in the bed, but he forced himself, and saw that he was attached to wires that led to monitors of every kind with machines that hummed or beeped steadily in the background. Those non-human sounds were the only noise he heard, otherwise it was deathly quiet. When Dr. Bernstein spoke, he lowered his voice to a hoarse whisper, "Before you see him you should prepare yourself. He is on intravenous antibiotics and steroids to reduce the swelling in the brain. You will also notice a tube that goes down his throat. This goes into his lungs and breathes for him. It delivers breath every few seconds." His tone had changed from sympathetic to professorial. There was even a touch of pride as he explained the hospital's equipment.

Dr. Bernstein opened the door and they entered the room. The doctor used the Purell dispenser to disinfect his hands and Jeff did the same. Then Jeff forced himself to approach the bed. He closed his eyes for a second and shook his head. "The poor kid. How did this happen to him?" he mumbled. Danny looked so pale, so vulnerable, so much a very sick, very helpless child. Jeff felt a wave of sympathy, followed by remorse for having assumed Danny had done something wrong. Was this child the danger he was trying to protect Griffin from? What had he been thinking?

He stared at him, then turned to the doctor.

"Does he feel pain?"

"No. He's in a coma. Even if he were awake, he would be heavily sedated or he wouldn't be able to tolerate the breathing tube."

Although at first Jeff had to force himself to look at Danny, once he did he couldn't take his eyes off the boy. He looked away just long enough to notice a screen above

Danny's bed with graphs composed of different-colored lights. Seeing him looking at it, Dr. Bernstein said, again in that same odd tone of a teacher instructing his first-year medical students, "That is a monitor that tells us his vital statistics. There are electrodes on his chest and a blood pressure cuff that cycles every fifteen minutes. He also has a blood pressure monitor in the artery of his wrist. If there is a problem, if his heartbeat slows or changes, if his blood pressure is altered, an alarm will go off and the nurse will come over immediately. If it is serious, she will call for the code blue team."

"Code blue?"

"That is a group of doctors and nurses on emergency call to try to revive a patient whose heart stops."

Jeff nodded. Now he was staring with alarm at a piece of metal that seemed to be sticking through the top of Danny's head. "What is that?" he asked, frowning.

"It's an ICP—an intercranial pressure monitor; it monitors the pressure so that the swelling in the head doesn't crush the brain."

He had gone too far. "Crush the brain?" Jeff repeated, horrified, raising his voice above the hum of the machines and the doctor's hushed tones. "Is that a possibility?"

"Uh, no, probably not. I mean, that's why we put the ICP in, to avoid that."

There was a chair next to Danny's bed and Jeff lowered himself into it. "Look, this is a lot to take in. I'd like to stay with him for a while. Would that be all right?"

"Yes, of course. You can stay with him as long as you like."

"At some point I'd like to speak to the attending physician."

Dr. Bernstein looked a little nervous but he said that of course Jeff could see her. He informed him that Dr. Gillian Flynn came in to see her ICU patients every morning. Jeff said he would be there to meet her.

When the doctor left, Jeff turned again toward Danny. He saw his chest moving up and down as the breathing machine fed him air, and took in all the wires and machines that were keeping him alive. He couldn't bear to keep looking at him so he took a deep breath and looked away, trying to process everything that had happened. He thought of Marcia and knew how devastated she would be to learn of this, how it would be even worse for her because she hadn't been at his side. He turned his gaze again toward Danny, unchanged, so still. A nurse came to his side.

"You can talk to him," she said.

"What?"

"You can talk to him. Take his hand. Rub his arm. Speak to him."

Jeff was confused, tentative. "I thought he was in a coma; the doctor said he's unresponsive."

"Well, yes, he is. But no one really knows what he can hear or not hear. Talk to him. It can't hurt him and it might help you."

Jeff looked up at her. "I'm Maria Hernandez," she said. "I'm one of the nurses here. I look after him."

"Thank you," Jeff murmured. She smiled, reached out to squeeze his shoulder and moved on to another patient.

Jeff's eyes fastened again on Danny. He didn't know what to say. The gulf between what he'd felt just a few hours ago and what he felt now was too great, and to him it seemed awkward, even self-indulgent, to acknowledge it. What good would that do now? He had missed his chance to do the right thing for this boy. But he knew he wouldn't be going home that day, or any day, until whatever was going to happen, happened, or until Marcia arrived. He left the room and took the elevator to the main floor so he could use his phone. He called Berta and told her that he might not be able to come home for longer than he'd thought. "Can you manage?" he asked her.

"Don't worry, Mr. Jeff," she said. "I can stay. I will take good care of Griffin. You take care of Danny till Mrs. Marcia gets there."

Jeff went back upstairs and returned to his place at Danny's side. "I'm sorry, Danny," he whispered, not wanting anyone to hear him. He couldn't think of anything else to say so he leaned back in the chair, took Danny's hand in his own and squeezed it lightly. He didn't expect any reaction and didn't get any. When he released it, it flopped down, as though lifeless. Then he reached over and with his fingertips, very gently rubbed Danny's arm.

36

After a while Jeff got used to the eerie quiet punctuated by the steady hum and rhythmic beeps of the machines. He must have dozed because the nurse who had spoken to him earlier had been replaced by an older woman he hadn't seen before, and he hadn't noticed the change of shifts. He rubbed his eyes, stretched in his chair and looked over at Danny. He appeared the same. Jeff's stomach rumbled and he realized he was hungry. He looked at his watch and saw that it was a little after six in the morning. He hadn't had anything to eat since brunch the day before. He introduced himself to the new nurse, asked her where the hospital cafeteria was and thanked her when she directed him to it. It was on the fifth floor so he took the elevator down two flights. It was an average institutional cafeteria, Formica tables, unappetizing food including hot dishes that looked overcooked and were smothered in some generic tomato-based sauce, and cauldrons of thick, creamy soup. He decided on a cheese sandwich on whole wheat bread, then picked up a donut and a cup of coffee. He wanted to check on Griffin, but it was too early so he killed time by picking up the business section of yesterday's *New York Times*, which he spotted on a nearby table. He glanced at it while he ate and, after another half hour, called home to check on Griffin. All was well, Berta said. She was full of questions about Danny, and Jeff just reiterated that he was very sick and it wasn't clear what would happen next. He asked if Marcia had called and was disappointed, though not surprised, to hear that she hadn't—he knew she'd be out of contact. They had discussed it over and over, and he had convinced her that nothing bad would happen, that she could feel confident he would take care of everything. He had believed that, but only up to a point. This was something they had never even imagined—just as they had never imagined that Eve might die on the delivery table. How could they have had such bad luck again? He felt like they were cursed.

He thought he should make a hotel reservation and checked hotels.com on his phone, looking for a place as close as possible to the hospital. There was a Hilton just a few blocks away and he drove there, registered and brought his bag to his room. He was tired, but he didn't lie down, though he was tempted, because he wanted to go back to see Danny again and catch the attending physician on her morning rounds.

Back at the hospital, he took his place once again at

Danny's bedside. Nothing had changed. Looking at him so still and unresponsive, he wondered if he would suffer brain damage if he lived. This was one of the questions he wanted to put to the doctor. He had picked up a newspaper at the hotel and taken his iPad from his overnight bag so he was equipped to pass the time while he waited. He looked at the top stories in his *New York Times* but found he couldn't concentrate. He stared again at Danny. He remembered what the nurse had advised so, awkwardly, self-consciously, he leaned over to talk to him. He didn't know what to say so he just started narrating what was happening. "Hey, Danny," he began, "so I'm here because Marcia is in South Africa and she's in the bush in a kind of retreat with one of her writers so I can't reach her to tell her about you. You know if she knew, she'd fly right back as soon as she could get on a plane, right? I mean, that's the only reason she's not here, you know that, don't you?" He looked closely at Danny's face to see if any of his words seemed to register, but it looked as blank and still as it had before he spoke. I don't think he can hear me, Jeff thought, but the nurse was right, I can't know for sure. He continued to talk. It made him feel a little better. She was right about that too.

Another hour passed and still the doctor hadn't appeared so he left the room and asked the nurse when she might arrive. She had already come and gone, he was told, while he was away. Surprised she had come so early, and disappointed, he sat down again at Danny's bedside. He didn't know what else to say to him, so he read the paper out loud, commenting on the different stories that he thought Danny would find interesting, telling him about movies he'd seen and a new television series he might like. He promised to take him to see *Hamilton* on Broadway when he recovered, saying whatever came into his head just to talk.

Several hours went by and he was beginning to feel hungry again. He thought he'd return to the cafeteria, grab a bite, then return one last time to see Danny before going back to the hotel. He was tired and needed to sleep, he thought, though he wanted to be sure he'd return early enough the next morning to see the attending physician. As he was gathering his things, a new nurse came over to Danny. She nodded at Jeff but wasn't friendly, though she did seem efficient, which was what he cared about. He asked what she was doing as she checked Danny's chart hanging above his bed. She explained that it was time to add medicine—more antibiotics and steroidal anti-inflammatories—to the fluid and nourishment that were flowing into Danny's veins. Jeff nodded, watching her bustle about, injecting something into a tube that was attached to the IV bag on a stand next to Danny's bed. Just as she finished they could hear another patient call out in pain and the nurse left Danny's room and rushed to his side. Jeff got up to go and was glad to leave—the cries of distress from the other room were unnerving.

When Jeff returned after his dinner he sat down next to Danny's bed again and once more tried to speak to him. "So, Danny, I'm going now, okay? I just got some dinner and I'm going to my hotel but I'll be back early tomorrow morning. Maybe you'll feel better by then. Maybe you'll have your eyes open. I hope so." He paused. "Look, I know my being here wouldn't be much comfort to you if you were awake, but I promise, Marcia will be here soon. Just hang in there, okay? Don't give up on us."

As he turned to leave another nurse approached Danny and reached for the IV bag. Jeff was curious so he asked her what she was doing. "Oh," she said, fussing with the bag, "it's time to add antibiotics and anti-inflammatories to his IV."

"Are you sure?" Jeff asked. "I mean, a nurse came and did that less than an hour ago."

The nurse stopped and checked Danny's chart. "No, you must be mistaken. She was probably just checking to be sure the IV was inserted properly and wasn't causing problems. His chart doesn't show any recent medication."

"No. I'm sure. We spoke and she told me what she was doing. I didn't see her write anything on the chart. Another patient needed her and she broke away to go to him."

The nurse hesitated. "Do you know the name of the other nurse?"

"No. But you can check it, can't you? I don't want him to receive any more medication until you are sure it isn't duplication. I assume that could be dangerous."

The nurse narrowed her eyes—in her view this was clearly just a meddlesome family member slowing her down. She knew the type, she thought, but she left to check Jeff's story and he sat down again, determined not to leave until this was settled. When she came back twenty minutes later, she was full of apologies and self-justifications—the chart hadn't been filled in, she pointed out; it wasn't her fault.

After this episode, Jeff was reluctant to leave so he remained in his chair, sleeping on and off during the night, waking with a backache early in the morning when the nurse checked on Danny again. He looked at his watch and realized the doctor might soon appear so he alerted the nurse to ask her to wait for him, went to the men's room, washed his face, glanced ruefully at the stubble that had already appeared, and returned to his seat.

He didn't know what he was expecting from the attending physician. His desire to see her was probably just a symptom of his helplessness, he thought, wanting to speak to the most senior person, as if that gave him some control over the situation. It didn't. She was a woman who looked only a few years older than Dr. Bernstein, who was at her side. She seemed efficient but cold and also seemed to be in a rush. He was happy to notice, however, that she did use the Purell dispenser as soon as she entered the room. Then she introduced herself as Dr. Flynn and put on a pair of gloves before doing a very brief examination of Danny. She turned to Jeff and, in response to his questions, repeated everything Dr. Bernstein had said in a brisk, mechanical voice, offering neither hope nor comfort. She made him angry, bringing out in him the reaction to rudeness or arrogance he always had, which was to challenge it. But he knew that Danny was at the mercy of these people and he had to avoid antagonizing them. He restrained himself, with considerable effort. He thanked her, but stopped her as she started to move off to her next patient.

He explained, as nicely as he could, that he wanted to return to the hotel to shower and change, but was afraid to leave Danny's side after what had happened with the nurse. Now he seemed to have her attention. She made a note on the paper on her clipboard and assured him that the mistake was an unusual event and wouldn't be repeated. She would speak to the head nurse, she said. Jeff looked at Danny again and ruefully shook his head.

"If the antibiotics are going to work, when would we start to see some improvement?" he asked.

She pursed her lips thoughtfully. "I think we would see some change by tonight or possibly tomorrow," she said. He couldn't bring himself to ask about possible brain damage.

He thanked her and left for the hotel. Once there, he showered, shaved and changed clothes, stopped in the hotel coffee shop for breakfast and returned to Danny's room, taking up his vigil once more at his bed.

Danny didn't show any change all day. Jeff followed the same routine as the day before, once again sleeping in the chair next to Danny's bed. Maria, the nurse who had suggested he talk to Danny, asked if he wanted to lie down—she said they could provide a cot for him—but he thanked her and said he was fine where he was. She smiled at him and patted his shoulder. "How's the conversation going?" she asked.

He smiled back, appreciating her kindness. "It's not really a conversation. That takes two of us. But I'm trying."

"Good," she said. "Keep it up. Later you can ask him if he heard you."

"If there is a later," he mumbled.

She patted his shoulder and moved on.

He called home again when he broke for supper and Berta said he shouldn't worry, Griffin was fine. Once again he gave her the same report about Danny—nothing new. He checked on Danny again after dinner, hoping he would see something, anything, that would show he was going to pull out of this. No change. Jeff settled again into his chair and dozed off. Somewhere in the early morning when the room was even quieter than usual he woke suddenly to the loud noise of an alarm clanging. He looked up, bleary-eyed but worried, and realized it was Danny's. The nurse wasn't in the room so he got up and ran to the nurses' station shouting for help. A nurse darted out from another room and was at Danny's side in an instant. She checked the monitors and adjusted one of them. "Don't worry," she said. "It's just a wire that came loose. His stats are the same." Then she bent down and looked closely at Danny. "But how did the wire come loose?" she murmured. "Did he move?"

Jeff bent down too as his heart stopped racing. He stared at Danny's arm, the one he had rubbed the day before. It seemed to be closer to his body than it had been. "His arm," Jeff said. "Doesn't it look like it's in a different position?" They both looked closely at Danny again. Jeff took his hand and squeezed it. He felt a slight movement. Was it a response? "He moved!" he shouted, as the nurse smiled and hushed him at the same time. "He moved. I'm sure of it."

"I'll get the doctor," she said, hurrying off. "Talk to him. Don't stop."

"Danny, Danny, it's Jeff. Can you hear me?" Danny opened his eyes. "Listen, you're in the hospital. Don't be scared. I'm here with you and Marcia is coming. She's coming soon. The doctors are taking really good care of you."

Danny blinked. Jeff couldn't tell if he understood anything he said but he was thinking that surely this was a sign the antibiotics had kicked in. A young doctor, a different resident, came in to check him. Just as she arrived the blank look on Danny's face turned to one of panic. His eyes opened wide and he grabbed for the breathing tube, trying to pull it out. The resident restrained him and called a nurse, who helped her tie his hands to the bed. Danny was weak and he couldn't put up too much of a fight. The doctor added something to his IV, all the while talking to him, calmly telling him not to panic, he wasn't choking, he needed the tube to breathe, she was giving him something to make him feel better. Within seconds, he seemed to calm down; his body became less rigid and his eyes closed.

"Is he okay?" Jeff asked.

"Yes. I just gave him some more sedative so he can tolerate the tube. We'll try to remove it soon to see if he can breathe without it, but we can't do that yet. But you can allow yourself to be happy, Mr. Naiman. I know he's scared and he's uncomfortable and he may be in pain, but he's alive, and he's beginning to recover. Look at his hands."

Jeff glanced down and saw Danny's hands, no longer purple and mottled, but looking almost normal. The relief that flooded through him was so strong it surprised and exhausted him.

"He'll sleep for a while now," the resident said. "Why don't you take a little break?"

"I want to be here when he wakes up. I don't want him to be alone."

"Come back in about an hour. He won't wake before that."

Jeff went back to the hotel. He longed to sleep, but he resisted, stopping in the hotel coffee shop for a strong cup of coffee instead. He called Berta to tell her the good news.

"Listen, if Marcia calls, just tell her that Danny is in the hospital and she must come home immediately. She should come straight to the hospital. You have the address, right?"

"Yes, Mr. Jeff. But I'm sure she will call you when she hears."

"I know, but I'm not allowed to have the cell phone in the hospital room so she might not be able to reach me right away. Tell her he was in a coma but he just woke up."

"Thanks to God. I'll tell her."

Jeff picked up another coffee to go and returned to the hospital. The curtain around Danny's bed was closed when he got there and he could hear several people ministering to him. He hurried to the nurses' station to ask if Danny was all right. The nurse on duty reassured him, saying they were testing the breathing tube and if they could remove it, it would be done shortly. Jeff waited impatiently, pacing up and down in the hallway until the group started filing out of Danny's room. Jeff recognized Dr. Bernstein and also Dr. Flynn. She nodded at him and smiled as she passed but Dr. Bernstein stopped to talk to him. "It's good news," he said. "He's awake and he knows where he is. We tried to turn off the ventilator to see if he can breathe by himself, but his breath is still a little ragged so we're leaving the tube in for a few more hours. But I'm pretty sure we'll be removing it by the end of today."

"But that tube terrified him. It made him feel like he was choking."

"I know, but he has enough sedation now so he can stand it, but not enough to knock him out. You can talk to him and he understands. He can even answer. We have a whiteboard and a pen he can write with. Would you like to try?"

Jeff nodded. Dr. Bernstein called the nurse over and asked her to bring Jeff the board. Jeff walked over to Danny's bed. Danny's eyes were open but he still had most of the tubes and wires attached to him, and looked so frail and weak. "Hi, Danny," he said. "You gave us quite a scare."

Danny looked at the board that the nurse had just put in Jeff's hands. "Do you want to say something?" Jeff asked. Danny just barely nodded his head yes, and Jeff propped the board up and gave him the pen. Danny was weak and exhausted, and he struggled to grasp it and write. His message was hard to read, but Danny had managed two words.

I'm sorry.

"No. Please. You have nothing to be sorry about. I was just trying to say how glad everyone is that you have woken up. You were in a coma."

Danny didn't respond. "Are you in pain now?"

Danny wrote, *Where Marcia*

Jeff explained again, saying that she would come as soon as she got the news. Probably by the next day or the day after. "Is there anything I can get for you? Would you like a magazine or a book or, I know, how about an iPad?"

Danny looked very tired. He shook his head, then wrote *need sleep* on the board and closed his eyes.

Jeff took the board away and put it on the windowsill for later. He noticed that Danny's blanket was rumpled and he straightened it and pulled it up. "I'm going to go to the hotel and take a nap too," he said, not sure that Danny was still awake to hear him.

37

Marcia's retreat had been a great success. After spending three days with her author, she was more convinced than ever that she had discovered an impressive new talent. She'd had several ideas, however, for structural changes she felt were needed and she had worried that her author would resist or resent her suggestions. But she found they worked well together and had reached a happy understanding by the end of the third day. She was relieved when they decided to return to Cape Town a day early. Although she was eager to get home to see Griffin, she also felt sad that she couldn't stay longer. It was such a beautiful country. It seemed foolish, even wasteful, to have come so far and not even see one wild animal. She should have gone on safari for a few days, she realized, and considered the possibility that she might change her plans and add an extra few days to her trip, as soon as she checked in with Berta to be sure all was well at home. She might not get another chance.

Her cell phone, which she had left in her suitcase in the hotel's storage room, was dead so she didn't immediately get any of her messages. But when she checked in at the desk to get the key to her new room, she was handed several slips detailing multiple phone messages from Jeff asking her to call him as soon as she was back. The sheer number was alarming—there were six messages in three days. She knew something must be wrong and, fighting her growing anxiety, she quickly gave the hotel operator the number for Jeff's cell phone. There was no answer and her worry mounted. She then gave the operator her landline number at home but there was no answer there either. Berta is probably out with Griffin for a walk, she tried to tell herself. It doesn't mean anything bad happened. But it didn't calm her. She plugged her phone in and waited a few minutes until it turned on. When she checked those messages, she heard a series of urgent, panicked calls from Jeff, informing her that Danny was very sick and telling her to return home immediately. The last message suggested she call Berta for an update. Her fear mounting, she tried Berta's cell phone and this time she reached her. Berta told her to go straight to the hospital, Danny was very sick, he had been in a coma, but he had just woken up. Jeff was with him. When she realized that Danny had been near death and that no one but Jeff, who didn't even like him, was at his side, she was beside herself. It still wasn't clear exactly what condition Danny was in. He had been in a coma. How was he? Was his brain damaged? What had happened to him? Berta knew so little—not even whether it had been an accident or an illness. She asked the hotel concierge to get her on the first flight to New York, and managed to get on a flight that left at 7:55 that same evening and arrived at 10:25 New York time the next morning—a trip of about 20 hours. She sent an e-mail to Julie in New York asking her to book her a car and driver to meet the plane and take her straight to the hospital. She didn't want to drive herself, fearful that the combination of her exhaustion, jet lag and anxiety would be dangerous.

She tried to picture how Jeff would behave in this situation. He was at the hospital, she thought, so that was good; after all, he might have just said it wasn't his concern. But he wouldn't do that, she corrected herself. He didn't have any love for Danny, he wished he wasn't in his life, he even blamed him for all the problems in their marriage, but he wasn't a monster. He would have realized that Danny had no one else and that he had to show up, even if it was just so he wouldn't be embarrassed when the doctor called. But Danny needed more than a dutiful appearance from Jeff. He needed someone to advocate for him, to sit by his bedside, to hold his hand, even if Danny wasn't conscious enough to know Jeff was there. She would have done that but she knew Jeff wouldn't. She could imagine what Jeff would have done. He would have come to the hospital, gone to the nurses' station, looked in on Danny, probably even felt bad to see him lying there half dead. He would have talked to the doctor, told him or her that his ex-wife was really the boy's guardian and would surely come to the hospital as soon as she could get there. He would have encouraged them to do whatever was necessary to save Danny, and then what? Would he have left? Probably he would have, she thought, he'd have needed to get back to work or maybe he'd been worried about Griffin, or maybe he'd just wanted to be out of there. He'd have satisfied his conscience by going to the hospital and looking like a decent guy to the hospital staff, and then he'd have left.

But something nagged at her as she pictured this scenario. It seemed to paint such a cold portrait of her husband, and staring at it in her imagination, she didn't recognize Jeff in it. On some level, even as she bitterly assured herself that yes, that's what he would do, she couldn't really believe it. As had happened so many times since that terrible day Eve died, Marcia thought of her, pictured her, imagined her sorrow about what had happened to her child. Marcia felt guilty yet she knew she wasn't at fault. This was yet another dirty twist of fate, almost as if they were cursed. And why, if this had to happen, did it have to be while she was away, when she so rarely traveled? There was no answering these questions, no point in wondering and imagining. She just had to get to Danny.

They were the longest twenty hours of her life, but eventually her plane landed, she passed through customs, following the crowd in a dazed way, and as soon as she was permitted to use her cell phone she tried Jeff again, but again she couldn't reach him. Where could he be? Berta had told her the name of the hospital so she called and asked for the nurses' station on Danny's floor. The nurse who answered seemed to be in a hurry to get off and barely seemed to know whom she was asking about. Marcia repeated his name several times and asked to speak to someone who knew his condition. The only information she could get was that Danny had been in a coma for three days and was now awake. His status had changed from critical to stable and his breathing tube had been removed just an hour ago.

"Thank God," she said. "Does that mean he's no longer in danger?"

"I'm sorry, ma'am, but I am not authorized to give any more information," the nurse said. "But when you arrive you will be able to speak to the attending physician, who will answer your questions."

Marcia was about to hang up but then asked, "Is my husband there?"

"I don't know," the nurse answered, her impatience evident in her tone.

"Okay. I'm on my way. Please tell Danny that I'll be there in a few hours."

"I'll see that he gets that message."

She tried not to worry too much on the drive. She hadn't slept well on the plane and was relieved she had thought to get a car and driver. She gave the driver the address, leaned back against the seat and tried to sleep. She was exhausted, but she couldn't drop off. She felt peeved with Jeff and she wasn't sure why. She knew from Berta that he was at the hospital and she knew from all the messages he left that he had tried to reach her. He'd done nothing wrong. It was just . . . just that she wanted so much for him to be the other parent, for them both to be the surrogates for Danny that Eve was for Griffin. She wanted it to have worked out differently, for them to still be together, for her marriage to be intact, for Jeff, when she wasn't there, to be the loving parent Danny needed during this crisis. And, she thought, she wanted for Jeff to still love her in spite of everything that happened. But she asked herself again, did she still love him? She didn't know. She'd thought a lot about him while she was away. And she knew, if she was still asking that question, their story wasn't over yet. She still believed if they could just forgive each other and if Jeff could somehow find a way to accept Danny, they might still have a chance. She closed her eyes and adjusted the pillow behind her, trying to get more comfortable.

The next thing she knew the driver was calling her name. She opened her eyes groggily and took account of where she was. They had arrived at the hospital. The driver was asking her to sign the payment voucher. She didn't even glance at the price, just told him to add a 20 percent tip and then signed it. She climbed out of the car, straightened her skirt, patted her hair and walked into the hospital lobby. The receptionist told her Danny's room number and what floor he was on, and she hurried to the elevator. She didn't know exactly what she'd find and she caught herself hoping, in spite of everything, that Jeff would be there. She prepared herself for disappointment with the thought that he'd known she was coming today and would probably be back at work, relieved to be out of it. She nodded, as though she'd been having a conversation and was agreeing with herself. Squaring her shoulders, she exited the elevator and, following the signs, walked down the hall checking the room numbers as she passed, searching for Danny's room. She could hear her shoes tapping on the polished linoleum floors. A nurse approached her and asked if she needed help and she told her she was there to see Danny. The nurse's face broke into a big, friendly smile. "Oh, he's just around the corner. We had a big scare with him, but you'll be pleased to know he's out of bed right now, taking a short walk for the first time since he arrived." She pointed down the hall as they turned the corner. Marcia saw Danny from behind, walking away from her, wearing a hospital gown that hung loosely on his thin frame. He was taking painful, slow steps, his IV on wheels, rolling next to him, his frail body leaning on a nurse, or maybe it was a doctor in scrubs, who was supporting him. She hurried to his side. "Danny," she called. He stopped and slowly turned around to look at her, his face pale. "Marcia," he whispered hoarsely, with a smile and an exhalation of breath that sounded both tired and relieved. She leaned over to kiss him and that's when she noticed Jeff, who smiled sheepishly.

"Oh, I thought you were a doctor," she said, confused.

Jeff shrugged. "I had to wear this before and I just got used to it," he said apologetically, indicating his scrubs. "He's okay now, Marcia," he continued, noticing the worry in her face. "It's been a rough haul, but he's going to be fine." Jeff put his arm around Danny's shoulder.

Danny smiled gratefully at him and, feeling weak, leaned harder on his arm.

"I'm so sorry I wasn't here, I didn't know," Marcia said.

"That's okay. Jeff was here the whole time," Danny said. She looked up at Jeff. She wanted to say so much and so did he, and maybe, later, they would. But for now, Jeff spoke not to her, but to Danny. "Let's show Marcia how well you can walk," he said. "Marcia, it will be easier if you support him on the other side." She did, gingerly putting her arm around him, and, slowly, the three of them headed back to Danny's room.

"How's Griff?" Danny asked.

"He's fine," Jeff said. "He'll be so happy when you're home." He stole a look at Marcia.

"He'll be happy when we're all home," Marcia said.

38

SIX MONTHS LATER

It was Friday, usually a day Marcia was able to leave work soon after lunch, but today there had been several late meetings. Just as she was finally gathering her papers, she was saddled with an urgent phone call from a distraught author whom she felt she had to mollify. She had tried to pass it off to Julie, but the author insisted on talking to her. The call delayed her for fifteen more minutes. When it ended, even Julie was gone. When Marcia was finally out the door she hailed a cab, hoping that would be faster than the subway. She stopped on Broadway and picked up a barbecued chicken, a few potatoes to bake in the microwave and some fresh green beans and rushed home. Berta had said she couldn't stay later than five-thirty tonight and would, she knew, be waiting with her jacket on, ready to leave. Marcia was eager to be home, looking forward to the weekend. As she expected, Berta was at the door, holding a wriggling Griffin, ready to hand him over.

"I'm sorry. I came as fast as I could," Marcia said as she took him in her arms and gave him a hug.

"He had his bath," Berta said. "He's ready for dinner. See you Monday."

"Yes. Thanks so much."

She put Griffin down. He was a toddler now, walking around on sometimes unsteady feet, needing constant supervision. She had childproofed the apartment as best she could, but he was still somehow always capable of finding something that might be dangerous, either to him or to the furniture. She put some pots and serving spoons on the floor for him to bang while she unpacked the groceries and washed the potatoes. That diversion didn't last long so she followed him into the living room and sat on the floor with him, watching him try to push a round peg into a square hole. He got frustrated after a few tries so she showed him how to do it correctly, and the next time he did it himself. She clapped her hands, grinning at him. She was helping him with the next piece, a triangle, when her phone beeped. She checked her texts and saw it was from Danny and texted back. A few minutes later, the front door opened and Jeff walked in.

"Hi," he called from the hall.

"Hi," she answered. "Griff, Daddy's here," she said. He beamed and started running toward the door, and she took his hand so he wouldn't fall.

"Hi, buddy," Jeff said, scooping him up in his arms.

He kissed him, then leaned over to kiss Marcia. "Good day?" he asked.

"It's better now," she said. "How about you?"

"Same." He looked down the hall toward the bedroom.

"Danny home?"

"No. He just texted me. He's in the park with one of his friends."

"Who?"

"Tom Duncan, from school, He lives nearby."

"It'll get dark soon, shouldn't he be coming home?"

Marcia smiled. "He said five more minutes."

Jeff hesitated. "How much time is there before dinner?" he asked.

"It's fast tonight. Just barbecued chicken. It can be on the table in ten minutes."

"Maybe I'll go meet him and walk home with him," Jeff said sheepishly.

She knew he was trying to be casual, but actually he was worried. Ever since Danny's hospitalization, Jeff worried if Danny wasn't home when he arrived.

"He's fine, Jeff. He's on his way."

Jeff took a baseball glove from the closet and headed out. "I'll be back in ten minutes, I promise."

She nodded. He had managed to go from hostile and indifferent to overprotective all at once. Only extremes for my husband, she thought affectionately, shaking her head and smiling. All in all, I prefer it this way. She pricked the potatoes with a fork, then wrapped them in paper towels and put them in the microwave. She would have dinner on the table in ten minutes but she knew only she and Griffin would be eating it.

And she was right. Danny and Jeff came in thirty minutes later but she didn't mind. Now that Danny was playing baseball again, he needed the practice.

RISKING IT ALL
by Nina Darnton

About the Author
- A Conversation with Nina Darnton

Behind the Novel
- "Celebrating the Unplanned Life": An Original Essay by the Author

Keep on Reading
- Reading Group Questions

For more reading group suggestions
visit www.readinggroupgold.com.

 ST. MARTIN'S GRIFFIN

What was the inspiration for your book?

I have been fascinated with the question of surrogacy ever since the Baby M case when a surrogate mother refused to turn over the baby she bore and had contracted to deliver to the baby's father and his wife. In that case, the surrogate was also the biological mother of the child and she felt unable to give her baby up. It was the infancy of surrogacy and people took extreme and passionately held positions on both sides. When the father and his wife sued for breach of contract, the surrogate fought back and ended with a visitation agreement that recognized the rights of both parties. It was a King Solomon–like situation, and the emotions, ethics, repercussions, and needs of all parties were fascinating to me. I always knew I would have to find a way to write about it and finally this story formulated in my mind.

Did you have any interesting experiences while you were researching your book, or getting it published?

I spoke to several women who had gone through the surrogacy experience. I used to worry that surrogacy was a kind of rent-a-womb arrangement that was basically rich people using the bodies of poorer ones, but I learned a lot about it and found that many surrogates want to perform this role for a variety of reasons. I became much more sympathetic to the women and men who were deeply saddened by their inability to conceive and for whom surrogacy was their last best chance. I tried to express this conflict in the book.

Is there is a book or books that most influenced your life?

There are three books, all of which I read before my eighteenth birthday, that influenced my life. Each affected a specific part of my development and I am so grateful for all of them. Of course, as I grew older many other books were relevant in the development of my thinking, but these early ones started the process.

The first is *Black Beauty*, by Anna Sewell, which I read when I was about twelve years old. I had always loved animals—we had dogs and cats and birds as children—and, coming as I did from a gentle, loving home, I had never realized how cruel people can be to helpless animals. *Black Beauty* opened my eyes, moved me, upset me, and made me determined to do what I could to love and protect all animals whenever I could.

The next book that affected my life was *The Good Earth*, by Pearl Buck. It expanded my horizons from my Brooklyn neighborhood all the way to exotic China, left me with a lifelong interest in and fascination with other cultures, and was the first book that raised my consciousness about women's suffering and unfair treatment. Of course at that age I thought that suffering was confined to China. It took a few more years (and a few more books) to realize how universal that abuse is.

Finally, when I was sixteen, I read *Marjorie Morningstar* by Herman Wouk. The story of a young middle-class Jewish girl like me, I identified with her in a visceral way. I too wanted to be an actress. I too dreamed of falling in love. Whereas the other books moved me because they were far from my own experience, this one reached me because it seemed to speak directly to me about my own life and dreams.

"Celebrating the Unplanned Life"

A few years ago, my husband hosted a book party to celebrate the publication of my first novel, *An African Affair*. The book is a thriller based in Lagos, Nigeria, where I lived with my family nearly thirty years ago. In his toast, my husband pointed out that I accompanied him to Nigeria even though it meant giving up work on a graduate degree in developmental psychology—and this, after I had given up Yale Drama School where I hoped to train as an actress in order to move with him to New York City, when he started a job at the *New York Times*. He went on to list all the other career opportunities I gave up in order to marry him, raise our children, and follow him, a foreign correspondent, around the world.

It was a moving toast. But in listing all the things I had given up to be his wife, he forgot to mention all the things I gained. Now I am married and in love with the same man I fell in love with more than half a century ago at the University of Wisconsin. We have three wonderful children, all of whom came to celebrate my book. I have seen and experienced more of the world than I ever dreamed of.

But there's more, and this is the part that I want to stress: everywhere we went, I found something interesting and exciting to do. I tried out different careers the way today I might try on a new dress. I found a developmental psychologist in Africa and did a cross-cultural study with him that ended in my getting the degree I thought I had abandoned. I acted in plays with the community theater in Nairobi. I started to write articles and ended by

being a journalist, writing about Nigeria, Poland, Spain, and then theater, movies and fashion in New York City. And finally, the experiences of thirty years ago in Nigeria—when I had no idea where my life would next take me—found their way into my first novel. Finally, in writing *Risking It All,* I took the subject of surrogacy that had interested and challenged me for years and by exploring it I came to understand it and to change my views about it. I suddenly was interested not just in the truth that facts provide, but in the heart of the truth which, in my opinion, is only reachable through fiction.

I want to raise a toast to serendipity, to self-invention and to the virtues and value of an unplanned life. I'm not claiming it's the only route to a happy life—far from it—but it's definitely another one and one that we are not always told about. There is so much emphasis on making plans, especially for upwardly mobile, middle-class children. We have to get good grades because next is job hunting or graduate school and then we start interviewing and then, well, then there's the next forty years in whatever profession we've chosen. Often, it isn't the profession that gives us the most satisfaction.

When I meet young people straight out of college, agonizing about what to do next, I try to tell them first to calm down. Then I ask what they enjoy doing and suggest they look for a job that follows their interests. It doesn't have to lead to anything. It doesn't have to be a "career path." That will come. It is just important to take a step into life and to let the current pull you for a while.

Sometimes it tosses you onto a shore you never even knew existed.

I have a niece who vowed since she was a small child that she would take care of her grandmother (my mother) when her grandmother got old. My mother was living in an assisted living facility in Arizona. My niece grew up there, but had moved to Massachusetts. The rules of the facility allowed people to stay there as long as they were largely self-sufficient or could be cared for by a spouse. After several small strokes, my mother didn't meet those conditions and my father was unable to care for her on his own. My niece, who wasn't sure what career she wanted to follow, decided to move back to Arizona and take care of her grandmother.

Everyone objected. What will you do? we asked. How will you support yourself? How will you find a career? But she insisted. She got a temporary job as a teacher in a local school, rented a house and invited both my parents to live with her. Along the way, she found she liked taking care of elderly people. When my parents died, she opened a care home for the aged, which became one of the most popular in town. It was so successful, she opened a larger one. She had found that this was more than a job, it was a calling. Now, back in Massachusetts, she is enrolling in a PhD program in gerontology. She found herself and her career not by searching for it, but by following her heart.

My trajectory too was unplanned. But by staying open to new experiences and opportunities, I built a life I never would have dreamed of had I followed my original path.

1. Marcia has to work hard to convince Jeff to try surrogacy. What do you think of his objections, especially those that relate to his feeling that it's somehow not "natural"? How do you feel about surrogacy? If you were unable to conceive a baby in any other way, would you consider finding a surrogate?

2. How much did you know about alternate ways of becoming parents before you read this book? Did you learn anything new from your reading? Did it change your opinion of surrogacy?

3. Marcia and Jeff are upper middle class professionals. Eve is a poor, high school dropout who is a single mother. Do you think it is exploitive to take advantage of her need for money by paying her to have their baby?

4. Marcia's relationship with Eve was contractual but it grew to be emotional as well. How much do you think she owes Eve and is it worth the price she has to pay?

5. After the tragedy, Jeff and Marcia react in very different ways. Do you think men and women often handle family crises differently?

6. The decision Marcia makes moving forward after the tragedy threatens her marriage and the welfare of her new baby. Why did she do it? Do you think she made the right choice? What would you do?

7. How do you feel about Jeff's desire to help Danny financially but not take him into his home? Given that Jeff said from the beginning that he didn't want an ongoing relationship with another family, is his reaction reasonable?

*Keep on
Reading*

8. Marcia is shocked that Jeff has an affair. Do you think that she is partly responsible for alienating him by not considering his feelings or point of view and fighting so hard for Danny's? Do you think he should have remained faithful and tried harder to work things out, regardless of his feelings that she had chosen Danny over him?

9. Is there anything that Marcia could have done differently to help Jeff accept Danny?

10. At first, Marcia wants to adopt Danny because she feels guilty and responsible for him. Later, even though he is difficult and creates problems, she starts to love him. What do you think is the explanation for this?

11. When Danny gets sick, Jeff goes to the hospital because he feels he has to. When he leaves, he has undergone a major change and so has his relationship with Danny. What happened?